THE
ORIGINAL

THE ORIGINAL

NELL STEVENS

SCRIBNER

LONDON NEW YORK SYDNEY TORONTO NEW DELHI

This edition published in Great Britain by Scribner,
an imprint of Simon & Schuster UK Ltd, 2025

Copyright © 2025 Nell Stevens

SCRIBNER and design are registered trademarks of The Gale Group, Inc.,
used under licence by Simon & Schuster Inc.

The right of Nell Stevens to be identified as author
of this work has been asserted in accordance with the
Copyright, Designs and Patents Act, 1988.

1 3 5 7 9 10 8 6 4 2

Simon & Schuster UK Ltd
1st Floor
222 Gray's Inn Road
London WC1X 8HB

Simon & Schuster Australia, Sydney
Simon & Schuster India, New Delhi

www.simonandschuster.co.uk
www.simonandschuster.com.au
www.simonandschuster.co.in

A CIP catalogue record for this book
is available from the British Library

Hardback ISBN: 978-1-3985-3338-7
eBook ISBN: 978-1-3985-3339-4
eAudio ISBN: 978-1-3985-4030-9

This book is a work of fiction.
Names, characters, places and incidents are either a product of the author's
imagination or are used fictitiously. Any resemblance to actual people
living or dead, events or locales is entirely coincidental.

Typeset in Palatino by M Rules
Printed and Bound in the UK using 100% Renewable Electricity
at CPI Group (UK) Ltd

MIX
Paper | Supporting
responsible forestry
FSC® C013604

<dedication>

A translation issues from the original—not so much from its life as from its afterlife ... And indeed, isn't the afterlife of works of art far easier to recognise than that of living creatures?

—WALTER BENJAMIN,
'The Task of the Translator'

But lovers, and Kenyon knew it well, project so lifelike a copy of their mistresses out of their own imaginations, that it can pull at the heartstrings almost as perceptibly as the genuine original.

—NATHANIEL HAWTHORNE,
The Marble Faun

Prologue

There was a painting my family set on fire. It burned to ashes, and then it came back.

It was a portrait of a haggard old lady—though I believe she was in fact only thirty-two years old—on her knees in a field of mud, holding a blazing torch above her head. Her face was covered in open sores. Her eyes were closed. She had the expression of someone who knew she was dying. Before her on the ground was the mangled corpse of a pheasant. The canvas was very white around the flame, dark everywhere else: the mud, the dying woman's body, the bird. I believe it was one of the ugliest paintings that ever existed.

The title of the painting was 'The Drag', which was written on a little plaque screwed to the bottom of the frame, beside the date 1747. The event depicted took place, supposedly, in the thirteenth century. The name of the artist, if it had ever been known, was long since forgotten; there was a single looping 'C' in the lower-right corner, or a shape I imagined might be a 'C'.

The woman portrayed was my many-times-great grand-mother Hodierna, who was the kind of person who adopted stray kittens and gave her clothes away to vagrants. She invited orphans to dinner and donated great sums to good causes. If nobody had stopped her she would have given up the family's whole estate, a great house called Inderwick Hall and three-hundred hectares of parkland in a boggy corner of Oxfordshire. Her husband, my many-times-great grandfather Geoffrey, was a notorious brute who never did a single kind thing in his life.

The story goes that my grandmother Hodierna, on her deathbed, saw a wounded pheasant from her window and was so moved by the sight that she begged my grandfather Geoffrey to do something after her death for the afflicted and disadvantaged of the parish, be they beasts or men. It was approaching nightfall, but still she could see the pale grey underside of the bird's wings flapping in the darkness. Geoffrey looked at her, his poxed, shrivelled, pitiful wife, and said he'd continue all her charitable works and would even take in the bird, would nurse it back to health himself and—laughing—vowed never to eat pheasant again if, at that moment, she could rescue it herself. (Do you believe this story?)

Grandmother Hodierna, miraculously empowered by the strength of her compassionate urges, got up from her death bed and lit a torch from the fire burning at the foot of her bed. She dragged herself out of the house and, on her knees, clutching the torch, she crossed the garden to the first muddy field of the estate, where the pheasant was flapping hopelessly in a rut, wing broken. She saw it was a hopeless case and that nothing could be done to save it, so she kissed its head and broke its neck without a moment's pause. (What about now?) And because my Uncle Geoffrey was a liar and a cheat and not to be trusted, and since, in stories like this, people do this kind of thing, Hodierna placed a curse on the family. If Geoffrey or his descendants ever again ate pheasant, the family's sons would perish or become impotent and the line of male heirs would fail. Then she died. The burnt-out torch slid from her hand and she fell forwards, beside the twisted corpse of the bird she had killed.

(This story has been told and retold over the centuries, and each time, surely, the particulars must have shifted in some way, each telling nudging it towards greater strangeness, or greater earnestness, or forgetting some little detail, until, I imagine, it came to bear no resemblance at all to what really happened. And yet, there was this horrible painting of Hodierna: a fixed point. And after many years of dithering back and forth, I find, now, that I believe it all, the whole thing, whole-heartedly, in whatever form the story has come to take.)

There was a room at the back of my uncle's family home, past the gun room and the kitchens, near the servants' quarters, where all the unwanted belongings were kept. It was where my uncle's family put the painting, and also, when I was sent to live with them at the age of nine, where they put me. Hodierna in 'The Drag' was one of the first people I saw when I arrived, before I met my uncle, my aunt, my cousins Eliza, Charles and Teddy. Each night I stared up at Hodierna dragging herself through the mire until I fell asleep. The following year I learned to paint, and 'The Drag' was the one of the first canvases I copied: a portrait of the woman who foretold the end of our family. I copied it over and over in secret, working my way through ochre and brown paint in vast quantities, a little yellow and some white around the torch, dark green for the pheasant's broken neck. I learned so much from it: how to mix the exact shade of the mud on the family estate, how to make human skin look at once alive and on the verge of death, what despair looks like, and resolve.

Generation after generation of my family refused to eat pheasant in memory of Grandmother Hodierna's curse. And then came the autumn of 1886, when I was twelve years old, and a roasted pheasant appeared one night on our dinner table. Too much time had passed. My cousin Eliza had died of consumption the previous year and the household was still mourning; in the face of this tragedy, the story of 'The Drag' had lost its urgency. There had been a hunt that day, and many birds shot, and it was a waste not to enjoy the spoils. Nobody gave any thought to the painting hidden away in my room. Nobody believed in curses any more. Later, when a gamekeeper asked my uncle whether it was true he should be sending birds to the kitchen now, my uncle, irritated and embarrassed, remembered the existence of the painting and sent someone to my room to have it destroyed. I watched from my window as a bonfire was lit in the field beyond the formal gardens and the painting set atop it.

That night, I lay in bed beneath the spot where Grandmother Hodierna's portrait had been. The space above my head felt weighty and unpleasant. I had the sensation that all that empty space might somehow fall on me. I went to my closet and took out one of the copies I had painted and placed it in the empty frame. Hodierna looked down on me again. After that, I slept easy.

The next day, a maid came in to make up my room and saw that the painting had come back, had been burned and was now, miraculously, returned, as it always had been, as though it had never been obliterated. Word spread amongst the servants and then, eventually, to the family. The household gathered in my bedroom to survey, astonished, 'The Drag'. The painting was back from the dead.

What followed was a kind of collective breakdown, everyone suspecting everyone else of having done something weird, but unable to say exactly what, or who. It was a shared hallucination, the painting. It was a kind of madness the whole family entered into. To talk about it would be to make it real.

What happened next was that my cousin Charles ran away to sea and after some years was presumed drowned. And then my uncle died. And then my cousin Teddy died, and there were no more male heirs. And then even stranger things happened, and my copy of 'The Drag' remained above my bed, untouched, unmentioned, though I often thought of the night they burned it, of the flames flaring up from the dark field by the house like Grandmother Hodierna's torch all those centuries ago, as though the painting was the thing that was wrong.

The moral of this story is: never underestimate the power of a generous woman.

The moral of this story is: the things you wish to hide might have other ideas.

The moral of this story is: sometimes a copy is mightier than the original.

Part One

Autumn 1899

THE NEW CHARLES

There he was, lying flat on his back, an open leather diary obscuring his face: my cousin Charles. He was perched atop a frayed chaise longue: wider than the bench beneath him and very tense, arms straight by his sides. He seemed nervous, even hidden as he was, even from a distance. His breaths were fitful, pushing the round of his stomach and chest up towards the ceiling, which sagged and loomed, damp, too low.

I stood in the open doorway, my aunt behind me, and said, 'Charles?'

There had been a series of downpours that day and the whole of Rome was filled with the smell of rain, the stirred-up water of the Tiber, the pungent old stones of the city. My aunt and I were wet through after walking from our hotel, eager for a warmth we didn't find in my cousin's cold rooms on the Via Margutta. It was shadowy, a single lamp barely fighting off the darkness. The fire was unlit.

'Charles?' I said, again. 'It's me, your cousin Grace.'

The windows rattled as my aunt and I stepped forwards, and I thought he would turn to us then, would let the diary slide from his face and reveal him. We had last seen each other thirteen years previously, when I was twelve and he was seventeen. The long-lost cousin of my childhood ran through my memories in short trousers and long socks; later, awkwardly, in the adolescent fashions of an artistic pretender, lanky and vague and smoking a cigarette.

'Charles?' I said. 'Is that you?'

His hand twitched a little, but the rest of him remained still.

He had sent a note to our hotel saying he was sick and could not, after all, join us for dinner. He had a fever, he'd said. What was exposed of his skin was a high pink. His forehead, looming over the diary, shone with sweat. And it was true there was a close, unhealthy air in the room, the smell of a person who hadn't been outside for days, who had been living on—I sniffed—a diet of beer and potatoes. There was another smell too, so familiar it took me a moment to identify as turps; there were canvases heaped in the far corner and a collapsed easel by the fireplace, upended like a shipwreck.

The new Charles was an artist, as the old Charles had been.

'Charles?' said my aunt, still hovering near the doorway.

I was surprised to hear her use his name. She had been in a bad temper since arriving in Rome, repeatedly grumbling that it was a fool's errand, that this person, this stranger who had written to her purporting to be her long-lost son, would without doubt turn out not to be, would be some crazy person, delusional, or a fraudster after our money. I'd campaigned to accompany her in part because the idea of a crazy person or a fraudster was intriguing, but mostly because I had business of my own in Rome, though I kept that fact a secret from everybody. Since nobody at home could plausibly claim I would be missed, it had been agreed that I could come: my aunt was fragile, having been recently bereaved twice over and herself in poor health, coughing all night and cantankerous all day. She would need company. I packed my own case. Nobody saw what I brought.

My aunt had done nothing but complain the whole way and had, up until that point, refused to leave the hotel to see anything or visit anyone. When the message came about the cancelled dinner with the crazy person or fraudster we had come to see, she had looked pale, on the verge of tears, and insisted we call on him at once. He could be dying, she said; this could be our only chance, and since members of our family had started to die at an alarming rate in the preceding months, it was hard to dismiss the possibility. There was some part of her, despite herself, that believed this person might really be the man we'd assumed had already died.

Now, she seemed nervous to approach him. 'I have come to see you, Charles.' She seemed uncomfortable saying his name, stumbling on the L, lisping the S.

He did not reply, though the rising and falling of his chest quickened.

Beneath the little leather diary he was vast, an enormous man in every dimension. Even the size of his jaw seemed notable, and surely I would have remembered encountering such a jaw, surely it would have loomed large in all my memories of him, surely it would have been something people said about him in the intervening years: *Your long lost cousin Charles, presumed drowned at sea, with his enormous chin, his enormous face.* Nobody had mentioned it, and in my memories, though my memories were not to be trusted, his head was ordinarily-proportioned, his cheeks if anything a little hollow, his movements light. This new, broad Charles was balanced precariously on the very narrow couch and I could not believe he had been there long. It looked—I almost laughed into the cold, quiet air of the room when this occurred to me—as though he had prepared a *tableau vivant* entirely for our benefit, as though on hearing our footsteps coming up the stairs, he had arranged himself pitifully on the chaise longue and covered his face, assuming the position of an invalid and a man far smaller than he was. The whole scene felt on the verge of collapse.

My wet clothes were coarse against my skin, prickling; it was cold enough that the hairs on my arms were raised. And there was something else, too, despite myself: excitement. And despite myself: suspicion. Was it too much, too insistent, that the diary across his face was embossed with my cousin's initials: *C.R.I.* Charles Robert Inderwick? And there it was, too, on his cufflink, *C.R.I.*, and there, too, *C.R.I.* stitched across the breast pocket of his threadbare brown jacket. But then, hadn't Charles always loved his initials? He had loved to mark himself across himself in that way.

His breathing quickened again when he realised I was approaching. The pink sinews of his neck bulged over a gulp. Somewhere several floors below us, someone dropped something heavy, and moments later emitted a deep, low, bottom-of-the-belly laugh. Rain was hitting the windowpanes in a thick, clumsy patter. I felt suddenly aware of the three of us, the new Charles and my aunt and me, suspended in the wooden box of his room, surrounded by other things happening.

'Charles,' I said. Silence. 'We are here.' Silence. 'We have come to see you.'

Nothing, still, just the rising of his chest.

I glanced at my aunt, who jutted her chin forwards impatiently. She looked a little feral, ready to launch herself at him, hungry.

'I'm going to take the book off your face now,' I said, half expecting him to jump up like a corpse leaping out of a coffin.

I took the diary as lightly as I could, pinching it between forefinger and thumb, keeping it at arm's length as I slid it across his forehead and cheeks. The paper, very fine, stuck to his sweat and I had to jerk it away more forcefully than seemed appropriate. Loosened, the pages swelled over his nose, drooped down a cheek and then fell open in the air. I looked around for somewhere to set the book down. I had the feeling it was contagious somehow, that I should not breathe too close to it. I crouched and placed it on the floor.

My aunt and I both stared at my new cousin's face: red and grey, broad, furrowed across the forehead, eyes closed. I looked from him to my aunt, awaiting the verdict. I was used to relying on others to do my recognising for me.

The face of my new cousin, I could tell, was nothing like the face of my aunt as I saw it then, nor what I could vaguely picture of the face of my late uncle or my late cousins', Charles's siblings, Teddy and Eliza. But then, I thought, nobody in our family looked much like anyone else; we had always seemed mismatched to one another. I searched my memory for any suggestion of my old cousin's face—I had spent enough time staring at it, hadn't I, in those long, lonely years of my childhood?—but I found only flickers and hints, pinched skin between his eyebrows, a determined way he had of setting his lips together. The skin between the eyebrows of my new cousin was pinched. His lips were set determinedly. I had no idea. I had no idea.

His chest rose and fell, as my cousin's chest had used to, as people's chests in general did. One of his fingers twitched. He opened his eyes.

'Well?' I said. I was jittery. I didn't like being so near to him. 'Is it Charles, Aunt?'

My aunt closed the distance between us in a few steps and looked again, this time for longer.

My new cousin's eyes were very light, pale grey or pale blue, it was hard to tell in the dim room, and they were darting across the ceiling, avoiding both our faces. She touched the back of one of his enormous hands, and only then did he turn his head to look at her, his expression bemused, lower lashes watery.

'Mother,' he said, though he had always called her *Mater*. 'It's me. It's Charles.' His voice was strangely light; I had expected something booming, equivalent to his size, but I thought then that I remembered it being that way, musical and weightless. It dislodged a memory of how he had said my own name, Grace, as though I were indeed a graceful person. He held out a hand to my aunt, a gesture that looked unnatural from where he was lying, and she took it, and it seemed to me that something passed between them. There was laughter again from the rooms below us, several people this time, and I wondered whether I, too, in the fizzing, vertiginous moment, might laugh. Somebody clapped and I waited for my aunt to speak.

WHAT WE KNEW

What was certain—what we all knew and agreed upon—was that the last anyone had seen of my cousin Charles was thirteen years ago. Until then he had lived with my aunt and uncle and his brother, my cousin Teddy, and his sister, my cousin Eliza, until she died, and with me, causing minor and less minor ruptures within the family. After that he was gone.

There had been a time after his departure, a year or even more, when things had been calm, when even my presence, usually such an irritant to the family, had seemed more tolerable. My aunt and uncle had always been ill-matched and uneasy in each other's company, and I sensed they were almost grateful to have me there; had I not been, with Eliza dead and Charles gone and Teddy away at school, it would have been harder to ignore the unused expanses of the dining table, the creaking cavities of the house, their mutual disdain. And so, the troubling circumstances of my arrival, my parents' unspeakable difficulties, were suddenly forgivable.

The days took on a convalescent quality, as though we had all been very sick: breakfast was served late, with large quantities of fruit; my aunt took up walking, striding out with the dogs in the late morning, calling them to her as she had, once, called her children. She met with her lawyer (she was always meeting with her lawyer) to clarify certain points relating to the management of the estate in the absence of her eldest son, and this project alone seemed to keep her occupied. My uncle slept a great deal, and though he continued to drink sherry with his doughy, red-cheeked friends, they all seemed less rowdy, less obviously drunk and less mean now that Charles was not there to rile them.

If Charles was mentioned at all, it was in bland and neutral terms: he was at sea, would return shortly, would likely eluci-date his long-term plans in his next letter. The apoplexies and accusations and explosive arguments that had dominated the months before Charles left were over, and in their place was this expansive quiet. It was as though everyone chose to believe that Charles had been the only problem, and that now he was gone, we could proceed as a normal household: my aunt, my uncle, their coterie of friends, lawyers, servants, dogs—and me.

I was thirteen that year, though young for my age and permanently discombobulated. I had known for a long time that I had an unusual difficulty with faces, a sort of blind-ness when it came to people's features, but I felt it becoming worse and worse to the point that, with the exception of the immediate family and a few of the servants, I could recog-nise almost nobody without the help of context. Some were easier to fix in my mind than others, especially if they were unusual-looking, very beautiful or strange or interesting in some other way, and I was helped by clues in dress and voice, by the way people smelled and walked and laughed. But of those whose appearance I'd learned well enough to single out, I was still unable to recreate any kind of mental picture of them in their absence. It was a source of particular agony to me, at that time, not to be able to recall my parents' faces. I could think only of hair colour, my father's dark brown, almost black, my mother's glossy red, and the shape of it as it fell around their foreheads. I could think of my mother's eyes, knowing they were blue, knowing they were relatively large and ringed with pale lashes, but I could not see them. A sort of wateriness took over. I could not do it.

Charles, before he left, had always noticed when I was uncertain and had acted as my guide to the wild social landscape of Inderwick Hall. Without him, I hid myself away, forever scared that the strangers I saw might in fact be friends. The only person I saw willingly was a boy called Bobby who had started work in the stables, whom I learned to identify by his horsey smell and uneven, loping walk and by the fact that he was always pleased to see me, always had some little joke or story to share, and seemed to like my company. The rest of my time I spent imagining Charles's new life, where he was, what views he might be gazing upon at the very moment that I was staring at the umber surrounds of the house.

Charles: who paid a servant a year's wages to let him paint her in the nude.

Charles: who kissed his sister Eliza on the lips as she lay dying of tuberculosis, and never so much as coughed.

Charles: who once read a pornographic novel in church.

He had been known, even to me as a child, for drinking

more than he should, for shameless behaviour and provoking people. Before I was sent to live with my uncle, my mother, when lucid, never mentioned his side of the family without making hushed reference to my 'awful cousin Charles'. And he had been particularly awful in his final months in the house, appearing red-eyed at breakfast smelling of dinner, smoking and secretive and sensitive in the mornings, vanishing for days on end and the returning to ask my aunt for more money, provoking my uncle into violent outbursts about duty, propriety and moral fortitude. They had argued about everything, my uncle and Charles, had seemed like perfectly opposite characters: where my uncle was unimaginative and loud, Charles was deft; where my uncle was blunt, Charles was sharp. My uncle roared and Charles laughed, and when my uncle demanded Charles deny a transgression—that he had been gambling or sneaking around or associating with someone he shouldn't—Charles never did, would simply agree that he had done it, and that made my uncle angrier still.

But Charles was known, also, to me, as my very great friend, my one ally in a house of hostile strangers, and had taught me everything—what I thought of then as everything—that I could claim, at thirteen years old, to know.

Charles: the one person in the world who had been truly and relentlessly kind to me.

Charles: who I missed with the fervour of a pilgrim for a favourite saint.

What we knew was that, after a particularly painful argument between Charles and his father—so painful that none of us knew what, if anything, it had been about—my awful cousin resolved to go to sea, which was exactly the sort of thing that awful young men like him resolved to do, and then he had done it.

Letters came from La Rochelle. Letters came from Madeira. *Dear Mater, Dear Pater.* He was seeing the world. Learning much about trade, about seafaring, about men. He sent his respects to his family. Looked forward to seeing them all when the opportunity arose for a return. Mindelo. Caracas. He had plans to sail from the Port of Santos to Valparaiso on a ship carrying a cargo of coffee, a perilous route around Cape Horn, about which he felt both trepidation and excitement. Nothing, then. The family began to worry. At last, two years after he left: an envelope with a Chilean stamp.

He was improving his mind, he said. He assured them that they would find him, on his return, almost entirely re-formed. He had been spending some time in Chile thinking deeply about his life, and felt he had seen, now, enough of the world. He would return to Europe—to Paris or to Rome—to study painting, which as they well knew had always been his passion, and which he now felt he could pursue earnestly and honestly. He understood this was likely not his parents' preference, but he hoped they would nonetheless accept it, since he was in all other ways now an entirely reputable person and those undesirable aspects of his character, which his father had laboured so hard to correct, were now utterly erased. He was determined to have a respectable career as an artist. He would even get married if they wanted him to and they could decide on the girl. He asked if they might restore his allowance, which was the first I'd heard of it having been cut off in the first place.

We knew that on the thirteenth of December 1888 he boarded a steamer called *The Magellan*, which took him from Valparaiso to Lisbon, where he found passage on *The Margaret*, bound for Civitavecchia. My uncle set off for Italy to meet the ship, with a view to dissuading him from his ludicrous passion for painting and bringing him home to assume his responsibilities as heir to the Inderwick estate. But at Civitavecchia, once all the passengers had disembarked, there was no Charles. My uncle waited until the very last cabin boy had left, just to be sure, then made enquiries with the passengers, interrogated the Captain, interviewed the crew. It was confirmed that Charles had boarded the ship as planned. It was confirmed that he had been present at stops along the way: at Gibraltar, at Monaco. But nobody knew what had happened to him since. He had vanished. The only explanation—the awful explanation—was that at some unseen, unexpected moment, he had fallen overboard into the Mediterranean and drowned.

In light of this news, my aunt became grey and rather cruel. When my uncle returned home, he, too, was different: tight-lipped and highly strung. It seemed they could no longer tolerate each other's company at all. My uncle took rooms in London, and they did their best never to meet. Nobody mentioned Charles's flaws. Nobody seemed to remember the pranks and provocations. The surviving son, my cousin Teddy, had always been reserved, a little foppish but certainly not at all artistic; by dint of temperament alone he should rightfully have always been the heir. He had finished school by then and was managing the estate on behalf of his father, keeping neat tallies of income and expenses, responding promptly to correspondence. But now it seemed that it had been Charles—my absent, awful, much-missed cousin Charles—keeping them together all along.

My presence began to trouble them again. My uncle, on a rare visit to Inderwick Hall, looked surprised to see me there and asked, 'When is she going home?' My aunt, who became vague and distracted when forced to contemplate logistical questions relating to me—a fabric bill, some suggestion that perhaps I should be educated, a request that I be allowed to visit my mother and father—replied, 'They'll be collecting her soon,' and I assumed by 'they' she meant my parents, and I assumed she was lying, though I couldn't be sure. I did not know whether being collected by my parents was something I longed for or dreaded.

I was old enough to understand that I was a reminder to my uncle's family of the parts of themselves of which they were most ashamed. There I was, a child who lived with them because my parents were mad; there I was, a child who behaved in unusual ways, who said the wrong things, who always looked lost, because perhaps I, too, was mad. There I was, a suggestion, an accusation even, that there was something mad about all of them, as though I wafted an unpleasant odour of insanity over the family.

I was both too strange and too similar. I did not belong there, and yet there I was, belonging. And while I had been useful for a while as a body at the table, a distraction from other absences, my continued existence now seemed to strike my aunt as insulting. That I was there when Eliza was not, when Charles was not: intolerable. How dare I be there? She began to check on me several times a day, as though at any moment the redeeming point of me might be revealed. I became more secretive about my secrets: my paintings, my growing awareness of the sort of person I was.

Charles was gone, presumed dead, and that was all we knew for nearly a decade, until everyone else started dying and the business of an heir became pressing. First it was my uncle, who keeled over on Christmas Eve, 1898, in the middle of Russell Square. And then, more upsettingly, Teddy: after twenty-seven years of good behaviour, Teddy found his time at the head of the family overwhelming. The experience released a previously dormant nonsense from within him, and he began drinking too much and spending too much and talking very quickly; he acquired a yacht the day after his father's funeral and two more vessels in the subsequent weeks, and then, on his way to see his purchases and learn how to sail them (having never once seen the sea, let alone sailed it), experienced chest pains and a tingling sensation in one arm. He was dead by the time his carriage reached the coast.

This left my father as the beneficiary, and since he was resident at a lunatic asylum in Dorset, a madman with no expectation of producing a male heir, the situation was considered undesirable. My aunt met again with her lawyer, Mr George, to enquire about the possibilities of trusts and exclusion clauses, of altering the terms in her late husband's will by which the Inderwick fortune was to be inherited; there were some distant cousins, the Forrests, who might have among their number a more suitable heir. But it was no good. The thing was not to be altered; the order of succession was iron clad. My father's institutionalization was not disqualifying. My uncle's family had been blinkered and uptight for generations, but they had possessed enough self-knowledge to know that allowing disinheritance over such a trifling thing as a little madness would compromise the lot of them.

My aunt sent for more lawyers, for my late uncle's friends, for anyone who might tell her differently, but they all surveyed the papers in question and acceded to Mr George's opinion. After all, Mr George was at pains to add, it was not impossible my father might yet produce a male heir. This idea horrified me and my aunt in equal measure, for different reasons.

Thwarted, she became despondent, and despondency turned to a general worsening of health until she seemed only precariously attached to her own life and wits. She began to make strange decisions and say strange things. She paid a spiritual medium to visit her in her bedroom and would emerge in manias of optimism (She would herself bear another child! It was not too late after all!) only to slide into deepening depressions, which could only be alleviated by another visit from the medium and a strong dose of her drops. Sometimes I caught her looking at me with an intensity that suggested she felt I was keeping a secret from her. Naturally, this made me wonder which of my various secrets she suspected.

I watched her back—through keyholes, as the medium sat

beside her and clutched her hand and whispered odd promises, or from the other end of the dining table over the tops
of untouched dishes like the rooftops of a town between us,
or askance as we rode out side by side on cold mornings to
'check on the estate', though I had no idea what we were looking for and she seemed to notice nothing except the uneven
ground beneath her horse's feet. An awful desperation em-
anated from her, which she blew out in puffs of steam into
the cold air, and which settled over me so that I, too, began to
feel increasingly frantic. Life could simply not go on as it had
been: the house too cold, my aunt too cold, the air too cold
and I, too, was becoming cold, cold even to the things I cared
about—painting, mostly, and one or two people. It had been
going on this way, impossibly, for far too long: and surely,
surely something now had to change.

I thought this daily. I tried to stay warm. I planned my
own plans, worked on my own work, secretively, as I did
everything. I had begun a money-making venture, an experiment that felt outlandish but compelled me nonetheless,
the idea that I might be able to turn my skills as a copyist of
paintings into money, and might use that money in turn to
alter my own fate. I was tentative, embarrassed by it, but it
was enough to keep me busy, to prevent the freezing effects
of hopelessness from taking hold. I worked. I waited.

And then something did change.

A letter came, postmarked from Saint Helena—later we
hauled an atlas from the library to the dining room and
gazed at it, a tiny speck in the expanse of ocean between two
continents—addressed to my aunt by name. She seemed

hesitant to open it, as though she sensed the much-longed-for change was imminent and was suddenly afraid. She tapped fitfully at her boiled eggs, briefly feigned a headache and then tore at the envelope in a rush.

The writer was a solicitor in Jamestown, Saint Helena, who wrote on behalf of his client, a gentleman who had read notice of my uncle's death in a copy of *The St Helena Guardian* and who, after many years of travel and adventure, was keen to reacquaint himself with his family. The client's name was Charles Robert Inderwick, who enclosed warmest wishes to his mother Irène Inderwick, his brother Teddy and—I felt winded to see it—his dear cousin Grace. He had such happy memories of Inderwick Hall, and in particular his beloved old horse Roger. If my aunt was willing to send money enough for travel expenses, the attorney wrote, then Charles Robert Inderwick was intent on coming home.

The effect this letter had on my aunt was something like opium—a kind of stillness fell across her face. And to me, too, it felt momentarily paralysing: a ghost had appeared at the breakfast table, and neither of us knew how to react.

'My medium told me this would happen,' she said, several hours later.

What we knew was that my aunt sent a chequebook and a letter of cautious interest, saying that she was naturally intrigued by anyone claiming to be her son and who knew the family names, the house, even Charles's favourite horse. On receipt of this, the man who said he was my cousin travelled first to Dakar and then to Casablanca, where, when presented with his bill after staying one night in the Royal Mansour

Hotel, he instead bought the entire business with a banker's note from a bank the Inderwicks did not in fact use. The first the family heard of this was an anxious letter from the former owner of the Royal Mansour, alerting us to the confusion and requesting clarification on where the funds for the hotel were, in fact, to be drawn from. But by that point, the new Charles was already in Rome, and my aunt and I had already made plans to travel there to meet him.

'And are you really him?' she had said that first night, without letting go of his hand.

The new Charles shifted uncomfortably on his little chaise longue. 'I'm pleased to see you after all this time, Mother.'

'Mater,' my aunt said. 'You always called me Mater.' There was something corrective in her tone. It was the voice she used when telling the dogs to get off the bed.

'Mater,' he said then, and that was when my aunt's expression changed, and even I heard it, the fluttering familiarity of the old Charles's voice, the cadence just so, long-lost, much-missed and now, suddenly, upon us.

'It's you,' my aunt said. 'It's really you. I knew it. I knew it. I knew it would be.'

And so, then, that was what we knew.

THE THREE GRACES

The attractions of Rome were threefold to me. Rome was Rome of course, a welcome change from the Oxfordshire mud that surrounded Inderwick Hall, the dull trudge of October towards November. I was delighted to be elsewhere, never having been abroad before, never having seen much of anywhere beyond a few towns and villages in the south of England and, occasionally, London. And I was delighted to be in Rome, specifically, where autumn seemed to have a gilding quality, orange trees shedding leaves onto cobbles that glowed wetly under illuminated storefronts, and where, on turning a corner, I found myself confronted by something at once familiar and startling, the Spanish Steps exactly as I'd seen in pictures in the books in my uncle's library. It was like reading in a novel a perfect description of an idea you'd thought had been entirely your own. The long shadows thrown by carriage lamps across the Corso made everything seem wilder and more crowded. The colours of everything—the clothes of the Italians, the ochre-stoned buildings, even of me, my own hair, my own shoes—seemed rich and dark and intriguing.

Second, there was the intrigue of the possibility of my long-lost cousin.

And then, also, last and clandestine, there was the chance that I might make a sale.

I had been copying paintings in secret for many years, ever since my first year in my uncle's home. It was Charles, in fact, who had taught me, though inadvertently at first. I had arrived, nine years old, an orphan with living parents, and found myself reviled in my uncle's house. The shame of my situation I well understood. But I had not known until I arrived that I, like my parents, was an odd person. My aunt and uncle had loathed it, had found it affronting, the way I talked, dressed, looked too directly at people. Teddy and Eliza had kept their distance, too, if not hostile then certainly suspicious, resentful. Charles was the only member of the household who had found me entertaining, who had complimented the clothes I'd brought from home, who had asked how I was when I came to the breakfast table red-eyed, who had been kind.

I'd been passing by his bedroom. The smell of turpentine stopped me. I went to his door and would have burst in, since I knew him well enough by then to do so, but heard voices and so paused. Through the keyhole, I could make out the swell of his back, his shoulders, a glimpse of a palette hooked over his thumb. Beyond him: his easel, a small board pinned to it. And beyond that: one of the house girls, Emma, who was older than me and older even than Charles, nineteen or twenty years old, and particularly recognisable to me by a large mole on her jaw. She was naked, standing alone, facing him and the door, and so me. There was some navy-blue fabric draped over a chair, a makeshift backdrop, and the curtains were drawn. She had another mole, or some sort of birthmark, dark, on the side of her ribcage. Her hands hung tensely by her sides, as though keeping them there required some effort. Her face: mild, somewhat entertained, quite embarrassed.

'Someone's at the door,' she said. 'I can see shadows on the doorframe.'

Charles swung around to face me. 'Who is it?' he said. 'Who is it? Don't come in.' Dark pink patches had appeared on the skin of his neck, the way they did whenever he fought with his father. He fiddled anxiously with his collar.

'It's me,' I said. 'It's Grace.'

'Don't come in,' he said. 'Don't come in, Grace.'

And I didn't, not then, but later, when he had gone out with his father, I did. I found his portrait of Emma on the board on his easel and took it, though the paint hadn't dried, running as fast as I could down the stairs, third to second, the yellow landing, second to first, blue landing, first to ground passing by the red landing, green room to library to oak room to entrance hall and then all the way around past the dining room and kitchens and gun room to my room, and slamming shut the door behind me. Even there I felt anxious of discovery, so I went into the little side room beyond, an unused boxy space that had once been the sleeping quarters of a servant's servant, and there with my back to the door I scrutinized the painting.

I did not know why I was so curious about it, the way Emma looked in it, the thought of the dim room, the drawn curtains. I only knew that it interested me and that I wanted to think about it longer. From my bedroom I retrieved watercolours and in what from that day on I thought of as my painting room, I copied it as closely as I could into my workbook, before replacing the original back where it belonged in Charles's room. A few weeks later, Charles, who had taken it upon himself to teach me some Latin amongst other things, was flicking through my pages of scrawled-out declensions when he came across the copy. He held the book away from him and squinted, then said, 'Oh, you copied my picture of Emma,' and I checked his face to find he was not angry, in fact seemed entertained. 'I'll teach you how to paint, if you want,' he said, and I said that I did want that, and we started that very day, in my uncle's library, copying Raphael's 'The Three Graces' from a book on the Old Masters, which Charles found amusing. He tried to make me laugh—'Which one are you, Cousin Grace, or are you a fourth Grace, just beyond the frame?'—and I frowned, at work on curves: buttocks, bellies, hairless pudenda. That night, alone, I made my first, inexpert copy of 'The Drag'.

My uncle was in almost every way a philistine, but he had inherited from his father a significant library of books on paintings, including instruction manuals on technique and colour, encyclopaedias of provenances and biographies. He kept the collection up-to-date out of filial duty if not genuine interest. And so there, in the unpromising surrounds of Inderwick Hall, which was itself surrounded unpromisingly by boggy fields and sickly coppices and uneven roads to less depressing places, I began my education as a copyist. Charles instructed me on some basic techniques: how to mix various tones of skin, the browns and whites and pinks and greys and darks of the human body, how to use brushstroke to convey texture as well as tone, how to imagine the bones beneath the flesh in order to get the body right.

Repeatedly, Charles urged me to paint from life. A red-streaked apple, placed in a blue bowl. A stuffed fox, mounted on oak. His horse, Roger, stationed outside the window and stamping impatiently. I muddled through these commissions, got all the proportions wrong. A hand—his hand—laid out motionless on the arm of a chair, which in my rendition had an air of decomposition: skin too white, shadows too green, the fingers amorphous, knuckles undefined, as though it was painted by a person who had only a vague idea of what hands were and had never seen one.

Worse: Charles's face. Worst: my own. I scrutinized my features, scrunching up my eyes to stare at my reflection in the glass, and thought: *Eyes. Those are my eyes. My eyes are eye-shaped.* There, too, was my nose: a solid thing, its hard ridge rising up beneath the skin, nostrils opening out around a nervous inhalation. Lips, creased as un-ironed linens. *Here is a face, which is no less real than any other real thing.* And then I turned to my page, brush poised, and the certainty would fade like smoke. There was simply nothing there. There was no face at all.

Charles was first horrified, then fascinated, and ultimately highly entertained by my distinctive stupidity with faces. We sat together in the window, looking out at people coming and going from the house and he would test me: 'What about him. Did you ever see him before?' and I would shake my head, no, and he would hoot and stamp a foot and say, 'That is your uncle's great friend Marcus, visiting from London, who sat opposite you at dinner last night.'

Charles's incredulous delight helped to lessen the enormous shame I felt about my limitations in this regard, though I remained embarrassed by my inaptitude as a painter from life. I wanted desperately to impress him, and so, whenever he set me a task, a green-glazed vase of diaphanous poppies, a plum on a gold dish, I asked that he paint beside me. I found that if I copied what he painted, rather than the subject itself, I could do it almost perfect justice. I understood then that these were separate skills, to observe and record from life, and to copy. At one I was risible, but the other there seemed some hope of mastering. When he realised what I was doing, Charles set us up on opposite sides of the room, so I couldn't see his work.

'Don't make me paint real things, Charles,' I said, at last. 'I don't enjoy doing things I'm bad at.'

'We're bad at everything until we learn to do better.' It was the sort of thing his father said to him, chiding, condescending, and I could tell he regretted telling me something so predictable.

'You know it is worse than that.'

'Yes,' he said. 'You have a sort of blindness to the real world. It's very strange.'

After that, I showed him my copies of 'The Drag' and he nodded and accepted that I would always be a copyist.

I worked from the reproductions of lithographs in my uncle's books, or from postcards or pictures in the newspaper, with no sense of the original brushwork or texture or scale. In those early days I painted everything on the same small boards, no wider than my forearm and only a little taller, no matter how big the original: Botticelli's 'Primavera', Da Vinci's 'Last Supper', shrunken and stashed in my painting room.

The first time I worked from memory, I stayed within the house. At the halfway point between the ground and first floors there was a small mezzanine we called the red landing, where a portrait of my great-great uncle hung. The painting was large—his dimensions were life-size—and to copy it unobtrusively required memorizing it first, and working alone in my room. I imagined the portrait as a grid, and each time I passed it would commit to memory a single square, the brushstrokes abstracted like a kind of map. What I saw no longer looked like the lowered eyebrow of a scowling man; rather, it was a giddy, light patterning of browns and reds, flecks of white like crests on waves and a glowing, sunny triangle of pink that was in fact the topmost corner of a nose. I worked that way, in tiny increments, for weeks, until my great-great uncle was doubled, perfectly replicated in my painting room on the first large canvas I had ever attempted. I showed it to Charles, full of pride and giddy for praise; he looked at first baffled, asked what I was doing with the picture of Uncle Alexander, and then laughed, a full-bodied, true-hearted hoot. 'You're a little magician,' he said. 'You're a machine!'

Shortly after that, he left without saying goodbye and there was nobody left to show my copies to. Copying was a habit both too precious and too embarrassing to declare to anyone, and besides, who would have cared to know?

I sensed—knew—I had an unusual talent (sometimes I heard Charles's words again, 'A magician! A machine!' and felt myself grow a little taller), and one that would unnerve people: to be able to see a painting from the inside out, so to speak, and reproduce it as though from the original artist's long-dead hand. It was a kind of possession, not so much mechanical, as Charles had thought, as spiritual.

And I was ashamed as well as proud: it seemed damning, somehow, to admit that I could make a piece of fruit on a plate look like fried egg, a piece of mounted taxidermy like a rug, and yet could depict Vermeer's 'The Music Lesson' to a fault, from memory, having spent two hours staring at it on a visit to the London home of my aunt's cousin, who had married a Duke. The hosts had taken great pride in showing the painting: the black of the floor tiles, the slightly crude evocation of marbling, the astonishing brightness of the girl's skirt, a red so bright it was, in fact, orange. They had set up their tea table beneath it, and I kept my eyes trained on its details, the glow of the red skirt in the varnish of the cello, over the heads of the Duke and Duchess. In the foreground, a rug draped from a table in thick, weighty folds. They gave us almond cakes, and I surveyed the way that, in the picture, the mirror above the instrument showed the reflection of the player's face at a surprising angle, light on the forehead and the side of the nose, glancing. Black tea with bergamot. In the painting: the frayed edges on the blue footstool. It was a kind of inhalation.

Later, at home, I looked up its exact dimensions in one of my uncle's encyclopaedias, thought carefully about the glazes. I laid out a palette of madder lake, Verdigris, carmine and large amounts of yellow ochre, and in the confines of my painting room, I reproduced Vermeer.

I was incapable of making something from nothing. It seemed miraculous to me that anyone could. Hence: the appeal of art in the first place, I supposed.

I was not a generator.

I was a conduit.

But by then it had occurred to me that perhaps I could make money from it nonetheless.

I had for years by then engaged in a mutually-beneficial system of exchange with my friend Bobby who worked in the stables. He was younger than me, had just turned twenty that year and was keeping a sick mother and two younger siblings with his wages. It had started out with the two of us swapping stories: he would tell me about girls in the village, one of whom, Rosamond, he was in love with though he didn't seem to realise it. I would tell him in return about the goings-on in the hall, my aunt's mannerisms, my uncle's foibles. We were both intrigued by the life the other led; I loved his easy interactions, his closeness to other people, his comfort in his own skin, and he seemed to find the eccentricities of my home life exotic. Later I told him, too, about my work: at first nothing more than that I was painting and wanted to make some money from it one day.

Then he started getting me pigments from town in exchange for knick-knacks I pilfered from the house. A tube
of vermilion for an embroidered Indian elephant. Rose
madder for a little porcelain dish in the shape of a boat. He
was good natured about it and uncomplaining and always
brought exactly what I asked for. We both understood he
was getting a good deal out of it, that he sold the items for
more than the paint cost him to buy, and that this made him
uneasy. Once, he tried to give me some money alongside
the requested raw umber and I panicked, the sight of the
coins in his hand mesmerising and horrifying. Part of me
wanted to snatch them. There was almost nothing I wanted
more than money, because I had seen by then that it was
the key to everything else you could want, but for that very
reason I could not bring myself to take any from Bobby,
from his mother and sisters. I waved him away and acted
unconcerned, though really the interaction troubled me terribly and I thought about it for a long time afterwards, half
regretful, half relieved.

The next time we met I gave him a miniature, a copy
I had done myself of a 16th-century portrait of my aunt's
grandmother, very fine; I had taken particular care over it.
He took it unquestioningly and came back with the new
brushes I'd requested, as though it were like any of our other
surreptitious transactions. But it seemed to me those brushes
were miraculous, better than any I'd ever seen, purchased
with money I might as well have printed myself. I had taken
a significant step, and one that could not really be undone.
When I wondered aloud if he'd had any trouble selling the

item, he shrugged and said no, there was an antiques dealer in Oxford who had been very pleased with it.

It occurred to me only then how unforgivable it was to have asked Bobby to sell the fake. Had the fraud been discovered, the consequences would have fallen on him and not me, and I felt terrible and guilty and avoided him for a while afterwards, then later told him I was very sorry for asking him to sell things for me. He shrugged and said he didn't mind at all and would take whatever I wanted him to, so long as I was certain the items would never be missed from the house. I nodded and felt no better, I resolved that the next time I sold a copy, I would do it myself.

I had read an article in my late uncle's newspaper, which a boy from the village continued to deliver after my uncle's passing, about the thriving trade in counterfeit paintings in Paris and Rome. This business, the article's author suggested, raised certain questions about the value of authenticity in art, and whether, if a buyer could so easily be deceived by fakery, they might perhaps deserve to be. The piece was written in a wry tone, taking particular pleasure in stories of ignorant Americans who believed they had stumbled across a genuine Da Vinci. It also made mention of an anonymous dealer known to operate by the Spanish Steps in Rome who was infamous, in art circles, for taking advantage of unsuspecting tourists, selling upwards of fifty Botticellis a month. And it was surprisingly simple, a matter of writing a few letters to journalists, to learn his name.

I contacted the dealer as soon as I knew I was going to be in Rome, laying out my terms as clearly as I could. I tried to act like a person who knew what they were doing, who did this sort of business all the time, and who was simply offering an opportunity. I would visit his gallery at such and such a time, I would have only one piece available for viewing, I would accept no payment less than—and so on. It felt like a game, sending off my letter from the familiar dullness of Inderwick Hall, surroundings unchanging except for a limp seepage of greens into browns as autumn progressed. When the dealer replied, it seemed that somehow, from afar, he had changed the nature of the light in my room. Everything looked sharper, more clearly defined. I felt purposeful and alarmed.

I wrapped 'The Music Lesson' in several layers of cloth and buried it at the bottom of my trunk. I had chosen it largely because it was small, but nonetheless when my aunt saw my luggage on the morning of our departure, she rolled her eyes and asked who I thought I was that I would need so many different outfits for such a short visit.

'I hope you know, Grace, that you won't be attending any parties. All you'll need is a thick coat.'

I said I understood, and thought perhaps I should look disappointed, though if my aunt had given the matter any thought she'd have known parties saw me at my worst, worse even than large family dinners, at which I could be trusted to say something awkward and spill a staining drink onto white cloth and introduce myself, as though for the first time, to a treasured family friend. I had no hopes of attending parties in Rome.

My private engagement was of a different quality

altogether: thrilling. The project of selling the painting was as compelling to me as meeting my cousin and perhaps even more so, because though I missed and yearned and hoped for the Charles I had known almost more than anything else, in the case of the copy, there was money involved.

THE COPYIST

That first night in Rome, after our encounter with the new Charles in his hot-aired room, I did not sleep. My aunt went to bed and I sat alone feeling blurry and strange and up-ended. From my window, I could see the cluttered rubble of the city, a few windows glowing with a lit fire inside, vines twisting up walls and across arches, a drizzling haze above. Rome seemed impossibly vast, stretching out all the way to the dark hillside beyond the terracotta rooftops, and time passed in lulls and leaps. As the sky lightened towards dawn, everything seemed depressed in a way it hadn't the previous day: the shopkeepers and servants trudging past doorways, clumps of decaying leaves at the roadside. The buildings all seemed to sag, as though on the verge of disintegration.

I opened the window. There was cold coffee left over from the night before and I drank it, tonguing loose grounds against the back of my teeth. It was time to go. It was time to sell my painting. I almost lost my nerve until I didn't.

I left the hotel holding the canvas of 'The Music Lesson' awkwardly under one arm. As I followed the scribbled instructions the dealer had sent detailing the route from our accommodation to his gallery, I felt my attention being pulled in two directions, blearily, as though in thinking too clearly about only one thing I might have to confront that it was really happening, and might run away in fright. So I thought about the meeting to come, what I should say and how I would act and the idea of coming away from it with money in my hands. But I thought, too, about the rooms where we had found my cousin the previous evening: the scattered canvases in the corner, the little initialled diary balancing on his face like a ball on the nose of a performing seal. Already the memory of it seemed foggy, as though we had all been drunk.

There had been a long silence after he first spoke, as I waited for my aunt to deliver a verdict. I had anticipated something large in her reaction, an immediate negative or positive: screaming delight, screaming fury. I had anticipated the thrill of a mystery being solved. It would be exciting, of course, to discover it really was Charles after all those years, my dear old friend, much changed, much loved, back from the dead. But I couldn't help but think it would be exciting, too, if it turned out not to be him after all. I had grieved Charles long ago and by then was used to a life in which I depended only on myself; if this was not the real Charles, there was considerable consolation in the idea of encountering a man who was mad or wild enough to try to fool a mother into believing a stranger was her son. I was accustomed to mad people, and often felt that I was one of them, but still: the situation was exhilarating.

The dealer's premises looked shut when I reached them, windows shuttered, and I thought for a moment of turning around, retracing my steps back to the hotel. The gate to the alley beside the building was ajar, slamming and opening and slamming again in the wind, knocking little dusty chips of plaster off the wall. I stood and waited for a decision to come to me.

'Grace Inderwick?'

The voice came from the back of the dark alley; a door had cracked open, showing a slim rectangle of light and a hand grasping the handle. For a moment, still, I couldn't move.

'Grace Inderwick?'

I did not have time to think about my life, about what it had been and would continue to be if I did not take this step, do this thing, make a sale, acquire money of my own. I couldn't take that moment to play through in my mind all the many miseries, small and large, that would go uninterrupted: the grey-gold house, my precarious position within it, my eternal indebtedness to the unsympathetic family, my own strange nature forever strange and undeciphered by anyone other than myself. But I felt it, I think, as a sort of shock that propelled me towards the open door and forced my name out of my mouth.

'Grace Inderwick,' I said. 'Yes, that's me.' I tripped on something unseen in the dark, a step of some kind, regained my balance, coughed, stopped on the threshold. 'The Music Lesson' was digging into my armpit. The dealer had stepped back from the door into the room beyond: dim, candlelit.

'Do you always do business at six in the morning?' said the dealer.

It had been embarrassing suggesting the meeting time in

my letter, but I hadn't known what else to do. There was no other hour I could guarantee I'd be free from my aunt.

'Not always,' I said. 'No.'

He gestured that I should come in. I did, in one large stride, and I tried not to react to the smell of tobacco in the room, so strong it filled my throat and made me want to cough, and so reminiscent of my father that I felt disoriented for a moment, as though in stepping through the doorway I had somehow stepped back into my early childhood. The dealer jutted his chin towards a chair, its wicker seat frayed and sagging, and gently nudged a cat from an armchair that he lowered himself into. In Italian, he called over his shoulder to someone unseen, asking for coffee. I couldn't make out the floor beyond where we sat; I couldn't see the walls at all.

'Except, of course, you've never done any business in your life,' he said.

'That's not—' I began, though I didn't know what it wasn't, and stopped.

I was unsure what to do with my face and found that I was smiling—out of nerves or out of awkwardness, I wasn't sure. He lit a match and then a lamp, illuminating his face enough for me to see the lines in his yellow, creased skin around a grim-set mouth. 'I can always spot a fake,' he said.

In the new light, I could see more of the room and found that it was bigger than I'd assumed, and fuller. The walls were crowded from floor to ceiling with framed canvases, and when the dealer noticed me looking towards them, he angled the lamp in their direction. I had the impression of finding myself in front of an enormous audience, like a dream

of appearing naked in front of one's family—and all the more
so because, the longer I looked and the more I made out, the
more of the paintings I recognised: Botticelli next to Raphael,
above Tintoretto, below Dürer. Masterpiece after masterpiece.
It seemed I had wandered into the most significant art gallery
in the world.

'My clients are grateful,' he said, 'for the range of stock I
carry.' He gestured at the walls but did not look away from
me. He seemed to be assessing me, as though I was the item
to be valued rather than the canvas that was clamped, now a
little sweatily, under my arm.

The clink and clatter of cups on a tray grew louder, and
footsteps, and then a woman appeared on the shadowy far
side of the room. She began to move towards us, and as she
did so there was a loud crash, the sound of something shat-
tering, and the woman swore. She bent over and picked up
whatever had broken, placing it on the tray. When she reached
us, she presented cups of coffee alongside the unmistakeable
blue-and-white shards of a Ming bowl. The dealer picked up
a fragment and I wondered how long it would be before he
began to shout, or cry; it was a jagged triangle showing the
bulging eyes of a dragon whose head was now severed from
its body. He turned the piece over in his hand then tossed it
onto the floor, where it shattered further. His expression did
not change from its fixed frown. Looking down I realised
the soft white beneath the glaze was not porcelain but thin,
dusty plaster.

'Piece of shit,' he said.

He took a cup of coffee for himself and I reached for one

too, thinking that I should seem confident, assertive, having some idea of wanting to appear at ease in the gallery. Then I thought I should have waited to be passed one, that it had been a reprehensible rudeness to reach over and grab it like that, and I panicked and replaced the cup on the tray, spilling a little as I set it down. The dealer looked at me. There was a silence that felt very long. He took the cup and held it out.

In that moment it seemed to me that this small thing, this misstep over the coffee, was now the most important event in my life, overshadowing the sale of the painting, the return of my cousin Charles: they were nothing compared to this humiliation of taking and returning a coffee cup, unbidden. I had revealed myself to be hesitant and uncertain and strange, and there was no coming back from it.

When the dealer said, 'So. Show me,' I did not immediately know what he was talking about.

The painting. I nodded. I unwrapped 'The Music Lesson', trying to perform the care and pomp of someone handling the original, trying to muster the confidence I had hoped to display with the coffee, trying to hide the shaking in my hands.

The dealer bent over the canvas as he might a glass of wine and was quiet. Only when he stepped back did his expression began to change. The frown softened, the set of his lips began to turn, and at last he smiled a large, large smile and I felt my own lips widening in response, as though we were sharing between us a very private, very tender joke. The coffee was no longer the most important thing. He had seen my painting and was smiling. He reached behind him to the table without looking, his fingers floating towards his cup. When he found it, he lifted it to his mouth without taking his eyes off the painting. He was grinning so broadly the rim knocked against his teeth. He didn't drink.

'This painting is a good old friend of mine,' he said, his cup still hovering.

'You've seen it before?' I asked. 'You've seen the real one?' I pictured the dealer in the Duke's house on Hyde Park, standing where I had stood to look up at the Vermeer, breathing the same air.

'I've seen the painting you copied this one from,' he said. 'I know it very well, because I painted it myself.'

Some Truths About Copies

To be duped by a copy is embarrassing but perfectly natural. We all want to believe we are in the presence of an original.

A good copy reveals itself to be fake by its perfection. The original is imperfect, as all art must be.

A perfect copy is imperfect, but not in the way the original is imperfect. A perfect copy, therefore, always differs from the original.

If the value of an original is in the discernible hand of its artist, the value of the copy is in the copyist's powers of empathy.

To create originals requires vision. To create copies requires second sight.

Anyone duped by a copy should thank the copyist for making possible their fantasy.

Copying preserves, recycles, disseminates. It is therefore an act of tremendous generosity.

And if the copyist occasionally thrills in deception, who could blame her? Who could begrudge her the enjoyment of a little power once in a while?

Sometimes I have made a copy that I think is better, even, than the original, and have had to start over.

PUTNEY

In our berth on the ferry from Calais to England, my cousin and I surveyed each other's knees. His: bulbous like banister finials, the fabric of his trousers stretched so taut across them it shone. My thighs seemed stubby and insubstantial in comparison, and I thought of how he had seemed as he approached the boat: monolithic, a black monument in the sea mist. He carried his own bags, even the canvases, and seemed nervous to let anyone else touch his belongings. He looked ill at ease, still, now, after several days of travel in our company: too big for his seat and also somewhat cowed. With each roll of the ship he flinched, as though bracing for a storm that didn't hit. It had been raining overnight but the sun had broken through and was sending occasional spears of light through our half-curtained porthole. Beyond it, the sea churned greyly. I became aware that I was fidgeting, bouncing my leg on the ball of my foot. My aunt, beside me, was pretending to be asleep.

We had planned to stay for several more days in Rome, and several weeks in Italy, visiting acquaintances of my aunt in Florence and Milan and returning from Genoa, but my aunt had risen the day after meeting Charles with a mania for home. This was entirely unreasonable—we had spent a total of seven days traveling from home followed by a single night in the city—but also entirely predictable, to the extent that I had arranged to see the dealer that morning in case things happened exactly this way. My aunt was an uneasy traveller and an uneasy guest, uncomfortable anywhere that was not Inderwick Hall. She sent down for a courier as soon as she woke and announced that we were departing at once, that my cousin's ill health could only be addressed by the trusted family doctor in England, that to delay would be an inexcusable foolishness. When Charles responded to her summons and appeared at the hotel, dishevelled, it became clear my aunt's urgency was not driven only by homesick-ness: she wouldn't stop touching his hand, could barely drag her eyes from his face. It was as though she expected him to dissipate if she did not hold onto him herself. And so our belongings were packed, carriages ordered, and we left Rome that same day.

My cousin had seemed jittery, anxious, especially once we reached the port, and my aunt had been anxious in turn, fussing around him and patting his forehead a lot. He was too ill to eat anything, he said. Could barely even swallow water. Seemed reluctant, again, to look at either of us directly.

'Go away, Grace,' my aunt had said. 'You're making him uneasy.'

I had plenty of time, over the days that followed—disembarking at Marseille, the long trip north, first to Paris and then Calais—to stare into space and imagine all the

many things I would do now that I had my own money. The
dealer had paid me exactly what I had asked, and I had the
impression he would have given me more. His manner, once
he had shown me the fleck of blue paint he had added to
the red rug in 'The Music Lesson' as a clandestine signature
of sorts, had been avuncular. 'We are linked, you and I,' he
had said, at one point. 'We have been inside the same painting.' I had parted with a lightness under my arm where my
copy had been, and a sort of weightless feeling of immense
wealth, and on top of it all, a letter of introduction to a man
in London who would be pleased, the dealer said, to facilitate
more transactions between the two of us. If I was able to copy
certain specific paintings, he said, there would be even more
money. Some items had been requested by clients willing to
pay good prices: Courbet's 'Le Sommeil', Van Eyck's 'Arnolfini
Portrait', a few others. He could always sell a Venus and it
didn't matter whose: Titian, Botticelli, Velázquez, Veronese,
Holbein.

I felt bolstered by the transaction, though I could not put
into words quite how. I had a sort of fizzing energy that kept
me awake, even when the rocking of the carriage was stulti-
fying, even at night when I felt nauseous with tiredness. The
money I'd made was no vast amount but it was enough to
contemplate for the first time in my life what I would choose
for myself: what clothes, what food, what books. And I could
buy more supplies, and paint more copies, and so make more
money, and more, and more.

I had thought about money so much and for so long, and
could get quite worked up over it. My burgeoning awareness

of it, of how it worked, how it could be got or lost, seemed to me the defining feature of my growing up.

That my father was poor compared to my uncle was something I'd known even as a young child, though what it really meant I hadn't understood. My father was a younger brother who had neither wed money nor joined the clergy; instead, he married my mother, a penniless woman from Dorset he'd met only by chance, and moved to her village, a place called Sixpenny Handley. His family had retaliated by shrinking his allowance and writing him out of the will, but he had enough, nonetheless, to cover our necessities. We lived in a cottage that had belonged to my mother's family for generations; her parents had lived and died there, as had theirs, and it was expected that mine would, too.

I knew these facts but never gave them much consideration as a child. My life was my life, my parents my parents, ordinary because they were mine. I never thought to question what mechanisms whirred beneath the surface of our family life, by which food appeared on our table and firewood in our baskets. I did not pause to imagine the hardships we were spared because we could afford these things, nor did I know the things we did not do (travel, entertain, eat much meat) because we could not afford them. Though we did on occasion see my uncle's family, most frequently at funerals, I hadn't known how to read the ways their money was written across them: their clothes, transport, many servants. I felt no curiosity about any of it until my parents' difficulties led to them being taken away and I moved to Inderwick Hall. Only then did I learn about money.

There, I wondered who lived in all the rooms in the house, which was large enough to accommodate a family ten times the size of ours, and for a long time I supposed there were vast numbers of inhabitants who never left their rooms. I wondered who the ate all the food left on the table after we finished our meals, sliced ham curling drily towards the ceiling, little sandwiches staling in the warm air after tea, carcasses of chickens and turkeys half shredded and half intact after dinner, and sauce congealing in jugs. I wondered why the members of my uncle's family had so many clothes, so many hats and so many little trinkets spread all over every available surface. What were they preparing for, I wanted to know. What event did they anticipate for which it might be necessary to possess a little dish made of cut glass, decorated with a pair of acorns made of gold and mother-of-pearl, too small and too fragile to hold anything at all? The answers came to me slowly. The rooms were for nobody. The food was for nobody. There was no purpose to most of the things they owned.

I began to see these things very clearly because I was a person who belonged nowhere; I was neither staff nor within the inner circle of the family. It was like viewing a segment of rock—as I did, once, in a museum in Oxford— cut top to bottom and stratified. They were all fixed in place: my uncle's family at the top and all the rest of the household arranged below them: friends, lawyers, butler, and then the footman, housekeeper, cook, head house- maid, lady's maid, parlour maid, kitchen maid, scullery maid, laundress, housemaid, stable-boy. Me. And though

I told myself I was on the outside, felt myself to be outside of it all, I was at the same time trapped in the rock with the rest of them, some kind of fossilized worm—I saw that, too, in the museum, and imagined its death, the avalanche of sediment, the eternity that followed—out of place and stuck there.

I felt, when I really thought about it, that I wanted to smash the rock to pieces, but I also felt I wanted money more than anything in the world. I had no allowance, since my parents' meagre funds were spent on their care and my uncle preferred to cover my expenses himself; nor did I ever expect to have one. My parents had nothing to leave to me beyond the cottage where we had all once lived. I would inherit nothing more from them.

Wealth was as arbitrary as shifts of mud and residue millennia ago, and as immutable. My uncle was no more deserving of his wealth than Bobby and his family were deserving of their poverty. I saw, in snooping through my uncle's papers, both before and after his death, that the history of the family's money was a history of grabbing: land, freedoms, goods. There were questionable interests abroad that had been sold at politically opportune moments at great profit. Closer to home: rent, rent, rent from our neighbours. Rent, from the farmers we allowed to till the soil we claimed was ours. Rent from Bobby's family, which was paid with the wages he earned working at Inderwick Hall. It was grab after grab after grab. My great grandmother Hodierna had seen it for what it was. But then: look what happened to my great grandmother Hodierna.

I saw it all and at first I said nothing, because who could I have said anything to? It seemed to me that everybody in the family must already know it, though they pretended they did not. Later I mentioned it to Bobby, who seemed amused and irritated in equal measure and pointed out I had never done a day's work in my life. I made a promise to myself, then, to make my own money, and not just that, but to work to make it. This fantasy of wealth was at times all-consuming and more powerful still was the fantasy of wealth without guilt. It had such glorious implications: freedom from so many different things.

From the start I knew the only chance I had of realising this dream was to sell my copies. Which, now, I had begun to do. And to have achieved this thing I had imagined for so long was suddenly destabilizing.

Opposite me in the berth, my cousin's eyelids drooped and then fell shut. His head tilted back. His mouth cracked open. I surveyed, then, the angled cluster of his lower teeth, the stubble splaying over a mole on his chin. It was not a feature anyone had ever mentioned about my cousin Charles, this mole. Was it was the sort of thing that, despite my trouble with faces, I might reasonably have remembered?

I thought then about how, when I first arrived at Inderwick Hall as a child, my uncle made casual reference to a mole on my face. I had been bemused. I'd had no idea what he was referring to, and as soon as I was left alone I went to the mirror, and there it was, just as he said, a dark mole beside the inside corner of my left eye, positioned almost like a tear. And though it had surely been there my whole life, though I had seen it every time I looked at my reflection, I had never noticed it before. The feeling then of being revealed to myself was almost pleasant, exciting, that there could be something new about me without anything changing at all.

Perhaps Charles had always had this mole, unseen by me and so familiar to his family that they never found it worthy of mention in his absence.

I wondered: if I spent my new money on better quality paint, would I be able to charge more for my next copy?

I wondered: when and how might I find an opportunity to view Courbet's 'Le Sommeil'? The dealer had given me the addresses of four people in London who were under the impression they owned the original.

I wondered: if I bought something utterly frivolous with my copying money, some sort of intricate hat for example, would everyone ask where I'd got it from, would I have to hide it, would it be enjoyable to own an intricate hat that could only be worn in private, and how would I face any-one, really, Bobby or his family or any of the Inderwicks' tenants, anyone who was hungry or overworked or late to pay rent, knowing that when I had been in possession of my own money, that was what I had done with it? And yet, I imagined the hat.

I wondered: how many copies would I have to sell before I could afford to live alone?

My cousin's eyelids snapped open. I looked away too late. Our eyes met and my looking away made it worse: he had witnessed not only the staring but the attempt to hide the staring, and the whole split-second interaction felt too intimate; I had given myself away. I felt unpeeled. Perhaps he was recalling, at that very moment, my parents' madness, and wondering. I frowned at his boots, then at my aunt's boots, then at my own boots. And then, reluctantly—it felt inevitable—I lifted my gaze to meet his. He blinked. I blinked. He raised his eyebrows a fraction.

Reaching into a pocket, he took out a sheaf of papers and a pencil and began scribbling something. I did my best to act unconcerned, tried to become interested in what was happening out of the window, the unruly swell of water. I looked at the ceiling, where the paint was thinning and patchy. I looked at my cousin's knees again.

He flipped his page around. What I saw at first was a chaotic collection of lines that refused to cohere. And then from amongst them I made out a pair of eyes, and below one of them a black mark I registered as a mole, and from this came to understand he had produced a sketch of me as I must have looked in the seat across from him. Underneath the picture, he had written: *You look different.*

'Different to what?' My voice sounded loud in the silent cabin. The ocean beyond the window seemed suddenly stiller.

'To what I expected.'

'It has been thirteen years.'

'And you're my cousin Grace.' He didn't say this as a question, but there was an uncertain angle to his mouth once he closed it.

'Yes,' I said. 'I am. We used to—' I stopped. 'We spent a lot of time together when I was a child.'

'Yes,' he said, and then, 'You're Aunt Sophie's daughter. How is Aunt Sophie?'

I had not mentioned the name of my mother in his presence, and neither had my aunt.

'You look different, too,' I said.

'It has been thirteen years.'

'She died last year,' I said, and my cousin looked—what was his expression?—afraid, horrified, something like that, before collecting his features back into their dour, organised frown. 'My mother,' I said. 'She died in a lunatic asylum. They told us she jumped into the fire in her own fireplace and though they fished her out as soon as she was discovered, she did not survive her burns.'

'And your father?' He offered no condolences. He turned over a new sheet of paper and began drawing again, then paused. 'Forgive me, I forget his name.'

Was it plausible that a man might forget his uncle's name, after thirteen years at sea?

'My father is still in his asylum,' I said. 'He has been there, now, for seventeen years,' and at that point my aunt, who had been peaceably following our conversation behind closed eyes, seemed to feel things had gone far enough and commenced a loud performance of waking up, stretching her legs, yawning and saying she felt sick, demanding ginger tea.

Charles did not say another word for the rest of the sea journey. When my aunt, later, really did drift off to sleep, he flipped his page around and showed me another drawing, a face, eyes-closed, that I understood be my aunt's because he had labelled it 'Mater, eavesdropping'. He smiled a small, quick smile that felt like a sort of peace offering. It wasn't until much later, after we had disembarked the boat, found a carriage and reached the outskirts of London, that he spoke again.

His demeanour had changed entirely at the sight of the city: the grey smoke and the applause of the horses' hooves on cobbles, the air inside the carriage tasting murkier, the occasional wafts of cooking smells, body smells, smoke through the windows. He became alert, sitting up very straight and staring intently out of the window. My aunt, who had been fussing about which hotel we ought to go to, recalling that last time she had stayed at Claridge's the sheets had been yellowed, and her friend had recently told her that the service at Brown's had gone horribly downhill, turned to him and said, 'Well, Charles, what should we do?'

He seemed surprised to have been asked, his lips forming the beginning of an answer and then swallowing it.

'Really, I think you should decide, Charles,' my aunt said.

And he said, 'Putney.' His own eyes widened when he spoke, as though it was a surprise to him too. He was sweating again.

My aunt looked astonished. He might as well have suggested we all go back to Saint Helena. 'I beg your pardon?'

'Is there still an inn at Putney called the White Lion?'

'I'm sure I would not know,' said my Aunt. 'We have no business in Putney, Charles.' And then, firmly: 'We have never had business in Putney, Charles.'

For a second I thought he looked forlorn. 'No,' he said.

'But I should like to see it, all the same. Would you do this for me, *Mater*?'

And he said the word, then, with such precision, much more like a man who had studied Latin since the age of seven than he had the night of our first encounter in Rome, that there was no arguing with it, and I thought I did remember him saying it just that way when he was younger, could hear his youthful voice embedded in his speech now. We asked to be taken to the White Lion by Fulham Bridge which it turned out did still exist although, our driver remarked, it had been almost entirely rebuilt three years previously—a fact that seemed to cause Charles some dismay. And so it was decided that my cousin would spend his first night in the country in thirteen years not in Mayfair, as my aunt would have chosen, nor even in Bloomsbury, but in the White Lion by Fulham Bridge in Putney.

Until then, my experience of London had been limited almost exclusively to those large, leafy neighbourhoods on the west side of the city where members of my aunt's extended family kept houses: the Duke, who we saw once a year at Easter, in his large house at Hyde Park Corner and various of my aunt's nieces who had married into the kinds of families who lived on garden squares in Pimlico. Three times in my life I had visited the National Gallery. I had once, as a child—with Charles, now I thought about it—been allowed to see an opera; we were given instructions to see whatever was playing at the Royal Italian Opera House but Charles instead took us to the Alhambra. We saw *Die Fledermaus*: entertaining, if a little hard to follow.

I had never crossed any of the great bridges over the river, and though I had come close to it, I'd never even seen the Thames, which was vaster and darker than I'd imagined, a horrifying expanse of black beneath us, since it was nightfall by the time we reached Fulham Bridge and the smell coming up from it was rotten and thick. I knew, of course, of all the bodies that washed up on the banks, and all the many others who were hooked up out of the water from boats; it was the sort of thing that was mentioned, periodically, in the papers, as something between a blight and a curiosity of the city. But I hadn't thought, until that moment, of the smell of them, all that flesh and brain bloating and stinking into the air.

I could still smell it when we reached the White Lion, and stepped down from the cab with my sleeve pressed over my mouth. By the door to the inn, a girl about ten years old, dirty and small, was begging. When I smiled at her she frowned and, a second later, bared her teeth. She said something to a boy leaning against the wall nearby that I understood was hostile and then she stood up and moved away.

My aunt hesitated in the cab, waiting until the girl had disappeared around a corner before descending. She looked at the door of the inn, and then up to the roof, and then at Charles, who was waiting, arm extended, ready to guide her down. 'If you would be so good as to refrain from buying the place,' she said.

We were given three adjoining rooms, and refreshments in a little parlour with a view of the street, and I could see my aunt's dismay at Charles's choice fading. By the time she had finished her tea and was surveying the view from the window, carts loaded with produce and a newspaper boy shouting news of a murder, she seemed in fact quite entertained, invigorated even, by the novelty. There was an unnerving kind of energy to her, as though she was drunk and pretending hard not to be. She seemed too earnest and too quick to be pleased, but her hands shook whenever she wasn't holding on to something and it made me uneasy.

That night I felt, even with the door closed, even in bed with the covers over me, that my cousin was too close. The places we'd slept on the journey back through France had all been larger, grander; the walls had been thicker. Here it seemed to me that at any moment Charles might appear at my bedside. As though he could still see me. I thought I could hear him snoring—a relentless grinding sound, the flap-flap-flap of a loose soft palate; when I closed my eyes I was taken back to the ferry, Charles asleep and his open mouth revealing the dark cavern of his gullet—but when I pressed my ear to the wall I realised it wasn't that. The inn was above an underground station; trains were moving beneath us, rat-tling, rattling, and there was something horrifying about all that movement happening out of sight, below us in the dark; I thought again about the bodies in the Thames, the smell, and then about my aunt, the way she looked at Charles as though she wanted to eat him. The buoyancy I'd felt about the sale of my copy, about the money, faded into a churning sense of unease, and I found that I kept getting up to check the money was still there, a bankers' note folded tightly around coins in a purse at the bottom of my case. I had the sense that something calamitous was about to happen, and though by then I was dizzy with fatigue, I found that I couldn't stay asleep.

Then I heard a noise, a definite noise, from the next-door room: heavy footsteps crossing the floor, and a pause, and after that, hinges turning.

I cracked my door just wide enough to see the blur of my cousin passing down the corridor, then I crossed to the window and peered down, waiting for him to emerge onto the street below. It was quiet and black outside, and then there he was, faintly illuminated by the lamps still burning in the inn's front parlour. He bent over into the cold and coughed out plumes of his own white breath before starting off across the road, looking back once in a way that suggested he feared and expected he was being followed. It was only then it occurred to me that I should follow him. I lit a candle and threw a skirt over my nightclothes, and a coat, and slid my feet into boots without lacing them. I ran out to the corridor, then: a second thought; I dashed back, dug into my case and found my purse, from which I took a couple of coins. I left the rest and the unfolded note scattered on the table, and even in my rush to leave, there was some small part of me that noticed this and thought: that was a mistake.

By the time I left the inn, Charles was some way down the street, the bulk of his shoulders only just visible in the dark, walking the brisk, purposeful walk of a man who knows where he is going. I followed as fast as I could, noting without slowing down that the beggar girl was back, huddled beside the doorway of the inn, the boy beside her. I kept my feet light on the cobbles and stayed close to the house fronts, eyeing each doorway I passed as a potential hiding place. My breaths came quicker and I covered my face against the smell, which seemed weaker—or perhaps I was just growing used to it—but still troubling, sticking in the back of my throat.

Charles made a series of turns down streets and alleys, dark and dark and darker, the buildings getting closer together and hiding places fewer and further apart. Sometimes I thought he was about to swing around, and I would jump backwards—I knocked my elbow against the brick of a doorway and drew blood—but he didn't turn around, kept striding onwards.

Then he stopped by a house indistinguishable from all the other houses, ramshackle and black, except that its door-knocker hung from one corner and the paint on the door was, I thought, a peeling shade of green or grey; it was hard to tell exactly in the brief light-flares of Charles's matches as he lit his pipe. He stood outside it for a long time, breathing heavily and smoking. At first I thought he was lost. I pressed myself into a doorway, expecting at any moment that he would charge back in the direction from which we had come, but he waited and seemed to be deliberating. Twice he approached the house as though to knock and then fell back. Once, he turned away and began to walk in the direction of the inn. And then, swiftly, he spun on his heel and tapped lightly— just the faintest knock—against the door.

A glow appeared in one of the upper windows; someone had lit a candle. Then a woman stuck her head out and peered down. 'Who's down there?' She spoke quietly, but her voice carried across the stone street.

'I was wondering—' Charles began. He was nervous. His voice had the same tremor it had had on that first meeting with my aunt, girlish.

'Who is that?' the woman said again.

'I'm looking for Arthur Watts,' said Charles. 'Or a relative of Arthur Watts. Does Arthur Watts still live here?'

There was a long silence. The woman withdrew her head, briefly, before poking it out again. 'He's dead,' she said. 'Wife and son too. There've been no Watts people here for years.'

Charles, whose face was invisible in the darkness, was quiet.

'Who is it that's asking?' the woman said.

More silence, and more, and then Charles said, 'I'm sorry to trouble you. Thank you. I'm sorry to disturb you.' At first he didn't move, and neither did the woman above him, then she muttered something vague and he shrugged and began to walk back in my direction. The window snapped closed. I held my breath as he approached, resisted the childish urge to close my eyes. His footsteps grew louder and then stopped.

'You can come out, Cousin Grace,' he said. 'We can walk back together. It will be safer.'

I think for a moment I did close my eyes, then took a breath through the fabric of my cuff and found that I was irritated more than embarrassed. As I stepped towards him, what I heard myself say was not an apology, not even an excuse, but, 'Who is Arthur Watts?' in a voice that was bolder, more accusatory, than mine had ever really been.

Charles, looking mild and very tired, simply said, 'A friend,' and gestured that we should walk on down the road.

'I'm sorry.'

'For following me?'

'For the loss of your friend.'

'You're not sorry for following me?'

'I was curious.'

He did not seem to want or expect anything more from me. 'And you're no stranger to sneaking around in the dark.'

I looked at him, at the outline of him, just decipherable as a person against the black brick of the buildings we passed. 'What do you mean?'

'I mean that I'm no stranger to following people who sneak around,' he said.

I said, again, 'What do you mean?' though I was feeling uneasy by then, and almost did not want to know.

'Did you not think I would be curious about you, too, Cousin Grace? Imagine my surprise when, upon arriving early at my mother's hotel, I should see you scurrying off down the road by yourself.'

I said nothing.

'That man you visited at the Spanish Steps, the one you sold the painting to, is a known crook,' he said. And when, still, I was speechless, at once indignant and ashamed and at a loss for words while my heart hammered guiltily in my chest and my cheeks flushed hot in the cold air, he said, 'But perhaps you already knew that, Cousin Grace,' and he walked on a little ahead of me in a way that made further conversation impossible. When we reached the door of the inn, the beggar girl had returned—a relief, I'd thought perhaps she might have left, that I'd missed my chance—and I slid the coins from my pocket into her sleep-loosened fist, and she startled awake, ready to fight, and then when she saw it was me simply squinted through half-shut eyes and said nothing, and Charles watched, and he too was quiet.

INDERWICK HALL

When I woke to daylight, my purse was as I'd left it the previous night, open on the table, but the money was gone. At first I thought it must be my mistake, that perhaps I had moved it somewhere when I'd returned to my room; perhaps I had swept it onto the floor as I fumbled through the dark to reach my bed. Or perhaps I had hidden it, sleepily or asleep, somewhere I couldn't remember. Or, worse still, perhaps I had only imagined the money in the first place, perhaps it had been an elaborate fantasy of which I'd convinced myself. A kind of madness.

The idea of anything else—that someone could have come into my room and found it, and having found it, taken it— came to me only slowly. I had left it out on the table. I knew I had. When I had returned after following Charles, it had still been there. I had reached out and felt it. I had checked. And then, because the candle had burned down and because I was so tired and because I was, after all, there in the room and what could go wrong if I was right there, I had left it as it was and fallen deeply asleep. So: somebody had come in overnight while I was unconscious. So: who could it have been, who else could it possibly have been, but Charles?

It was a source of both shame and irritation that my first instinct had been to doubt my own sanity.

The journey out of London felt twice as long as usual, the road wetter and bumpier, the carriage more jolting and cold. My aunt still seemed feverish and would not take her eyes off Charles, would not stop talking to him—or rather, at him, about him, about how much he would find changed in the old house and how much was still the same, how we had replaced almost all the staff since he was last home except for Ferris, of course, my late uncle's man who no longer appeared to do any meaningful work but who was kept on nonetheless, as much a fixture of the place as were the fountains and the yew trees and the rose gardens and the lake. His horse Roger had been sold, an awful thing but how could they have known, and he would find there were several good replacements in the stables. Did he know that we had dredged the lake? Had found a lot of pottery that seemed very ancient, a couple of helmets from the civil war? He could try them on, if he liked! And oh, how delighted everyone would be to meet him. How thrilled Ferris would be to see him again! There were some distant cousins staying who would be beside themselves. She named them carefully, first and last names, and sketched out little portraits: Emily Louise Forrest, pale, you might even say wan, reddish hair; Magnus Peter Forrest, Charles would remember Magnus of course, such a gentle young man, blue eyes, very tall; Mr George, of course; Charles surely recalled Mr George the solicitor, though he had working with him now a new young colleague, Mr Barnard; and then there would be my late uncle's friends, who she could never persuade to leave.

And so on. And to think that all these friends, old and new, would find Charles so substantial, so mature! It would be beyond anyone's imagining. To have him home after all this time! And on she went, and on.

I, too, could not stop looking at my cousin, but he did not look at me, not even once, not even when I asked how he had slept.

And then we arrived, at last, at Inderwick Hall. The driveway was long and straight as an arrow from the gatehouse to the hall, and the lower branches of the yew trees lining the way were bare, so we could see the house several minutes before we reached it, growing, looming, the ivy around the sides of the wings first just a haze, and then a rippling green, and then, finally, I could smell the thick earthiness of it and hear the wind lacing through the vines, rain tapping the leaves, the door at the main entrance rattling ajar as though the house was breaking open, a broadening crack. The carriage stopped; the horses ground their hooves into the gravel.

I always felt a churning unease on seeing the front aspect of the building, the way it seemed to tilt forwards at you, casting a shadow that was too dark and too long, the way the wings on each side reached graspingly outwards as though trying to claim more ground. The sight reminded me, inescapably, of my first arrival, when I had been alone and my parents gone. I had allowed myself on the journey to imagine my uncle's house as a castle, something from children's stories, where everything would be gleaming and people would be pleased to see me. It had been sunny that day, spring, and the Oxfordshire lanes had been blossoming and noisy with birds and I had somehow not noticed the mud, the cows wading knee deep through floodwater, the unchanging palette of brown and green and brown, which not even the hawthorn blossom and cow parsley could disrupt. The gatehouse. The yew trees. I had imagined my uncle and aunt, hearing the sounds of the wheels on the driveway, would rush down to meet me, to say how tired I must be, and how hungry, that there was tea waiting, and cake, and perhaps—why not, I was nine, I had been uninterrupted in my fantasy for the full two days it took me to get there—there would be a puppy for me, something helpless and floppy, as I had once seen in the village, slapping its big paws on the grass as it trotted after a girl who was walking hand-in-hand with her mother.

It took me years to understand that it was not the house itself that was hostile, that there was nothing innate to the bricks, the clusters of arched windows, the twisting pillars that led up from the entrance to frame the stone crest at the very top, that was particularly unwelcoming or harsh. It was only the family: my uncle and aunt, who loathed each other, who were uncompromising in everything except the fact of the marriage and who were sometimes cruel, too, because they could imagine no greater hardship than what they themselves had experienced and so felt their own lives had been cruel to them, and my cousins, who were young and knew no life except the one they lived. There was between them all such a coldness, a lack of mutual understanding, that the house could not help but emanate it. As a child approaching Inderwick Hall for the first time, I understood at once, before even passing the last yew tree, that there would be no tea, no puppy awaiting me inside, and it seemed, it really did seem it was the house that repelled me.

There had been nowhere else to go. I dismounted my seat alone. I pulled my trunk into the entrance hall—it scraped the flagstones and the sound echoed along the corridor and up the stairs but I heard nothing else, no footsteps, no voices— and wandered, alone, through the green room, which smelt of cigars, the library, which smelt of old paper and damp and the soft, vegetable odour of flowers left too long in a vase, the oak room, which smelt of wet dogs and gunpowder (and all of it smelt of turps, everything, everywhere, turps, drifting down from Charles's room at the top of the house, though I did not know the smell well enough to recognise it then), the entrance hall again, until I was found, at last, by Ferris, crouching outside the locked gun room, with my back to the wall, waiting, waiting, waiting for something good or bad to happen.

Now, the house looked almost unchanged, as though Charles had never been gone: the darkness, the tilting, grasping, the extravagance of its shadows. Since Teddy's death, it had begun to slide into a state of disrepair; my aunt had given up patching leaks and replacing rotten window frames; she had allowed ivy roots to worm too deeply into crevices. Still, the façade gave nothing away.

It was silent in the stationary carriage and then my aunt said, 'Here we are,' without taking her eyes off Charles, who was looking unwaveringly at the hall, eyes narrowed, his lower lashes clumped and wet.

'Are you crying?' I asked.

My aunt pinched my arm. 'Be quiet, Grace.'

'The air is cold,' said Charles. He shook his head a fraction but didn't blink.

None of us moved.

'Here we are,' my aunt said again, and then a footman opened the door, and we all shifted a bit, none of us wanting to be the first to descend until I could bear the awkwardness no longer and stepped down. My aunt followed, and when Charles finally emerged, she gripped his elbow as she guided him towards the house, as though at any moment he might take off like a wild horse across the fields. When we entered the hallway to find what was left of our family gathered at the bottom of the stairs—the second cousins, the staff, Ferris, the lawyers Mr George and Mr Barnard, the four friends of my late uncle who were called, by all of us, 'the uncles', and who never seemed to leave—there was a long silence. And then Ferris, who had turned almost white, stepped forwards from the cluster of faces and said, 'Welcome home, Sir,' and Charles looked shaken, almost spectral with nerves, only stuttering short thanks, his body seeming to shrink away from its own surface. For a while nobody said anything else, each looking round to gauge others' reactions, and then Mr George exploded.

The man we had brought home was not Charles, Mr George said.

He did not look like Charles.

His eyes were lighter than Charles's eyes.

His voice was, admittedly, very like the real Charles's voice but his accent not quite the real Charles's accent.

His head was enormous. His head was simply enormous.

The response to this was a general uproar. My aunt became emphatic, more energetic than ever, and she would surely have seemed too spirited, manic, even, had she not been hotly supported by Ferris, who seemed drunk with the shock of it all. My aunt insisted Charles be accommodated in his old rooms at the top of the house because they had the best views of the estate—*his* estate, she pointed out, which he had come home to claim—and he deserved uninterrupted sight of what belonged to him. I had wandered up there in the years of his absence and had seen for myself the whole expanse of the lake. In the winter when the branches were bare you could feel the full force of low sunlight coming in off the water; the room glowed with a strange, rippling light. When one of the uncles suggested Charles should stay in the village, or else, as a compromise, in the servant's quarters, my aunt became so agitated she almost fainted, and had to be given a double dose of drops.

Once she recovered her senses, or the semblance of them, she gave the cook instructions to make a lavish series of meals in Charles's honour and even before the maid had unpacked her cases, she was sitting at her desk writing out invitations to a dinner to celebrate the return of her long-lost son. In the library, in the corridors, in the dark passages between the gun room and the back stairs, Mr George and his allies (at this point: three of the uncles, many of the senior servants and Mr Barnard) began to say she was mad, and Ferris mad, and the couple of second cousins who had dithered but had come down on her side, too, were mad, and

the other uncle who was hedging his bets was mad, and me,
I was as mad as the rest of them if I didn't speak up soon
for the cause of plain sense; everyone who agreed with my
aunt was mad.

A Brief Discourse on Madness

There was nothing new or surprising to me about madness. I had grown up with it, or rather under it, my parents sliding gently towards eccentricity, and then surpassing even that, becoming entirely unhinged. It was a project they embarked upon together, a game they played for which nobody else knew the rules. My mother would one day wander into the village without a skirt on, and the following day my father would take a walk entirely nude. I could not, even years later, discern which of them was the instigator, if either of them was. He would eat only red foods for a week—berries, tomatoes, raw meat if he could get it—and in response she'd eat only blueberries, figs, plums, pungent cheeses with blue veins threaded through them. As a child, I thought of it as a kind of love letter they wrote to each other, as though each night they whispered across the pillow, 'Wherever you travel tomorrow, I will not let you go there alone.' They even, over time, began to resemble each other, which my mother pointed out to me once, how their faces had gradually fallen into sympathy with one another, though when I looked between them I found myself only confused. It was true, I thought, if I really concentrated my attention, that his eyes had taken on her knowing askance-ness, that her smile had become crooked in exactly the way his was. When I looked away, or closed my eyes, I could picture neither of them, and in that way they looked the same, too: vague.

For many years, nearly the whole first decade of my life, I simply did not question it, the madness of my own family appearing utterly banal. My mother sang from the windows to the birds, my father dug holes in the garden to serenade moles, and other people—their reactions, their stares and gasps and, later, their interventions—seemed to me the ones who were deranged.

I remember my father bursting into my bedroom not long before he was taken away, carrying a covered dish on a tray. 'Grace,' he said, 'Grace, I have brought you your inheritance,' and then, with a flourish, he removed the domed lid to reveal an empty plate, which on closer inspection was flecked with toast crumbs. I thought about it all the time, that moment, that plate: 'Grace, I have brought you your inheritance,' and then there it was, empty, nothing at all except, perhaps, for madness.

Insanity seemed inevitable. It lay ahead of me, and all around, as bleak and immovable as the marshy fields that surrounded my uncle's house, as definite and depressing as a crumb-flecked plate. I was in the habit of checking myself for it, to see whether it had come for me yet, or more accurately, how far it had progressed. Was that strange dream, which had taken me several minutes to shake off upon waking, the beginning of it? What about that lapse in memory—a misplaced glove, a miscommunication—was that it? I had been sure I'd left the money there, on the table in my room at the White Lion, and yet maybe not, maybe I was wrong, delusional, had perhaps imagined the whole thing: the soft-edged note folded over coins in my purse, the dealer's dark gallery by the Spanish Steps, perhaps even 'The Music Lesson', and why not all of it, why not Rome and my cousin, entirely?

My parents' derangement had, in the final months before their incarceration, become increasingly focused on the idea of having another child. It had started as a preoccupation with my safety and with the idea that something terrible would happen to me, the empty plate of my inheritance re- placed, in their minds, with a series of miserable deaths. I was not allowed near fire; in the cold months, I shivered beside an empty fireplace. Food was a choking hazard, and so I was hungry, given milk to drink and pureed fruit. Strangers, or really any person at all other than my parents, would murder me. I was not safe, I was not safe, and they must have more children to replace me when, eventually, inevitably, I was taken from them. They must have another one of me.

They set upon the project of creating my sibling loudly and increasingly publicly. When they were found, naked and entangled, on the roadside by the house, the extended family decided enough was enough, and my parents were sent away to separate asylums, and I went to my aunt and uncle in Oxfordshire. My parents never saw each other again, though my mother was pregnant by the time she reached the asylum, and gave birth to—I believe—my sister, who lived a day or two and then died before it had been decided what should be done with her. Years later, my mother jumped into the fire and my father simply waited, never seeing anyone and spending his days rocking a pair of small throw pillows in his arms. I heard that, several years after my family was dispersed, there was a huge fire in Sixpenny Handley. Almost none of the buildings remained.

In my uncle's house, I waited for my madness to surface, and I painted copies, and I became aware of all the ways that I was already mad, a long list that included but was not limited to: the way I dressed, the way I spoke, the way that, as I stumbled through the strange and unfamiliar world of Inderwick Hall and as I yearned and yearned for my dear, mad, familiar parents, I could pass a person I had met several times before—my aunt's maid, for example, or a friend of my uncle, and have no idea who they were.

I liked, as a child, to decorate my own clothes in the style of paintings I had seen, pasting little glass beads to the sleeves of my coat to look like Henry the Eighth in the portrait by Holbein the Younger that had been in the newspaper, or draping white cloth over my head as I had seen the women do in Vermeer pictures.

At my parents' house, I had spoken to everyone in the same manner: my parents the same as the vicar the same as the maid the same as the rag-and-bone men who used to come by with items they'd stolen from the people in town, the same as the travelling players who arrived in the village once a year to perform an inscrutable drama that referenced, variously,

Julius Caesar, Jesus feeding the multitude and some satire about local politicians. I was taught no rules in this regard except the rule of being, generally, a pleasant person who did not trouble others and who was untroubled by them. I had not known, before I moved to Inderwick Hall, that to see the family lawyer emerge from a consultation with my aunt and say, 'Why are you so sweaty? Have you been running or are you sick?' would be considered an affront.

I had been accustomed, too, to moving freely, eating what I liked whenever I was hungry, reading the books my father brought home from his library club as soon as he was finished with them and sleeping in the same bed as my mother, though I had my own room down the hall. I was not at all used to the rhythms of the new house, which ran almost despite its inhabitants, and to which we were all expected to succumb. After dinner, when the men moved to the library and the women to the green room, the table was cleared. Later, before the staff retired to bed, it was laid out for breakfast. The sun rose. Food was brought into the dining room, set out. The family arrived: ate. Later, the food was cleared away: crumbs swept, smears and stains wiped, eggshells and apple cores bucketed for the pigs. The table was laid for lunch. Food was brought in, set out. The family arrived: ate. The table was cleared, and then laid for dinner. The sun went down. Food was brought in. The family ate. The men moved to the library, the women to the green room. On my first day in the house, having been awake and terrified all night, I slept through breakfast then wandered into the kitchen mid-morning and asked the cook for an apple.

This was reported to my aunt and uncle, who reacted as though I had casually asked for a dagger in order to drive it through their hearts.

When I passed the cook in the entrance hall the following day, I did not recognise her. She had taken off her cap and apron and appeared to me, without them, an entirely new person. She asked if I had been sufficiently fed that day in a tone I did not understand was sarcastic and I answered, as I would have answered my parents, or a rag-and-bone man, or a lawyer, that I was not hungry just then, and thanked her for asking. This too was reported. This too was mad.

I simply never knew who anybody was. Not a new problem for me, but newly horrifying, separated as I was from my mother, who I only then realised had ushered me through my encounters with the world while whispering a running commentary: 'Here comes our friend Mr Wainthrop, and ah, look, let's wave to that kind gentleman who helped your father mend the gate. And, see, here is the doctor just leaving church.' Without her, I was at sea. I began to creep through the house, furtive as a rodent, sticking to its quietest places and keeping my head down for fear I would encounter a strange and looming face in the hallway—which might be a stranger but might be a cousin, might be a servant who the previous day had bathed me, might be a friend of the family who had given me a birthday present—and disgrace myself with blankness. I missed my parents hotly and angrily, and at the same time, began to fear that if they came to rescue me, I would not know who they were.

But there was Charles. Charles, who was distinctive to

me long before the others were, because he was the only one who smiled.

Charles, who had come to understand the ways in which I was and was not mad, was and was not any madder than anybody else in our family, and who had, after a time, begun, of his own accord, to whisper, when we were together: 'And here is Mrs Arthur, who is the new cook, and who asked you yesterday whether you liked carrots; and here comes Mr Williams in a bright blue coat, who is writing a book about the house; and over there, looking at you sourly, is Mrs White, who is Mater's dear friend who has come to stay for the week.'

I loved him for that, and for other reasons.

And now he had returned, and was amongst us, meeting nobody's eye and shuffling apologetically into rooms through which, as a younger man, he had paraded, laughing; rooms he had once made lighter and brighter and more tolerable.

Charles was back, and everyone else went mad.

COPY OF A SELF-PORTRAIT OF CHARLES ROBERT INDERWICK

I barely saw Charles in those first few days at the house. He kept to his room for the most part and had his meals sent up to him, claiming to suffer from severe headaches, which was reasonable since whenever he did emerge everybody started shouting. The only glimpses I got of him were at dusk, when he would sneak out to the old rose garden, which my window directly overlooked. There, he was out of sight of the best rooms in the house, which had views of the fountains and the new rose garden, but he must have known that my room was right there on the ground floor, and that I would be right there, too, wiping my breath from the other side of the glass.

He meandered, listless and enormous, between the flower beds. Then he stopped, his back to the house, unmoving. The sky was very clear in those evenings, dusk-dark and blue, and against it the straggling branches of the flowers looked precise and jagged. Amongst them, Charles looked statuesque, a half-finished rendition of a man, implausible almost. A bird whistled. Charles looked up, whistled back.

I imagined going out to him, saying, 'Do you remember

when you took me to Oxford, to see the stuffed dodo bird?'
or 'Do you remember when you gave me paint brushes?' or
even, 'Do you remember your portrait of Emma?' But the
questions sounded accusatory, like tests, and besides, there
was only so long I could be alone in his company before I
would feel compelled to accuse him of taking my money.
There was something too decisive about mentioning that,
as though I was declaring war. There could be no undoing
it. And so I too stayed in my room, and watched him slouch
amongst the dying flowers and light his pipe—a bright white
spark—and stay there until I gave up watching and went to
bed. I emerged only at meal times, propelled by habit to sit at
the table and listen to the family cacophony. Twice I received
notes under my door from Mr Barnard, inviting me to take
the air with him, which I fed to the fire. I spoke as minimally
as I could, except to Bobby, who tapped on my windows
to ask for gossip about what was happening in the house,
what had transpired in Rome, and also to pass on details of
a conversation he'd had with Rosamond, who had said some
very funny, very winning things, and who had invited him
to attend her socialist meetings, and did I think he should
accept? I told Bobby he should go to the socialist meetings.

The atmosphere throughout the house was one of jangling
tension. I found myself fidgeting compulsively at the table,
my heel bobbing up and down, fingers reaching to pull at
hang nails. The skin where I had grazed my elbow in Putney
had scabbed, and I found I could not leave it be, picked it open
compulsively, so that day after day my sleeves had brown
dots of blood at the elbow.

My aunt had written to several friends whose allegiance she felt she could depend on, and to more lawyers, and a former servant who had worked closely with Ferris, and to an old friend of the family, too, inviting them all to the house at their earliest convenience. Servants brought in flowers for the dinner she was determined to host; an excessive amount of wine arrived. At the breakfast table, she spoke at length about who should sit next to whom, and the ideal timing for her speech. She made it clear that she absolutely did intend to make a speech.

Mr George, having regained some equanimity since the night Charles had arrived, murmured that she might like to wait until after more enquiries had been made; that perhaps Charles might be too tired from travel and his abrupt change of scene to enjoy a large social event; perhaps it was an event best held in springtime, rather than this oppressive autumn that was turning, now, frosty and inhospitable. One evening, after drinking a lot at dinner, he raised his voice again. Certain phrases—'Can't you *see*?' and 'Simply preposterous'—were audible even from behind the closed library door, where Ferris argued just as forcefully against him: '*Plain* to see,' 'the *very* same face, manner, bearing,' and it was 'shocking to blight the happy moment this way.' The following day, my aunt let it be known that Mr George's services were no longer required by the family. Mr Barnard, who was barely older than me and had the demeanour of a puppy taken too soon from its mother, could carry on alone. And besides, she had sent for more lawyers. Mr George began loudly slamming books around, pretending to pack up his papers but in reality only disordering everything to create more work for Mr Barnard.

On occasion, people turned to me and said, 'Well, Grace?'

The first time this happened it was Mr Barnard, who appeared suddenly at my elbow and too close, so that I could smell the milk from his tea on his breath. I knew what was being asked of me. It was widely known that during our years together at Inderwick Hall, Charles and I had been close, that he had been distant with his siblings and parents to the extent that I had probably spent more time with him in those years than anyone else in the family. And so, now, a verdict was required from me, as it was from everyone, all of us lining up on one side or another.

'Well?' I said. 'Well.'

'Well?' said Mr Barnard, and he moved closer still, so that the toe of his shoe was touching mine.

I stepped away and thought of Charles, now, the solid expanse of his shoulders amongst the spindly stems of the roses. I thought of Charles, then, the glimpse of his back through the keyhole of his bedroom and Emma naked beyond him. 'I am not good with faces,' I said, which was the closest thing to an admission I had ever made in public but was also the sort of thing said by people who were, in fact, better with faces than I was.

'You must surely recall your cousin, Grace,' Mr Barnard pushed, and the others did, too, subsequently—'You were so close, you and Charles! You loved him so much! You were always trailing about after him!'—and I found myself floundering, found that I was reluctant to say anything, let alone what I really thought, because what I really thought—what I was beginning to think—felt like a betrayal.

In truth: I was swayed. The certainty of Mr George, of the three uncles, of almost everyone, really, who was not my aunt or Ferris or one of their select recruited allies, was compelling. This man, this new Charles: could he truly be my cousin? He was not remotely like my cousin.

I tried and tried to remember Charles's face as it had been when I last saw it. I thought perhaps I could see the shape of his mouth, perhaps the way his eyes tightened at the edges when he smiled and even when he wasn't smiling but was thinking about smiling. But what I saw most clearly were the creases on his jacket when his back was turned, the fair hair at the nape of his neck over skin that went brown at the first glimpse of sun in springtime. He had been lean—lanky, even, the way boys often are in the later years of their adolescence, before they accrue the heft and breadth of their fathers. Sometimes I thought I was remembering something else distinctive about his appearance, only to realise that it was to do with his voice, or his clothes, or something he had said.

I thought about the mole on the new Charles's skin, and about the entirety of the new Charles, too, the largeness of him, the way his silhouette looked at dusk, and I thought: *I do not remember you.* I thought: *I do not remember you more than I do not remember most people.*

And I thought: *You stole my money.* The new Charles had stolen my money, which my real cousin would surely never do.

People started to arrive—my aunt's guests, her friends and Charles's—and they, too, said, 'Well, Grace?' and I found that, still, I could not say out loud what I was thinking, though it would have been of no consequence, not really, to speak. When Bobby came by my bedroom window one morning, tapping gently on the glass again, I told him, panicked, that people were asking me what I thought. 'What is it that you think?' he asked, and to him I said something closer to the truth: that if I could just be left alone, if I could just have a day, several days, of uninterrupted silence, I might be able to see things clearly, might find a memory of the face of my cousin, a true memory of him, in which eyes and chin and nose and mouth were all correctly placed and shaped, that would make everything definite.

'I'm sorry, then,' he said. 'I'll leave you be.'

And I had to say no, no, I didn't mean him, I didn't mean to be left alone that second. But that it was a feeling I had, a feeling of general noisiness, something buzzing in my ear that stopped me from being able to think straight about anything. 'I'm just not good with faces, Bobby,' I said, at which he laughed and repeated a story he'd told me many times, about how, when he first came to work at the hall, I only recognised him if he happened to be leading a horse somewhere. We'd had long conversations about his family and his life while my aunt's mare stamped and huffed beside him, but if ever our paths crossed and he was alone, wearing different clothes or somewhere unrelated to his work at the stables, I did not acknowledge him at all. It took a full six months before I could reliably recognise who he was, horse or no horse. I struggled with some faces more than others, and I had struggled with Bobby's in particular.

'I thought maybe there were two of you,' he said, which was the end of this story. 'Twins, one friendly and one cold.'

I looked at Bobby's face as he leaned in through the window and thought: he has eyes, he has a nose, lips, which I can see quite clearly. I tried to fix it all in place in my mind, the way I would a painting, but when I turned my head away, the memory dissipated like smoke. If I could not hold Bobby's face in my memory for even a few seconds, what hope did I have of summoning my cousin's?

In the end, though, Charles's face appeared to me as I was passing the bottom of the stairs and glanced up to the red landing: there it was, my lovely young cousin Charles, exactly right, exactly as he was, and I jumped, would have screamed had I not, after arriving in the house as a child, trained myself out of screaming. It was a painting. A portrait of Charles. A self-portrait, in fact, since he appeared in it looking intensely forwards, the thumb of his left hand angled through a palette, his arm draped over his knee. Beside it were my aunt and Ferris, in the process of removing the painting of my Great Grandfather Alexander and replacing it with Charles's likeness.

I remembered the painting, though I realised then that I hadn't seen it for several years, had entirely forgotten about it. Charles had painted it himself to mark the occasion of his seventeenth birthday. For a while it had hung in the red room, beside a dour and too-dark portrait of some ancestral hunting dogs. After that it must have been sent off to the attic, or the gun room, or somewhere in the house I never went. But here it was, now, here he was: my cousin looking golden-skinned and really quite beautiful, seated at an easel in front of an ivy-hung white wall, the sky orange and white behind his head in the manner of skies in paintings, though it had never looked like that over Inderwick Hall. His hair was foppish and tufty. His eyes were so dark it was impossible to see their colour. There was a self-consciousness to the whole thing, a suggestion in the expression that he had both enjoyed and worried over the performance of it as he painted. It was not badly done, I thought; there was skill and care and even pride in the brushwork.

'Charles!' my aunt shouted. And again, 'Charles!' And then, though it was unnecessary since already people were gathering, sticking their heads out of the library, the green room, round from the entrance hall, to see what the commotion was, 'Everybody! Come!'

From the top of the house, the faint thud, thud, thud, of somebody descending.

'Charles!' called my aunt. 'Come down and be recognised.'

Overhead, floorboards creaked.

The household assembled, my aunt's new guests along with the rest, nay-sayers included, and me. My aunt, standing on the red landing, glanced towards the upper floor at someone out of sight and I imagined Charles there, waiting, hovering, not yet able to see the painting that was facing those of us on the ground floor.

Did the portrait, in any way, resemble the new Charles?

'You'll notice,' my aunt said, looking from the wall to the

foot of the stairs, 'the portrait of Charles. I have placed it here for us all to view. There is his likeness on canvas. He painted it himself, on his seventeenth birthday, and we all agreed at the time what a marvellous likeness it was.'

I thought back to Charles's seventeenth birthday, a few months before he went to sea, when things had been bad, at their worst, in fact, my uncle always shouting and Charles caught up in something unreachable to me, angry and absent and when he was not absent, too busy writing hurried letters to spend time with me. I had no recollection of anybody saying the painting was marvellous.

'I have here, in addition, a photograph of Charles taken on the occasion of his thirteenth birthday and which you will see captures the very same essence of Charles that you see in the painting, though admittedly he appears still rather boyish.'

She took a couple of steps down towards us, extending the photograph in her hand. Mr Barnard took it from her, looking uncomfortable and passing it quickly to one of the uncles.

'And here, now,' my aunt said, 'is Charles himself.'

Nothing happened and people looked uneasily around. My aunt glanced up the stairs.

'Here is Charles himself,' she said again, more sternly, and above us I heard a heavy step, and then another, and then there he was, the new Charles standing beside the painting, looking mortified. He seemed surprised by its presence there, and when he studied it something seemed to give way in his face. I thought for a second he might cry. He shook his head, averted his eyes.

'As you can see,' my aunt said. 'It's a perfect match. There can be no doubt.'

The new Charles fixed his eyes somewhere above our heads. The uncle in possession of the photograph lifted it up.

'See here,' my aunt said, pausing to cough, 'where the jaw-line is clearly the same. And here, the same pattern of hair falling just so. And his eyes—you can see for yourselves, of course—his eyes are unmistakeable.' She looked unsteady, and a servant darted forwards to hold her arm. 'And look, now, see how Charles is embarrassed, and he sucks in his lower lip a little, and you can see the same, the very same, in his self-portrait, and again,' she waved in the direction of the floor, 'in the photograph, the very same.'

I looked from the painting to the fleshy face beside it, and around me I sensed everyone else doing the same thing, and then craning their necks to see the photograph, which was being passed around, from the uncle, to Ferris, to another uncle. The new Charles was bigger, of course, and that was in some ways the only thing I could see: the vast discrepancy in size between the two men. But then people did get bigger, didn't they? That was a normal sort of a change, the waxing of the figure into middle age, and he was thirty now, and looked it.

The photograph had reached Cousin Magnus, who was beside me. I scrutinized the small, earnest face in the image: a little blurry, one eye covered by a sweep of hair. The sharpest element of the whole thing was a vase on a table by his knees, but nonetheless, I thought as I looked, perhaps my aunt was right. Perhaps there was something shared and distinctive about the way the hair fell. Perhaps their jaws followed the same square route around the chin. Perhaps even the posture was the same, the new Charles's reticence and the Charles in the portrait's uncertain seat at the easel and the boy Charles in the photograph, out of focus and pale, their sucked-in lips. The longer I looked the more it seemed apparent: it was the same face, it surely was; they were the same, Charles then and Charles now. She was right. She was not the mad one after all.

Nobody said anything and my aunt began to look flustered. She twisted her hands in front of her stomach and scrunched up her mouth. Behind me I heard a tut, a sigh; it was Mr Barnard and one of the uncles, catching each other's eyes and smirking a little. Then somebody stepped forwards—a man of about thirty whom I struggled to place but later understood was the son of a family friend who had, at one time, attended school with Charles—and then forwards again, and then ran headlong up the stairs, catching the new Charles in a tight hug and slapping him on the back and saying, 'Charles, I've missed you! Charles, it's really you!' The people around me seemed jolted into action, began to talk, and someone else said, 'Well, yes, it clearly is him, isn't it?' and Ferris clapped his hands against his thighs triumphantly and said, 'Precisely, precisely, this is exactly what I've been saying.'

Hooked over the friend's shoulder, my cousin's face was a blank, his jawline buried in the man's jacket, his eyes closed.

SOME TRUTHS ABOUT COPYISTS

The copyist is invisible, a kind of vacancy, a channel between the beholder of the art and the original artist. In this sense, a copyist is simply not there.

The copyist says, 'Do not look at me.'

The copyist says, 'Look at how invisible I am.'

The copyist says, 'Do you love me? Don't you love me? Don't I exist? Do I exist?'

A Dinner in Honour of Charles Robert Inderwick, Returned from Many Years at Sea

The dinner party was not huge, though it was hugely stressful, hugely wearing to everyone involved. There were only thirty guests but my aunt had decorated the house in the style of someone even wealthier than she in fact was. She had invited people from town, notable academics and one of the college deans, but also relatives from London—the Duke was in attendance—and, most affronting of all to the rest of the family, several journalists. My aunt led them on a tour of the house, pointing out the contributions made by various generations of Inderwicks, the fourth floor added at the beginning of the century, the Roman pottery in the green room that had been collected by my great uncle, artefacts hanging in the library that she waved at casually, saying, 'Those are from abroad. We had land abroad, once. Quite a lot of it.'

'My niece,' she said, 'can tell you more about the artworks, if you care to know about the artworks.'

They turned to me. I nodded a small nod and looked at my aunt, who had never before conceded that I had any particular knowledge about anything. The group had stopped beside a small watercolour of the lake, quite nicely done and hard to copy, though I'd tried many times, on account of the layering, the unpredictable way the colour pooled and dried.

'This is a small watercolour of the lake,' I said.

Later, at the dinner, I found I was seated beside one of the journalists, a man only a little older than I was. On my other side was Mr Barnard, whose presence I was so accustomed to ignoring I might as well have been in the last seat at the table.

'And you were there, I understand, Miss Inderwick, at the moment when mother and son were reunited in Rome?' the journalist said.

Charles was seated at the head of the table, next to my aunt, and I watched him tentatively holding his knife, glancing at my aunt's fingers as she handled her own cutlery. He prodded the fish, swiping the blade through the flesh, uncovering bones in the manner of a painter spreading base colour on a canvas. (A memory of Charles doing just that, laying out an arced smear of ochre as he told me, in an agitated voice, about an argument he'd had with his father about the kinds of friends he was making in London.) He lifted a loaded fork to his mouth and set it down, murmured something polite in response to a question I couldn't hear. He lifted the fork again, parted his lips, then let it fall back to his plate. It struck me then that I had never seen him eat.

'Yes,' I said. 'I was in Rome.'

'And how does it feel,' the journalist continued, 'to be reunited with your cousin after all these years?'

I thought about the beer-smell in the room where we'd

found him, and the diary and the narrow chaise longue and the way my aunt had said, 'And are you really him?'

I had turned the phrase over in my mind ever since: *are you really him*, when it would have been neater, would have made more sense, wouldn't it, to ask *are you really you*? To ask *are you really him* was to ask a person whether they were somebody else, and my cousin was himself, surely, or he was not.

How did it feel, I wondered. It felt like someone amongst us was the mad one, but none of us knew who, and maybe it was all of us, each mad in a specific and complicated way. Why should anyone doubt that my aunt was correct, that she was able to recognise her own son? Why should I, of all people, doubt it, when I could not remember my own mother's face, let alone my cousin's? And yet there was doubt: people doubted, I doubted, sometimes even Charles himself looked doubtful. It felt as though we were all missing something.

'Wouldn't you agree, Miss Inderwick?' a voice said in my ear, and I turned to realise that Mr Barnard had been speaking to me. I tried to think what he could possibly have been saying, and came up with nothing, and smiled.

'I suppose it's a rather complicated feeling,' the journalist continued on my other side. 'Rather mixed emotions. A cousin returned, an uncle lost. I was,' he added, 'very sorry to hear of your uncle's passing.'

Charles was drinking, now, and too fast, hiding his face behind his wine. I watched the muscles of his throat twitch as he swallowed. I waited for him to put the glass down, and when he did, he picked it up again almost at once. And he had always liked to drink, that was consistent at least; he and I had once got quite drunk together when I was about twelve, and we had walked down past the formal gardens out to the fields and passed a bottle back and forth between us, and he had talked a lot about his father, how much he hated his father, how much he wished to be free of his father, and then he had stopped and said, 'I'm sorry, Grace, to complain about my father when you cannot be with your own.' I had told him I didn't mind, that his feelings about his father had no bearing on my feelings about mine, and when I said so he'd looked oddly at me, and said, 'You don't think quite like other people, little cousin.' After that my memory of the event is hazy.

'At least, I've always thought so,' said Mr Barnard.

My aunt's speech was, in the end, less combative than I'd anticipated, in part because she wanted the journalists kept entirely in the dark about any uncertainty surrounding the new Charles's identity. She stood and coughed, at first for show, to stop people from talking, and then the coughing seemed to take hold of her and she was immobilised for a few moments. By the time she caught her breath, we had all been silent for too long, had been staring at her for too long, so from the beginning the speech felt freighted, and nothing she said could possibly live up to the strange tension at the table. Charles was the only person to look away, bending his lips to his glass and fixing his eyes on the window, as she spoke about the great strength of character of the Inderwicks, of the adversity we had faced in recent months following the loss of her husband and younger son. My mother was not mentioned. She framed the return of the Inderwick heir to the family home after many years at sea as a sort of moral reward, a just and fitting acknowledgement by God or providence that the family was made up of good, lucky people who deserved good luck.

'Welcome back, Charles,' she said. 'We are so very lucky to have you home with us, at last, at long last. At long last.'

Charles had cleared his throat and then looked panicked when the silence that followed my aunt's words became the kind of silence that indicated he was expected to speak.

'Thank you,' he said. 'Thank you. This is . . . I am . . . That is all.' His cheeks had turned very dark pink. He drank again.

'And maybe they'd be right to!' said Mr Barnard, now, and again I turned to look at him. There was nobody seated to his other side; he really did seem to think that he and I were having a conversation about something.

'And what next for the Inderwick family?' the journalist asked. 'Has Charles discussed his plans with you at all?'

When I next looked over to Charles's seat, he was gone, his chair angled back from the table, a napkin crumpled by his plate. I glanced at the journalist and at Mr Barnard and, saying nothing, pushed myself back and left the room as fast as I could, before my aunt had the chance to call me back. As I left I saw the journalist glance around, attempting to make eye contact with one of the distant cousins, before turning to study a painting of a goldfish behind him on the wall. Mr Barnard began to listen intently to a conversation that was happening on the other side of the table, nodding as though he had been part of it all along.

The rest of the house was dim and quiet, the floral

decorations already wilting in their vases. I passed the hall to the kitchen where they were preparing some kind of overwhelming pudding, and the oak room, where my uncle used to lurk when he was forced to visit the house and wanted to avoid my aunt. I poked my head in but Charles wasn't there, and it was only when I felt disappointed that I realised how anxious I was to see him. I was annoyed, then, that I had so instinctively wanted anything to do with him. Still, I couldn't face returning to the dinner, where I was certain the journalist and Mr Barnard would be poised, ready to pick up their own threads and throttle me with them as soon as I sat down.

I left the house, passing the fountain and the new roses and the shrub-lined paths of the formal gardens which grew darker and darker the further I moved from the lights of the house, until I reached the low wall that marked the edge of the fields beyond. It was too dark to see in any detail, but I felt for grooves and footholds in the brick, hauling myself up and then astride it. The wall had been a favourite spot of mine ever since I'd first come to Inderwick Hall. It had felt secret, my own discovery, since nobody ever went there except me, though I hadn't minded when after a while Charles had started to join me.

I ran my palms across the brick, cold, slightly wet to the touch. The moon broke through cloud long enough for me to see a herd of cows grazing close by, wading ankle deep in mud and occasionally pissing into the wet earth. Between me and the house, the shrubs looked black as water, late summer flowers decaying on the stem. In the new rose garden, pink petals that had turned crisp brown were now soggy and smelt of rot.

'I seem to keep running into you in the dark,' Charles said. 'Are you hiding?'

He was standing a little further along the wall. The orange end of a cigar glowed in the dark, illuminating his nose, the hillock of his chin.

'Not hiding, just not present at the party,' I said. 'Are you hiding?'

Charles leant his weight against the wall and said, 'God, yes.'

I tried out a sentence several ways in my mind, and then said, carefully, 'People are still saying you're not the real Charles.'

'Let them say that if they want. My mother knows I am. Ferris does. Her friends do. And you do, of course. You believe in me, Grace. What those others think doesn't matter, really.'

He was drunk. There was a looseness to the way he was speaking that was new, a little unexpected flair. He seemed suddenly so like the old Charles, rakish and irreverent and confiding in me, that I felt a rush of familiarity and relief. In the dark I couldn't see any of him except what small slivers of skin were lit when he raised a hand to smoke, but his voice—I felt myself smiling into the blank night—I remembered his voice, it was just the same, the way he said, 'You do' and the way he said, 'Grace.'

'But I think what the others think does matter,' I said. 'If you want—' I hesitated; it felt crass to say the word, but then,

I thought, Charles *was* a little crass (and after all, hadn't he stolen from me? Hadn't he, in doing so, started the conversation?) '—money.'

He stiffened a little. His breath had a hard edge to it when he exhaled.

'It matters if you want money,' I said.

He said nothing. Back at the house, a door opened; I could just make out voices of the guests. They were exclaiming over something, perhaps the pudding, perhaps the absence of Charles, and then the door slammed shut. A cow squelched through the mud near us and snorted.

'I remember you so clearly,' Charles said, 'as you were then. Pale little scrap. Terrified all the time but talking as though nothing scared you in the world. You know, I didn't quite recognise you at first, in Rome. You seemed so different, but now I see you're just the same. You were the best thing about being here, in those last few years.'

I nodded, pointlessly, in the dark. It made me feel suddenly very young, very small, to be remembered as young and small.

'It was me who persuaded my parents to rescue you in the first place, you know. I don't think I ever told you that.'

'Oh.'

'I want you to know I was always on your side,' he said. 'That's all.' He was speaking intensely, had turned in my direction and raised his cigar; he seemed to be searching out my eyes.

'You think your parents rescued me?'

'Well, they did.' The hard edge was back again, ringing his words.

'Then you must not remember that time as clearly as you think you do. You must not remember what it was really like.'

'What was it really like?' he asked.

'It was not like being rescued.'

He sucked on his cigar. 'Well, you'll be safe enough now at least, with Mr Barnard.'

'What do you mean, safe with Mr Barnard?'

'When you marry him.'

I laughed, so loud and suddenly that I surprised myself. 'I'm not going to marry Mr Barnard.'

'Oh.'

'I'm not going to marry Mr Barnard,' I said again, and then, to my horror, found myself asking, 'Am I?'

He paused again to smoke and then said, 'I think it is expected that you will. By him, at least. And by my mother. You hadn't noticed?'

He moved along the wall towards me, breaking sticks underfoot. I felt too hot despite the cold air and wondered if I'd had too much to drink. With each step he took closer to me, I felt there was some rising expectation, and I didn't understand what it was, what was being asked of me. I thought of making a run for it back to the house, tried to calculate how quickly I could dismount the wall and break away towards the shrubs, but he was right there beside me, I could smell his tobacco, and something about the way he was standing—too close now, and tensely—made me certain I shouldn't do anything that might upset him.

'Do you?' I said, after a while. 'Do you want money?'

I felt a weight fall on my forearm and it took a moment to

realise it was his hand. His fingers lay against my wrist, very hot, slightly clammy.

'Everyone wants money, Grace.'

It had not until then occurred to me to be afraid of him.

Part Two

Winter 1899

Copy of Gustave Courbet's 'Le Sommeil', Oil on Canvas, 1866

Standing in front of Courbet's 'Le Sommeil'—a copy of Courbet's 'Le Sommeil', since the original was owned by an anonymous collector in France, too scandalous for public view—I wondered, again, whether it was I who was the mad one.

The painting: two female figures lie naked on a bed, one brown-haired, one blonde. They are artfully dishevelled, legs entwined, the face of one leaning towards the nipples of the other. Both appear asleep. The scene is arranged to suggest the artist has simply happened upon them, has guilelessly wandered in, as though he, and by extension all of us now seeing them, could quietly back out of the room without waking them. And it was vast, seemed to fill the whole room, and so it seemed to say, or rather to shout: *this is what is happening on the other side of this wall, behind closed doors, in places you are not, and have not been invited.* And it seemed to say: *this is the secret nobody has ever told you.*

I thought of my parents, naked by the roadside.

I thought of my own life, of certain naked people I had known.

I thought of myself, naked. A memory of examining myself in the mirror as a child and realising I was just a body, like everyone else, an assortment of limbs arranged around a pulpy middle, and in realising this, understanding something about mortality. A memory of, later, lying naked in a hidden corner of the gardens at Inderwick Hall, and I was beside another person, entwined so that our limbs had become confused and I could not tell by sight alone which of the four legs belonged to me, and in realising this, under-standing something about familiarity and lust.

I felt suddenly, phenomenally sad and for a moment won-dered whether the task I'd undertaken, of memorising this work, inch by meticulous inch, so that I could later copy it, was beyond me.

It had taken some effort to get there, though I'd been grate-ful for the distraction in the aftermath of the dinner, when the atmosphere in the house had, if anything, worsened. Mr George had departed, more people had arrived who backed my aunt's case; Charles had chosen to absent himself, saying he wished to consult with a lawyer friend he knew in Plymouth and leaving directly the morning after the dinner. I half thought we would never see him again, though in his absence the arguments continued, my aunt threatening to throw out anyone who disagreed with her, and the people who disagreed with her threatening to have her committed to an asylum.

Nobody seemed to care what I was doing, so I gave Bobby a carved-bone picture frame and a silver trinket box and in return he brought me a large order of paint, a roll of

unstretched canvas and two new brushes. I wrote letters
to the four owners of the Courbet copies, whose names the
Roman dealer had supplied to me, angling for an invitation
to view their painting. I was a student of art, I said, with a
great interest in the female form, which I noted to myself was
not in fact a lie. To my aunt, I said I was travelling to London
to consult a doctor about my pains, which was certainly a
lie, but she nodded distractedly. She did not ask what my
pains actually were or seem surprised to discover I suffered
from them. Nor did she ask how I would pay for the trip. She
waved a hand at me as though I was telling her something
she already knew, then resumed talking to somebody about
something to do with Charles. I was left undisturbed to pack
and arrange my travel. I supposed that for this I should be
grateful to my cousin.

In the past, when I had tried to beg small freedoms—an
unaccompanied trip to Oxford, say, or a chance to go back
to Dorset to see my mother's friends—I had been apologetic,
had tried too hard to argue my case to my aunt, and in doing
so had hardened her against me. I had made her feel weary
of the whole conversation before she'd even begun to speak.
Her natural feelings about me had always been hard, since
she liked nobody except her own children and disliked me in
particular for my strangeness and my familiarity; I gave up
trying to soften her animus and turned my attention instead
to overriding her instincts to thwart me.

Since Charles's arrival, I had studied the way he stood his
ground, even when he was nervous, even when he was sweating, and the way that his few, terse words never included an

apology or an offer to compromise. From him I learned not to say, 'Might I go to London, aunt?' but rather to inform her I was going. It had worked better than I had dared to hope, and so for that lesson, too, I was grateful to my cousin.

There had been no reply from two of the owners of 'Le Sommeil', and one wrote back demanding payment in advance of viewing, which left the fourth, who had asked a lot of questions about who I was and what I wanted, had seemed instantly suspicious and yet continued to respond to me, in shaky handwriting that suggested the author was elderly. Over the course of four letters and several weeks, I concocted a wonderful history for myself: orphaned, inherited immense wealth, trained in Paris with several fashionable artists, returned to England to take ownership of the family home whilst continuing to pursue my work. I added a few details I thought might appeal to the owner of a painting like 'Le Sommeil', about the conservatism of the art world, of how difficult it was to view work of real vision and daring in this country, of how stifled I felt by the lack of spirit and daring in English painting. Eventually, when I'd almost given up hope, the invitation came.

The house was on Queen Anne Street and looked ordinary from the outside. The old man who greeted me there, Mr Barnes, seemed ordinary too, at least at first, leading me from ordinary hallway to ordinary parlour and through to a smaller room where the painting filled almost a whole wall. The only item of furniture there was a small stool placed directly before the canvas. 'I had to have it,' he said, a little too quickly, not quite in control of himself when it came to the painting. 'As soon as I read of it, I knew I had to see it, and as soon as I saw it, I knew I had to have it.' I nodded. 'I'm not a man to buy great artworks,' he added, 'but this! Well. You see. You understand.'

I found it hard to look at him directly; there was a sort of mania to him when he talked about the painting, a curatorial fervour that reminded me of my aunt, the way she talked too quickly about Charles, the way she looked at Charles, the way that, even when she was not talking about Charles, was saying something mild about the weather, about the menu for lunch, she seemed to be talking about Charles.

Mr Barnes referred to the painting not as 'Le Sommeil', and not even as 'The Sleepers', but as 'The Two Friends', a title which I tucked away in my mind to laugh about later. 'Here they are,' he said, 'in repose. 'The Two Friends'.' As though, perhaps, this was the sort of thing friends got up to all the time: a friendly nap, this naked embrace. As though only a filthy mind would think otherwise, and only perverted eyes would be drawn to the proximity of pink lips to pink nipple or the dark shadows of the bodies' creases. He loitered nervously at the edge of the frame, scanning my face. He was waiting for a sign that I understood the painting, I could tell, and that in understanding it, I understood him. I tried to remain expressionless and thought about the people at Inderwick Hall who had said, 'Well, Grace?' and then waited with such urgency for me to speak, and I felt all over again that I did not want to give myself away, not to anyone, not even over a painting.

I could sense it coming, could almost see the word forming on his lips, and then he said it: 'Well?'

'It's very nice,' I said. And then, when this appeared not to satisfy him, when I realised he would never leave me alone unless I performed for him a little, I said: 'What good friends they are!'

The painting was bigger than I had expected, an enormous undertaking; it would require the mixing of vast amounts of pinks and beiges for skin and a considerable outlay of white paint, more than Bobby had brought me, since what was not skin in this painting was pale bed linen. I tried to keep my focus on practicalities, on the cost of the materials and on contemplating the canvas, patch by patch, square by square, committing it to the strange, volatile part of myself that would later regurgitate it. I tried not to think too much about the whole, about the bodies themselves, about the crook of the brown-haired woman's knee bending over the fair-haired woman's hip. When considered as an accumulation of brush strokes and tone, pigment and oil, browns and reds lightened with whites and yellows, piece by piece, each mark was meaningless, an abstraction, a leaf falling from a branch into a pile of other leaves, and there was nothing there to make me flush—and yet I began to flush—and nothing corporeal, nothing close and hot and female and strange and bodily that would trigger something like giddiness—and yet I could feel something like giddiness rising in me. It was a familiar sensation and yet still it took me by surprise.

I did not think, really, that the thoughts and feelings I had about women made me mad, but perhaps the thoughts and feelings of my parents had not struck them as mad either.

I knew that the feelings I had about women were the feelings men had about women.

I was less certain whether the feelings I had about women were the feelings most women had about men.

I had found, once, while sneaking into Charles's room in search of art supplies, a plain-bound book which contained within its covers a novel called *Autobiography of an Artist and his Exploits in Lust*. In it, a painter detailed his sexual encounters with various young models, and the word 'frig' was used a lot. I had felt warmly towards my cousin then, knowing that he and I had more than just painting in common, shared too this interest in bodies, in women, and I looked forward to his return from sea. Reading the book made my face hot, made me glance, and then stare, at the maid washing the windows of my room, her body occasionally flattening against the wet glass, the yellowed cotton of her smock turning grey and the faint outline of her torso becoming less faint. I took the book back to my bedroom, along with two tubes of cadmium red paint and a little bound collection of autostereograms: pages of frantic, meaningless patterns that, if you stared at them with just the right balance of concentration and vagueness, revealed pictures hidden in their midst.

At the time, having no other way to pursue this interest, I had turned as I always did to painting, to repeating and repeating the Madonna as portrayed in the chapel, the ruched dress falling against the groove of her breastbone, the hand, the fingers of the hand, pressed below her throat. I could paint it in my sleep. Later, I'd had encounters: once with a woman in the village who had seemed to recognise something in me that I was still myself baffled by, and had invited me to join her for lunch. It had been an oddly formal affair, and when it was over she seemed relieved, as though she'd done her duty by me. There had been a second time, with the daughter of a business associate of my uncle who had passed me a note at breakfast, and another at lunch, and then finally at dinner had held me in her gaze as she had announced she was retiring with a headache. I had waited five long minutes before saying I was very tired and needed to go to bed. She had been waiting for me by my bedroom door. We had run through the gardens—it was a hot night in August—to their most undisturbed spot, where the shrubs became thicker and taller and the ground began to slope down to the lake, and it was something I thought about all the time afterwards, long after her father's business dealings with my uncle had soured, long after I learned she had married, the way her hair had brushed against my collar bones, the way the skin beneath her breasts had smelt sour with sweat.

Courbet was not good at portraying weight, I realised, and it took some effort not to correct this for him in my mind as I continued my study. In a painting that was so much concerned with draping, with limbs on top of limbs, bodies on a bed, hair on a pillow, everything in it seemed to hover uneasily. Even the cup on the nightstand seemed to be floating, a string of pearls wafting through the air behind it. The figures in particular looked weightless, more in the vein of Botticelli goddesses drifting towards the frame than two real women embracing heavily on a real bed. I tried to hold it close, this floating quality. It kept my own feelings at bay.

The comment Charles had made, the night of the party, what he had said about Mr Barnard, had been bothering me. I had been unable to shake the uneasiness, a sense of having been oblivious. It struck me that perhaps my aunt *had* been mentioning marriage to me with an increasing urgency; it was the sort of thing I ignored when she spoke to me, because her plans changed so often and she frequently forgot the things she'd said. It was certainly true that after my mother's funeral (an extremely quiet occasion, not publicised for obvious reasons), it was the first thing she had said: 'You need a husband, Grace. You absolutely need a husband.' She wanted me out from under her feet. She wanted more men around. She wanted less responsibility on her own shoulders. I had nodded and, until Charles raised it, forgotten all about it. It had seemed so abstract as to be irrelevant. It was simply not what I was looking for.

I wasn't, now I interrogated myself, opposed to the idea of a husband. If it meant I could leave Inderwick Hall and commence a different kind of life, I was open to it. But I was fully aware that marriage would be an effort, something I'd have to work at. When I thought of women, of the way I felt about women, I felt smooth, I felt certain, it was like copying: instinctive and serene. When I thought about husbands, I felt exhausted.

I stepped back and looked at the sleeping figures in the painting of 'The Two Friends', the tiny squares of brush-strokes cohering into shimmering flesh, and I thought about the complete vacancy of a human being that was Mr Barnard, and I thought about Charles, leaning against the wall in the dark and smoking his cigar and saying, 'Everyone wants money, Grace.' The legs of the women in the painting were slightly different colours; one had pinker, paler skin, the other slightly yellowed. They held each other. The hand of the pale one on the calf of the ochre one was the only heavy thing in the painting.

I could get married, I thought. I could do it, if it was the right thing to do. Or I could leave the house on Queen Anne Street and go home and set to work on a copy of Courbet's 'Le Sommeil', setting out all the legs, the hands, the fingers, all the rumples in the sheets and the dark blue beyond just so, just as it was, and make some money from it and then perhaps I could do something—do anything—else.

A LIKENESS

'An artist is coming.'

The voice made me jump; I snapped my notebook shut, breaking a stick of charcoal. 'What?'

'An artist is coming,' said Charles, again. He was standing in the doorway to my room, obscuring what was left of the grey winter light and looking mournful, as though an artist was the worst possible thing that could arrive.

I had never shown him to my room, nor suggested he might be welcome there, though he had been, of course, in the years before he left. His presence now was an imposition. I had been busy, very busy, making plans for my Courbet, acquiring additional paint and a frame for the enormous canvas, sketching out in charcoal the lines, each exact, and recalling and recalling and recalling every small detail of colour—the lip of the glass vase on the nightstand, same grey, exact same grey, as the shadow in the bedsheet behind and just below it; the palest pink of the lips of the paler woman as dark as the darkest part of the nipple of the darker woman—which I repeated to myself as a kind of prayer, and as I took him in, I still could not shake 'Le Sommeil'.

When I looked out of the window behind his head, at

clouds rolling towards the house, what I saw were blousy bedsheets under naked bodies; when he set a cup of wine on the edge of my mantelpiece, I thought of the blue-and-orange goblet at the brown-haired sleeper's elbow, and of the string of pearls leading to its rim. When I saw his feet, booted on the rug, and my own, angled away from him, my mind turned again to the entangled legs of the two friends: their dark soles, the neat grooves between toes, the shadowed hillocks of their ankle bones. Everything else—the real world—was muffled and removed from me, my ears full of persistent and colourful music. Or, rather, I felt I was removed from the world, as distant and uninvolved with the goings-on in the house as a painting on a wall.

It had not escaped me, even in this state, that there was an increasing air of carnival about the place: journalists were as frequent guests as lawyers (the news about Charles's uncertain identity had got out, inevitably; the journalist I'd sat beside at dinner had published a wry and slightly cruel little article in the local paper about us all, taking pains to note my parents' misfortune as he sketched out the family history), and I had the constant impression that at any moment somebody might break into tears, or song, or some act of terrible violence. But still, it was a shock, and unwelcome, to be confronted by the solid reality of my cousin in my doorway when I had been so happily entranced by 'Le Sommeil', to see him so firmly planted on the floor, his silhouette against the light of the window so black.

'An artist is coming.' I tried to discern from Charles's expression whether this was the opening of a joke, whether he was going to reveal that he knew where I had been, that I had visited the Courbet and fabricated my pains, that he had uncovered yet another part of myself that I had assumed was secret. I glanced around to check there was no evidence of my work on view: the canvas, stretched in sections on small, temporary frames that could fit in the painting room, even when wet; the paints in a box buried under napkins of the sort that might, plausibly, have been used for monthly blood; brushes washed and drying behind the curtain, a window cracked to air out the odour of turps.

'An artist?' I said.

'Yes. Coming here, to the house. To draw a likeness of me.'

I felt a flicker—just a flicker—of jealousy, then, and shame that I had ever thought he might call me an artist. But what I said was, 'How charming.'

'Where have you been, Cousin Grace? I've not seen you.' He looked reproachful, and for the first time I thought perhaps he was scared of something. He seemed to sense that I had seen this and flashed a smile. 'You, who are my only friend in this cruel world.'

'You've been away,' I said.

'I've been back quite some time.'

'I've been busy,' I said, and then added, 'unwell.'

'Ah yes,' Charles said, and his eyes darted to notebook in my hands, the spill of charcoal dust down from its fold onto my lap, and then beyond me to the painting room, though surely he could not know, how could he possibly know, there was anything unusual within it. 'Your agonies.'

'Pains,' I corrected.

'Your pains. I hope they are easing.'

'They are not,' I said.

There was a lightness to him that I hadn't seen before. He was smiling again, as he had earlier, in an effort to displace nervousness from his face. It was almost shyness, a kind of silliness. There had been no sign of this side of him when he was with my aunt, or the uncles, the lawyers, the journalists, when he was stern, and gruff, and met nobody's eye. And I hadn't seen it during the two conversations we'd had alone: both in the dark, when he, too, had seemed dark and definite. But the way he was smiling, the way he was lightly thumbing the side of his wine glass as he looked to and away from me, reminded me—for a strange moment I couldn't think who he was like, and then it came to me, so that I, too, was smiling—reminded me of him. Young Charles. He who had been my only friend in this cruel world. He who would have constructed a sentence exactly that way: too much, to cover up the extent to which it was true. I ground the charcoal dust between my finger and thumb and streaked a smudge across the leather cover. When I looked up again, Charles had come further into the room.

'The artist is not to see me,' he said. 'They have told him to look at my self-portrait from all those years ago, and the photograph, and at portraits of my father and grandfather and so on, and make a likeness of how I might look now. And then there is to be a comparison of this imagined portrait with me as I, in fact, am. And it is going to prove the point one way or the other. It is some scheme of Mr George.'

'I thought Mr George was gone.'

'Back again. Summoned by the uncles. They are deter-mined to humiliate me.' Again, a grimace rapidly replaced with a grin.

'Why should it be humiliating?' I said. 'I expect the artist will rule in your favour.'

'Perhaps,' he said, and took his glass and moved to leave the room. On the threshold he paused, and I saw his eyes move to 'The Drag' over the bed. A small smile moved his lips. 'That awful painting. Still here.'

I had forgotten, during the conversation, how anxious I was to have my privacy back, to return to my own thoughts, but remembered it now.

'Yes,' I said. 'It's still here.'

'I'm glad you're back,' he said, and then, finally, moved out of sight.

The artist, when he arrived the following day, did at least give the impression of impartiality. He introduced himself as James, without a 'Mr.' before it, or a surname after it, so it was unclear whether this was a first or second name and I couldn't tell if he was being overfamiliar or rather cold. Even as he handed off his coat and hat, he waved away the uncles and Mr George when they thanked him for his efforts, and similarly distanced himself from my aunt when she mentioned, apropos of nothing, that many years of eating a foreign diet can cause remarkable weight gain in a person, and that such things were surely of no account, though they could perhaps be forgotten by a man in the artist's position, given only historic portraits of a slender boy to work from.

James was at pains to emphasize, he was not here amongst us for one thing—confirmation of Charles's identity—or another—confirmation of Charles's fraudulence—but merely to cast light, objectively and artistically, upon our predicament. He came to us in the spirit of truth, being famous for his courtroom sketches and renderings of faces, in particular; he was sought after by the police, who frequently issued his imagined portraits of suspects to the papers; several criminals having been caught based on likenesses he had drawn from witness descriptions alone.

(For this reason, he became at once an object of some fascination to me: he possessed a skill exactly matched to my own weakness. Where I was blind to faces he had second sight, could see their past, their present and also their future. I thought perhaps that if I could see how he worked, I might be able to see faces the way he did, might dislodge whatever it was that stopped me seeing clearly.)

He had brought an entourage, which nobody had expected: several assistants and his daughters, too; the older one around my age and the younger two, twins, about ten or eleven years old. Charles and I had observed their approach through the window of the topmost parlour, next to his bedroom, from where we could see a procession of servants and luggage trailing from the carriage at the gate to the house and culminating, finally, in the artist himself, wearing a black coat and black hat, with his daughters by his side. Charles was under strict instructions to keep himself hidden from the artist, and I had been tasked with being his gaoler.

'Look at him,' Charles said, so close to the glass that it

misted, 'look at him,' and I looked at the surprising crowd and at the man himself, at the way he seemed to take everything in—the house, the people, the weather—as though he was appraising its value, and I found that I could not help but look, too, at his oldest daughter, who was fiddling with a scarf knotted jauntily around her neck and staring out towards the muddy fields. She glanced up at the house and I stepped back.

'You should stand away from the window,' I said to Charles. 'He might see you.'

Charles didn't budge. He wiped his breath from the pane. 'Go down,' he said. 'Go down and see what is happening.'

What was happening downstairs was mostly consternation about where all the unexpected guests were to be housed, but what was also happening was that the artist's oldest daughter, whose name, I learned, was Ruby, was standing there, glancing at things and nodding when being spoken to and smelling faintly of cigarettes, and nobody else seemed to be distracted by this, seemed to think that anything about it was extraordinary, seemed to notice that she was the loudest thing in the room even when she was saying nothing. She had a clear, strong brow and hair that was twisting away from its pins, hands that were broad and long and agile, drumming silent rhythms against her thighs, and a way of being in her clothes that seemed casual, somehow, a scarf knotted jauntily beneath her chin. I was very distracted. I thought she was very extraordinary. She did not look at me.

'What is wrong with you, Grace?' my aunt said, swatting a hand in front of my face in a way that suggested I had been staring.

I shook my head. 'Nothing is wrong,' I said, and beyond my aunt, Ruby blinked, nodded at something her father said, moved a loose hair away from her cheek.

James was led away upstairs, and my aunt said something about dinner plans; again I shook my head and followed, anxious I would miss some wisdom from James about faces, anxious I would miss something about Ruby's face, which was turned from me now as she ascended the stairs.

'Grace,' my aunt said. 'Grace,' and I left her and followed them.

Mr George was showing James and his entourage Charles's youthful self-portrait, which had been hung in the upper gallery alongside paintings of my uncle and grandfather and great grandfathers, one after the other, aging and aging and aging into the past the further down the line they walked. James kept his daughters close to him at all times and appeared to be training them in his trade; he pointed at details of the portraits and murmured to them. I could make out only a few words: 'bone', 'droop', 'hollow', 'jowls', and pressed forwards, closer to them. 'Imagine the eye socket,' James was saying, 'the diminishing muscle and sinew, here, and the discolouration where the bone edge sits below the thinnest skin.' The daughters nodded and the younger ones scribbled in little sketchpads. Ruby looked around, unconcerned, and then, for the first time, noticed me. I met her eye, and when she did not blink or glance away, I stepped back, and then back again.

'You look flustered, Cousin Grace,' Charles said, later, when everyone had gone to dress for dinner. We were in his upstairs parlour again and he was smoking, holding a pipe in one hand and a glass of port in the other, which he was sipping fast. He had taken off his jacket and tie and unbuttoned his shirt at the collar as though the weather outside were very hot, and not chill November rain. A tray of food had been brought up for him, since he was barred from the communal meal, and every now and then he set down his pipe to poke distractedly at onions and bacon.

'They keep sending me meat,' he said. 'Is it so hard to remember, still, that I won't eat it?'

He had always been that way about meat, it was true. The whole time I had known him he had refused it, though he would sometimes eat fish. It had been one of many things about him that enraged his father, who had been driven at times to violence by Charles's repudiations of pork, beef, especially game.

'So do you,' I said. 'You look flustered.'

He was looking at me strangely, with an expression somewhere between amusement and suspicion, and I made myself stare out of the window to avoid meeting his eye. I watched a raindrop slide jauntily down a pane.

'No,' he said, 'I mean, you look *very* flustered,' and, unable to tolerate his attention on me any longer, I sprang up and said I had to go down for dinner.

I was no less flustered downstairs. Ruby was seated beside me and, though no conversation was required from either of us while James held forth on his recent successes with the police, I found myself wordless and gormless and not hungry. I pushed my food to the edge of my plate and drew lines in the sauce with my fork. Ruby was barely eating, either; she turned over a slice of ham and scraped at the underside with her knife, then set it aside. The smell of the meat was suddenly too much. It was intimate, salty, lip-coloured, and I felt embarrassed, felt Ruby's distaste for the ham must reflect a broader distaste, for my silent company, or my smell, or for the whole of me. She declined dessert. She declined coffee.

'Would you like bread?' I found myself asking.

She looked at me again, the same, unblinking stare. 'Bread?'

'Are you hungry?'

'I've eaten,' she said, gesturing to the sideboard from which dishes had yet to be cleared.

'Barely.'

'Neither did you.'

'No,' I said. 'So I was thinking about having bread.'

'I would not like any bread,' she said. 'Thank you.'

And I was flustered when, after the meal, James led us to back to the upper gallery, where his assistants had already set up his tools, his inks, the photograph of thirteen-year-old Charles propped up beneath the self-portrait, and the uncles, Mr George, my aunt, Mr Barnard—oh, yes, there he was, Mr Barnard, still there—and I were invited to take seats around him in the manner of a musician about to give some kind of recital. Ferris hovered, mothlike, at the back. James's youngest daughters had been sent to bed but Ruby was at his elbow, passing her father his black ink, his cloth, his blotter, his thin nib, his grey ink, his thick nib, his blotter again, until, at last, he nodded, sighed, closed his eyes, opened them, dipped his pen and began to mark his page. I could sense the audience stiffening, as though he was about to make a speech. And then he did make a speech.

'The eyes!' he began, and I almost clapped. The eyes! He was going to tell me what I needed to know. 'One thinks of the eyes as an unchanging feature, unmarked by time. But in fact, the eyes can change shape, brightness, even colour. Eyelids droop, cataracts obscure, lashes thin, irises pale.' I repeated this silently to myself: eyelids, cataracts, lashes, irises. 'The true unchanging element of the face is not the eyes, but the nose.'

The nose! I became aware of the blur of mine at the bottom of my vision, intruding on everything I turned my head to see. If I closed one eye, and then the other, I could see its sides, the hazy outline of its profile. Mr George touched his without seeming to realise he was doing it, and then so did Mr Barnard, and so did I, and so, even, did Ruby.

'Naturally,' the artist continued, 'deposits of fat, or damage to skin might change its outer appearances, but the structure of the centre of the nose, that is to say, the ridge, protuberance, symmetry, septum and so on: this is the true landmark, so to speak, of the face. So, it is with the nose that I begin: a nose that is clearly and distinctively represented in my subject's self-portrait and in his childhood photograph, and which is shared by his father, his grandfather and so on.'

'What about violence?' asked one of the uncles, and there was a clatter at the back of the room that made everyone swivel round. Ferris was straightening, having dropped his pipe.

'Violence?' asked James.

'Might not violence alter that inner structure of the nose?' said the uncle, whose own nose was flattened to one side.

'Violence, yes,' James said. 'A broken nose is unlike the nose it was before the breakage. Likewise, the burning of the whole face in fire alters its appearance rather drastically. Likewise, scarring caused by sword-strike, lightning, chemical explosion.'

My aunt emitted a distressed chirrup.

'I deal with probability, Sir,' James said, turning to the uncle in question, 'not fortune-telling.' His page was blank, and then there, in the middle of the white paper, he drew a nose.

'Does that look like his nose?' one of the other uncles murmured to Mr George, who said nothing.

Ruby's nose, I noticed, was long and somewhat asymmetrical, leaning slightly towards the left side of her face. It made her look sharp, unwavering. I stared at it and stared at it and thought, *I will remember this nose*, but when I closed my eyes to test myself, I could only hold the image for a second, and then it faded into something cartoonish and approximate.

'Teeth,' the artist said. Teeth! I turned to him for my next lesson. 'Teeth remain similarly consistent, notwithstanding loss to decay and, yes, violence and disaster and so on. And the structure of the teeth affects the external appearance of the mouth, even when unsmiling, even with lips entirely sealed. To this we can with reasonable certainty add a philtrum, which, regardless of weight gained or lost, will be constant in its proportions, its length and depth and position, from childhood to old age.'

Ruby's teeth were very straight and small. I had glimpsed them when she spoke. I looked at her lips and tried to imagine her small, straight teeth underneath them. The lips themselves were full and wide and a little brittle-looking, there was something brickish about them, sharp, and just then—like a kind of miracle—just as I was watching, her tongue darted out between them for a second, dark pink.

'Cheeks, chin, eyelids: these are features prone to change, to sagging or bulging and so on. I will allow in my depiction for both sagging and bulging to occur, since it is my understanding that the subject is now—' he turned to my aunt, '—thirty?—' and she nodded, 'when such downward and outward transformations are likely to commence.'

Ruby's cheeks, chin, eyelids: smooth, freckled, taut and in this moment turning, turning away from her father's page, shadow sliding over her cheekbone, eye socket, brow, turning, now, to look at me directly. I stood up. She watched me stand. Faces could wait, faces in general could wait, but not this one. I walked to the door and she watched me. Nobody else seemed to notice me go, all staring rapt at James's page, and once I reached the hallway I waited and I heard the legs of a chair scrape against the floor, and three neat footsteps getting louder and the door opening a crack, and then wider, and then there she was.

She closed the door behind her.

'Are you like me?' she said.

I nodded. 'Yes.'

'Good.'

'Won't your father miss you?'

'He doesn't mind.'

She said nothing else, and from the other room we could hear her father start up again, holding forth on the chin or the forehead or hairline or some other thing that no longer seemed worth caring about because Ruby was extending a hand to me, and when my palm touched hers I felt as though I was taking flight. As we walked together through the shadowy dark house to my room I thought of 'Le Sommeil' and of how nothing in it seemed to have any weight except for the woman's hand on the other's leg—and I had thought this was a weakness, the hovering limbs and hovering buttocks above the bed, hovering pearls above the cup, and hadn't understood that it was like that because that is how it is, because the hand was not heavy on the leg but lifting it up, lifting everything up, a magic trick of a touch, and I watched Ruby's feet lift off the floorboards with each step, the curve of the arch of her boot, and I felt her hand against my hand and we were floating, floating, everything, both of us, floating.

A Brief Discourse on
Rose Madder

I'd ordered paint but not enough, which is why when I was halfway through my copy of 'Le Sommeil', I began to use rose madder, a fleshy pink pigment, floral and lovely before it went onto the canvas and then insubstantial after. It faded fast, like a bruise; it would mark my copy as a fake within a few years, if not months, though would hold out long enough to make a decent sale. But it was what I had and so I used it in vast amounts. Rose madder for the flowers, for the red-pink bedsheets beneath the white; rose madder on cheeks and buttocks and nipples and the soles of feet. Fleshy pink upon fleshy pink. Skin on skin. Rose madder.

There are ways to navigate the world by colour alone, by landmarks in pink, the innermost reachable parts of a person, an open mouth or the lips of the vulva parted by finger and thumb: rose madder.

A postage stamp: the queen's face in pink, pink eyes blank like a statue's eyes, ringed in pink rings and attached to the letter that said, *Your mother has died, she has jumped into a fire,* and latent, resisted, un-thought-and-yet-insistent, the pink of a burn. I did not think about that pink, I did not think about that pink, but sometimes that burn-pink thought about itself inside my brain.

When I came to Inderwick Hall as a child, I spent many hours at my bedroom window looking out at what was then called the rose garden, later the old rose garden, and I watched the gardeners' rhythms, moving in and away from the flowerbeds like a tide, fertilizer, water, pruning, training, and I sometimes went out and followed them around, asking the names of the flowers. Gloire de Dijon, a salmony yellow. Old Blush China. Adam. La Reine. Souvenir de la Malmaison, pale as an eyelid.

The tail and nose of the pet rat my father had given me for my sixth birthday, who had been named Horatio, who had liked to eat strawberries, so that the pale-grey fur of his cheeks looked bloodied and sweet.

In my uncle's library I had found the *Century Cyclopedia of Pigments,* and read about *Rubia Tinctorum*, a plant that had, confusingly, unpromisingly, small yellow flowers, but whose roots produced the deep red madder dye. I had even, once, gone looking for the plant, had dug up dandelions and celandines and found only pale brown roots, or unearthly white, like peeled eggs. I could not find *Rubia Tinctorum* at Inderwick Hall, but still, whenever I saw a plant with small yellow flowers I paused, I noticed, and sometimes I'd take the time to uproot it, in search of deep red below the surface.

I had picked at the scab on my arm so relentlessly that what was left was a raw sheen on the skin, smooth as the interior of a rose petal, labial-smooth, smooth as the frozen lake in winter, pink.

Ruby, and the parts of Ruby that were pink, that seemed freshly squeezed from a tube of rose madder: her lips, yes, the rims of her eyes, yes, cheeks and nipples and vulva, yes, but also her nail beds, darker than the surrounding skin, and also a scar that ran over her collar bone, which I did not ask about but ran a finger down to feel its ridge, the way it erupted out of her like an impertinence. And the groove around her nostril was pink, and the blood vessels sprayed across the palm of her hand when I held it to my face, pink, and it was lodged in my mind, that phrase I had thought about fading—*rose madder fades quickly, like a bruise*—lodged in my mind the way that faces were not, and even then, even in the midst of all the pinkness with Ruby, I was grieving the fading, the lack of remembering, the way that over time the base colour came through, the white or the ochre, and the red-tones dissolved and then, eventually, the sun came up.

COPY OF A LIKENESS OF CHARLES ROBERT INDERWICK, AS HE MUST LOOK NOW, AS ENVISIONED BY AN ARTIST WHO HAS NOT ONCE SEEN HIM

I could smell the smell of Ruby all over my hands, metallic, and I was almost nauseated with the thrill of it when my aunt walked into the breakfast room waving a black-rimmed notecard and said, 'Grace. There you are. Your father has died.'

It was morning. It was raining, loud as applause against the windows and leaking in through a patch above the curtains; damp wallpaper was folding inwards like a petal. Breakfast had not yet been served when Ruby and I reached the table, anxious to appear ordinary, not looking at each other, resisting the urge to place some part of our bodies in contact, my finger against her elbow, knee to knee, the heel of her boot against the toe of mine. She was wearing clothes from the previous night, though she had thrown a shawl over the top and nobody seemed to notice or pay her particular attention. When we reached the table we moved to opposite sides. People were drifting in, filling seats, and the space between the two of us felt surprising, unmooring. Everyone was in an agitated state because of what the artist had drawn, and though I hadn't yet seen it myself, I understood enough from the atmosphere around the table to know that it should be a day of lying low and staying out of people's rages. When James himself appeared and sat beside Ruby, the room went very quiet. But now here was my aunt, sailing in with her letter.

'Did you hear me?' she said. 'Your father. Dead.'

Ruby, across the table, was trying to catch my eye, trying to communicate something but I found I could not look at her.

'Yes,' I said.

'Well then.'

'Does it say how?'

'Yes.'

My aunt appeared healthier than she had in weeks, sharp and upright and direct. There was an unnerving lightness to her; it seemed she herself had not absorbed the gravity of the news. She extended the sheet of paper to me and as I reached to take it I became aware, again, of the smell of Ruby on my fingers. It felt like the wrong thing to do, to touch a letter about my father's death without washing my hands. I held the page as lightly as I could while I read, in the neat apologetic handwriting of the director of the asylum in Dorset, that my father had leapt out of his bedroom window three nights previously and nothing could be done to save him. Plummeted, he wrote. It was inexplicable, he wrote. My father had been in a wonderful mood just beforehand, he wrote.

A wonderful mood. Plummeted. *I have brought you your inheritance.* Crumbs.

When I looked up the room was full of uncles and my aunt was telling them, too, that my father had died, and I noticed at once a strange look on their faces, an unusual sharpness in the way they considered me. I could not bear to consider my father's death any more than I had been able to consider my mother's, what his final moments must have been, what strange ideas had led him to jump, what the air might have felt like as he plummeted through it, and I found that I was thinking about this even as I told myself I couldn't, thinking about the sensation of soaring and falling, about the sudden horrifying encounter with the ground, and I thought, too, about whether even then, even as he fell, even as he landed, he had considered me.

The uncles muttered condolences darkly. I found I had nothing to say in response, or rather, that I had only strange unsayable things to say, and I felt childlike, the way I had when I first arrived at the hall, when I had said everything that occurred to me and had learned that this was a mad thing to do. When the food was brought out, pears and bread and some sort of curried egg dish, I couldn't eat. I was aware that Ruby was still looking at me and, worse, that Charles had come in, too, and was being told the news. All I could think was that I needed to leave the table, but even as I said this out loud, asking as meekly as I could to be excused for a moment, I felt their new attentiveness settle over me, a sudden collective interest turned upon me like the torchlight in 'The Drag'.

I walked away from them back to my room, which was quiet and smelt of me and of Ruby. A wedge of grey daylight sliced through dust from the window, and when I stood there to look out at the gardens, I saw Bobby, a way off, crying beside the rusty deadheads of a Great Western Bourbon rose. It was raining still, and his hair was wet, his face was wet, and I thought at first he must be crying because my father had plummeted, and then I thought vaguely that Bobby didn't know my father, had never met him, would surely not have been informed of the news. So, Bobby was crying for some other reason. He looked up towards the house; I raised a hand but he didn't react. I thought of the way the light bounced off the windows in the mornings; I was waving behind a white sheet of reflected clouds, and Bobby, crying, would have no idea I was there. I turned away. I thought I should do my own crying, though I found I could not.

My bed was dishevelled, sheets peeling back from the mattress, because Ruby, when she had slept, was a restless sleeper, and when she hadn't slept had been occupied with disarranging the sheet and the pillows and me in particular. I stood beside it and began to fold the linen, to tuck it back into place and smooth its creases, and for a while this was wholly absorbing, the folding and tucking and smoothing, the gentle work of undoing, as though, in returning the bed to the state it had been in the previous evening, I might also return myself and the world to a moment before my father had died. 'Grace, Grace,' my father had said, 'I have brought you your inheritance,' and he had revealed that empty, crumb-dotted plate. And then the bed was made, and I found I was staring at its blank, white sheets, and I was an orphan.

I thought, sometimes, about what might have happened had my sister lived. I'd never met her, and she'd been days-old when she died, but I enjoyed the fantasy of imagining her life. She would have grown into herself by then. She would have started to seem like the person she might be as an adult. She would have looked like me, or like one of my parents, and even in their absence, even if everything else had stayed the same and my parents had stayed mad and I had been sent to my uncle's house just as I was, I would have had someone familiar. Without her, I was alone.

A soft knock at the door. I turned, dreading whoever it was, hoping it wasn't Ruby, who I suddenly felt I wouldn't know how to talk to. Then, when I saw it was Charles, I was crushed it wasn't Ruby.

'I want you to know that I loved your father, Grace.' He didn't ask permission to come in. 'I'm so sorry to hear what has happened.'

'I can't imagine you knew him much, did you?'

He padded towards me and then closer still, and then sat on the edge of the bed, depressing and creasing the sheets.

'I did. I visited him, you know, just before I left. He wasn't well, but I took him to the sea and we talked about catfish. He talked a lot about you. About the stories you used to make up and your night terrors and your little pet rat Horatio and the clever, odd things you used to say. He was delighted by you, just delighted. I wanted to tell you that.'

I was startled to hear Horatio's name: Horatio, who I thought of often, whose long-clawed fingers he used to rub together, whose yellowed front teeth protruded from under his upper lip, whose shuddering whiskers and lips used to settle into something that, as I child, I could not believe was anything other than a smile. Grey, white-speckled. His downy, scaly, pink-pink tail. Nobody at Inderwick Hall had known of him, had spoken of him, I didn't recall telling even Charles about him; I had been alone with Horatio's memory for so long that hearing his name then felt as though Charles was referencing something from a dream.

'Horatio,' I said.

'Yes.'

'And what was my father's name?' I said.

Charles looked at me, and then up at the painting of 'The Drag'. He seemed to be calculating something and I felt at once I had done the wrong thing, betrayed his friendship somehow. He fiddled with a loose thread at the edge of the sheet and seemed determined not to meet my eye.

'I'm sorry,' I said.

'For what?'

'For asking.'

He opened his mouth and seemed about to speak, then closed it. I watched his neck swell as he swallowed. Then he said, 'James. Your father's name was James. I'm sorry that the fact it slipped my mind at first offended you.' He was speaking very formally and I wished he would stop, was about to say something to that effect when he went on. 'Now, do you want me to fetch Ruby?'

'Why would you fetch Ruby?'

'Because you're in love with her?'

At this I laughed so loud I surprised both of us, and that

surprise displaced, for a moment, my upset and awkwardness over the previous conversation. 'Charles, I don't know
her at all.'

'Yes, but,' he said, and again opened and shut his mouth,
and then murmured, 'you do know her a little.'

How much time did he spend stalking through the hall-
ways of the house, ear pressed to keyholes? How much time
did he spend surveying us? Did he do it to everyone, or did
he do it only to me?

'Charles.' My heart was beating very hard. For a moment,
I thought perhaps I would burst into violent sobs, just so that
something would happen—I glanced to the gardens where
Bobby was still standing, no longer crying but breathing
heavily enough that I could see his shoulders shift up and
down, pacing slowly between the rose beds—and then the
urge passed, and I saw that Charles was smiling.

'Grace.'

Whatever hesitation I had seen in him had vanished. He
seemed definite again, and calm. He was saying something
very loud with his eyes, was looking at me with such certainty I felt a restful kind of hopelessness, calm as a hare in
a trap. I had thought many times of what it would be like to
be found out, and I had never imagined it would be like this.
I met his eye.

'Do you think it is a madness, Cousin Charles?'

'No.' He said it so quickly. He reached forward to put his
wide hand around my forearm, and at the touch I thought of
Ruby. 'Grace, it is not a madness.'

When I looked again at the gardens, Bobby was gone, and

it seemed all too much, all too laughably much, Ruby, my father, Charles, me.

'Have you seen the picture yet?' I asked. 'From last night?'

'No,' he said, and lifted his hand from my arm, 'have you?'

'No.'

'Do you want to go together?' he said, and I did, because there was at least some interest to be had there, some answers to be sought out, and it would be me who would get to do the seeking, rather than him; and because my room felt crowded, suddenly, with him and with me and with everything he seemed to know about me. I was becoming aware that I had, until his arrival, wandered about with secrets wrapped around me like scarves that kept the cold at bay, and now he was here and even though it was supposed to be the other way round—it was supposed to be *us* discovering *him*—he was sauntering casually into all the most private parts of myself. I felt agitated and exposed and in need of distraction.

James's sketch had been left in the upper gallery, untouched since the previous night, tacked to a board and propped up on an easel. Empty chairs were clustered around it, uneven and disarrayed, giving the impression that everyone had left in a hurry. The sketch itself, though drawn in dark inks, looked insubstantial in the daylight: spindly lines spidery on the page, clustering around a shadowy neck and tangled hair. We stood and surveyed it together, the eyes staring out of the white page and the broad cheeks and, wait, how could this be, the mole on the chin, and the several other chins below that chin, and then Charles let out a loud and throaty laugh. I looked from the page to his smiling face and then back to the page again and it was so clear that even I could see it.

'Well,' I said.

'Isn't it!' he said.

'It's you,' I said. 'It's exactly you.'

Charles's face looked out at us from the page, almost smiling, and even to me it was clear, it was laughably clear.

Charles shook his head and, just for a second, looked glibly upwards. 'I've nothing to thank the artist for, I suppose. He has done his job rather too well.' He reached out and unpinned the paper from its backing, before rolling it up into a tube and tapping it into his palm a few times, as though it were a cane. 'Shall we?'

As we left the gallery and walked back to the blue landing and began to descend the stairs, I became aware that everyone was stopping their conversations as we passed by, and that they were looking at Charles. This in itself was not strange; they were constantly looking at him, and now that that the artist had drawn his face, it made sense that they would look all the harder. He had proven his case on the terms they had set for him and the debate was over for good: Charles was really Charles, and they were surely ashamed at having made him feel so unwelcome and also resentful and embarrassed.

But they were looking at me, too. I could feel the precision of their attention, that they were noticing me in a way I had never previously been noticed in the house. It settled over me like drizzle as we walked past the oak room (my aunt was talking shrilly to my second cousins about her plans for

Christmas and the new year, but stopped when we passed and they all looked up) and the library (two uncles, deep in conversation with James, who was flanked by his younger daughters, but not Ruby, and they, too, stopped, turned, watched me). It could not be—could not only be—that my father was dead, because none of them had cared about him when he was alive. It had to be something more than that, and I felt myself getting agitated as we walked, imagining all the things that might have changed: perhaps they had all found out about Ruby, perhaps it was not just Charles who knew, or perhaps they had somehow discovered my copies, and which would be the worse of the two, I thought; which would feel like the greater violation? I had the sense as we rounded the corner past the green room (a servant lighting a fire, and I wondered where Ruby was) of a rising panic, of having all at once too many secrets and too much to lose and being far less good at hiding them than I had thought I was.

When we reached my room, I pressed the door closed behind us and said, almost to distract myself, 'Congratulations. It's over then. The argument.' Charles nodded but before he could respond I found I was not at all distracted and said, 'Everybody is behaving very strangely towards me.'

'Naturally,' said Charles. He moved towards a chair and then to the bed, where he sat. 'Naturally they are.' He patted the rolled-up sketch against the mattress.

'I don't see anything natural,' I said, and waved my hand and, God, again, there was the smell of Ruby, it caught me off guard, made me lose my train of thought, and I wondered where she was, whether she was still in the house or hiding in a guest room or whether she had already left in advance of her father, and the thought crystallised: was there any chance that she had betrayed me somehow? 'Was it Ruby?'

Charles frowned. 'Ruby?'

'I'm not in love with her. I barely know her. It was just something that happened.'

'Why are you talking about Ruby?'

'Why should they suddenly be so interested in me, if it's not to do with her?' I asked.

'Grace, don't you know?' He got up and went to the window. Beyond him were the gardens, the paths Bobby had trodden earlier, all the wilting roses. The trees had lost their most of their leaves and sent spindly, grasping branches up behind his head.

'Don't I know what?'

'Don't you know that if I were not me—that is to say, if it should have happened that on some technicality I were not able to prove my identity to the satisfaction of a court of law—then, in the absence of any male heirs, and my mother, your aunt, being currently in possession of all legal titles, and your father now having died, then the heir to the Inderwick estate would become—' he paused, and seemed to be checking my eyes for a sign that I knew what he was going to say, '—you.'

Some Truths about Copies

Everything in language is a copy of a real thing.

Every memory is a copy of the remembered event.

Everything done for the second time is a copy of when it was done for the first time, and an attempt to bring back something lost.

The second night Ruby and I spent together was a copy of the first time we did it, except this time I knew that my father was dead, and this time, too, I knew a little how it would be with her, how she would arch her back and how she would be expert with her left hand and clumsy with her right. (She had written me a note—in fact two, the first asking whether I wanted to be left alone, and the second, when I'd said I did not and would welcome some distraction, exuberantly filthy, lewd and irresistible and incorporating a sketch, a little paper copy of how she and I had looked together. Below, she asked whether she could return to my room, and I had read and re-read and re-read it, agitated, anticipating, until at last there she was.)

Afterwards, as we lay with our legs entwined and our hair falling on the pillows in wild clouds and were very quiet together, what I pictured was Charles on the other side of my door, straightening as he stepped back from keyhole and turning, padding softly away into the dark house. I thought about how he had never once apologised for his intrusions into my life, large and small, and I thought about how, in all the scenarios I had ever imagined and feared in which this part of me was exposed, the part of me that liked women the way men liked women, I had never imagined that the person to expose it would be so kind.

In the days after Ruby's departure I returned to my Courbet copy, while the household's mood clenched and unclenched around the artist's confirmation of Charles's identity and nobody talked about my father. I hid away from all of them and thought about Ruby as I translated, stroke by stroke, the image of the painting in my mind into an image of the painting on canvas, and I did not think of plummeting.

The work was vast, stretching almost the width of the painting room, and I had to arrange a scaffold of furniture in front of it so that, should anyone come in, I could throw a curtain of sheets across it. Nobody ever came in, not even to the main room, not even Charles. I had not said goodbye to Ruby, because I did not know how to behave like a person around her in public, and though it might have been possible to do it had Charles not revealed to me that he knew what he knew, it felt truly out of the question now that I knew he knew. So instead

I painted as I listened to the thuds and shouts of the servants removing their luggage, and I painted as they gathered in the hallway to exchange thanks and payment, and I painted after I felt the faint vibration in the floor that meant the large front door of the house had opened and shut.

I was under no illusion that I would see her again. It was not something we had discussed; it had not even been mentioned that we should write to each other, though I had taken the trouble to note down her address all the same. In place of a future meeting, my mind replayed the two nights we had spent together, seeking out each small detail, and I painted my copy of the two women in bed.

Charles had said, 'Because you are in love with her,' when he talked to me about Ruby, but he had said it to be polite. It was a euphemism. I was not in love with Ruby and had been honest when I said so, but meeting her had made me think about being in love in the same way I had thought about it, for a while, after my encounter with the daughter of my uncle's associate that August evening in the garden under the plum trees.

When we fall in love with a person, we start to copy them. Following Ruby's departure, I began to knot my scarf a certain way—and it happened to be the way that Ruby did it, with the knot at the side of my neck—and found that when I did so, I felt clearer and more deliberate and more like myself.

When we fall in love with a person, we fall in love with the copy of them, inexpertly done, that we carry around with us whenever they aren't there.

PUTNEY AGAIN

I was feeling guilty, which is why I went to Putney. Or: I went because I was feeling incensed. One or the other, or both.

My father's funeral had been so broadly awful for all of us that, when we returned to the house, I was allowed to stay in my room with almost no disturbance at all, save for the delivery of food, for two weeks. I didn't even go to breakfast, but ate pieces of toast, cold, which were left by my door. During that time, I thought about my father and mother and about the funeral, where the clergyman had been unable to disguise his discomfort at eulogizing a man who had died by his own hand, and sometimes the thought of Bobby came to me, too, the mystery of Bobby crying in the garden and why I hadn't seen him since; I thought about Bobby's life, which was only partially imaginable to me, his mother and sisters, his work with the horses, his friends in the village, Rosamond and her socialist meetings; and then I turned back to the funeral again, and my grief settled into a kind of furious energy. I wanted to change my life. I wanted to change my fate, more than anything I wanted to change it, and it almost didn't matter if I was the mad one, since there was no escaping one's inheritance, not really, and the day-to-day task of continuing to be myself was immutable.

Day and night, I painted the Courbet. I stared so hard at brushstrokes in pink and white and beige that I could no longer see the shapes they formed, and when I slept, at unusual hours and in short bursts, I saw the colours mixing on the palette: cadmium red, rose madder, yellow ochre, raw sienna, lead white.

When I emerged, the painting finished but still not dry, I was greeted by my aunt looking unusually sympathetic. She had been unable to disguise, even at my father's funeral, her triumph and delight about the confirmation of Charles's identity. She had spent the service gazing at him with a hunger that seemed adjacent, uncomfortably, to lust, smiling and shaking her head and then fixing her face into gentle grief again when she remembered where she was. Her buoyancy translated into an unusual indulgence where I was concerned. It was she, in fact, who suggested I return to London to consult the doctor again about my pains; I heard her later telling the uncles that my physical suffering was exacerbated by grief, and she hoped I would be given laudanum drops. She had benefited greatly from drops herself, she said, and so had many of her friends.

I performed some reluctance to go—would she not, I wondered, need my assistance around the house to finalise the legal matters relating to Charles?—and was briefly horrified when she seemed to give this real thought. But then, in the end, she insisted I leave. I thought perhaps she really did feel sorry for me, now that she was so happy about Charles being

Charles, though she mentioned, as I left, that if I did happen to be given drops, she wondered if she might take a few of them. I said I would make arrangements for my travel and took the opportunity to ask the housekeeper about Bobby. He had left very suddenly, she said, with an excuse about his father's health, and there was no indication of when he would return.

'Excuse?' I asked. 'Why would it be an excuse?'

'Well he's never mentioned a father before.'

This was true; I'd always assumed his father was already dead. But for the housekeeper I summoned a little indignation. 'It is not improbable that Bobby should have a father, Mrs Whitehead.' I gave instructions for my transport to London the following day, leaving after breakfast, and I mentioned, casually, as casually as I could, as though I had no reason to believe anyone would think it remarkable, that I would have rather a large amount of luggage with me. I had rolled up my Courbet with a sheet of linen and folded it over so I could fit it in my bag, which I knew would likely damage it, so I took paint with me too, and brushes, and together with my clothes and all the ordinary items I might need for the trip, it looked as though I was planning to travel for several months.

And then, the morning of my departure, just when it seemed as though everything might go smoothly, Mr George said, 'We have received a letter.' He marched into the breakfast room with the air of a town crier. 'A very significant letter.'

I was sitting at the very edge of the room, as unobtrusively as I could, but Mr George looked directly at me when he said this. I thought of Ruby, of the dealer in Rome, of all the many letters relating to my life that might have fallen, disastrously, into Mr George's hands.

My aunt turned from her boiled eggs. 'I hope you know, Mr George, that if this has anything to do with Charles, I consider that matter closed.'

Charles shifted at the mention of his name; his chair leg screeched along the floor.

'We simply await our moment before the judge to have it entirely finalised in law,' my aunt went on, 'and I do not appreciate any further interventions on the subject.'

She reached across the table and took Charles's hand, which was just too far away for the gesture to look natural; it required him to shift again—another scrape of his chair— and rearrange his plate and coffee cup. Charles's face was arranged very neatly. He tucked his lips inwards and widened his lips.

'Respectfully, it is not closed, Madam,' said Mr George, gripping the paper in his hand all the tighter. 'It is not closed at all. We have received this significant letter, a letter from a concerned member of the James household, which calls into question the character of the artist, Mr James, upon whose sketch we all placed such weight. And enclosed with the letter,' he said, 'was this.' He took from the envelope in his hands a photograph, very small, with scalloped edges, only slightly larger than a postage stamp, and placed it on the breakfast table. One of the uncles gasped and my aunt made a noise somewhere between a whimper and a groan. Ferris, who had been standing with his back to the sideboard, leant forward to see and then stepped suddenly back, almost losing his balance.

Charles withdrew his hand and said, 'Excuse me,' and his chair screeched again as he pushed himself away from the table. For the first time since I had met him, he looked small. As he left the room, he cracked his elbow on the doorframe and I heard him swear under his breath. He closed the door after himself and I imagined that he was standing behind it, rubbing his elbow and listening as we leaned in to examine the photograph on the table.

It was a picture of Charles, and it was immediately apparent that this was the exact image the artist had drawn in the gallery: it was the same pose, the same light falling and the same shadow creeping around the cheek; the same clothes. There were, printed in tiny lettering along the bottom, the words, 'Boswell and Sons: Photographers and Imagers,' and an address in Valparaiso, Chile.

'It was a hoax,' said Mr George, once we had all taken it in. 'It's preposterous. That man, that artist, that Mr James, simply copied this photograph. He had us all fooled. He had us all fooled!'

'What are you suggesting has occurred, Mr George?' my aunt asked, sitting back in her chair. There was anger in her voice, though Mr George seemed too excited to notice. 'We have no reason to believe the words of an anonymous writer, over those of my own son.'

'That man,' he said, nodding towards the door through which Charles had left, 'that impersonator, that imposter, is not your son.'

I wondered who could have sent the letter, toying briefly with the idea that Ruby might have, before thinking more seriously of James's many assistants who had bustled around with his belongings and fussed over the firmness of the cushions on his chair and amongst whom, it seemed reasonable to imagine, there was someone who might have become aware that things were not quite what they seemed and felt moved to enlighten us.

'This photograph is clear proof,' said Mr George. 'The imposter must have supplied the artist with this photograph in advance.'

My aunt took the back of a teaspoon to her eggs, rapping the tops of the shells sharply without looking at them. 'And what motive do you ascribe to the artist?' she asked. She was very pale. Her lips pressed bloodlessly together around each word. 'Why would he go along with such a plan, when he was paid quite generously by us to give an objective rendition?'

'Well that's obvious,' said one of the uncles, leaning in to pick up the photograph and inspect it. 'The man was bribed.'

My aunt smiled, as though this was an answer she had hoped for. She peeled shards of eggshell and arranged the little jagged pieces around the rim of her plate. 'Well, Charles has access to no money whatsoever at present, as you well know. He has not a penny to spend on anything, let alone bribery. He is dependent on us for everything, absolutely everything, until the matter of his identity is finally laid to rest in court.'

I thought I heard, then, a slight thud from the other side of the door, and I thought about what Charles had said when he and I had seen the drawing—'He has done his job rather too well!'—and the words were out of my mouth before I even knew I would say them: 'He did have some money,' I said. 'He did have money.'

I did not know, until that moment, that I wanted to betray Charles. I was surprised by my own fervour, a kind of thrill that shot through me at the opportunity of ruining him. Charles, who had only ever been kind to me. Charles, who had said, 'It is not a madness, Grace.' Why was I so excited at the thought of causing him pain? I had not hesitated when I saw the chance. Charles, who had stolen my money.

Mr George turned to me first, and then my aunt, who looked incredulous, and then the uncles, one by one, and they all seemed surprised that I was there, and more surprised still that I had spoken, when I had been assumed to be almost mute with grief ever since the funeral. I tried to remember the last time I had said more than 'Good morning' to any of them.

'He did have money,' I said, again, and took a breath, and inhaled the sulphurous smell of my aunt's peeled eggs and coffee steam and somebody's sweat. 'I know he had money, because he stole money from me.'

That was the start of the next great uproar, and in the chaos following my statement, I slid the photograph of Charles into my pocket. My aunt began to gesticulate at Mr George, and Mr George to remonstrate with my aunt, and the uncles to take the sides they had taken from the start, and everything became very loud. It was only a matter of time, I knew, before my aunt, in her incredulous fury, would think to question why I, who like Charles was supposed to be dependent on her largesse, had been in possession of any money to begin with. I slipped out of the room unnoticed—no sign of Charles on the other side of the door—and hauled my luggage from my room and into the carriage waiting for me outside, almost as though I had planned the whole thing: the getaway, and the trouble just beforehand.

We drove towards the train station and I toyed with the photograph of Charles, fiddling and softening its edges and staring at the face, his face, or if not Charles's face, then some-body's. When I turned the breakfast conversation over in my mind, I was surprised at how angry I was; how something latent had revealed itself so readily, and how enraged that something was. I found I was unable to stop thinking about it, even when I was away from them all, even as the train reached London, even as I was bouncing and swaying in the back of the cab crossing the river.

I had no money to pay for somewhere to stay and had been nervous to broach the subject with my aunt lest it focus her mind on the implausibility of the whole venture. And so di-rectly upon arrival I went to the home of the art dealer whose details I'd been given in Rome. It was a modest little house by the river in Southwark, yellowed brick that was blackened towards the upper floors, and inside the light came in from above the water. I waited in a small parlour that smelt of modelling clay and paint thinner, until a sickly-looking man appeared, shaking my hand limply and immediately asking to see the Courbet. I unfurled it, lifting off the linen, and at once he pointed out several spots on the canvas that had been damaged in transit. I gestured to my bag and explained I'd brought the paint, but he waved a hand dismissively and said—it was the first full sentence he spoke to me—'My buyers won't know the difference.' He said nothing else about my 'Le Sommeil', neither good nor bad, and I felt deflated. After my weeks of labour there would be no praise, no admiration. I felt embarrassed for having expected it.

'What will come next?' he asked. 'A Van Eyck?' and I said yes, that was right, that was what the Roman dealer had suggested. And then silently he handed over forty-two pounds in cash, which was more money than I had ever seen in my life.

The effect of that money, as soon as I touched it, was like laudanum.

I went at once to a hotel; it was a place I once walked past as a child, on the same trip when Charles and I had gone to the Alhambra, which had struck me then as the absolute height of elegance—two ladies at a table in the window with bright hats, laughing and laughing over some unheard joke—and which had stayed in my mind ever since. It was the sort of place I would go, I'd promised myself, when I had money. I was relieved to find it more or less as I remembered, well-lit and warm and there was still a table in the window with a view of Saint Paul's Cathedral, though no laughing ladies.

I offered a name that was not my own, though I wasn't completely sure why, and paid up front. And once the porter had led me to my room and retreated through the door, pulling it shut, I was alone. I paced around, touching all the surfaces and peering into the mirror at my own looming face and looking out of the window at the rooftops and eaves and smoke blooming up towards the blotchy city sky. I sat in the chair, which had springs that pushed up against my legs and a back that was too upright to be comfortable. I stood up. If I tried not to listen to the sound of my breathing, I could hear the wheels of vehicles and hooves of horses passing by on the street, occasional shouts, dogs barking, and further off, music.

I wanted to sit still. I wanted to occupy this space I had paid for where nobody else could find me, where not a soul knew they could find me. I wanted to enjoy it. I wished I had asked for coffee to be sent up, or some sort of cake, but it had occurred to me too late that I had the means to pay for that sort of thing. I wished I had brought a book with me. I could have luxuriated. I could have fanned out the money and touched it and been listless and proud for a while, in the way I had always imagined I would. But I found I could not luxuriate. I could not sit still. I took out the photograph of Charles again.

I had glimpsed him as I left Inderwick Hall that morning. He had been standing in the window of the upstairs parlour, his face striated with a reflection of clouds and briefly blackened by a passing crow and though he was too far away for me to read his expression, I sensed that he was miserable, deeply miserable, more miserable than he had been since first arriving in the house. I did not let myself feel sorry for him. I repeated to myself that he had stolen my money and lied to my face, that he was a stranger who had wormed his way into the heart of my family and tried to take an inheritance that was—it turned out! Extraordinarily!—rightfully mine.

But I could not, even in my most furious moments, really believe he was a stranger. I doubted, even then.

I went down to the street again and hailed a cab. Perhaps it was doubt that took me to Putney.

Copy of a Portrait of Arthur Watts

It took no time to find the house that Charles had visited; it was so fast, in fact, that I came upon it before I was ready, before I'd thought through what I wanted to happen. In my memory, the route from the White Lion to the green-grey door had been longer, had involved more turns and darker alleyways, but I was upon it in minutes: the doorknocker hanging from one corner on a single screw. I doubted myself and looked around for the doorway where I had hidden, but there it was, exactly as I remembered, and the old-flesh-river smell was just the same, the feel of the street underfoot, and before I could wonder longer, the door opened and a man stepped out. It was as though the house had come to find me, and not the reverse.

The man who emerged was in his thirties, wearing the kind of suit I associated with clerical work, though I wasn't sure why, wasn't sure I knew anyone who did clerical work or what they wore to do it in, and he stopped short when he saw me. 'What is it you want?' he said, and though the words were hostile, his tone was not. He seemed, the longer he looked at me, concerned. He looked up and down the street, as though expecting I might have handlers nearby. 'You've lost your way, Miss.'

I thought of Charles in the night, calling up to the woman in the window. 'Arthur Watts,' I said. 'A friend told me I might find people who knew him here.'

A woman appeared behind the man in the doorway; perhaps the same one who had spoken to Charles, though I stood no chance of recognising her if she was. She looked irritated, and even more so when the suited man simply gestured at me helplessly and said, 'I have to work.'

'Arthur Watts?' the woman said, as the man walked past and away from me in the direction of the river. 'Have you something to do with that great big man who came asking for him in the middle of the night?'

'Yes,' I said, 'I have something to do with him. He's my cousin.' An odd thing to say, I thought, as I said it. I sounded so sure.

'His people are all dead,' she said. 'I told your cousin the same.'

'All of them?' I asked. 'Are all of them gone?'

'His sister lives on Montserrat Road, or used to. It was she who sold us the house when Arthur died. Mrs Alice Clawson. The others, though, are dead.'

I repeated the name to myself, Mrs Alice Clawson, Montserrat Road, Alice Clawson, Montserrat Road, and was already beginning to turn when the woman called out after me.

'What is it you people want with Arthur's memory?'

'I don't know,' I said. 'I don't know, I'm sorry,' and I turned

again and continued to walk as though I knew the way to
Montserrat Road. When I had turned a corner and was out
of her sight I began to ask passers-by the way and discovered it was close, only a few minutes' walk, which was lucky
since it had started to rain and I was wearing only a thin
coat, something decorative I'd hoped would impress the art
dealer, though that meeting already seemed a lifetime ago,
and breakfast at Inderwick Hall even longer, and the wind
was finding its way in at the seams. The streets got cleaner
and wider as I walked. The smell of the river thinned and
waned. The rain got wetter.

I found Mrs Alice Clawson, a woman with long red hair
and nice clothes, standing in the garden of her house. I'd been
waved towards the building, one of many on the road, newly-
built with grand little frontispieces carved in stone over the
doorways, by her neighbours, and then ushered incuriously
through the house to the back door by a maid, and there she
was, wandering in the drizzle, plucking dead flowers from
bushes with her bare hands. In the moment before either of
us spoke, I thought of Charles and tried to imagine what connection he could possibly have to this woman, this stranger,
into whose garden I had wandered.

When I explained why I was there she seemed unsurprised. 'Mrs Lloyd told me someone had come to the old
house a few weeks ago, asking after him.'

'Yes,' I said. 'I'd like to know who he was.'

She showed no sign of moving us in from the garden, and
offered neither shelter nor refreshment, though I could see the
maid hovering in the doorway looking uncertain. The rain

got heavier, running into her eyes, and only then did she lead me to stand under a little canopy stretched over a wooden frame like an upturned canvas. 'I like it out here,' she said. 'I find the house so blank. These new houses, you know. There's nothing in them. They all look alike.'

'It's a very nice house,' I said. I thought about Inderwick Hall, the way it creaked and cast shadows over everything, and about the portraits of all my ancestors all over the place and Grandmother Hodierna's ghoulish face looking up from the mud in 'The Drag'.

'I moved here with my children when I married my second husband. He was—he is—very fond of the house. He likes things to be predictable.'

'It feels lighter here,' I said.

'My husband is not an excitable man,' she said, as though the relevance of this to the question of the house was clear. She looked up at the dark sky and the rain and the horizon where you could just make out the chimneys of factories, blowing up black clouds of smoke. 'Before I married again, I lived in the old house with Arthur and his wife. And, well, at least here in the garden there's a little old ground underfoot. I dug up a piece of pottery the other day. Could be Roman, or it could be ten years old. You find, when your family dies and when your husband is very orderly, that you get a little obsessed with digging up old things. Or at least, I have found that. You know, looking for roots.'

The wind flapped the canopy and shook little curtains of water down in front of us, and I realised that what she was saying, what she was trying to say, was that she was sad.

'My parents died,' I said. 'And my sister, a while before that.'

She nodded. 'So, you understand.'

I nodded in turn, though I wasn't sure I really knew what confidence had passed between us. Still, she seemed so frank and so unquestioning that I pressed on. 'I'm afraid I don't know what I want to know about Arthur. But my cousin knew him, and I would like to know about my cousin. My cousin is something of a mystery to me.'

She gave no sign of being surprised, nor of being particularly interested. 'Arthur knew a lot of people.'

She told me about her brother and I pretended not to be cold. He had been a journalist and wrote for a local Putney paper, she said. He mostly covered crime, several murders, fraud, and had enjoyed some success in tracking down elusive witnesses. In particular, he had loved uncovering confidence tricksters. In his spare time, he liked jigsaw puzzles and detective novels. He had married a German woman whose father was a printer at the paper, and they'd had three children in as many years, all girls. And then two of the children fell ill, and shortly after both the adults, and within three weeks they were all dead, leaving only the baby, who had been sickly and weak since birth and lived only half a year after her parents died. She delivered all of this in a flat, inexpressive voice, as though reading a train timetable aloud, or a weather report.

I tried to imagine this man, this married journalist with three young children, and who he would have been thirteen years earlier, and who he might have been to Charles. The two of them would have been boys: sixteen, seventeen years old at most. Try as I might, I could not picture Charles—the Charles he had once been, restless, troublesome, irreverent—interacting with this man; not my awful cousin Charles who when home had painted girls in the nude and read offensive literature, and when away had surely not spent his time doing jigsaw puzzles in Putney.

'Well that was my brother,' Mrs Clawson said, 'in a nutshell.'

'I have a photograph of my cousin,' I said. 'Perhaps I could show it to you, and you could tell me whether you ever saw him with Arthur.'

I took the picture out of my pocket. Its edges were curling inwards and I tried to flatten them in my palm. There was something very sweet about the tiny image of Charles, its smallness capturing a vulnerability that was normally obscured. A drop of rain found its way through the canopy and landed on his chest. Mrs Clawson took the picture, then looked at me with a strange, new intensity, and then looked back at it.

'What was his name?' she asked. 'Your cousin.'

I paused. What could I say? That I did not know his name? That he was not really my cousin? 'Do you recognise him?'

'Yes,' she said. 'He is much changed. But yes.'

'What was his name?' I asked, and my heart was hammering, then, and I realised it had almost stopped raining, the drops had slowed to a delicate thrum, and the wind had dropped, and in the new calm my body felt too loud.

'Charles,' Mrs Clawson said. 'His name was Charles.'

The maid, in that moment, built up the courage to interrupt us and offer tea. I looked towards Mrs Clawson to see
whether she wanted me to accept or leave, then I asked for
coffee. Mrs Clawson asked for shortbread. 'And bring the
picture of Arthur, too, Mary, from on top of the piano.' Her
voice had become warmer. She was speaking more quickly.

'You're sure?' I said. 'His name was really Charles?'

'Quite sure, yes. He looked different. Thinner. But I'm
sure it's Charles. He was a very close friend of Arthur. They
were—they were very close as young men.'

'How did they know each other?'

'Oh, gambling I think. Or at least, something Arthur preferred I didn't know about. Charles was so rich, of course;
Arthur was rather dazzled by that. Charles was always
throwing money away on horses and dogs. And on Arthur
too. He was always giving Arthur things.'

I realised I was looking at her dumbly. All I could think
to say was, 'And you're sure his name was Charles?' again.

The coffee arrived, and the shortbread, and the picture of
Arthur from on top of the piano. It was a photograph of a
young man with a broad forehead and thin lips, wearing a
dark jacket and holding a newspaper out as though he had
been disturbed while reading it, and the rain started up
again, and when the maid had left us alone Mrs Clawson
turned to me and looked very deep into my eyes in a way
that made me think she was going to ask something of me.

'You know,' she said, 'Arthur would have died for Charles.
He was devastated—it broke his heart—when Charles left.
There was some bad business with money and it caused us a

lot of trouble, me in particular you understand, since it was my money that was taken, and then after that Charles simply disappeared.'

'Charles took your money?' I asked, and the morning's breakfast table returned to me for the hundredth time that day: Mr George, my aunt, what I had said.

'No,' she said, 'not directly. Arthur took it from me and gave it to Charles, because Charles told him some story of tragedy and desperation and whatever else. Charles was supposed to pay him back but never did, and it was all I had to keep me and the children fed and warm. I was a widow, you see.'

Would Charles really do this? I wondered. Could he really have stolen money like this? But by then of course I knew he could.

'I know this must be distressing to hear,' she said.

'What would Charles have wanted money for?' I asked. 'He always had money. There was never a problem with money.'

'I'm sure nobody would like to hear this sort of thing about their cousin, even if—' she paused, 'if their cousin is a mystery to them.'

She wanted me to speak more, I could tell, to tell her something about a man who she, too, must surely find mysterious. She took a bite of shortbread, and then another. A crumb stuck itself to her lower lip. I thought of all the many thoughts I'd had about Charles and could find none that would offer her what she wanted.

'How much money did he take?' I asked.

'Twenty pounds,' she said.

'Twenty!' I felt an apology form on my lips and found it hard suppress it, to resist the urge to claim responsibility for Charles. But it was brewing, getting louder in my head. 'I'm sorry.'

She shook her head. The crumb fell from her lip. So, an apology was not what she wanted. 'I remarried,' she said, as if that was an entire explanation. And then, 'I remarried, perhaps more hastily than I otherwise might have.' And then, quickly, as if to distract me from the bleakness of what she had revealed about her life, about my cousin's dire impact on her life, 'If you want, I could send you to visit one of Arthur's friends. A man called Randal Bryson. Rather a character, I think. Or at least he used to be. Randal could tell you more, if you want to know more, if you tell him I sent you. If you really want to know about that.'

'I do want to know about that.'

'And you'll be kind to him?'

'To Randal Bryson?' I was taken aback. I searched her face before I said, 'Of course. Of course, I'll be kind.'

She nodded a small, sharp nod and I wondered why she trusted me to be kind and what she saw in me that made her accept what I said, and what value she was placing on kindness, and what, after all that time, she felt she had paid for with those lost twenty pounds.

'It wasn't a bad match,' she said, 'my marriage. There is nothing wrong with my husband. I don't want you to think there is.'

'I don't think there is,' I said, though I remembered how she had looked in the garden when I'd first found her, alone in the rain, digging for shards of old pots, and thought: she is bored out of her mind.

'Did he really come back?' she asked. She looked brighter, then, eyes vivid, as though she might cry. 'Did Charles really come back asking for Arthur?'

'He did.'

'Arthur would have been so happy,' she said. 'He'd have been so happy to know that.'

WEALTH

The second most surprising thing about Randal Bryson's house was that people there kept offering me cigarettes—but the most surprising thing of all was the art on the walls. The paintings clustered, packed frame to frame in the vestibule where I gave Randal Bryson's name, and Mrs Clawson's, and explained she had told me to see him. They were figures in the classical style, mostly, many Adonises, the occasional Christ, but what was most striking was that they were all asleep. Jacob on his side, knee bent, face turned towards the crook of his own arm, his nakedness obscured only a little by draped red cloth, the clouds above him grey and low, and beyond, the winged figures of his dream. Adonis reclining, almost in the nude, so that his ribs splayed upwards like a bird's wing, and one of his hands fell across his face. Several Endymions, some with cherubs, Diana or Selene, some alone, and all stretched back in deep, muscular sleep. And some of them were dead, not sleeping: Hyacinth in Apollo's arms, Abel tipped backward over a rock like a reclining cat. Amongst them were famous paintings I had seen in catalogues and newspapers, a couple I had even seen myself in the National Gallery. The copies were reasonable, I thought, though in some the paint had faded—I thought guiltily of my rose madder—and everything was yellowed by tobacco smoke.

I was led, after a moment, into the larger room, where I discovered to my mortification that I had arrived in the midst of a party. Men clustered around tables, clinking glasses, occasionally hammering fists on the wood, occasionally erupting in loud roars of laughter. I scanned the room and saw not a single woman present, though when the guests glanced up at me they simply nodded in my direction and continued to smoke and laugh and thump their hands. Some of them smiled and held out cigarettes and I announced, to a group gathered around the first table by the door, 'I'm looking for Mr Randal Bryson.'

And soon a man came forwards, a broad smile on his face, and shook my hand as though I were one of them, an old friend, and said 'Welcome to my home' in a way that suggested I was simply another expected guest, and then explained, in the same sanguine tone, 'We're having a party for the shortest day of the year,' and then, just as placidly, 'I'm afraid I have no idea who you are.' I introduced myself apologetically, and he waved a hand in the air when I tried to say something about intruding on his time. He ushered me to a table by the window. Though the curtain was drawn, the fabric fell open just enough that I could see the lamps being lit along Shaftesbury Avenue. Crowds were already arriving to eat before the theatres opened. On the shortest day of the year, it was quite dark already and the city looked bright and close, intrusive; as though the cabs and omnibuses might crash through the walls of the house.

A servant came to the table and brought brandy in slim glasses, and though I never drank it at Inderwick Hall I did then, aware, as I had been all day, of the pleasant textures of my new money, which I was keeping in a leather pouch strapped under my clothes around my waist. I felt it whenever I leant forwards, a small pressure like a reassuring hand. And it seemed like a person with money strapped to her stomach might enjoy a glass of brandy at a party for the shortest day. It seemed like a person with money might take all of this in stride. On the walls, the faces in the paintings kept their eyes closed, and right by the table was a copy of Caravaggio's 'Sleeping Cupid', all black paint and cracked varnish, the startling light falling on the flesh of the stomach and leg.

'Would you like a cigarette?' asked Randal Bryson. He lit two and held one out to me before I replied. A tail of smoke flicked upwards from my fingertips when I held it. I tried to move my hand around it as the men did, smoothly and unthinkingly. A person with money would surely raise it to the side of her mouth, would surely fold her lips around it as though murmuring a confidence to a friend. When the servant appeared with an ashtray I forced myself to wait a moment before setting it down to smoulder on the table.

'I've come to ask about Arthur Watts,' I said. 'And about a friend of his called Charles.' I did not give a surname, since Mrs Clawson hadn't, and I felt there was a chance Charles had been deliberately protective of it. 'They would have known you a long time ago. Thirteen years if not more.'

Randal's eyes narrowed briefly, and he seemed to be

assessing something about my face. Then he nodded; something had been decided. 'Yes, I knew Arthur.'

'I'm sorry,' I said. 'I should have begun with condolences.'

'Yes, you should have. He was my best friend.' He didn't look angry, and continued to blink slowly. He raised his glass in the direction of newcomers entering the room.

'Did he ever talk about a man called Charles? Did you ever meet a friend of his called Charles?'

Randal drained his glass. 'Arthur's Charles? I met him once, just before he left. We were all very young then. This place still belonged to my father.' He gestured around at the tables of men. 'And then I think he went to sea. I think that was the story. There was some fuss, something ugly about money going missing.'

'Yes,' I said. 'He went to sea. But I think,' and I glanced around us and felt bolder than I ever had, the brandy creating some space between my thoughts and my worries, between my head and my feet, 'I think it's possible he and Arthur were in love with each other.'

Randal nodded and said, quite loudly, 'Oh, yes, of course. Besotted.'

The scene then revealed itself to me like one of the patterned images in Charles's collection of autostereograms: I found that, turning again to the people around us, alarmed by Randal's audible candour, and studying once more the smoking, smiling men, what I saw were hands extended to other hands, feet knocking and stroking other feet, and there—how had I not noticed before?—one man leaning across to kiss another's cheek. And then all at once I saw

kisses happening everywhere, and caresses that were impossible to misread, and the light was dim and gold, and made
everyone look quite beautiful; the men were not all young but
the hue and smoke gave everyone a kind of energetic glow.
It was the first time in my life I had seen a man kiss another
man like that, and it had been so nonchalant and tender,
so unabashed and so deliberate; it gave me a sense of such
sudden safety I thought I might burst into tears.

'Is this a Molly House?' I was surprised by my own words
as they left my mouth; I hadn't even known that I knew them,
and Randal's eyebrows shot upwards.

'Times have moved on, you know, just a little, in recent
years.'

I thought of my copy of 'Le Sommeil', the sleeping
women entangled on the bed, my beautiful work, which
was somewhere else now, in strangers' hands, perhaps already sold, beginning to fade. In its place I had the money,
extraordinary money, and here I was in this rich place,
which seemed wealthier and more golden than anything I'd
seen at Inderwick Hall, and which made me feel an intense
hunger for what I already had. I'd spent so much time in my
uncle's house considering wealth, considering its uses and
its arbitrariness, the ways it defined and defiled people. I'd
seen villagers shiver while our fires sent up smoke like flags
waving from the chimneys of the house. I'd seen servants—
and really I was troubled by the word itself, which I could
not see written down without thinking of ants, of crawling,
and then, seamlessly, of 'The Drag', Grandmother Hodierna
crawling through the mud, her final indignities in the name

of some small redistribution of resources, and why was it that Bobby was crying in the old rose garden?—disciplined for taking a piece of discarded bread from our breakfast table. I had seen people with not enough giving even more to people who already had too much, and had vowed as a child, and repeatedly since, to burn it all down to the ground.

But then here was wealth. Here was money, illuminating this bright room full of men. Look what money could do.

'I'm sorry,' I said. I realised too late that I was very drunk, and thought about Charles reaching out with his large hand as he said, 'It is not a madness, Grace.' It was Charles who had inadvertently led me here to these people, who were not mad either, and for whom I felt a rush of love, though I knew none of them and none of them knew me, and I felt suddenly that I loved Charles and even, astonishingly, loved myself.

'Charles was Arthur's great long-lost paramour,' said Randal. 'He could be devastatingly boring about Charles, once he got started, absolutely devastating. How Charles bought him this or that, how Charles was just so funny, but then whenever he tried to tell you one of Charles's jokes, of course it seemed that you needed to have been there at the time. And, God, he went on and on about how Charles had surely always meant to pay him back, must have been in real trouble just to up and vanish like that, would come back, surely, with the money, wouldn't he, come back? On and on.'

'I see.'

'But we're all like that, aren't we? Horribly boring about the people we love. I'm like that about Arthur, you see. He was to me what Charles was to him. My one and only. Would you like another cigarette?'

There was a slight spin to the room when I shook my head. 'What was Charles like, when you met him?'

'Oh, beautiful,' said Randal.

I took out the photograph of Charles, ragged and now a little washed out by rain, and showed it to him. 'And this was him?'

Randal frowned a little when he saw it. 'Is that him?'

'Well, is it?'

'The years have not been kind to him, if so.'

'I think he looks very nice,' I said, feeling offended on Charles's behalf and once again—it seemed to keep happening that evening—surprising myself. 'I think he's beautiful still.'

Randal looked amused. 'Well then,' he said. 'There you go. Beautiful. Are you in love with him?'

I laughed and then suddenly worried I might throw up. I put a hand to my mouth, and then to my stomach, my money. 'I've had too much,' I said. 'I've had too much to drink.'

'You should know, we don't make good husbands,' said Randal. 'Broadly speaking. We're not what people really desire in a husband, people like me and Charles.' He paused and folded his hands around his glass. 'But we're not the worst husbands either. Broadly speaking.'

'I'm not in love with him,' I said. 'I'm not like that. I'm like you. I'm like you.'

And Randal just smiled and said, 'Well, that's for the best,' and offered to call me a cab.

Fantasies

I dithered about returning home. I contemplated simply disappearing, as Charles had done. I had woken, thirsty and stinking of tobacco, in my hotel bed. I could smell the smoke on the skin of my hands and in my hair, could taste it around my tongue and on my lower teeth. Daylight was beginning to glow in the loose folds of the drawn curtains, which meant I had slept late; it occurred to me that it was my birthday. I pieced together the events of the previous night, Randal Bryson's party, the cab swaying and rocking as it took me in the direction of the hotel. I had felt sick, horribly sick. When the driver had asked whether I would like to stop for air, I'd said instead that he should take me to Montserrat Road.

There had been no light in the windows of Alice Clawson's house, so I counted out four five-pound bank notes in the glow of the cab's swaying lantern. Twenty pounds, which she no longer needed but had needed years before. Twenty pounds, for the lack of which she had married a boring man and moved to a boring house and lived a boring life. I checked and rechecked the amount, losing track of the numbers, and when I was sure, I stuffed the money through the letterbox, note after crumpled note, while my driver surveyed me gloomily and said, 'You ought to get back in the cab, Miss. You oughtn't flash that kind of money about round here, round anywhere.' As we moved off, I imagined the notes lying inexplicably on the mat, a bemused maid encountering them before sunrise, and only then thought I should have placed them directly in her hands, or at least in an envelope with a letter. It was too late to go back. I rested my head against the jolting wall of the cab and allowed myself to be bounced and rocked into something like sleep until we reached the hotel. And then up the stairs, shoulder sliding along the wall to stay upright. And then into bed. And then the daylight, thirst, awake again.

Perhaps I should run, reinvent myself, never return to Inderwick Hall. I thought about the rooms I might take, somewhere noisy and bright, Covent Garden perhaps, somewhere that lit up at night, brilliant as a painting, the chiaroscuro of the electric lamps in darkness, and full of people who would interrupt your thoughts; somewhere unlike the silent marshland around Inderwick Hall where, on winter nights, the blackness was so uninterrupted I sometimes felt I was falling into it. I could live right at the top of a building where sunlight came in through high windows and I could set up a little studio there, an easel and some paints, and I wouldn't have to put anything away at the end of the day. There would be nothing to hide. I lingered in this fantasy the way, as a child new to Inderwick Hall, I had yearned to go home.

My hotel room had a view of St Paul's and I sat up in bed to look out at the dome and the clouds behind it and

I embroidered the daydream further: how, when my time was my own, I could make more work and therefore make more sales; there was, surely, no upper limit on the number of customers for a glowing Caravaggio, a detailed and mischievous Velázquez. Everybody wanted to own something exceptional, didn't they? And so, it wouldn't matter about the inheritance being Charles's; the mirage of family money on my horizon was of no consequence. It had never been and was not mine—it had never been theirs! I thought, again, of the grab, the grubbiness of that money and told myself I did not want it, could not want it, and anyway, I would not need it. Charles was welcome to it, though it wasn't really his either, wasn't really anything to do with us, had all been plundered and stolen over centuries.

I could be rich in my own right and I could move from my Covent Garden garret rooms to somewhere grand—a house in Piccadilly, say—and I could take up smoking in earnest, learn how to hold a cigarette properly, and wear, perhaps, very nice tailored jackets and trousers, and, God, why not, I could take a lover and live with her, could find Ruby again or someone like Ruby, and we could drink brandy like I had with Randal Bryson. I thought, in detail, about sending out invitations for a party—*Miss Grace Inderwick and Miss Somebody-Whom-She-Loves request the pleasure of your company at a soirée, champagne and fireworks at nine, cigars and dancing to follow, carriages at any time you like and please be interesting, please be fun, please be a surprising and exciting kind of person.* Why not, I thought, why couldn't I, and there was something so desperate in me that I felt agitated by the idea, upset by it, almost sick, and had to shake myself back to the present moment, the hotel room and the bed sheet across my legs and the dome of the cathedral bulging beneath a dotted cloud of starlings, the sound of the bells ringing out for a funeral.

How unbearable, the thought of a different life. It propelled me back to the one I knew, and I felt a kind of relief at the mindlessness of packing my things, returning the room to the state in which I'd found it, descending to enquire after transport. I would return to Inderwick Hall, at least for now. Only for now.

I had the feeling on the journey home of driving fast to-wards a cliff; there was something self-destructive in going back, and I was aware, too, that I did not know quite what I would find. I had left them in uproar over the photograph, the fraud, the money. I had made everyone think that Charles was not Charles, for which he would likely never forgive me. I tried to piece all these Charleses together: the golden cousin of my childhood years, the frowning man who had come back with us from Rome, who was sometimes so polite and sometimes so furious, and then Mrs Clawson's Charles, Arthur Watts's Charles, an in-between, a lover, a thief and then gone. They floated, distinct, and when I tried to bring them together they sprung apart again, as though caught in the act.

But now I knew they were all one and the same, that Charles really was Charles. It had been confirmed by Mrs Clawson, who had looked at the photograph and given the correct name. But what could I say? Who could I tell? Because to offer this explanation was to reveal another secret about him, which was not mine to tell, not ever, not when he had so carefully guarded my own. And for all I knew, by the time I got back, Charles would have been sent packing by the uncles and Mr George, never to be seen again. There would no longer be anyone in the house whom they disliked more than they disliked me, and I would never have the chance to apologise.

And then, as soon as I stepped down from the carriage outside the house, Charles was the first person I saw, and all the different Charleses in my mind tucked themselves away behind his face. He was looking out from his parlour window, exactly as he had been when I left, as though I had been gone no time at all. Before I could react he had lifted a hand, was waving, mouthing something I couldn't see. There was an urgency in his manner that filled me with dread. Was he so furious he simply could not wait to tell me so? But the way he had gestured had not seemed angry, exactly.

I felt my money strapped against my stomach as I walked inside, and put a hand there. It was very quiet. I paused, expecting to hear footsteps from the top of the house, floorboards creaking below Charles as he rushed down to say or do whatever he had been gesturing about. But for that moment, at least, there was no sound. My aunt was nowhere, the uncles were nowhere, and when I put my head around the open doorways of the studies and library, I found the lawyers were absent too. In the kitchen, the cook was listlessly ladling soup. A maid was lighting fires. She looked up and said, 'Welcome back,' and I tried to place her. She looked extremely young and a little—only a little—familiar.

'Thank you,' I said, and tried not to get flustered, not to redden with the embarrassment I had felt a thousand times of not recognising a person who recognised me.

'Hannah,' she said. 'I'm Bobby's sister. You came to visit us at our house once.'

I was quiet, thinking of the sickly little girl I had seen at Bobby's house, how desperate and small I had thought her then, and thinking that she seemed not much bigger or stronger now. She nudged the lit kindling under a log and blew just enough to spread the flame.

'Are you old enough,' I asked, 'to work like this? You cannot be nine years old.'

'Your aunt allowed it as a special consideration to Bobby,' she said, and though I tried to correct her, to say that wasn't what I meant, that my concern was her for and not the work, she carried on, 'Things have been very quiet in your absence, Miss Inderwick. Your aunt has taken to her bed and sent almost everyone away. Your cousin—that is, Mr Charles, or, well, yes, the gentleman upstairs, is keeping to himself. Upstairs.'

'I'm sorry,' I said, to fill the silence.

'You might perhaps,' she said, 'if you speak to your aunt, you might perhaps ask her whether she prefers to cancel the party.'

'Party?'

'There was to be a party for New Year's Eve. And the cook and the gardeners and the musicians and all sorts of people need to know, and the invitations have gone out so if we are to cancel, it would be helpful to be told.'

It was three days before Christmas, just over a week until the year ended. I nodded. 'I'll find out,' I said.

'And Miss Inderwick?'

'Yes?'

'Bobby needs a friend. If you've a moment, I believe he needs a friend.'

She turned quickly to the fire again as though embarrassed, and I realised I should never have left without seeing him first. I took my case to my room but found the silence there unbearable. I tried to steel myself to see my aunt, who would surely ask me about the provenance of the money Charles had taken from me, and since I still could not think of a reasonable explanation, I delayed. Whenever the house creaked or the wind blew ivy stems against the windowpane I imagined it was Charles approaching, and though I was in some ways anxious to see him, in some ways keen to begin the process of putting everything right between us, the thought of his excited waving through the window, the not-knowing what it was that he wanted, made my heart pound. Instead, I put on my thickest coat and went out to the stables.

Bobby was shovelling manure into wheelbarrows. It was steaming in the cold and at first he was so absorbed by the rhythm of the work he didn't notice I'd arrived. When I said his name, two of the horses looked up but it was only when I repeated myself that I got his attention.

'You came back,' he said.

'Yes,' I said. 'Of course.'

He shrugged. 'I didn't know.' Absentmindedly he reached his palms towards the manure, as though it were a fire.

'I saw Hannah,' I said, 'at the house.'

He nodded. 'She just started.'

'She's too young,' I said.

And just like that he was crying again, crying just as heavily and miserably as he had been in the old rose garden, and I looked around a little panicked in case anyone else saw him like that.

'Bobby,' I said. 'Bobby.' But he didn't seem to be able to stop and was holding his face in his hands so that he couldn't even see me. I hooked my arm through his and half pulled, half guided him away from the stable block, out down the smaller entangled paths that ran behind the formal gardens, past a statue of my great, great grandfather Rufus dressed as a Senator, done in the classical style in marble greened with moss, and through the straggling, bare December fruit trees towards the back wall until we reached the gate, and on the other side of the gate, the cows. Their nostrils were surrounded by haloes of steam and they were crunching frosted grass and furrows underfoot. I leant against the wall and breathed my own hot breath towards them and listened to their exhalations, their peaceable, infrequent lowing, and Bobby did as well, or at least seemed to, since after a while his crying stopped, and his breathing slowed.

'What is it, Bobby?' I asked. 'Nobody's here now. What's going on?' and after a moment longer, he told me what had happened.

A man had come to the village and stayed in one of the rooms over the pub, claiming to have some business up at the hall, and claiming, in fact, to be a dealer in antiquities (I

stiffened at this). And Bobby had heard him speaking one
night at the bar and thought of course of me, of the paint
orders he sometimes fulfilled for me and of the trinkets I
passed him in return, and he had begun to wonder whether
this dealer might not be able to help him with the sale of some
of these trinkets. He'd gone home at once to fetch some of the
things and the dealer had taken some of them and had paid
him very handsomely for the silver box in particular. After
the transaction they had shared a drink together. Over beer,
the dealer had mentioned that he in was in fact in need of a
partner in a trading matter: he was in possession of a very
fine marble potpourri vase, a real original item, bronze legs
like ostrich legs and heavy as anything. He had a buyer in
London very interested, which was all well and good except
that the dealer had sudden and urgent business on the con-
tinent and could of course not travel with this valuable and
bulky object. If Bobby were inclined, the dealer was willing
to sell Bobby the vase at an extremely favourable rate, taking
into account their pleasant rapport and the convenience of
the vase being taking out his hands at an opportune time.
He would also pass to Bobby the details of the buyer, who
would purchase the vase at twice what Bobby was being
asked to pay.

'Bobby,' I said. 'Bobby.'

And Bobby had thought, then, of the money he had saved
up at home from his work at the stables, which he had been
putting by to pay for his mother's medicine and perhaps even,
silly really, but perhaps even his marriage one day, if that
were ever to happen, not that he assumed there was anyone

who'd have him. And he thought of the money the dealer had just paid him for the silver box and the other little things, and he thought that if he put this together with what was at home, he had just enough to buy this vase, which would in turn get him twice as much, just as soon as he wrote to the buyer in London.

'Bobby,' I said.

And the vase itself had been a very fine thing to look at, an extraordinary thing, dark red marble with those bright golden-coloured ostrich legs, and when you lifted its lid and replaced it again there was a real echoey thud that went right through you and seemed to say, again, how expensive a thing it was, how much money it was worth. And it was so heavy! Really, you couldn't lift it as just one man, it was so heavy, and the dealer wouldn't let him try for more than a moment, in case harm should come to it. 'You see,' the dealer said, 'why I can't take this with me to France! Why I need a buyer for it now!' And Bobby could see and said he would be right back and would the dealer be so good as to make a note of the buyer's details, and they could shake on the deal right then and there. And so Bobby went home to get all the money he had in the world and brought it back and gave it to the dealer, who counted it carefully, and pointed out in fact that there was an extra shilling there, which he returned to Bobby with a gracious nod, along with a slip of paper naming a Mr Wise of Forth Street, Edinburgh. 'I thought you said London,' said Bobby, 'I thought you said the buyer was in London,' and the dealer shook his head in disbelief at his absent-minded error, and crossed out Edinburgh and wrote, instead, London. And then the dealer said Bobby should come back with another man in order to transport the vase home.

'Oh, Bobby,' I said.

And naturally, when Bobby returned with a friend, the dealer was gone. And naturally, when they went to collect the vase, they found it was not heavy at all, only nailed down to the table so as to seem so, and they found it was not marble but a bit of varnished wood, and not bronze but just a little paste, and the rich metallic thud of the lid closing was got about with a bit of misshapen cutlery and a tin plate tucked inside the bowl, and when they tried to pull it off its perch it fell apart entirely into a mangled heap of dust and splinters and tangled bits of wire. And the money was gone, and even the silver box was gone, and Bobby had spent every last penny his family had on a worthless piece of nothing, had ruined them, had believed in a fantasy of greater wealth and in doing so had ruined them, and so Hannah had come to work at Inderwick Hall, even though she was only eight, in order to recoup some of the loss, and Bobby could not stop crying in public.

'How much was it, Bobby?' I asked. 'How much was it that you gave to that man?'

'Twenty pounds,' said Bobby, and started to cry again, which was unbearable because it seemed to me it was somehow my fault, or at least that I was no different, no less villainous, than the dealer Bobby had met, peddling highly varnished tat to people who only wanted to believe in something better. I wanted to feel that I was different, less villainous, and part of me immediately began to insist that I was, because when I did my copies it was more like a kind of homage, adulation even; I aimed for my work to be exact, just as good, and to contain within it whatever it was that made the original worthy of copying in the first place. Surely there was something worthy in that? This question went unanswered, though, and Bobby continued to cry.

He didn't fight me much when I gave him the money, only protested weakly and then seemed to lose energy even for that. He folded the notes into his pocket, swallowing shallow, hiccupy breaths, and didn't ask how I'd come to have it, let alone why it happened to be about my person in that moment. When he left, he didn't look back and didn't know, I think, what to say, and I was relieved not to have to respond to his response. I leaned against the wall and breathed and waited for a feeling of having done something good; I expected at least a low glimmer of pleasure, some faint sense of satisfaction in having helped my friend. The cows snorted and farted and stumbled on buried roots and I did not feel good. I felt tired. The money had been the last of my Courbet payment, leaving only a few coins of change from the hotel, and the feeling of the empty purse against my stomach was accusatory, like a prod.

And yes it was good to help Bobby, and yes it was good to repay Mrs Clawson, I knew these things were good, but still. It had been a mistake to come back. There was nothing for me at Inderwick Hall, and never had been.

But then, Charles was there.

'Happy birthday,' Charles said. I hadn't heard the gate open. He looked bright-eyed. Still agitated, as he had looked through the window. 'I wasn't sure if we would see you.'

He was lifting his lips into an unconvincing smile, seeking out my eyes and leaning against the gatepost in a way that seemed calculated to appear casual. He lit a match, which took him several tries in the exposed air, and dipped the flame to his pipe. 'Did you get what you wanted?'

I tried to understand, from his expression, what he was talking about. He made me feel utterly transparent, as though he had glanced at me and seen everything, the trip to Putney, Randal Bryson, giving the money away, the hotel, coming home, giving money away again.

'For the Courbet,' he said. 'I thought it was a fine copy, very fine.'

I nodded. 'I didn't know you'd seen it,' and then, because I could feel irritation rising, defensiveness turning to anger, and wanted to quash it. 'I'm sorry. I shouldn't have said what I said about the money.'

The word was starting to lose its meaning for me; I had thought about it too much and its pronunciation, its spelling, started to feel implausible. Munny. Muney. Money.

'Oh.' He shrugged. 'Well, I shouldn't have stolen your money.'

I said, 'Charles,' just as he said, 'Grace,' and both of us paused.

And then he said, 'Grace, I have a question I must ask you,' just as I said, 'Charles, I must tell you where I have been,' and then, again, the gulp of silence.

I wondered what to say next, how to answer his question. He would want to know, of course, what I had done in London, what I had learned about him. And I wanted to find words to express to him that he was safe with me, just as he had made me feel safe with him, that these were secrets we could keep for each other. And I wanted to say, too, that if he hadn't stolen my money I probably would have just given it to somebody anyway, since I didn't seem to be able to keep hold of it no matter what I did. And I wanted to say that we would find a way to prove his identity once and for all, that I would help him. I wanted to say something grand and forgiving about understanding why he felt the need to trick us all with James and the drawing, that if he had been anxious the experiment would fail and cast unnecessary doubt upon him, it might have seemed simpler to arrange things in his favour, and that he shouldn't feel any shame about that, either, not with me, who understood him and was on his side.

I opened my mouth, ready, and cold air rushed in.

'The question I have for you is this,' he said. 'Will you marry me, Grace?'

Part Three

Valparaiso, Chile, 1888

ASHORE

Land felt shaky underfoot. He missed the rolling solidity of the ship as soon as he stepped off it, found himself reaching out for verticals: trees, walls, doorframes, the shoulders of his shipmates as they wandered, like dreamers, through the port. He felt sick, the way he had used to feel sick at sea when he first left home, seasickness and homesickness combined, a sort of madness that manifested in the guts, and he was tired—the last days of sailing had been brutal, there had been a strange illness on board that laid men out for weeks at a time with fever; the crew had been reduced to a skeleton who had kept double, sometimes triple, watches, fourteen, sixteen, eighteen hours on to four hours off, he had been unwell himself—and sometimes when he looked down and saw his own hands he was startled, thinking that someone had reached their arms around him from behind. It took him a moment each time it happened to come back to himself, to feel his way back to the inside of his own body.

He had been traveling for two years by then and was used to the drunkenness of coming ashore. It was a sensation of sleepwalking while awake, everything unsteady, the men from the ship would cluster together, replicating the rhythms of their sea lives, waking at the same times, eating at the same times. Gradually the crew would realise there was nothing holding them together and begin to dissipate, a few at first and then all of them, scattered across the country and the globe, taking work on new ships, new routes. They would likely never see each other again. But for now, they walked in step as they unfurled from the ship, stumbling together towards the town.

He sniffed the air. He liked the smell of land, the variousness of it. At sea: salt, hollow air, rotting fish, sharp body odour of himself and the other men. On land: extraordinary array of perfumes of people on the street, orange oil, peppermint, smoked chili pepper, animal dung, onion sweated on a low heat, wood smoke, damp dog, sharp body odour of himself and the other men, women. If he thought about his parents at all, of his home, it was in those first moments of inhalation on solid ground, when he could not help but imagine a homecoming, the port at Liverpool and the gulls circling over the dark skyline of mills and the smells of England, of home: beer and fried fish and the peculiar and distinctive dampness of English leaf mulch. It was clear to him how it would be, the enveloping autumnal greyness (it had been autumn when he set sail, and in his mind's eye it was autumn there still and always would be, the country frozen exactly as he had left it, his mother's mouths still agape, his father's small eyes stretched wide, his little cousin looking on, pale and silent), and then he shook his head a little and stepped onwards into this new country, a place that was not—yet, thankfully, not yet—England.

'Will we go to an inn?' said a boatswain, a man whose forearms he admired and thought about sometimes, the way the veins roped around the muscle and over the bones of the wrist.

They all agreed that they would go to an inn. There were several by the port that catered to sailors coming in off the seas: cheap food, cheap beer, girls milling around outside looking the men up and down as they approached. In Valparaiso they dressed well, the girls; he had noticed that at once, the skirts very full, ankles in bright stockings, and even the ones who were old or sick had good hats and smart expressions: a way of looking that was at once shameless and mild. Shameless was a word his father used a lot, and it had taken him some time to realise it was not a bad thing to be. He noticed he had started thinking of his father again, which he preferred not to do. It was a consequence of coming ashore, and of doing so while sober: his father, his mother, his old life taking hold. He had a sudden urge to paint the girls by the inn, which was a thing he would have done before, when he was the person he was when he had not yet left home. The passing thought of paint was pleasurable, the suggestion from somewhere at the back of his mind that he was still a man who might do that, might mix vermilion in oil for a lip, aquamarine for a frothy skirt.

The crew would fall on those girls like dogs on mutton bones and he wondered how they must seem to the girls, for whom the arrival of a new shipload of men, reeking of themselves and each other and half rabid with desire was a daily, even twice daily occurrence. To the sailors, after the months they had passed with only each other for company on the journey from Rio, save a dark and freezing stop off at Port Stanley, the women seemed miraculous, like ghosts. Or at least that was how they seemed to him. On his first few landings (he mapped them out for himself: Madeira, Mindelo) he had gone after the girls like everyone else and had found the experience disheartening. The girls had seemed so lively, so real, calling down from balconies as the men approached, but then when you got them into bed a kind of miserable inertia took hold of them and they lay there and you felt monstrous, really disgusting, putting your hands on them. And for what? Where was the joy in it? It wasn't for him. That was what he said, afterwards, when anyone asked: 'It's not for me.' Nobody had ever questioned him further.

It had always surprised him, the tenderness with which the other men treated him. They could be rough with each other, brutal even, would come to blows over the slightest of slights. But with him they always lowered their voices, patted him on the back, babied him even. When he had started out, an ordinary seaman (and an idiot, he had known nothing at all; they had taken him on at Liverpool simply because he had spoken well and mentioned the names of some friends of his father), they had kept him at a wary, almost respectful distance. They had shown him how to do things he had claimed already to know, but otherwise ignored him. Then, midway through his first voyage, he had been offered an opium pipe by the carpenter, and nothing was the same after that. He vanished. Or the world did. He spent the next year and a half intoxicated. It was the horrible irony of his seafaring career that the more he'd learned of the sea the less able he had been as a seaman: at his worst he had been nebulous and stumbling, lower even than the lowest apprentice, except vaguer, stupider, moving in a drugged fog even on clear days. And through it all, the men had been so kind to him.

He had begun to refuse opium on this last voyage. Something had broken in him. There had been no vision of Jesus beckoning him towards sobriety, no clarifying conversation with a trusted friend, which were the kinds of things he'd heard reformed drunks say, but the storms had been so wild, the ice and wind and cold all around so bleak, that he had become exhausted by himself. Withdrawal had made him sick. He had been laid out for days, but the men kept his secret for him and told the officers it was a fever, the same one the others had.

Now, they approached the bar: ragged flags flapping wetly outside and the smell of unfamiliar tobacco in the pipes of the men at the door. They ordered food from the inn keep ('Whatever is good here, and lots of it, hot,') and he felt himself begin, ever so slightly, to calm. There was always a moment at sea when he began to wonder if the world had perhaps ended—he imagined they would navigate towards the shore and find it gone, that the land had slipped underwater or disintegrated, and they would never again stand on anything solid. It felt so possible to him when the skyline was always the dark, dark grey of the water, he almost expected it. And then to have arrived where they had arrived, there in Valparaiso, where the buildings clustered brightly down towards the water, painted sunset colours, orange, yellow, pink; to be on land and amongst strangers and anticipating new flavours: nothing could be more reassuring.

He listened to the percussion of Spanish spoken around him in the bar and, though he was sitting, felt unsteady again, thought he might throw up, stumbled back to the door for fresh air. He stood there, looking out at the sea, which looked tame, pretty, even, pale blue and twinkling in the light, coughing up soapy waves towards the town; deceptive. He took a breath. Felt better. Thought to return to the table. And then was sick, copiously, all over his boots.

Straightening, unsteady again, anticipating the surge of a wave underfoot that did not come, he staggered away from his vomit and then stumbled. He reached forwards, gripping the shoulder of a man in front of him, and righted himself. He realised too late that this man was not, as he'd assumed, one of his crewmates, and though wearing the salt-stained clothes of a man who had long been at sea, was not somebody familiar after all.

'Sorry,' he muttered.

'No matter,' said the man, without looking back at him, and he was struck by the English accent, crisp and familiar and as out of place as some piece of food from his childhood: an apple, a plum. The man was smoking, staring at the water as he had been, wearing a green hat.

'Sorry,' he said again, and then, embarrassed, dug in a pocket for his pipe. Tobacco.

The man turned, watched him fumble. 'Do you need a match?'

He shook his head, patted his breast pocket where he

kept his matches. It took him several attempts to light one. 'Thanks.'

The man was still looking at him. 'Just arrived?'

'Yes.'

'From where?'

'Rio,' he said. 'Changed some men at Port Stanley.'

The man blew out, pushing his lips forward. There was a silence.

'And you?' he said. 'You've just come in yourself?'

'California,' the man said.

California! He had always wanted to see it. 'You're English,' he said.

'Yes.'

'Me too.'

'Yes.'

That was all the conversation they had, that day. Two strangers, reeking and unsteady, staring at the sea that had spat them up on the shore. He finished his pipe and returned to his crew, who were eating by then, meat pies and a kind of thick soup. They had thought of him and ordered some sort of vegetable dish, but he noticed the dispersal had already begun: some were off talking to the girls, one or two were asleep at the table, and he wanted a bed, somewhere nobody else was, sheets on a mattress, a pillow; a pillow! He wanted a bed more than anything in the world and asked the inn keep for one and only muttered 'Farewell' to the other men before he crawled up the stairs towards and away from them all. They wouldn't see each other again, not all together at least, and he did not know how to feel.

GREEN HAT

He woke alone for the first time in months. It took a moment to situate himself, to account for the silence, the absence of snoring and creaking, the jarring stability of the mattress beneath him. He had no idea what time it was; it had been mid-afternoon when he'd crawled in and fallen asleep, and it was daytime still, or again. It must be the next day, he thought; he had the feeling of having been asleep a long time. He went to the window and pissed into the pot while surveying the view: hillside; ramshackle, pretty buildings, ironwork on the balconies; some largescale engineering project underway in the distance, men bending low under the weight of metal girders and—if he held his breath he could hear it—calling to each other as they worked.

He felt sick again and crouched over the pot in case he'd vomit. Nothing came. His urine was dark yellow. He should drink something. He should drink something and make a plan.

The voyage from Rio had been bad, the men getting ill and the seas so rough, and he himself just rejoining the world after his intoxication, and Antarctica, a place he had never dreamed of, never wanted to go, where everything looked

black-and-white and blurred like a daguerreotype as you
blinked and blinked through the snow, and even the animals
were colourless, penguins like something out of a dream. It
had been so cold—he recalled the puffed-out cheeks of the
man he'd met yesterday, the wordless acknowledgement that
he had done something unenviable—he had thought only of
reaching Valparaiso. The other men had already made their
plans, he knew: some wanted to stay in Chile, to try farming
or trade; others would be even then negotiating with new
captains on new ships, haggling a wage.

And what did he want? What had he ever wanted? He had
left home on a whim after an argument with his father; he had
not known how long he'd be gone, or where he would go to,
had simply jumped on to the first ship that would take him.
The rest of the world had been unimaginable, and the decision had seemed unimportant, a sort of game. He had known
only England, only his childhood home in Oxfordshire and
the cold, echoey dormitories of his school, fields and cows
and pheasants, the grave of his sister surrounded by other
graves, his brother and cousin for company, though later he
had made friends of other kinds: London, gentleman's clubs
and the lights on the cabs, money changing hands over cards,
horses; he had fallen in love and that had felt sprawling and
absorbing the same way the city did, glowing, spires, the
cathedral, bridges like golden threads over the river that had
seemed to him, then—how funny to think of it, quaint even,
now he had been at sea so long—vast.

He sat on the bed with his knees pulled up, back to the
wall. Closed his eyes. Extended fingers to an opium pipe that

was not there, and imagined the drug taking hold of him, the sweet sensation of being cradled, of all his discomfort, pain, shame being pushed further from him, visible still but removed. Shameless. God, he craved it. He always would. It had replaced almost everything he had ever yearned for: former lovers, childhood food, his family. It was the long-lost love of his life. But it was gone. He was done with it. He could face himself, had to face himself, and the world, and his place in it, with clear sight.

He had to make a plan. Had to think of something solid. An image of the shoulders of the man in the green hat appeared in his mind; the curve of them, and the sea beyond. Then, a memory of the man's voice.

It was a nasty thing to feel lonely. It was an ageing thing. He felt so much older than he was. It surprised him whenever he answered questions about himself to say that he was nineteen. He had thought himself handsome, pretty even, before he left, but now when he caught sight of his reflection he saw someone far older, weather-beaten. He did not look like his father, which was something he feared, but still: there was a trench in the skin of his forehead, running right across it like a crack in a plate; his hairline was already creeping further from his face as though blown back by the wind. Lonely and old. Lonely.

You didn't notice it on a ship, or you didn't feel it for what it was. You were never alone and nothing was ever quiet, and even after he had forced himself sober he hadn't felt it. The other men moved around you like weather, and perhaps they didn't know you—not really, not deeply—but they also knew you better than anyone ever had.

Knew the sound of your breath just before you woke up. Knew to exchange their rations of cheese for your salt beef, since you never much cared much for meat. Knew the smell of your shit. There were moments, too, of real closeness, when you would talk about your pasts, families and disappointments and all the things you were running away from. Sometimes the men even fucked each other, though he never had; had peaceably rejected offers of that kind, not out of squeamishness, just a feeling that he didn't need it the way other people seemed to. So it was a different thing, the loneliness of being at sea. It was a companionable thing, shared and so diminished.

Here, now, he was sober and alone. He felt a sudden and horrible longing for his mother. He would find some paper, write something: *I am in Valparaiso, having arrived yesterday I believe and having sailed from Rio, stopping at Port Stanley where I am sorry to say my spirit was so depressed I did not write, having found the Antarctic waters to be nightmarish and colder than I ever knew anything could be. I am glad to have arrived, although I find that I am homesick.* He would write something like that. His mother had never been warm to him, but he understood her better from afar, the ways in which she had loved her sons and grieved her daughter, the ways in which she had sought to keep him from the worst of his father. He was anxious then that he might begin to think about his father again. And instead was interrupted, gratefully interrupted, by a knock at the door.

It was a girl. Blue skirt. He had seen her when he arrived. Inn keep's daughter perhaps. He thought she must be here to offer services, and began to rehearse, silently, his excuses. She was speaking to him in Spanish, which he understood but could not reciprocate. She was not offering anything, in fact. There was a man downstairs, she said, who was asking after him.

'Asking for me by name?' he said, first in English and then French. The girl looked blank. 'By name?'

It could only be the captain of the ship, making some awful request: 'Come back and work for me again,' or 'Come and help repair the ship.' He thought about refusing to go down, but the prospect of trying to convey that refusal to the girl was exhausting, and after a moment's indecision he just nodded, retreated to shrug on his sack coat—there was a punch of dismal odour when he put it on; he should find a laundry—and then reappeared. The excuses he'd thought of for the girl would work just as well for the captain: he was very, very tired; he was perhaps getting ill; he needed to be alone for a while, even while he dreaded his aloneness. He followed the girl down to the bar.

He could not see the captain. The room was busy already, full of men who were drunk and eating bowls of meaty stew. He caught himself thinking it must be later than he thought, afternoon at least, then remembered the relentless rhythms of port towns; it could be any time of day or night. He looked to the girl and said, 'Where is he? Is he outside?'

She jutted her chin forwards and said, 'There. He's there. Green hat.' Green hat, as though it was the stranger's name.

The man she gestured towards was not the captain. It was the man from yesterday who had offered him a match, the

English man who had come from California, wearing his green hat. He relaxed for a moment, spared an awkward conversation with the captain, and then tensed again. It could be nothing good, this stranger's attention. Whoever this man was, he had surely come because he wanted something.

As he approached, he tried to look as though he did not immediately recognise this man. He affected a bewildered, good-natured smile, and then, when the stranger raised his eyebrows in a slight greeting, a small nod, as though he were just then understanding.

The man in the green hat held out a hand. 'Glad to see you again.'

'How was it that you knew my name?' he said. It came out more hostile than he intended, than the situation called for. He smiled. 'I'm sorry, but I don't believe we know each other.'

'I asked after you once you'd retired. Your crewmates told me who you are, and a little about you. The vegetarian, they called you. And then they gave me your name.'

'And why was it that you cared to know about me?'

Green Hat opened his mouth and then appeared to falter. He took off his green hat, then put it on again.

He found himself stepping closer. 'Let's sit,' he said.

Green Hat put an arm to the small of his back, which made him start and reminded him of the fears he had felt, in the grips of fatigue and withdrawal, at the sight of his own hands. 'Outside. We can sit outside.'

There was some sort of parade happening along the seafront: people in bright colours were singing, a minister was present, several musicians playing unfamiliar instruments.

He realised, after a moment, that he recognised the music. 'Abide With Me'. Later, 'My Hope is Built on Nothing Less'. Later, a hymn about anchors the words of which he couldn't remember. Green Hat lowered himself stiffly onto a verge at the side of a path that sloped down to the harbour and he did the same. They both took out their pipes. Green Hat extended a match and this time, though he had his own, he accepted, leaning forwards and letting the other man cup his hands around the bowl. The wind coming in was strong and wild; it took several attempts to light it long enough to smoke from.

The procession passed further away, music softening into the sounds of the water and gulls and a clatter of traffic. New crews were coming ashore.

'Why do you care to know about me?' he asked, again.

Green Hat had become—was he, really?—pink-cheeked. 'I thought we could be friends,' he said. 'That's all.'

'Friends?'

'I thought so, yes.'

It was a direly embarrassing situation, and he wished he could think of a way to extricate himself. He considered simply jumping to his feet and running, but where was there to go? He knew nothing of Valparaiso or of Chile, and besides, his belongings were back at the inn, practical things but also sentimental, his diary and pen, paintbrushes, some clothes from home, and Green Hat would know where to find him. It would be an overreaction, in any case. It wasn't a situation that called for running away, though that was always his first instinct—there was his father's face again, looming, ever-present; it was more mortifying than that, boyish, as though he and Green Hat were both in short trousers, meeting up round the back of the chapel to share secrets, or stolen food. Friends. It was an embarrassing word.

'Do you,' Green Hat asked, taking pains to look out to sea rather than into his face, 'want to be friends?'

Mortifying. Disconcerting. The land still rocked him.

He was unbalanced. 'Yes,' he said. 'I do want to be friends.'

ALLOWANCES

Later, when he thought about it on the voyage back to Europe, he would struggle to put the events in order: how he and Green had come to fall so violently in love, the paintings, the house, the money and how it had run out. Without the ringing of the ship's bell to mark the changing of the watch (he still listened out for it: two strokes for one, five, nine o'clock; four for two, six, ten; three strokes for half-past seven in the last dog watch; eight for noon or midnight; a rhythm to live by; a rhythm to sleep, shit, wake and dream by) time felt shapeless. He stumbled through it. He had the sensation all along that he had wandered into another man's life. At any moment the rightful liver of the life might return to cast him out.

Still, he could recall moments very precisely: the first time he had seen the house, for example, the way the paint had been very fresh on the walls and how familiar it seemed, though he had never seen it before, and how full of possibility. He and Green had been spending idle days wandering Valparaiso, watching workers scale the hillside laying girders for a new funicular. They had not yet done anything but talk in noncommittal ways about themselves and their hopes. There had been a little note up in the window of the house saying it was available to rent, and he had stopped short to squint at it. And since it had been established between Green and himself that neither of them had any plans, that they both hoped never to board a ship ever again, what better to do than stay where they were, in the bright, dappled port town, in this bright, dappled house painted a shade of yellow neither of them would have chosen but which they both came to appreciate, like yolk and so sunny, even in the cold morning light? It had been his idea, not Green's, to share the house. Green had said yes at once.

He recalled in detail a conversation they had had about dogs, the dogs of their childhoods whom they had loved and what their names were and what their breeds were and what colours. He recalled preparing coffee in the small kitchen; how Green had laughed at him for not knowing simple things like how to heat the cups first, how to grind the beans fine enough: 'You can navigate oceans,' said Green, 'you can single-handedly sling a ship's worth of casks. But you don't know how to wash up a teacup without smashing the handle.' It was true. He knew almost nothing about the life they were making. There was a word for it, this life, and he bristled when he thought of it: domestic. A word for dogs and servants. And yet also something that, despite himself, he had craved and now delighted in. He, who had never been sure what he wanted, wanted this.

At some point, early on but later than he should have, he had asked the man in the green hat what his name was and confessed to calling him only 'Green Hat' in his thoughts. Green Hat had looked briefly offended. 'You don't know my name?' ('You don't know how to fold linen?' he asked. 'You don't know how to fry an onion?' Incredulity upon incredulity.) He asked Green how he could possibly have known it. Green had shrugged and said, 'One finds out things one wants to know.'

'Does one?'

'I do.'

That was true. Green somehow found out everything he wanted to know. It was disconcerting. And flattering. He remembered how flattered he had felt in those early days of their acquaintance. Green was a man whose attentions, when turned on you, made you feel rich. It was distracting, too. He felt disconcerted to realise how little he knew about Green.

Green's hands were large and he used them lightly; had waved one of them airily when asked about his upbringing—where he'd grown up, who his family was—and said, 'We have plenty of time to talk about that kind of thing.'

Green liked to eat. Liked to go out and come back with small, surprising morsels: cake, fish.

Green was a good cook.

Green smelled like parsley.

In the mornings, Green drank hot water with bits of fruit bobbing about in it, whatever was to hand.

Green seemed to know people, though they had arrived in Valparaiso only a day apart, tipping his hat to strangers in the street. Green had a knack for finding things they happened to need: food of course, but also books, a chess set. Bed linen. Flowers to put in the windows of the yellow house.

Green paid attention to details.

Green gave nothing away, though when asked, seemed not to mind: Green told him his name and they laughed about it, but it was too late; he could not stop thinking of him as Green Hat, and later, simply as Green.

He had wondered, idly, but still, whether Green was a confidence man. Perhaps Green had spotted how out-of-place he was amongst the crew that first day on land, a gentleman far from home, and thought he would make a good mark. It would have been a reasonable enough supposition and he wasn't, by then, naïve: he knew these sorts of things went on. Perhaps Green had been in Valparaiso far longer than he claimed, which would explain how he seemed so familiar with the place and its people. Perhaps Green was using him. The thought made him feel not angry but guilty.

'I want you to know I don't have any money,' he said. It was shocking to admit it; his cheeks were burning. Green looked up; he'd been tightening hinges on the back door of the house, which led to a dim courtyard where cats clustered. Green fed the cats pieces of cheese that he cut up very small for them.

'Oh, nor do I,' said Green. 'Are you worried about it?'

'I just wanted to make sure you knew,' he said. 'I've got nothing.'

So if Green was a swindler, he had been warned.

(And it was he, after all, not Green, who was suggesting things: let's take the house together, let's eat dinner together, and—a little later—let's both sleep in this room, in this bed, since it is getting so cold. It might have been Green who had made the first approach, but ever since, he felt, it had been he who was pursuing Green.)

Some people were reticent about themselves. If Green was that way, was a little mysterious about his life, well: he could understand that. He could understand why one might not want to revisit one's past. He tried not to think about his father. He tried not to think about his father. There were other thoughts, too, that were less unpleasant, of riding his horse round the lake and out across the fields, or of painting with his cousin, but those memories always led to other places, the inevitable dinner at the end of the day, his father's face at the head of the table, scowling and furious over something he'd done and been unable to deny: money spent, people met, food he would not eat. Green brought home a plant with long, red flowers like trumpets, which he potted in a coffee tin and placed by the front door, and he tried not to think about his father.

Kissing Green, a matter of getting the timing right. He had agonised over it for days. They'd not spoken about themselves in that way, though he'd noticed that Green never looked at girls and even without that, felt certain. He imagined the perfect situation might present itself. Ideally, they would both be drunk so they could pretend not to remember if they needed to. He thought he might mark the end of their first week together in the house with some kind of special meal, could get wine for the occasion, but even this he felt unsure of: Green was the one to find the food, the one to do the cooking. And besides, he had never paid any attention to what wines were good. He had always just drunk whatever was in front of him.

In the end, it was irrelevant. One morning Green came up behind him as he was smoking and began to unbutton his coat, his shirt, his trousers. He felt Green's large hands on his shoulders, strumming his ribs, gripping his waist. It was surprisingly rough. They didn't speak the whole time.

And to think he had been agonising over a kiss.

'And for money, what will we do?' Green introduced the question so lightly, as though he had simply said, 'And what should we eat for lunch today?' They were in their little garden, sitting on the ground with their backs to the wall and the sun in their eyes. Green was drinking hot water with halved cherries in it; he'd tried the same but found it made his stomach turn. They had just had sex.

His heart hammered. It was possible—likely—that Green would leave him once he realised the reality of his finances. 'I think I mentioned—I'm afraid—my father—I'm afraid I have none.' Perhaps Green would turn on his heel and leave there and then. Perhaps Green had forgotten what he'd said before, or misheard him. 'My father cut me off, after—after an argument.' A ginger cat jumped down from the wall and began head-butting his shin.

Green simply smiled in a way that suggested he felt he had been misunderstood and said, 'I have none either. My wages from California will last three more weeks, that is all.' The ginger cat moved its attentions to Green, which was something of a pattern: small creatures and humans alike seemed to trust him.

'I'm sure I could work at something,' he said. 'There must be something other than sailing I could do.'

'You barely know how to tie your own shoes,' said Green, but he said it kindly.

'I'll paint portraits by the harbour. A peso a picture,' he said. A joke. Green fondled the ginger cat's head while looking directly at him, so that he felt in some way it was he who was being touched.

They let the subject drop, and then, after a week had passed, could not help but pick it up again. They had gone for walks and stayed in bed, exploring, exploring, and he had talked about himself a lot. Had been indiscreet, really, though he felt—couldn't explain it—that talking to Green was like talking to another part of himself. Green was unshockable. Still, whenever he asked Green about his life in England, the replies he got were oblique and then patently dishonest, something about a family house in Wiltshire: he asked about the exact whereabouts of the house and Green was evasive.

He became self-conscious about this imbalance between them, and the self-consciousness irritated him. 'Why are you lying about this?'

'I'm not lying,' said Green.

They were in bed, naked, and when he looked at Green it seemed impossible that a man so bare and so beautiful could lie about anything. Green's stomach: convex and downy. Green's chest: hair and fat and muscle and, if you looked long enough, if you both lay still enough, a rhythmic puckering of the skin over his heartbeat.

'It's all right,' he said. Kissed him. Took his hand. Kissed that. 'It's all right.'

Only then did Green come out with it. A labourer father, drunk and unkind. A mother who worked as a cook in a big house, which was indeed in Wiltshire, so that had not entirely been a lie, there really had been a house like that, though he knew nothing more about it than its size and approximate location, a few small details his mother had shared. Green and his sister had been left in the care of an aunt in Borough.

Listening to Green's story, he had a sudden sense of dread. He imagined himself visiting that house in Wiltshire, as he easily might have done, if it had been the home of one of the young men he knew, and it would never have occurred to him to think of the woman in the kitchen who made the food, unless—and here he reddened just to think of it—he might have seen her in passing in the hallway and made a joke to his friends. He had been known to make jokes at the expense of servants. He couldn't bear to recall the details, only knew that he had laughed at their clothes or the way the spoke and it made him feel sick with himself. And one of those servants could have been Green's mother, and even if that was stretching things a bit, beyond what was likely, this scenario in which he had not only gone to the house but met the mother and said something vile about her, that wasn't really the point, was it?

He felt old again. His life, since he had left England, had been a series of lessons about how human other people were, even—especially—the ones he'd barely used to notice, and lessons, too, about how inhuman he himself could be. He felt sick. He thought of opium. He looked at Green, a steady presence, the up-down heaving of his chest like the roll of a ship over a wave.

'Where is your mother now?' he asked.

Green shrugged. 'Dead.' His father too, and his aunt, and a

twin sister who he had loved more than life had died giving birth to a son, dead also, and on it went, dead, dead, dead, until, thank God, Green ran out of relatives, and they were quiet for a while.

'So there's nobody,' he said, eventually.

'No,' said Green. 'Only you.'

Even when he was with Green, he thought about opium all the time. He didn't mention it and didn't ever do anything more than think. It felt like a betrayal nonetheless, as though he was fantasising about another lover. He spent a few minutes each morning recalling the sensation, the sweet, sweet peace of it, and would feel his breath slow and his body relax against the sheets, and he would know that at a certain point he had to stop, had to force himself back to the surface of his life, because if he stayed down there too long he would stop breathing. He would open his eyes. He would straighten his fingers, crack his knuckles. And then he would go down to the kitchen where Green would be making coffee or some sort of fruit tea, and they would kiss, lightly, and Green's beard against his chin, his neck, his chest, navel, groin, fuck, it was almost as good, wasn't it, bodies, care, not being alone? This was his new life. This was his new life.

'Could you write to your father,' Green said. 'About the money?'

The thought made him queasy. The idea that Green and his father existed in the same world, even. But it was awful, too, to think of his family, rich and alive, when Green had nobody to ask. 'What would I say?'

'Make something up.'

'Make something up?' He sounded slow, echoing Green like that. 'Make what up?'

'Oh, you know, the sort of thing he'd want to hear.'

'Lie to him?'

Green shrugged. 'Not if you won't like it. It was just an idea.'

He tried to meet Green's eyes to check whether he was upset, but Green avoided looking at him. He had the sense Green was embarrassed.

'I'll paint portraits by the harbour,' he said. Not a joke. It was the only thing he could think to do, and to prove he was serious he got dressed and went out (walking away from Green, a physical discomfort; the closest thing he could think of was a dentist pulling teeth: that nauseating, body-breaking moment before the tooth gives way) to buy black ink, cheap boards, a flimsy little easel, a set of tools made for tourists, really, ladies' brushes designed for little watercolour sketches of the environs, but they were all he could find.

'You think this will work?' said Green, doubtful and not wanting to show the full force of his doubt, though it was obvious enough.

He set up a little stand by the waterfront with a sign that said 'Likenesses!' but the portraits did not sell well. He was not bad at doing them, had always had a good eye for faces, and people did stop to peer over his shoulder as he worked, making comments to one another about this or that detail as though he could not hear them. (Was this what it was like, he wondered, to be a servant, to be a person like Green's mother, moving seen and unseen through the world?) But there was a dire lack of custom nonetheless; the kinds of people washing up at the Valparaiso port were not, really, the kinds of people who were minded to buy keepsake portraits of themselves. He had imagined sailors might like to send them to sweethearts or wives, but as someone pointed out to him quite early on, there was a photographic studio in Valparaiso, just a little way up the hill, Boswell and Sons, and who would choose an ink likeness when you could send a real photograph?

'I'll write to my father,' he said, dully, when he got home after a day of making not a single sale.

'No, don't. It was a bad idea,' said Green. 'I'll go along tomorrow and see if there's work to be had on the funiculars.'

'Don't do that,' he said. He reached out. Touched Green's forearm. There had been several fatalities on the funicular worksite since they'd arrived, men falling to their deaths from the scaffold, girders slipping and knocking people off balance. Even in passing they had seen horrible injuries and heard of worse. It was as bad as being at sea. 'Don't do that.'

He felt acutely the unfairness of it all. There should be an allowance made, he thought, for lovers. The world was awful. The sea was awful. Work of any kind: awful. The only thing not awful was he and Green in bed together and if people would just understand that—surely they did understand it; surely this, if anything, was universal—love!—and understand that it was the same for he and Green as it was for anyone, men and women, newlyweds, surely there would be some sort of allowance. A honeymoon. That was what he wanted. They should be allowed one. Anything else was awful.

He would write to his father for money. Once he said it aloud it did not seem so dreadful. He said he would make something up, as Green suggested, and after a moment Green brightened and said he would help with the letter, even write it if that would make it easier. They would do it together and get it out of the way and sent off, and then they'd forget all about it and continue as they had been in the yellow house, untroubled, wide awake.

Portrait of a Man in a Green Hat Drawing a Man in Brown

Green wrote the letter for him. Dear Mater. Dear Pater. Much improved. Man to be proud of. Desire, even, to marry (they had laughed about that). Life as painter. Make a real go of it. Study in Rome. Paris if they preferred. Respectable. Respectable. Please send money for passage back to Europe. Possibility, too, of reinstating allowance, being much re-formed and anxious of earning back trust and respect? Remain your dutiful, etc.

They had gone back and forth on the painter part. It was a gamble. Green had been in favour of a more outright lie, pre-ferring something along the lines of: 'desire to return home to be amongst you all, and if it pleases Pater, to manage the estate.' But when it came to it, he could not bring himself to say it when it was not—could never—be true. He could not go back to his family house with Green. And so he could not go back. That was all there was to it. (That was not all there was to it. More pressing, in fact, was the sense that, even if it was all made up, he couldn't bear to write anything that would give his father a sense of victory. A balance could be struck, he thought, between pleasing his parents enough to extract money from them, and preserving for himself the dignity of still aggravating them.)

So, the idea: dangle the possible return to Europe, which would certainly excite them and offer some reassurance that he would be once again within their sphere of influence and discipline, and would also perhaps bring forth from them a large lump sum of money, ostensibly to pay for his passage, but which they could spend instead on, for example, food; make general euphemistic assurances about his reformed character and willingness to marry, in order to indicate that the cause of the rift between father and son should no longer be considered an obstacle to the resumption of his regular allowance payments; drop in the painting part for his personal satisfaction but also to make the whole thing more convincing, since annoying his father was a core trait of his and a letter without any aggravation might arouse suspicions.

He'd told Green by then what had happened with his father—about the fight they'd had before he left, but only the scaffold of the thing: what the point of disagreement had been, what its consequences were. He hadn't found a way to convey the viciousness of it, which made the memory seem like some other person's: his father's eyes, entirely flat, dull, dead-looking, which made him seem like a stranger; his father's voice, expressionless and so quiet he'd had to lean forwards to hear.

'Sod,' his father had said.

There'd been no violence. That was the upsetting thing, really. If his father had raged and stamped and even pummelled him, it would have felt more ordinary. But it had been so horribly calm.

'Sod,' and then, 'You disgust me,' and then, in that same, flat voice, a litany of questions that made his skin crawl: 'Do you suck his cock, do you? Does he fuck you like a wife?' It had become more and more graphic, to the point that he'd wondered how his father had quite so much knowledge of the intricacies of what men did together in bed. He had simply stood in his father's study and listened and found that he had nothing to say. He might as well have been stripped naked; it could not have been more humiliating.

He didn't know for sure how his father had come to find him out. A servant had betrayed him most likely, probably Ferris. He'd been receiving love letters from a man in London, which he kept wrapped up in scarves at the back of his closet and got out to read only late at night. But somehow one of those letters had found its way into his father's hands, and the consequence was that he had left the house and never returned. He had written, once, to the man in London, not daring to say that his father now knew this awful thing about them and instead he was callous—it was dreadful, but what else could he do—saying only that the urge had come upon him to go to sea. And then had come the opium, the obliteration of himself as he floated from country to country about the world, and only later came the clarity, and Green.

They sent off the letter and they waited for a reply and ate a little less than they liked, just to make their money last, and knew that if things did not go as they'd hoped, if his father refused him money, they would have to go back to sea. Perhaps they'd find work on the same ship, he thought, miserably, but it was no life, and the intricacies of an existence at sea that he had missed at first, the ringing of the ship's bell, the shuffling-grunting-constant presence of the other men, he dreaded now. They had sworn to themselves they wouldn't go back to it. By the third week of waiting, they no longer had rent to pay for the yellow house. When the landlady came to collect it, Green went out to speak to her while he stayed inside, too ashamed to face her. He watched through the window as Green and the woman bent their heads together, saw the expression on her face shift from irritation to humour. By the end, they were both laughing, and she patted Green's arm in a motherly way before leaving.

'What did you tell her?' he asked, when Green came back inside.

'Nothing. Why? I just said we'd have it soon.'

He shrugged. Green smiled. He smiled. It was hard not to feel that Green could talk his way out of anything, could solve everything. The day after that, his father's letter arrived.

His parents were glad to know he was safe, having been concerned not to hear from him in so long. They were glad, too, to hear of his progress in reforming his character and his determination to continue his life in a manner that would please the family. The return to Europe was a sensible idea, and they certainly preferred that he travelled as a passenger, in comfort, rather than continue his ridiculous pretence of labouring as a common seaman. The money for his passage could be collected from the Valparaiso Bank with the enclosed note. ('Yes!' cried Green, more loudly than he'd

expected.) They hoped he would return at his earliest convenience, and preferred that he come straight to England so that
questions about his future could be discussed together, as a
family, and of course because he was much missed by all. In
expectation of this return, his allowance was reinstated and
he would be able to access his funds forthwith. ('My God,'
said Green. 'Look at that. Just like that.')

He knew he should feel elated, the way Green did, but he
was overcome with a full-body misery on reading the letter
and found it hard to meet Green's eye. He read and re-read
the line 'Come straight to England.' The thought—there it
was again, the smell of the rotting leaves by the docks in
Liverpool, that peculiar quality of drizzle in the air, England,
November—was visceral to him.

'But I can't,' he said, eventually. 'I can't go back to them.'

Green looked perplexed. 'You don't have to,' he said.

'It says so right there.'

'You're a man,' said Green. 'A grown man. And this,' he
tapped the letter so forcefully the edge tore off, 'is merely a
suggestion. There is no reason at all we cannot proceed to
Italy as planned. You must simply write and say so.'

'They'll be furious.'

'Darling,' said Green. 'Darling. If you find the right words,
you can do what you like.'

Green helped him find the words. Much gratitude to his
loving parents. Apologies, again, for having caused them any
anxiety on his part. Looking forward immensely to returning
to Europe, and humbly accepting their support in this matter.
Finds it better to travel direct to Civitavecchia from whence to

commence travel to Rome and begin his studies of art. Aware that his parents have justifiable reservations about this course of action, but anxious—extremely so—to prove to them, as soon as possible, that this is the correct course for him. If he could not demonstrate success within, say, a year, he would gladly return to England to take over, should it please his father, the running of the estate.

'No,' he said, 'don't put that. Don't put that bit about returning to the estate.'

Green's pen hovered over the page. 'I think we have to,' he said. 'It doesn't mean you'll need to go. It really doesn't.'

Off the letter went. They collected the money and he allowed himself to feel a little of Green's joy. They went immediately to buy food—thick cuts of salted pork for Green, a glut of custard apples for him, eggs, cheese, tomatoes, bread, beer, coffee—and took it home to the yellow house and ate while sitting on the floor, legs entangled, happy. He kept feeling for the money to check it was real. Thoughts of buying opium, inevitable, immediate, he pushed aside, and when they returned to him he leant forwards and kissed Green, harder each time.

'We'll take the rent round later,' Green said. 'We could put down a year's worth and not have to think about it again.'

'A year!' He imagined a year of life with Green in the yellow house and realised he had assumed that they really were going to Rome. He'd known, of course, that it was all made up, and yet part of him had already begun to imagine their life in Italy, had pictured himself really studying painting, and Green there too. Italy. He'd begun, almost, to crave it.

'What is it?' asked Green.

'What if we really went to Italy? I was thinking we could really go. Start something there. A life. Painting.'

Green smiled. Green stood up. Green was always so ready to say yes to him. That was what was astonishing, alluring, endearing.

'Then we'll go to Italy,' Green said.

The ship was called *The Magellan*. Green knew someone who knew the captain, and when they boarded it turned out they had both at various times worked with several members of the crew. It was a strange, awkward moment, walking past his erstwhile colleagues towards the first-class berths. They had planned a history for themselves before boarding: brothers—'No,' Green had laughed, 'best say cousins'—cousins, then, who had been conducting business for their grandfather in South America, and if pushed they would wave their hands and say something airy about gold mining, and they were now returning home for a family funeral. 'They'll leave us alone then, if it's for a funeral.' But here were people who knew them well, had slept alongside them, and there could be no pretence. They received, thankfully, no questions. The barriers in place between the seamen and first class passengers held fast. And his discomfort was eased when they found their way to their berth, which had been made up for them in advance by a steward, neat bunks and even, ridiculous, lovely, sprigs of dried lavender in a vase that was bolted to the table. It was almost impossible to imagine close by the men packed together in their hammocks, all shitting into the same pot.

There was nothing, really, to do. He had written to his father, confirming their travel plans—they would disembark at Lisbon and seek onward passage to Italy; he would send word then to confirm the next leg—and would not have to confront a reply until they arrived. They borrowed books from the captain but it was all poetry, which Green loved but he found exhausting. There were, occasionally, musical performances arranged by a particularly officious choir master in second class, but he found himself uncomfortable and self-conscious, could not keep his mind on the singers, was scared he would inadvertently reach for Green's hand, or knee, or thigh. They had sex a lot and slept a lot. They talked and talked and told each other every tiniest thing they could think of: from their most awful, unhappiest memories right down to the most trivial titbits of their former lives: Green told him the exact colour of a pair of leather shoes he'd worn at ten years old; he told Green about his mad uncle, whom he had visited once, and with whom he'd walked by the sea while the man had talked and talked and talked, dreadful, lovely nonsense about catfish and magnets and his daughter's pet rat. He felt, now the seal of Green's reticence had broken, that he and Green were collectors of each other; that nothing was insignificant; that everything should be lovingly stored.

He woke from a nap one afternoon to find that Green was drawing him. His inks and boards were spread out on the floor of the berth, and Green was cross-legged, holding up a brush and squinting.

After that, they drew each other over and over again. Green drew him lying down, and then smoking, and then when he began to draw Green in return they drew each other drawing. He drew Green naked, prone, astonishing. He drew Green in nothing but his green hat. Green had him wear his brown monogrammed jacket over a bare chest, drew him like that. 'We're getting fat,' Green said, staring at their images on the paper. It was true. They were. Week after week on board spent sleeping, eating; the only exercise they got was with each other. After the combined effects of opium and seafaring had pared him back to the leanest, smallest version of himself, he had begun to round out. In Green's pictures, his cheeks were full, jowly; a second chin had formed below the first like the strap of a helmet. Green had always seemed broad, magnificently so, but now they were the same size and still growing.

When they pushed their faces together in the looking glass that was nailed neatly beside the door, or put their portraits side by side, inky eyes glancing towards inky hands, the edges of the paper touching tentatively like fingers, he thought they both looked beautiful. He imagined what they might look like in a year, or a decade, two decades, the portraits they'd do of each other in Rome in gouache, in oil, charcoal smudges as their faces dimpled and wrinkled and warped, white chalk and the way their bodies would spread or shrink or furl, all the years stretching out ahead like water from the prow of the ship.

Part Four

The New Century

New Year's Eve, 1899

If there was one thing my aunt loved above all else, it was an ill-advised party. She refused to entertain the idea of cancelling the New Year's Eve event, which would mark after all not just the end and beginning of two years but of two centuries. If her party did not go ahead, she would be forced to attend someone else's, and if there was one thing she hated above all else, it was being a guest in someone else's house. She felt degraded by the experience of having to compliment other people's choices, having to notice some little detail to point out and admire. She hated saying 'Thank you.' So, despite the enormous family rupture caused by Charles, despite several snide newspaper articles about the fraudster who had convinced a mother he was her own son, which had drawn unkind conclusions about my aunt's mental state, despite all of it, there would be a party to celebrate the arrival of the twentieth century.

Her vision for this was a ball in the old style, and guests were instructed to come dressed as figures from history, which made sense to my aunt who thought that we could, in fashioning a kind of historical parade, say something significant about the passing of time and the thrill of change. It was a thesis nobody else completely understood, but my aunt was busy arranging a costume for herself; she was to be Lady Macbeth with bloodied gloves, and again, there was some question about whether Lady Macbeth was really a figure from history but nobody dared voice it. (A further question I had, also unvoiced, was whether there was something altogether distasteful in her choice, considering the situation.)

It had been a strange and sad Christmas during which my aunt had coughed and coughed and once or twice appeared to faint and had repeatedly requested that I share my drops with her. When she finally came to accept that I really had not been prescribed any, she sent for a doctor of her own, who brought her enough to kill a bull. After he left there were murmurings from the servants that he had diagnosed tuberculosis, but my aunt refused to discuss it, as she did any suggestion that we cancel the party, or the question of what should happen to Charles. He was still there in the house as my aunt's guest, lingering in his rooms at the top of the house, and she refused to countenance the idea of his departure. What she really believed, whether she had accepted the consensus that he was a fraud, was unclear, but her orders to keep him in the house were not. These were enforced energetically by Ferris, who had taken to roaming from room to room, pale-faced, and snarling at anyone who questioned Charles's continued residence in the house. My aunt spent the festive period alone with her laudanum, emerging at odd hours to give new instructions about New Year's Eve and then vanishing again.

'Why does the man even want to be here?' I heard Mr

Barnard mutter to Mr George. 'The household loathes him. He cannot feel comfortable.'

'It's a nice roof, as roofs go, to have over one's head,' said Mr George. 'And the man has a thick skin.'

Then Ferris appeared in the doorway, lips curling, and both the lawyers fells silent.

We lived like a family haunted, all of us creeping around the lower floors of the house and occasionally glancing upwards at the ceiling, imagining the spectre on the upmost floor. Charles never appeared. He did not even go to church. The servants took food up to his room, and coffee, and wine, brought down empty cups, plates almost clean save for smears of sauce. I saw them descending with the dirtied crockery looking stony-faced, as though the task demeaned them. I looked out for Hannah, worried I wouldn't recognise her still, and then eventually asked one of the housemaids, who told me she had left, suddenly, two days before Christmas. I looked out for Bobby, too, though he seemed to be avoiding me, walking the long way round to the stables to avoid passing by my window.

I was in a state of intense loneliness and misery. I'd been so pleased to find Charles was still there on my return from London, so gratified to have a chance to tell him I had solved the case, even if I had solved it to the satisfaction of nobody but myself. There had been a chance for things to be wonderful, really wonderful: we might have come up with a plan to bring certain witnesses to the house to confirm that they had known him in his youth and, like my aunt, recognised him still; there need not have been any mention of how, exactly, they had come to know him. And more than that, I had been excited to tell him that I had discovered his secret, his real secret, and that I would it keep it for him, as he kept mine. We could have been allies, and more than that, friends. Then he had proposed and ruined everything.

In my flabbergasted silence, he had ploughed into a wild and utterly unconvincing declaration of his affections, detailing how, since that first evening in Rome, he had known that our fates were entwined and how, the more he discovered of me—my 'talents,' he had said, for painting, for diplomacy within the family, for keeping secrets—the more he came to desire me. And the moment when I had announced that he stole my money? He described it as a revelation: it had been so wonderfully timed, so dramatic, and he had been filled with admiration at my boldness. My subsequent absence had been torture; he had been terrified that I would not return, that he would never be able to tell me how fervently he had fallen in love with me.

'I thought you understood me,' I said, after an age, during which the only sound had been the squelching and lowing of the cows. I was shocked—shocked by all of it, but most of all by the word 'desire,' which seemed so out of place that it had surely been an error, a dash of green paint on black, some kind of spill or smudge in his words. 'You must know it is impossible that I would feel this way about you. I thought you understood. You said—you said it was not madness.'

Charles had looked surprised and then embarrassed, as though I had said something stupid. 'It is not necessary to make a choice, surely? To love only men or only women? Many people, I think, can do both.'

And perhaps he was like that, and perhaps, therefore, it was not entirely impossible that he was telling the truth, that some odd thing had happened in his mind and he had begun to see me in this strange new light. And yet surely it was impossible, because he was delivering his lines so poorly. He had given me no opportunity to tell him what I knew, about his past, about Arthur, and I could draw only one logical conclusion about his motivations, which was that, having failed to convince the family that he was Charles, he preferred now to marry me and so get the money that way; it must have seemed just as easy, easier perhaps, than continuing to fight over whether he was or was not who he was. By the time the conversation was over, I was offended not just by his attempt to use me this way, and by his efforts to make me question my own nature, but also that he was doing such a bad job at it, that he hadn't tried, at least, to woo me more convincingly, to take even a moment's time over it, so that I might reasonably have believed, even had I not known what I did about his past, that somehow, miraculously, he had fallen in love.

'It is impossible, Charles,' I had said, and I had returned to the house and at some point he must have crept back up to his rooms, and I had not seen him since, not even on Christmas Day, not even at church.

Miserably, Mr Barnard's attentions had become more intense and more overt over the Christmas period; they seemed, like Charles's, not unrelated to my changed status within the family, the aura of money they saw around me now. Whenever I left my room he seemed to be there, and I had the sensation of being surveyed at all times, and began to worry how on earth I would escape again to look at the Van Eyck I was to copy, which had always been urgent and was now doubly so because I had none of the Courbet money left. There were only so many medical appointments I could claim before people would begin to ask more detailed questions, and I had a horrible feeling that somebody would suggest I be accompanied on my next doctor's visit, now that they were all newly interested in me, interested in what I did and where I went. The idea that I might one day have money was threatening my ability to make any money in the present, and I found that I could not sit still when Mr Barnard was there, staring at me. I had the impulse to twitch my hands around my head, as though I could flick away the irritant as I might a fly.

On Christmas day Mr Barnard held my arm on the walk to church, and I was reminded of a time in my childhood when my mother had brought home an injured crow and nursed it back to health; how, once she had set it free, the crow had waited devotedly outside our house and perched on her shoulder whenever she went outside, and at first we had thought it was charming or at least a little funny but then, eventually, the presence of the crow became maddening to her and she would dread going anywhere and when we did she would jump and flap about saying, 'Get it away from me, God, get it off me, that awful bird, get it off, off, off!' Eventually, my father went out and shot the crow off the gatepost. It had exploded into a cloud of feathers.

The only good thing about the attentions of Mr Barnard was that, once, returning from a walk with his arm looped through mine, I glanced up at Charles's window and saw that he was watching.

Mr Barnard proposed that, for the New Year's Eve party, he should dress as Henry the Eighth and I as one of his wives.

'Which wife?' I asked. 'Which wife are you suggesting?'

'Oh, whichever you like best,' he said.

'Which one died quickest?' I asked, but he didn't seem as offended as I thought he should be.

Nobody was looking forward to the party except for Mr Barnard and, presumably, my aunt. As guests began to arrive in the evening, there was an atmosphere of resigned dread in the household. Mr George was dressed as Charles I with a frothy white lace collar, several of the uncles were Julius Caesar, one of their wives was Joan of Arc; it struck me that there was a collective yearning amongst all of us to be put out of our misery. I was Anne of Cleves, in a costume based on the Hans Holbein portrait, which I had pieced together myself while staring up at Grandmother Hodierna in 'The Drag' for secondary inspiration.

We gathered in the hallway. I stood just by the entrance, watching the lights of carriages get larger and brighter against the black of the driveway and grounds, and fixed a smile on my face. There was wood smoke on the air and I wondered whether the stable boys were having a bonfire, as they sometimes liked to do; I thought yearningly of join-ing them, sitting beside Bobby and reaching my hands out to the warmth. The first guests came in, King Arthur and

Guinevere, neighbours from the other side of the village, and I bobbed in their direction and asked after their Christmas and accepted their condolences for my father's death, fiddling with the crucifix of paste gems strung around my neck. A few more people came after that, dressed as kings and queens, as though all of English history, all of what we were, was only that. I regretted Anne of Cleves. I should have dressed as Boudica. I waited for it to get busy enough for me to disappear without being noticed.

Except it never did get busy. The articles in the press about Charles had done more reputational damage than anticipated, and our more fashionable neighbours simply did not arrive. Those who did come looked sheepish, even dressed as they were; they wore the kinds of costumes that could, if necessary, be used to obscure one's identity. There were a lot of very large crowns. And everything else was off, too: the musicians were too numerous and therefore too loud; nobody could hear each other speak and because the event was not well-attended there seemed to be almost more violinists than guests. The food was copious but went cold and lingered, unappetisingly: steamed puddings stiffening by the fireside, souffles folding in on themselves. Cream was melting and drifting to the bottom of glasses of syllabub.

I had not been able to stomach alcohol since my night with Randal Bryson, but there seemed no other way of making it through the evening. I drank milk punch and, later, wine, and played an extended game of hide and seek with Mr Barnard, who was easily recognisable by his ermine collar and his enormous shoulders, which he had widened with rolled-up newspaper under his red coat. I wove from group to group in the library and oak room, never staying in one place long enough that he might catch up with me; when I glanced back I saw him standing on tip toe, scanning the rooms for his fourth wife. I knew, if I allowed him to reach me, he would have prepared a line that made some reference to wives or marriage and I dreaded hearing it. I thought of Boudica again, of an engraving reproduced in one of my uncle's books called 'Boudica Haranguing the Britons', in which she stood resplendent above a crowd, a girl tucked under her arm, and yelled at them.

There was fortune telling; the woman my aunt had employed to tell us about Charles was there, moving between clusters and offering predictions. She had tea leaves with her, but no means of making tea. There was, too, an enormous cake that nobody was allowed to eat, and which my aunt intended to throw against the door at midnight, a tradition I had never heard of. This went against the repeated advice of the fortune teller, who kept saying that whatever we were doing at midnight would be what we would do for the rest of the year, or even the rest of the century. It seemed my aunt would spend the twentieth century throwing cake at doors.

'Pick a book,' Mr Barnard said. I jumped. I had let my guard down for a second and there he was. We were standing in the hallway near the entrance, and I had been lingering by the wall, where some of my uncle's more expensive books had been arranged prominently in an alcove. 'Pick a book, open it to any page, and then, whichever phrase your finger falls upon will be your fortune for the year.' When I did not move, he reached across me to the bookshelf and gave me the Bible.

I let it fall open in my palm, the pages throwing up a churchy smell, and placed my finger on a verse in Ezekiel. 'And I will sanctify my great name, which was profaned among the heathen, which ye have profaned in the midst of them.' Mr Barnard and I read it in silence.

'What does that mean?' I asked, and he looked a little put out.

He took the book from my hands and was about to redo the exercise for himself, and I had no doubt he had rehearsed many times how to make the pages open to something about love or about men and women or marriage, something that would make the whole of my body shiver with awkwardness, when the atmosphere in the room suddenly changed. It was a kind of freezing effect, as though someone had thrown open the windows. People stopped talking. Heads turned. Charles was at the top of the stairs.

FORTUNES

I couldn't tell how long Charles had been standing there. He wasn't dressed for the occasion; he was wearing the shabby brown jacket he'd had in Rome, monogrammed and frayed, and no tie. He was staring mildly at everyone below and at the wreaths and the lights and the musicians and the costumes and at all the empty space between us, all the people who had not come. Mr Barnard, oblivious, flipped open the Bible and read, "Therefore shall a man leave his father and his mother, and shall cleave unto his wife: and they shall be one flesh." He looked up, smiling, and then glanced in the direction everyone else was staring. When he saw Charles he started so violently his crown slid off his head.

I thought I had never been more unbearably embarrassed—by my family, my costume, by my whole life. There was something about being looked at by Charles, even then, that made me feel obvious.

'My goodness,' Mr Barnard said, 'what is he doing here? He should be gone, long gone. Why is he not gone?' He addressed these questions to me with an urgency that suggested he felt I was to blame.

'He is my aunt's guest,' I said. 'Though I believe he was explicitly not invited to the party.'

'I should think not!' barked Mr Barnard, staring incredulously up at Charles. 'My goodness, I should think not!'

When Charles descended a step, Mr Barnard looked ready to turn on his heel and flee.

'He's just a person, Mr Barnard,' I said. 'He is not rabid, not contagious.'

'Someone should stop him. Shouldn't somebody stop him?'

'Stop him from what?'

Mr Barnard had paled and turned away from me, thrusting the Bible back into my hands. He made his way towards the library, muttering something about Mr George. I was alone, then, and dressed as Anne of Cleves in wimple and lace and paste crucifix, holding the Bible open to a verse about becoming one flesh, when Charles reached me at the bottom of the stairs.

'Good evening,' he said, and it became clear that he was very drunk. I could smell wine on his breath; he held the banister finial tightly, as though aboard a ship on rough seas.

I nodded. 'How are you, Charles?'

'Good evening,' he said again, looking around at everyone else and beaming in a menacing, uncomfortable way. 'Good evening, good evening.' He took a glass of eggnog from the tray by the door and downed it, wiping his mouth with the back of his hand, and then wiping the hand on his thigh. 'Good evening.' The thought of drinking eggnog at speed made me feel sick. I put down the Bible to reach for water.

There was a small disturbance in the cluster of people

standing behind me, which became a larger disturbance in the form of Mr George storming towards us. He stepped neatly around me and stood too close to Charles, leaning towards him to say, in a tone that was almost conspiratorial, 'Sir, the household is enjoying a celebration this evening. Perhaps I can invite you to take some refreshments in your room.'

Charles laughed humourlessly and too loudly. 'How thoughtful of you, Mr George. What an extremely thoughtful invitation.' He took a step back towards the table, where little concave soufflés were clustered, untouched, beside the eggnog jugs and glasses, and picked up the whole tray. 'I'll enjoy these in my room,' he said.

Mr George stepped forwards again, this time to block Charles's path back to the stairs, and said, 'Come now, Sir. This is not—this behaviour—please, be respectful.'

'Respect!' Charles was almost shouting. 'Respect! I'm delighted to know that, suddenly, you care about respect, Mr George. If we are being respectful, all of a sudden, then I'm sure you'll not mind if I stay and enjoy the party with the other guests. I find myself in the mood for—' he gazed again at the guests, everyone silently watching him, finally settling his eyes on me, '—company.'

Mr George's face: quivering with rage and timidity by turn. I had the impression that some small, boyish part of him wanted to punch Charles and that he was terrified he might really do it. He was opening and closing his fist in a way that reminded me of a fish in a net, gasping for air, the hopeless pulsing of it. The musicians were still playing, but nobody else was moving or making a sound; we all stood, rapt. Mr George opened and closed his mouth: a trout. There were footsteps behind us. Lady Macbeth appeared at my side.

'Charles,' she said, quietly, firmly. How astonishing it was that she still called him that, considering everything. 'Charles, you're making a scene.'

'Mater,' he said. 'It is he who is making a scene. I just came to the party.'

'Don't call her that,' snapped Mr George. 'It's an insult to her son.'

'My son—' began my aunt, and then stopped. She looked between Charles and Mr George. She seemed to understand that the time had come for her to make, or at least perform, a stand, but the notion only paralysed her. She looked exhausted and confused. She said, again, 'My son,' and nothing else.

It was at this moment that the fortune teller wafted obliviously in to say, as she had been saying all night, 'Whatever you are doing as the clock strikes twelve, you will do for the rest of the year!' It was a few minutes to midnight and servants were bringing round tapers, which we were all to light while my aunt threw cake at the door; and then they wheeled the cake in: an overly ornate cream-and-jam structure, decorated with sugar horseshoes and so large I questioned whether my aunt would be able to lift it without some sort of pulley system.

Charles sat down heavily on the bottom stair. 'You know my father told me something before I left,' he said, staring into the middle distance, 'which I swore never to divulge.'

My aunt stiffened and sought out his eye line. 'Then don't divulge it,' she said.

'About my brother,' said Charles. 'Excuse me, my late brother. About dear old Teddy.'

'Don't divulge it,' my aunt said. Under her white makeup, she had somehow further paled. She swallowed twice, quickly, suppressed a cough and bent awkwardly down so her face was close to his. She whispered, 'Don't,' but in saying the word another cough erupted, so that she spluttered wetly into his face. Charles flinched.

'I say brother,' Charles went on, speaking so loudly my aunt pulled back and almost lost her balance, 'but of course he was only a half sibling.'

Several people gasped. One of the Julius Caesars stepped forwards and laid a hand on Charles's elbow. 'Come now,' the man said, 'it's not—this isn't on—this kind of mudslinging.'

'Who was my brother's father, Mater?' said Charles. And then he looked—it was unmistakable, and in that moment seemed entirely obvious, like something I had surely already known, though I had never spelled it out to myself; the way they never seemed to leave each other alone, never seemed to maintain hostility with each other, that there was something audacious about their relationship—at Mr George.

Mr George wobbled as though someone had tried to trip him. My aunt looked unsteady, her lips pursed; she was holding on to the edge of the table to stabilize herself. Other people avoided looking at her, or at him, training their attention on Charles or the floor. Suddenly the musicians stopped playing, as they had been instructed to do shortly before the turn of the new year.

'That looks good,' Charles said into the new and horrifying silence, jutting his chin towards the cake.

'It's not for eating,' Mr Barnard said. 'Don't you dare touch it.'

Mr George, having had time to recover himself, stepped forwards. 'We've indulged your presence long enough, sir, and frankly, it's an insult that you are here at all. It is only as a courtesy that the lady of the house has allowed you tempo-rary residence while you arrange your journey back to Saint Helena. It is to Saint Helena you will travel to, is it not, Sir? Perhaps you might have more luck arranging your passage there from accommodation in London. I'm sure, even at this hour, we might spare a driver who could take you there at once.'

'King Charles,' Charles said, with that same, unkind smile. 'Has somebody already made a joke about losing your head, or must I? I think if my mother were going to marry you, she would have made plans to do so by now. It is over a year since my father's death. Was that your design? To worm your way into my father's bed, or should I say back into it, and see if she's still young enough to produce another heir of your own? Lord knows she doesn't keep you around for your skills as a lawyer.'

'Sir,' said Mr George. 'Sir. This performance has gone on long enough,' but there was uncertainty in his voice, and when he raised his hand to wipe a bead of sweat from his temple, his fingers were shaking.

'My father told me all about you, Mr George. People never knew, I think, that we were rather close, my father and I. Especially people who seem determined to deny he was my father at all, that I am really his son. But he told me about your troubles with the bar, naturally, and how, despite those troubles, he kept you on because he felt sorry for you. My father was a kind man, Mr George, extremely kind.' (Even then, even with everything else that was happening, I did note to myself that this was an unusual characterization of my uncle.) 'So I don't wonder that you've set out to discredit me, Mr George. You would prefer, naturally, to have someone at the head of this family who did not know that you are not an accredited attorney, who did not know what it was you did to get yourself disbarred.'

Mr George looked faint. Mr Barnard had the eyes of a madman, wide and gleaming, and was looking between Charles and Mr George as though observing the two of them playing badminton.

The grandfather clock by the front door showed a minute to midnight. The musicians were rustling and shifting, preparing for a fanfare. The twentieth century. It seemed fantastical. I had never felt my own ignorance so clearly, my own blindness to the future, and as I looked from Charles to my aunt, to Mr George, the flabbergasted Julius Caesars, Mr Barnard, jittery and crownless, my thoughts fell into a single refrain. What would happen to us all, what would happen to us all, what would happen to us all in the new century?

It struck me very suddenly that I couldn't stand to be with them a moment longer; I couldn't stand to be near them when the new year turned. I took a step back from the group, and then, when none of them seemed to notice, another. The door was in reach. All I needed to do was slip through it before any cake was flung and I could be alone with the night and the cows, and somewhere out there was a bonfire, warmth and ease and the whole yawning impossibility of the year 1900. I could already taste the air; how crisp and black and smoky it would feel as it hit my throat.

'Grace,' said Charles. 'Grace, where are you going?'

Eyes turning towards me. No chance of escape. I pivoted slowly.

'What is it that I should tell everyone about you, Cousin Grace?' He had taken another glass of eggnog, which was sluicing thickly as he gestured towards me.

'Charles,' I said, 'I have never wanted anything bad for you.' I wasn't sure what I meant by this and it wasn't strictly true, but I would have said anything, anything at all, if it stood a chance of stopping him.

'Let's welcome the new century by casting off secrecy, once and for all, Grace! Would you like to tell them yourself, or shall I?'

'Tell them what?' I said, very quickly, and Charles laughed.

I imagined, for a second, that perhaps it would not matter. Perhaps he could tell them whatever he wanted about me, about who I was and what I did and with whom, and it would come to nothing. I could run away as I had always longed to do. If only I had not given away my money. If only I had not given away my money. I didn't have time, in the moment, to loathe myself as fully as I wanted to: Charles's face was right there, his lips were right there, opening, forming new words, and all around were the faces of my family and familiars, my aunt's wide-eyed horror, the uncles, the servants, everyone looking at me. It felt as though Charles had proposed, in that moment, to peel back my skin in front of them all.

'I'll do it then,' he said. 'Our dear Grace here, my sweet cousin, who has for so long benefitted from the family's tolerance and largesse, has repaid your kindness by living a secret life, with secret dealings and secret interactions.'

'Charles,' I said. 'Stop. Stop it.'

He did stop. He smiled his gluey, drunken smile at me.

'I'll tell them,' I said.

'Go on then. Tell them.'

I nodded. I reached out and took his hand. It was heavy, limp and damp in my grasp. I laced my fingers through his, and felt my palm stretch, the knuckles widen.

'The secret is,' I said, 'it is, well, the secret is that Charles and I are engaged to be married.'

And then the clock chimed midnight, and the musicians began to play, for some reason, Bobby Shaftoe.

Copy of Jan Van Eyck's 'Portrait of Giovanni Arnolfini and His Wife', Oil on Oak, 1434

January. The air was cold and thick and the streets were shivering in rainwater that had fallen overnight. Though there were gas lamps all around Trafalgar Square, light bulging into the mist, I could barely see the other side of the fountain. It was early and the National Gallery was not open yet; I'd miscalculated how long it would take to reach from the hotel. I sat on the steps and watched my own breath unspool from between my lips and I tucked my hands between my thighs for warmth, and I waited.

There was something reassuring about being alone in the cold, about the sensation of icy stone on the other side of my skirt, of damp mist on my cheeks and, as I blinked, the shock of clarity when freezing air hit my eyeballs. My teeth began to chatter but I would have stayed there indefinitely, relieved simply to exist in my body undisturbed. When I heard the clunk and scrape of the gallery doors opening behind me, I was stiff and shivering but half reluctant to move. It was the calmest I had felt since New Year's Eve, when my life as I knew it had ended. I stood up. My shoes clicked crisply against the steps. I went inside.

The Arnolfini portrait was in Room Twenty-Five. An attendant led me up the main staircase and through the several corridors of Madonnas with crescent-moon smiles, proffering single exposed nipples to Jesuses who, almost to a fault, resembled Mr George. And then we reached the Renaissance, and we began in Italy, passing Botticellis and Michaelangelos and da Vincis, everything fluttering and gilt and bright, blue skies as though spring had already arrived; there were angels everywhere and squat, fat little Cherubs. Then we moved north, here we were in Bruges, it was Winter again and all the edges were crisp, the fruit was very round, the glassware very reflective, and there at last was Arnolfini and beside him a lady in green; they were hand in hand and staring down at me, much smaller than I had imagined.

I felt, when I looked at the painting, a sudden urge to burst into tears. I had first encountered it in a newspaper article several years earlier, the journalist objecting to some feature of its display in the National Gallery and in making his case arguing, too, how extraordinary an artwork it was: the unknown couple, Arnolfini and a woman who was perhaps his wife or perhaps his fiancé, perhaps pregnant or perhaps holding her gown in such a way as to make her appear so, and all around them a masterpiece of precision, a room and its furnishings so exactly rendered as to seem like a photograph. It was the beads hanging from a hook on the wall, the astonishing glassy roundness of them, that made me want to cry, and the wiry coat on the ugly little dog in the foreground by the couple's feet. Or was it the golden sheen on the chandelier, or those glowing oranges by the window? The fur trim on Arnolfini's tunic? All of it so tangible, so exactly right, the metal so metallic, the fur so furry, the ugly little dog so very ugly. And there, in the mirror behind Arnolfini and his wife, where you might expect to see an image of the artist at work, an easel and brush and a concentrated expression, there were instead two reflected figures entering the room, one in blue, one in red, only vaguely done because the scale was miniscule, so that the impression given by the scene in the mirror was of an interruption, of something that has not yet happened just beginning to happen, and the artist invisible, vanished from sight, like a copyist.

Everything had been so loud and wild and unclear, and now here was this painting, so still.

I sketched it several times, uselessly, since I knew I would remember the positions of everything anyway; it had already entered some part of my brain where even I could not quite access it, would only be able to reach when I was at my own easel. What I needed were instructions about brushstrokes and colour, so I found myself beginning to write a kind of verbal map: toe of left clog, Naples yellow and white, five ascending dots of raw umber increasing in size from a quarter to half an ant. Topmost panel of blue on the stained glass: cerulean and grey on pewter, a small cat's claw of shadow on the right-hand side, just below the halfway mark. Arnolfini's robe: caput mortuum and black and, again, cerulean in repeating ripples, a succession of dark horizons tipped sideways. It was useless and abstract, a mad kind of poetry, and in any case the success or failure of the project would rest on finding the exact shade of green of the woman's dress, which dominated the composition, ruched and riotous: cadmium, Prussian, viridian. I stopped writing and stood, instead, as close to the painting as I could without the tip of my nose touching the glaze, and I looked and looked and looked and for a while I thought of nothing else, nothing but ants and cat's claws and horizons, the precise combinations of oxidations required for gold and turquoise paintwork on a brown leather belt, and then, because I was helpless to fight it, I thought about Charles.

The consensus by the end of New Year's Eve was that, once again, Charles was the real Charles, and the consensus was also that everyone loathed him, even my aunt. There were no formal acknowledgements of this either way, not even from her, and no words of congratulations on the engagement, only a shocked silence after I made the announcement. And then my aunt glanced at the clock in a panic just as the twelfth chime of midnight sounded. She moved towards the cake almost despite herself. Three servants helped her hoist it aloft and stagger towards the door and the musicians, sensing that the timing of the twentieth century was already askew, began to play Bobby Shaftoe again, and just as she braced, ready to throw it, she looked at me, and I felt that she was seeing me for the first time in my life. Her face crumbled a little and her raised arms trembled, and it was only a fraction of a second's lapse but it was enough, the cake began to slide to one side of the platter, and then it collapsed, slowly, horrifyingly, a cascade of cream and bloody splats of jam onto the flagstones.

The painting. Spider webs of cracks in the varnish and the green, green gown of the woman. Was she pregnant? It was the story, the whole story of the painting if so. The voluminous gathering of fabric around her stomach; it seemed that she must be, and the more I looked the surer I felt, not convinced by the shape of her body so much as by her eyes, which looked past her husband rather than at him, and seemed so tired and wise that I could not believe there was anything she was ignorant about. She knew all the things I did not know, and specifically, surely, this studied neutrality was the expression of a woman who knew what things were done, and how, by men and by women who were married, or who were supposed to be married in order to do the things they were already doing, and which, it seemed, would soon be expected of me, if not by Charles himself (and now I frantically turned over what he had said, what was it he had said, about not having to make a choice between men and women, of how common it was to love both, and did he mean that was how he felt, or how he assumed I felt, and what would he ask of me, what would he expect or demand of me, once I was his wife?) then certainly by everyone around us.

Charles. Vicious and intoxicated, staring in astonishment at me and at the cake all over the floor and at my aunt, Lady Macbeth in cream and jam, who had started to cry, silently at first and then in embarrassing, grating sobs. He stood up too quickly and swayed, and then took my hand and tried to haul me up the stairs. In response, every part of my body set itself in opposition, pulling back from his grip and bracing against his force. It was beginning to dawn on me what I had done, what I had said, and how those few words would ruin everything, would lock me fast to a future that repulsed me, and I began to panic, tears rising towards my eyes, and Charles yanked on my wrist so hard I could feel the ligaments stretching. We tussled like that, neither of us wanting to admit that we were tussling, until I managed to twist out of his grasp and he almost fell backwards. Then, regaining his balance, he turned and took the stairs three at a time.

The painting. I looked at the hands of the couple, hers upturned and resting in his. I tried to feel my way into it, to sense what they must have sensed, the people inside their bodies, the heat and moisture of his palm against her knuckles. His cuff was threaded through with silver, hers with gold, and both looked like manacles weighing down the couple's wrists. There was a little figure carved into a wooden finial behind them, a monster or gargoyle, who looked disgusted, utterly disgusted, by the handholding that was taking place before his face.

'Charles,' Mr George had said into the space Charles had vacated at the bottom of the stairs. He looked exhausted, eyes pink around the rims, on the verge of tears. I never felt sorry for him but I did, almost, in that moment. He breathed heavily through flared nostrils. I found I couldn't look at him. 'The thing is,' Mr George said, 'the trouble is, there is only one living person in this world who could possibly know those things. There is only one person. And that person is Charles.' It seemed a foolish thing to say out loud to a crowd, a crowd that was still digesting the information only Charles could have known, but Mr George seemed dazed, oblivious to us all gathered around him, attending to his every word. The following day, before anyone else was awake, he left not only the house but the country, leaving a note to say he was taking a holiday. I doubted we would ever see him again. Mr Barnard, too, absented himself and sent a letter resigning his duties. I later heard that he had been seen driving off with Mr George and imagined the pair of them holidaying morosely together, somewhere with improving air, Switzerland or Austria.

The painting. On the wall above the mirror: writing. *Johannes de eyck fuit hic 1434.* I reached for hazy memories of the Latin grammar I'd taught myself from an old schoolbook of Teddy's: Jan van Eyck was here, 1434. There he was. Bolder even than if he had put his image into the frame. And I felt that I knew everything I needed to know about the painting, and van Eyck, because of what it told me about myself, about the struggle I understood by then was at the heart of me: I am here, I am not here, I am here, I am not here.

Charles. I lived in fear of seeing him, in those watery, thin days of the new year. I scurried between my room and the breakfast table, gathering up an apple, a piece of bread, a boiled egg, and then retreating to eat them behind the closed door of my room. There was only so long I could ignore the man I had declared was my fiancé, and I was aware, too, that he was trying to speak to me. He tapped on my door on three occasions, lingering long enough to show he knew I was inside, and each time I sat frozen in place on my bed, heart hammering, until I saw in the narrow crack between the door and the floor the dark shadows of his feet retreating. After the third time, he crouched down and nudged a piece of notepaper through the gap, folded over into a pellet. I opened it: a soft sheet crumpled like a palm and the words, 'Please see me.' But I could not face him. I could not face him.

And then, after several days, I did. I had just left my bedroom, feeling stifled and bored, and was heading as fast as I could for the gardens. It was early still, not quite light. The house was quiet. I had the idea of seeking Bobby out, since he was avoiding me as carefully as I was avoiding Charles, and I felt that things between Bobby and me, at least, were reparable. There was no need for awkwardness there, surely. But as I rounded a corner into the hall, Charles was coming down the stairs. He jumped when he saw me. Charles, who planned everything, had not planned this encounter. It took him a second to collect himself. I watched him rearrange his face.

'Grace,' he said. 'Grace, come to breakfast.'

'I'm going for a walk.'

'Come to breakfast.' He reached out and touched my elbow. The contact was light, a brush really, but it stopped me. 'It's raining outside. Come to breakfast.'

It was raining outside. It had barely stopped raining since New Year's Day, and water had begun to come in through the rotten window frames of my bedroom, making the wall below look glossy and mutable.

'I don't mind the rain.' I did mind the rain.

'Come to breakfast.'

And then there was my aunt, descending, too, and saying, 'Grace. Good. You've been skulking long enough.' Had she ever said, 'Good,' upon seeing me before? I didn't think so.

But there we all were, the three of us and two uncles and one of my distant cousins who I hadn't realised was still in the house, moving like a herd towards the breakfast room where the walls were leaking worse than ever, the wallpaper torn off in chunks. There we all were, sitting down to eat kedgeree in a silence I could tell Charles was desperately hoping might be companionable.

'The papers report snow,' he said, after a time, though I could see clearly that he was reading an article about himself, furnished by James's sketch and under a headline that punned on the words 'heir apparent'. There was something different about him. He seemed bigger somehow. When he picked up a fork it looked silly, like a toy, in his hand.

'I want to leave,' I said.

My aunt shook her head as though a fly was irritating her. 'You've only just sat down, Grace. You've barely touched your haddock.'

My heart was beating very fast. I had not known I was going to say it, though the phrase had been a constant refrain in my mind for days. But now, all of a sudden, it had escaped me. I said it again. 'No, I mean, I want to move out. I want to move to London.'

Nobody, then, was touching their haddock. They looked at me as if I had proposed we burn the house down. I laid out my case: in London I would have better access to my doctor so that I might achieve optimal health before the wedding and also—it felt bold, reckless even, to say it but I was feeling bold and reckless, a little unhinged even—I would like to be able to go to art galleries.

When I stopped talking my aunt took a bite of fish and before swallowing said, 'Well of course not, Grace. How silly.'

But Charles glanced up from the newspaper and said, 'I permit it.'

Something, a series of things, passed silently between Charles and my aunt. The muscles in my aunt's face locked into a miserable little smile that Charles met with a cleaner, brighter one, and he seemed to grow even as I watched, sitting taller in his chair, pushing his chin up. 'I permit it,' he said again.

My aunt, finally, swallowed. 'I do not think, Charles, that it is necessary or wise. Grace is very naïve. She knows nothing of London. And the money, for board, food—it's a waste.'

'It's my money,' he said. I looked at the headline on the page beside him on the table, the word 'heir', the word 'apparently'. His elbow blocked the article. 'It's my money, is it not, Mater?'

And so I went to London and Charles paid for it. A room was found for me in a boarding house with a view of Clapham Common, run by a widow called Mrs Roberts who filled the place with humane rodent traps that lured mice into little mesh cages; at night I could hear their claws against the walls, their squeaks of dismay. Each morning Mrs Roberts would gather her captives and release them in the undergrowth at the bottom of her garden. I struggled not to think that the mice were the true occupants of the house, the rest of us merely visitors.

The human residents were all young women of roughly the same age, all of us busy with some plan or another, all of us respectable and, in one of the favoured words of Mrs Roberts, 'gentle'; she turned away any girl who was not gentle. When Charles first told me he had found the place, having written to a friend who had asked his sister and so on, I took sudden and immense pleasure in imagining myself as part of this group. I imagined that I might, for the first time in my life, be one of a cohort of female friends in an easy, happy sort of way; I tried to picture the things friends did with one another. 'Here they are,' the owner of the fake Courbet on Queen Anne Street had told me, hadn't he, 'the two friends,' though of course I knew that having female friends would not be like that.

But when I arrived, I was gripped by awkwardness. I found myself avoiding the other residents in the halls and stairways. They were pleasant and cheerful, just as I'd imagined they would be, and seemed to want to befriend me, extending offers of dinners and wonderful books they had just finished reading and little cakes they got from the baker on the corner of our street. This was what friends did together, I learned: they ate small cakes and went on little walks. They seemed to expect to include me in their collective experience and there was something about the expectation that wrong-footed me. I was appalled by my inability to tell them apart, to know which of them I'd met before and which were new to me; they all seemed so simi-lar, in their neat coats and stylish hats. They were all called things like Annie and Bonnie. It felt impossible to explain to them my difficulty with faces and impossible to explain anything else, either: who I was, where I came from, what I was doing there. I simply did not know what I should say. I had no practice at being a pleasant person amongst pleasant people.

And so I shrank from them, almost wanted to bark when they came near me: I had so little time, I had so little time, so no, I could not spare any for them, and I hated myself for it.

I could not help noticing them, all the same. I was surprised and delighted by the easy, casual way they moved around each other, arms around waists, heads tilted against shoulders, and by their freedoms, which were, briefly, my own: they got up whenever they liked and walked to the river, rode bicycles, took omnibuses, went out to see plays.

'She's from the countryside,' I heard one murmur to another in the stairwell, when I had declined, yet again, an invitation to lunch.

My room was small and not well-lit. I arranged my easel by the window, which had a view of the tall trees at the edge of the common, spindly and leafless, and let in the noise of trains going by. I lined up my paints and brushes all along the sill. I went to all the way to Highgate to buy three oak boards for my van Eyck, fine grained and ten-years dry, and used a large portion of my allowance from Charles to pay a carpenter in Brixton to join them just the way I needed them joined; and I smoked a cigarette I had found beside the bathtub, forgotten by one of the other girls in the house, which made me feel sick, and with almost all the rest of my money from Charles I bought a new pair of boots from a shop on the high street that grated the backs of my ankles and which I loved regardless.

I was given three weeks of this life, of room and board and

modest spending money and the freedom to go where I liked. And then I would return to Inderwick Hall and get married to my cousin. An announcement had been put in the *Times:* 'The engagement is announced between Mr Charles Robert Inderwick, eldest son of the late Charles Henry Inderwick, and Miss Grace Inderwick of Sixpenny Handley, Dorset' and I tore it out and folded it up and tucked it into my pocket and though I never looked at it I felt its presence all the time. It was the heaviest scrap of paper in the world.

The painting. The painting was a contract. The man and the woman, locked together in the frame. They would get married. They were getting married, or perhaps had already been married. They would never, for all eternity, be able to drop each other's hands. It was horrifying, wasn't it, though I wondered what places and people the woman had left, in order to find herself there, in a rich, dark room with an ugly dog and globes of glowing oranges. Did she love him? Was she the sort of woman who could love a man? Or was that naïve—Grace is very naïve,' I heard my aunt say—was it all about money, since the painting seemed to me to be obsessed with money as much as anything else, how rich they were, how untroubled by whatever was beyond the stained-glass window? There was a sliver of a view, the tiniest, lightest brushwork, of fruit trees, and nothing else, though surely wherever they were in the world was troubled in all the ways England was troubled, and there were hungry people staring up at the branches, and desperate people calling through the crack in the window, and mad people. The face of Arnolfini's bride was a face that knew everything and felt nothing, I thought, and if I could just get close enough I might really understand her, might know what had happened, what she hoped for or dreaded and whether the reflected figures bursting through the door were bringing good news or bad.

Charles. Charles. Not only intruding on my thoughts but there, really there in the gallery, and standing beside me for quite some time though I hadn't thought to look up. He cleared his throat. He looked at me uncertainly. There was an apology somewhere between his pinched eyebrows.

'Grace,' he said. 'I'm so sorry to disturb you at work.'

The Opera Room

'You said I could have three weeks,' I said as we walked past the fountains and lions in Trafalgar Square. The clouds were rushing fast behind Nelson's column, making it appear to tilt horribly towards us. For once it was not raining and everything seemed quiet; our footsteps clicking intrusively along the road, Charles's rhythm slower and more certain than my own, and loudest of all I could hear the petulance in my voice and was aggravated by it. Charles's presence had turned me into a child, bargaining and morose.

'I did, and I meant it.'

'And yet here you are.'

'I have not come to bring you home, Grace.'

Birds were perched like sentinels along the railings outside St Martin-in-the-Fields. They shifted uneasily as we passed but didn't fly away, and I paused for a moment, half looking at them, half trying to gather myself and stay calm. There was a part of me that wanted to scream at Charles, to turn on him and rage and say cruel things to him and tell him I knew all his secrets and would betray them the way he had done to my aunt, the way he had done to Mr George, the way he would have done to me if I hadn't got in his way. He was smiling, as though he had said something that should reassure me, as though anything about his presence could be reassuring. I took a breath. I did not rage. The pigeons remained on their perch.

'Then why have you come?'

'I wanted to say something to you.'

'You could have written a letter.'

'You do not reply to my letters,' he said.

'Then it isn't that you wanted to say something, is it? It's that you want me to say something to you, and I don't want—' I stopped myself. I was aware I had started to speak very quickly. 'I don't want to say anything to you, Charles, because I don't think anything I say will be nice.'

He looked hurt and I felt guilty and then angry at him because of the guilt, and then guilty again. We walked in silence until we reached a pub, dark windows and dark panelled exterior, the kind of place I barely even saw, that was so far from my range of experience it seemed irrelevant, like a bird's nest in a tree or a fox's den or a stranger's house.

Charles stopped. 'Shall we go in?'

'In here?'

'You've not had lunch.'

I had been in the gallery all morning and some way into the afternoon. Without waiting for my answer, Charles shouldered the door, and I followed him. Inside, the bar was busy already, men jostling for service, still wearing their hats. There were no women that I could see, and I thought of Randal Bryson's house, and wondered briefly, optimistically, whether this place was like that. We waited at the bar. The

men were loud and they looked at me and cracked jokes that
made Charles flinch and move me towards a corner. It was
not like Randal Bryson's house and Charles looked uncertain
of his choice, a little panicked, until a barkeep appeared who
seemed to know him, nodding and raising an eyebrow when
he saw me. Charles's shoulders dropped and he called over
the hats of the men in front of us, 'We'll eat in the opera room.'
He guided me upstairs with a hand to the small of my back—I
wriggled it off—and I looked at the art on the walls, which
was very bad, sentimental paintings of women and children,
men with dogs, rosy-cheeked farmers, all of it original.

The opera room was empty, devoid of opera, and the art
on display there was of flowers in vases, poppies and some
chrysanthemums. We sat at a table beside a chequerboard-
glass window, little squares of orange and white that dappled
the tabletop and made me think of Arnolfini. Charles ordered
fried fish and two glasses of wine; he started smoking and
then seemed to remember me and offered me a cigarette. I
took it and twirled it, unlit, in my fingers, and watched the
dark, distorted bodies of pedestrians on the street below pass
in and out of the window's orange squares. Charles seemed
to be waiting for me to speak.

'I wish,' I started, eventually, and then a waiter, a teenage
boy with a jawline bubbling with spots, brought the wine. I
nodded, and smiled, and waited for him to retreat. 'I wish,
Charles, that you wouldn't always follow me.'

He raised his eyebrows. 'Oh,' he said. 'I went to your
room yesterday and they said you were always out. And I
came this morning, hoping to catch you before you left, but

you were just then marching along the road and you looked so purposeful and pleased, I couldn't bring myself to stop you. So I simply came with you to the gallery. And then you seemed absorbed, the way you were with that picture, standing right up to it, almost like you wanted to open a door and walk right inside it. I should have known you'd be working on something.'

'Well I am working on something. And would like to be working on it still.'

'I wanted to surprise you. I wanted to do something nice.'

'Charles,' I said. 'I'm not available for surprises.'

'Yes,' he said, 'the painting, I know. Very ambitious, by the way, you'll get good money for it. There's something complex in the glaze, isn't there? I should like, at some time, to learn exactly what it is you're doing in your mind when you work like that. But—'

'No, not just the copy. I have other commitments. I was supposed to meet somebody.'

He looked taken aback and I wished what I had said were true. I thought about the girls in the house in Clapham, about the barrage of invitations they'd sent my way. I should have said yes. I should have eaten little cakes with them. I should have made friends.

Now Charles was here and I'd never get the chance.

'I'm a person, Charles. I have my own life. You follow me. You watch me. You interrupt me. But you don't know me. You don't know me at all.'

'And yet it was you who said you'd marry me, Cousin Grace.'

'Stop calling me that. It's disgusting.'

'Cousin?'

'Yes.'

He shrugged. When he lifted his wine to his lips, he spilled a line of droplets on the over-varnished tabletop. 'Plenty of cousins marry. There's no disgust in it. Our grandparents were cousins, were they not?'

'Yes, and my father was a lunatic.'

'This is—this is besides the—it's not what I came to discuss.'

The wine was vinegary but I drank it anyway and felt, almost at once, its effects: a softening around the edges of my thoughts, a little less rage.

'I wanted to explain about the proposal,' he said. 'I know you are very angry with me, and I couldn't bear to think of you seething for three weeks from afar. I wanted to explain.'

'There's no need. I understand. I understood it, and I understand it still.'

'You don't.'

'You wanted the money and it seemed to you that you had lost what was yours, that your trick with the artist had backfired and that the family money would go to me. And you are greedy and not able to make your own way in the world and so you proposed simply to take it back by marrying me. I understood it.'

'I made my own way in the world for thirteen years.'

'And now you do not, and you rely on my aunt to keep you.'

'And yet you agreed to marry me. Rather publicly. I assume because you are wildly in love with me and could resist my charms no longer.'

'Charles.'

'It was, in the circumstance, not a bad gambit. But a surprising one.'

I shook my head. 'I could think of no other way. You were being vile.'

'I was,' he said. 'I'm sorry. I was angry with you all, and drunk.'

I had this idea of him as a man who never apologised, but really it was that he never apologised for the right thing. I finished my wine. The fish arrived. I couldn't bring myself to touch it. I watched as he delicately flaked off batter and flesh, and forked it into his mouth.

'Eat,' he said.

'No.'

He swallowed. 'We could release each other, if you wish,' he said. 'That is what I came to say.'

'Are you being serious?'

'Utterly serious.'

It was as though someone had drawn back a curtain. Suddenly there was light. The little dappled orange squares on the table in the opera room began to glow, as though it was not January but May and everything suddenly warmer. Charles was seeking out my eyeline and I took him in properly for the first time since he'd appeared in the gallery: his nicest jacket, his earnest beige shirt, a natty little neckerchief I'd never seen before, a hat when he never really wore a hat, even when the weather demanded it, and I felt for the first time since his return a rush of real affection for him. He had made mistakes, and I knew what that was like, and how could I possibly hold that against him when he was trying to make things right?

I thought of Arnolfini's bride dropping her fiancé's hand and walking right out the door towards the fruit trees and the sky, her green gown carrying her onwards like a ship, and this idea, this possibility of escape, made me want to lean forwards across the table and—ludicrous, hilarious, really—kiss him.

'It would be a scandal,' I said, thinking of the torn-out and folded-over announcement of our engagement in the newspaper.

'It's already a scandal. I am already a scandal.'

'That is true.'

And hadn't everything always been a scandal? My poor parents, scandalously mad. The way people had looked at us whenever we were in the village, even at church. My aunt and Mr George, lovers for countless years, the parents of Teddy, even! Poor Teddy, a posthumous scandal, oblivious in his lifetime. And Charles, who was still, even now, appearing in the papers, since the day in court was approaching when his identity would be confirmed by the family in front of a judge, thus restoring his rights to his inheritance, the money and Inderwick Hall. The scandal of the false heir would be put to bed and in comparison a broken-off engagement would seem tame, easily forgettable. So perhaps, really, there was nothing to fear. Scandal was a word that belonged to my aunt and I could simply shrug it off.

I could take my own path. I could emancipate myself, even, in some way or another. I would still need some family money, at least at first, while I got my business off the ground, but this new, mild, affable Charles would surely not object to that, perhaps might even enjoy investing in me; I could keep on the room in Clapham with his help and it would not be long, surely not be long, before I'd be able to pay my own way in the world as a copyist. There was possibility in that.

Wasn't everything a scandal, and so, by extension, nothing particularly scandalous? Who was it who decided these things, in any case? Who decided that a broken engagement between Charles and I, both by nature disinclined to marriage, was scandalous and not a man selling a very fine marble potpourri vase, a real original item, bronze legs like ostrich legs and heavy as anything, to Bobby, a man who had nothing, next to nothing and dependents at home? And what about my aunt and uncle, what about everything to do with them, the way they had locked up my parents for madness when really who was madder in this world than my aunt? And what about my work, surreptitious, not quite illegal but certainly not respectable, that was scandalous too, and what about me, what about all of me, who I was and what I thought about and the things I had done with women?

Everything was a scandal.

Money was a scandal, the haves and the have nots.

Having and having not was a scandal.

'We would need to do it together,' I said. 'It would need to be both of us.'

'I would still be your friend, Grace, if you were to choose not to become my wife.'

I nodded. The waiter had brought more wine though I hadn't noticed it arriving. I sipped it and found it less abrasive than the first glass. The longer I sat there, doused in sudden hope, the giddier I felt.

'Should we make a toast?' I said. 'To releasing each other?'

I raised my glass but Charles did not.

He dipped a finger into his wine and sucked it. A drop escaped his lips and ran down towards his knuckle.

'I wanted to say, Grace, that there is another way. We don't have to end the engagement. Perhaps there is a way of continuing it, of getting married, that might work for us both. For you, I mean. If you—if you find that—if, and of course this is unlikely, but if it happened that you were not, in fact, wildly in love with me after all.'

I looked up at his face, which was blank and broad and gave nothing away.

'What are you trying to say, Charles?'

'I am offering you something, that's all. No need to look so stricken, Cousin Grace. I'm offering you some freedom, if you'd like it.'

'It sounds like you are offering the opposite.'

I could feel my breath quickening and tried to stay calm. Still, the light began to dim again. It was January; it wasn't spring. I should have known there would be something miserable coming, because there was always something miserable coming. I had the feeling of having been tricked, and too late to understand it as such; a mouse in one of Mrs Roberts's humane traps, only just noticing it had been caught.

Charles reached out and tried to put his hand on top of mine; I jumped and snatched it away. His expression then was wounded, a little mystified.

He cleared his throat, moved his hand back to his wine glass. 'I'm saying that as my wife, I could offer you freedom you won't have if you continue to live with my mother. If you like your life now, in London, I'm saying you could have more of that.'

'But you were offering that before, weren't you? Weren't you saying we might release each other and be free?'

'I'm just asking you to entertain the idea of marrying me, Grace.'

'And what would be in it for you, Charles?'

'Is that any business of yours?' There was a sudden iciness in his voice. I was reminded of the Charles of New Year's Eve, hostile and unkind.

I chose my words carefully, feeling that the wine was coming between me and good sense. 'I am trying to under-stand what would be asked of me in return.' I wondered how cruel he had the capacity to be.

'Nothing,' he said. He wouldn't look at me. Stared forwards at the chequerboard of glass in the windowpane. Chewed his fish. Then stole a glance. 'Are you crying?' he said. 'You're crying, Grace.'

I lifted a sleeve, as casually as I could, to my cheekbone. 'No,' I said. 'No, I'm not crying,' and I was fairly sure I wasn't, but he had thrown me, and made me doubt myself, even my own eyes, even what was coming from them. 'You aren't sure of yourself,' I went on. 'You are worried, still, about what will happen in court. You're still scared of Mr George and the uncles. You have something that troubles you—you're still not sure—that's it, isn't it?'

Charles shook his head. 'I am perfectly sure of myself,' he said.

'I don't believe you, and I don't accept you.'

'You are choosing to break off our engagement?'

'Charles,' I said. 'Charles.' I imagined reaching over and slapping him, or more satisfying still, grabbing him by the cheeks and digging my fingers into his face and pulling on his jowls until his whole face stretched wide, wide, wide into a howl. 'You said—you said you had come to offer a mutual release from our obligation. That is what you said right at the start of this conversation. That is what you said you have come here to say. And now you are saying it would be me and me alone who would choose to end things, and you know, surely you know, that unless we do it together it would mean ruin for me. It would mean the end of things for me.'

He had wanted me to like him. It was almost a disappointment to realise it. He had wanted me to like him, had wanted to seem generous, offering me freedom, because if I liked him I'd be more likely to do what he wanted. He had wanted to seem nice. But he was not nice, was he? He had never done a single nice thing. He was a juggernaut of self-interest.

On the day of my tenth birthday, I had been sitting alone in the window of my room, twisting wires into a small model of a tree, which had been a brief obsession of mine at the time, those little wire sculptures, and Charles had come in. 'Happy birthday, Cousin,' he said. He reached out and touched my hair, a gesture I loved because it felt tender and ordinary in a world that was never either of those things. He nudged towards me a little packet, an inexpert wrapping job using pages of the newspaper tied with straw. Inside: a set of paintbrushes, each one monogrammed with my initials in silver. In the preceding months, Charles, fifteen years old, had taken a turn for the flamboyant, smoking thin, delicate cigarettes and getting everything he owned monogrammed in gold print. My uncle had made it known that he hated the cigarettes but profoundly adored the monograms, had gone so far as to have his own hunting gear labelled in the same way. And now here were my initials, printed very small and neat on the handle of each brush. 'A monogram is a wonderful thing to have, Grace,' he said. 'It makes you feel very sure of yourself.' I did not know what to say. Was flabbergasted. The brushes. The initials. The suggestion of personhood, of a name and an action, an invitation to purpose. It was the nicest thing anyone had ever done for me in my life.

For a moment I thought I remembered his face as it was then: the suggestion of a cheekbone, the way his newly-emerged facial hair had shadowed his upper lip. I squinted at the memory, tried to fix it the way I might a painting to be copied, but it folded in on itself. Then I looked to Charles as he was now, in the opera room, trying to make me marry him.

'Do you remember what you gave me for my tenth birthday?' I asked.

'Yes,' he said.

'What was it then?'

'The brushes, the monogrammed brushes.'

'What happened to those brushes?' I asked. 'They vanished.'

'I took them,' he said. 'Before I left. I needed brushes and I took them. I'm sorry.'

'They had my initials on them.'

I had been mystified by their disappearance at the time and suspected my aunt. It was the sort of thing she did. I had not once thought it could be Charles, who had never seemed the sort of man who stole things from anyone. Though he was, of course. The brushes. My money. Arthur Watt's money. He was a thief and always had been.

'So you are choosing to break off our engagement?' he said again.

I had said it would be the end of things for me, which was melodramatic but I felt nonetheless that it was accurate. The fantasy of running away would have to become, fast, a reality, and I didn't have the money yet. The Van Eyck was barely even underway. I was living on the allowance Charles himself had allowed me. My aunt would never forgive me for humiliating her son, and I felt utterly ignorant—'Grace is very naïve'—of how to go about anything, of how one found a home for oneself or paid for things, of how much anything cost, and I was friendless, had been incapable even of making nice conversation with the Annies and Bonnies in Clapham, and nobody would help me.

'Charles,' I said. 'I don't know how anything works.' I glimpsed my new boots under the table, lovely and regrettable; it was obvious to me then that I had overpaid for them.

'That is why I'm offering you another way,' he said. 'We continue. But I wanted to be friends, Grace,' and in his mouth the word 'friends' seemed so unfriendly, 'and I wanted you to know you have the choice.'

He began to count out, carefully, slowly, coins I knew my

aunt would have given him in exactly the same manner. He left them on the table. 'I should let you go,' he said.

'Yes.'

As we descended, Charles's weight creaking on the stairs behind me, he said, in a tone I could not interpret at all, 'I understand Mr George has gone to Italy.' I paused to turn and look up at him. He looked dejected, and I couldn't think what he wanted me to say. I continued on, past the awful paintings and towards the crowded bar.

It was raining again when we left the pub. I declined Charles's offer of a cab, pretending that I would go back to the gallery though I knew there was no hope of doing more work that day. I waited until he was gone, his bulk shrinking as he walked away into a crowd of umbrellas, before I began to walk. I noticed then that the leather of my new boots had at last begun to soften and was no longer cutting into my skin, and it made me want to cry all over again when I thought of this, of these boots I had bought that were now shaped to my shape. There had been some small hope in them, a possibility of adaptation, and now all I could think was of the many things I should have spent that money on instead. I paused on Vauxhall Bridge where the wind came off the river in punchy gusts and I looked down into the black, puckered water of the Thames, at the leaves and sticks and occasional pages of newspapers blown and floating on it. A seabird bobbed awkwardly atop it all. A boat passed by towards the docks.

Some Truths about Copyists

The copyist is not invisible to everyone. Some people see the copyist no matter what. These people delight in the craft of the copyist, are connoisseurs of copying. These people themselves have the sensibilities of a copyist.

The copyist is poor and has always been poor, since the copyist has no ideas of her own. Has never had any. Relies upon the generosity of others to create a semblance of meaning for herself. Unable to make anything for or of herself, she waits. She accepts the commissions she is given, by dealers, by clients, by her own life.

There was a good possibility, if the engagement had been mutually broken off, that my family would have come to accept it. Charles was Charles, and whatever he preferred would eventually be preferred by everyone else. But if Charles remained steadfast and I broke it off alone, I would never be forgiven. There was no question of whose side would be taken.

The copyist is a dependent. I thought about this obsessively in the days following Charles's visit—how in my copying life and in the rest of my life I depended on others for everything. It felt like a defining flaw, fatal.

The copyist is bound to accept decisions made by other people.

I had been resigned to the marriage in a way that seemed, in the aftermath of Charles's visit, like madness. I had said I would marry him in front of all those people on New Year's Eve and that had been that, the deal done, and everybody—myself and Charles included—had been astonished by it, and everybody—myself and Charles included—had nonetheless accepted that this was now what would happen. I had spoken the words. We would get married. I had never before truly understood the power of speech. I had trudged onwards towards this new, miserable reality as one who had never known anything else. But his visit had shaken something loose in me. If I had not been mad before, perhaps I was, then. He had dangled possibility in front of me, and I had imagined that he was saying I might be free, and in imagining that, I had imagined an entire life. And when he had withdrawn the offer, or revealed to me that it had never been meant, I could not go back. I could not return to the world in which I married him. I could not marry him. I could not marry him.

The copyist is a fantasist.

I had fantasized about my emancipation for so long, and had done it so intensely, that the sudden feeling of urgency was both familiar and strange. I could no longer rely on the goodwill of my aunt and I could no longer—had never been able to—rely on Charles. I returned to the fantasy and found it lacking.

Why had I never in my wildest dreams considered the basics? How much money would I need to rent a room? To pay for food, transport, laundry? How much I would need to save to support myself in old age, in ill health? These questions lay outside the remit of daydreams and I had ignored them and felt ashamed of myself.

Now, I counted what was left of the money from my allowance from Charles. Most of it was gone. How much would it pay for, this money? How many nights' lodging beyond my three-week reprieve, how many loaves of bread? I was ignorant. I was very naïve. I had no idea.

The copyist contemplates making a change, adjusting one small line, the direction of a gaze of some minor character in the background, opening the window just a crack, and knows that if she did so she would cease to be a copyist, and in ceasing to be a copyist would cease to be at all.

The copyist longs to be an artist, to make something of herself and for herself alone. This is the great shame and pathos of the copyist.

Something Complex in the Glaze

What I should have been doing, the only thing I should have been doing, was finishing the Arnolfini Portrait. Finish the painting. Sell the painting. Get the money. Break off the engagement. Be free, forever. And I had made a start of it, dutifully, returning from the gallery to confront the oak boards, sketching out all the items in the room, each in its exact right place, and then blocking out the darks and the lights, beginning to illuminate and illustrate. And then, after several days' work, barely looking up to notice the view from the window, barely even hearing the thuds of the feet of the other residents on the stairs and floorboards outside my room, there was a moment when the thing should have been done. Everything was correct in size and shape and position and colour, the brushwork was precise, the thinner paint beginning already to dry. But what I had done was not the Arnolfini Portrait. It was exactly like and nothing like. It was a photograph of the painting, as you might find in a newspaper. It was obviously and loudly fake.

I stared at what I had done and was astonished by it. I tried to strip back the paint but the ghost of what I had done still lingered, embarrassing and persistent and off-putting. I considered returning to Highgate for new boards but decided I couldn't stretch my money to cover it. I scrubbed at my work with so much turpentine I made myself nauseous and had to open a window, though the air was icy. I started again. And again. And again.

And time was passing. I had never before given much thought to the speed of my work. It had taken as long as it took, and in any case, I had always been someone with plenty of time. If I needed a month to perfect the folds in the lace of a Madonna, I took a month. Nobody had been waiting for my copies; I had simply finished them, allowed the paint to dry and then either rolled up or reused the canvas for what-ever came next. There had been things I had struggled with before—surely there had, there must have been, though in the moment I could think of nothing that had caused me significant difficulty—and I had simply taken the time that was required to get them right.

Alone in my room, I drew the crescent moon eyebrows of Arnolfini's bride. Branches extended from the trees to tap-tap-tap my open window and I mixed greens for the folds of her gown. 'Shall we go out for cake?' the women called to each other in the hallway. 'Do you want to go to the bookshop?' They were always about to go somewhere, or just coming in from somewhere, and the places they came from and went to were always enticing and ordinary and I felt in those moments that I hated them, that they were intolerably stupid and vain and uncaring, not one of them ever having had to paint a copy of a masterpiece at speed or marry their cousin. I also felt compelled to go out to join them each and every second, temptation like an itch. I wrote a long and convoluted letter to Bobby, all about London and the house and the other women and asking after his mother and Rosamond and the socialist meetings. I painted the line of light down the woman's nose, the sheen on the skin of the tip and the dark fold of her nostril. I tried to explain to Bobby how time seemed to be moving so quickly all of a sudden, as though I was falling forwards through it.

I should finish the painting. I should not do anything except finish the painting: bulbous oranges, dappled and matte; I painted a glut of them. I painted the glassy, chestnut eyes of the dog, eyes upon eyes upon eyes, each time feeling that something was not quite as it should be, that some speck of colour was off, that what, in the original, had been dizzyingly true, in my version was flat, only accurate rather than real. Clogs and clogs and clogs and clogs I painted, first on card and paper and then, in desperation, direct onto the oak, in case that was the thing that was making the difference, murmuring like a prayer as I flecked the cork soles, 'Naples yellow and white, five ascending dots of raw umber increasing in size from a quarter to half an ant.' Beads and beads and beads, in strontium yellow, barium yellow, zinc yellow. Caput mortuum on the folds of the robe, over and over, waves washing up on a shoreline.

And then, as I ascended the stairs of Mrs Roberts's house and encountered the other girls going down, I found myself pausing halfway to say, 'Could I join you this afternoon? For a walk?' Or whatever it was that they had decided to do with their time that day; I wasn't sure. I hadn't planned to ask, except that some part of my mind clearly had. I needed to finish the painting, and I could not finish the painting, and increasingly all I'd been able to think about was joining these women for a walk.

They glanced at each other. There was a moment's appalling silence. And then there was a little chorus of, 'Of course,' and 'We'd love that,' and, 'How marvellous,' and the thing was settled. We'd meet downstairs at half past two, they said, and we did, and I went with them to the bandstand, where we leaned against the railings and watched people and dogs and pigeons and squirrels passing by, and I listened as the women talked about their lives, which were various and interesting and about which they told wry little jokes at the expense of their bosses, their families, themselves. I wasn't sure quite how much was usual to ask, what was usual to say. I noticed a little ripple of surprise (worse? Disapproval?) when I asked 'And do you all have enough money?' but then after a moment they answered, and some of them seemed almost happy to have the chance to say they did or did not have enough.

'I am always worrying about money,' I said.

And then I told them I had difficulty with faces, a kind of blinkeredness when it came to features which made it difficult for me to recognise people until I knew them well, and that I was always worried about ignoring people I'd already met, or confusing them with someone else, and that if I had in this way or any other way offended them, I was sorry.

'Oh, yes,' said one of them. 'My father is the same.'

Just like that, as though it was nothing to be ashamed of.

After that I found myself telling them more than I thought I would about my life, about the engagement I didn't want, and that I was working on a painting, though I did not say what, and they nodded and said they had smelled the turps coming from my room, and they seemed at once interested and unsurprised.

'What would you rather do?' said one of the Annies, who had a job on Tuesday mornings reading correspondence at the Royal College of Veterinary Surgeons.

'I want to paint,' I said, not mentioning the kind of painting I wanted to do, and not mentioning the fact that I could and in fact should have been, at that very moment, painting. 'I want to learn how to be independent.' It was a shock to realise that I was close, very close, to saying: 'I want to be like all of you.'

It started to rain and the wind picked up, flattening the grass across the common until it looked almost white. We went back to the house. There were murmurings about going out for dinner. In my room, I found that I was jittery and tired; the effort of speaking and smiling and trying to be easy around the women—though I had, hadn't I, been happy, felt at ease?—had exhausted me.

I approached the easel with the air, I felt, of a lion tamer. I had the feeling that whatever happened next would be a fight, and all I wanted to do was crawl into bed, close my eyes and sleep. I kept thinking of things I'd said at the bandstand that were perhaps too odd or somehow regrettable—though none of the Annies or Bonnies had seemed to mind, not even the money comment, really, and had been kind. I tried not to think about the bandstand. I tried not to think about going to bed. I looked at the painting and pretended to be brave.

It scared me. I thought perhaps the task might be impossible. I had not thought to ask the dealer, when he mentioned the Arnolfini Portrait, whether it was actually possible to copy it. I had not thought to doubt myself, I who found everything difficult in life except for one thing, for copying, for this. And now it seemed it was indeed impossible, and worst of all I could not understand why, and worst of all I just wanted to give up, and worst of all I had done something foolish and regrettable two days' prior, which was that I had written to Ruby, inviting her to meet, and worst of all, here she was—here she really was, unmistakable even to me with her scarf tied just so and her cigarette-smell and her broad gloved hand extended—standing in my doorway, and what could I do, what choice did I have, but to turn away from my work and face her?

I had not entirely admitted to myself that I had sent the letter, though I had done it the very afternoon of Charles's surprise visit to the National Gallery, giving her my address and the dates of my stay in London and apologising for writing, for intruding on her life, providing in advance a series of excuses she might make use of should she need: perhaps she was too busy, or had made a new friend, or would be unable to come without attracting unwanted attention from her father. It felt like a weakness that I had written, breaking what I felt to be an unspoken agreement that Ruby and I were not to be too much to each other, and it was also patently an exercise in procrastination and therefore embarrassing.

And yet here she was, in my room, and here I was, daubed with cinnabar from sketching out the red inner rim of Arnolfini's mirror. None of the excuses I'd provided had pleased her. She had come to see me. I put my hand to my neck, where I had tied a scarf in just the way that she tied hers and said, 'You are here!'

The Ruby in my room was different to the Ruby of my memory. Not worse, nor exactly better, but sharper and more imposing that I remembered. There was a surprising bulk to her as she crossed the threshold, umbrella under her arm and her coat spotted with rain. It was just that she was a real person, I suppose: a flesh-and-bone reality whose hand cast a crisp shadow across the floorboards as she held it out to me. She was a well-dressed, smart woman of ordinary stature who nonetheless seemed enormous. She smelt of the outside: cold and smoky. Were we the kind of acquaintances who shook hands? Were we the kind of friends who kissed each other on the cheek?

'Are you busy?' she asked.

I rubbed my palms on my skirt but by the time I'd got the paint off, Ruby's hand had been withdrawn.

'No,' I said. 'Yes. But no, not really.' I gestured helplessly towards the boards.

'A copy?'

Ruby had seen me naked, had touched me and found my most hidden, interior parts, and still this was an exposure further than that.

'Not a good one,' I said.

She squinted as she surveyed it. 'No. Not a good one.'

'What's wrong with it, do you think?'

'The glaze,' she said, idly. 'You've not got it right at all.'

'I can't really bear to look at it,' I said. 'It's been wrong, wrong, wrong for a fortnight. I've only two days left.'

Ruby sat heavily down on my bed, pulled off her gloves and tossed them beside her. I found myself staring at them, formless fingers pointing towards her legs and towards me, and then at her hands, large, fingernails bitten to the quick. She took off her coat, shrugging it back behind her, and she wasn't saying anything, why wasn't she saying anything, did she expect me to know what to do? Should I just approach her, just kiss her, as though it was nothing stranger than offering a glass of wine or a cup of tea?

Without the need to sneak around, I had no idea how to proceed. If it was not hushed and secretive and dangerous, what was it supposed to look like?

I sat down next to her, heart pounding, imbecilic with awkwardness. I reached out and touched her thigh.

'You seem different,' she said, and unbuttoned her own chemise, was not wearing stays underneath.

'I am,' I said. 'Sorry.'

'Did you not want me to come? Your letter seemed so tortured I almost thought you didn't, even as you wrote that you did.'

'I am always worrying about money,' I said. 'I am always worrying about my work.'

I leant forward to kiss her, fumbling the approach but righting my course so that, by the time our lips touched, I felt clearer about how it was supposed to go. I sensed a split second's reticence in her, and then it was gone and things came more naturally: the heat of the bare skin of her breast; the shock of her cold fingers reaching up under my skirts, parting the fabric of my drawers. When she reached the inside of me she let out a little groan, as though she had been holding her breath until that moment, and though I was self-conscious and anxious and embarrassed by a hundred different things about myself, I found I could forget that, with her, at least for a while.

Afterwards, she lay on her back and stared at the ceiling. It was beginning to get dark outside and the rain was coming down harder. The room with Ruby in it felt golden and warm and I felt less overpowered by the smell of turps, less agonized by the presence of the oak boards on the easel, calmer. I was breathless still and when I thought of saying something, anything, some sort of pleasantry or compliment, I decided against it.

'When are you leaving?' Ruby asked.

'Saturday,' I said, as quietly as I could. It was Thursday then.

'And when are you coming back?'

I screwed up my eyes and made a sound that came out as a strangled growl. 'I don't know. It depends.'

'Depends on?'

Why hide anything from Ruby, who had seen all there was to see of me?

'Depends on whether I have to get married,' I said.

In the moment after I said it there was a knock at the door and the voice of one of the Annies or Bonnies said, 'Grace? Are you in there? We're going for dinner.'

Ruby and I, stark naked on the bed, frozen. The door that stood between us and the women on the landing was flimsy. You could hear everything through it; the slightest creak of the mattress, a throat being cleared. It was not locked.

Another knock. 'Grace? Are you in there?'

Quieter, another voice: 'Perhaps she has fallen asleep?'

And another: 'Shall we go in and wake her?'

'Perhaps she doesn't want to come.'

Louder: 'Grace?'

Quieter: 'Let's just go.'

Quieter still: 'She seemed lonely though, didn't you think?'

I glanced at Ruby, whose face did not move.

After that we heard softer murmurings, shuffling, the clomp-clomp-clomp of their boots on the stairs as they drifted away. Neither Ruby nor I had moved the whole time, but when they were gone, Ruby sat up suddenly and began reaching for her clothes. She shrugged them on without looking at me, pressing her chin to her chest to button her skirts and blouse, casting around for her stockings, which were stuck down the side of the bed.

'Ruby?' I said. 'Ruby, what's wrong?'

She shook her head. 'I feel that being engaged is something you rather ought to have mentioned to me before.'

'It's not—' I started. What wasn't it? 'It's not real,' I said. Pathetically: 'It's a mistake and a misunderstanding and the man is—well—the man is a man, and it's my cousin, and I don't see that it has to affect—'

'Your cousin!'

Her cheeks had turned pink while we were in bed together

and were now pinker still. She was taking short little breaths as she bent over to lace her boots, then straightened to snake her arms into the sleeves of her coat. She reached for her scarf and hooked it around her neck without tying it.

Pausing for a moment by the awful Arnolfini Portrait, she said, 'Some people are hurtful because they're thoughtless, but you are hurtful because you think too much. I've not met anyone like that before. It's unusual.'

'Ruby,' I said, 'I do not want to get married.'

She crossed the floor, opened the door and peered out; there was nobody else around. She stepped across the threshold, paused, looked back, jutted her chin towards my painting. 'You need to layer up the glaze.' Then she pulled the door shut behind her without saying goodbye.

I listened to her sharp, cross footsteps going down the stairs. At my window, I watched her leave the house and move towards the Common, pausing to light a cigarette without looking as she stepped into the road, so that a cyclist had to swerve not to hit her.

A Brief Discourse on Caput Mortuum

The key to the Arnolfini portrait was not the green, I came to understand, but the brown. You saw the green, could not help but see it and become distracted by the thoughts it stirred of grassiness and glass bottles and general feelings of spring and bursting forth and abundance, or if not that then algae and profound stillness. So it made sense that at first you thought the green was the answer to the painting, but no, it was the brown, the man's brown robe, the window frame, the mirror and the little dog: all resonant and alike, a kind of wave rising up over the woman in green.

And so much of the brown was not really brown, or not only brown, but a kind of purple that gave way effortlessly to blue: *caput mortuum*, which meant—my creaky, patchy Latin stretched this far—dead head. *Caput mortuum*, which was sometimes, in *The Century Cyclopedia of Pigments*, referred to as 'mummy brown' and which could be made from ground up pieces of Egyptian mummies, blended with white pitch and myrrh. An outlandish process for an outlandish colour: brown and yet not so, brown and yet somehow at the same time blue. I could not think of it without contemplating death: a paint made from corpses that resembled at once the colours of decay and also something of eternity.

Caput mortuum, which was more regularly achieved with iron oxide. Running through my mind as I painted: dead head, dead head, dead head, and I tried not to think about Ruby.

I tried not to think about Ruby, who had been right about the glaze. With almost no time left to finish the copy I'd tried one, and then another, and then glaze upon glaze, Verdigris over lead tin yellow, all while moving the paint, pushing the little grooves of it around, colour into colour, viridian into cadmium yellow, yellow into ochre, ochre into umber, umber into *caput mortuum*, blurring, bleeding ever so slightly from one stroke to the next, and it had all of a sudden come right. A magic trick. It had always been about the brown, and it had always been about the glaze. The oranges and the eyes and the chandelier and the green gown had all begun to glow in just the right way, and the copy had stepped forwards and backwards at the same time, as all good copies do, as though to say, *Here I am, real and vibrant*, and also to say, *I am nowhere, I do not exist, there is only one Arnolfini Portrait*. I thought of writing to Ruby to thank her but was scared of what she'd say in reply.

One of us, I wasn't sure which, had bled a little on my sheets while she'd been with me. I couldn't tell if it was monthly blood or if it came from a scratch, a nick somewhere intimate, a fingernail not bitten low enough. There was not much of it, a few dark streaks against the white that had already turned brown by the time I noticed the following morning. I checked my hands and there was a little brown smear on my index finger, but then when I held it up to the light of the window it looked more like paint. When Mrs Roberts came to collect my laundry I pretended to have none and carried on sleeping on the stained sheet.

When I thought of brown I thought of Inderwick Hall, of the fields around the house, where the cows were, and beyond that, where other patchy attempts at agriculture were made: wheat, sheep. The browns of the Inderwick estate were dark and deep and unending, and as a child I had dreamed about them, and in my early attempts at original landscapes I tried to render them in *caput mortuum*, a sort of despair.

When I thought of brown I thought of 'The Drag', where the brown was so deep and so wet it seemed as though it was consuming Grandmother Hodierna, would swallow her whole. And of course it had, it did. The grounds of the estate contained all the dead Inderwicks, Hodierna and Geoffrey and all the generations that followed. My cousin Eliza, my uncle, my cousin Teddy. Above ground, their headstones tilted and gathered moss, frost in winter and in the summer the dogs slept amongst them in the shade. Below the surface it was surely a riot of brown: the bones in soil, flesh falling away like leaf mulch. The soft earthiness of moles and worms and woodlice and there was a sort of comfort in that, in the sameness of it and the commonplace-ness and the familiarity. (My mother's bones would look the same, in a cemetery I had never visited. My father's bones would look the same. My bones, one day, would look the same.)

Caput mortuum: a sort of despair. But also, *caput mortuum*: an old friend.

The embracing *caput mortuum* of my new boots, worn to the shape of my own precise ankle.

Charles's jacket in *caput mortuum*, worn thin and distinctive, his initials insistent against the receding brown.

I gave up trying not to think about Ruby. I spent horrid hours in imagined conversations with her, in which I described how impossible my situation had been and she poked holes in my logic. 'Would it have been so awful,' she would say, 'if on the night of the New Year's Eve party, Charles had exposed you as a copyist and an invert? There are worse secrets to have, far worse. Nobody thinks female inverts are real anyway,' and I would say she was right, it was true, but could she not understand that secrecy to me was like my skin, and in the moment, when he had proposed to flay me, there was nothing I would not have said to stop it? Even the thing I had said: that I would marry him. 'And having said it,' she would press, 'what stopped you from unsaying it at once, from simply announcing at breakfast the next day that you had been confused by wine and wished to clarify that there would be no wedding after all?' and I would say that was a good question, yes, but really it came down to money—to the fact that I had none, that my parents' vacant house, which would have been mine, had burned down in a fire that had destroyed the whole village, that I was utterly dependent on my aunt's family, and if Charles had fought me about it, which I'd supposed he would, the options before me were marriage or destitution. And she would say, 'Well then you must make your own money,' and I would say how right she was, how very right she was, and I would look at the Arnolfini Portrait, at all the *caput mortuum* brown.

Dead head, dead head, dead head, I thought. Ruby was angry. Ruby was gone.

There was love, or the possibility of love, and then there was money and the possibility of money.

There was the lovely green, green gown of Arnolfini's bride, and then there was the brown of Arnolfini.

Escape Plan

Inderwick Hall was quiet, as it had been the last time I'd returned. There was no evidence of journalists nor a preponderance of uncles. Nobody came out to meet me when I arrived, not even a servant to help with my bags, not even Ferris emerging from some shadowed corner. I had a brief fantasy that they had all gone away, had decided to live different kinds of lives and leave me be to live whatever mine should be. Perhaps Charles and my aunt had gone to Rome. Perhaps there would be a letter from Charles waiting for me on a sideboard somewhere, calmly and firmly breaking off the engagement, giving some polite justification, releasing me back into the wild. 'Mr George has gone to Italy,' he had said, quietly and dejectedly, and there must have been something meant by that, something that my mind turned to, now, as I reached and reached for easy solutions. How easy it could all be. How swift.

The reality was unlikely to be swift: there was too much to do, and to be done secretly. The image I had in my mind was of my aunt's foot, which she often jiggled anxiously, but which she took pains to disguise with her skirts. She presented an image of taut control, and only when you knew to look for the tremor were you able to spot it. For these final weeks in my aunt's house, I would copy her. On the surface I would be calm, still, starchy. Unseen, secret: the panic, the movement, the jiggling foot. Unseen: my escape plan.

On my final morning in London, I had taken my Arnolfini Portrait to the dealer's house by the river in Southwark. The boards were heavy and cumbersome and not yet dry, so I used the last of my allowance to pay two boys to help me transport it in a cab. The dealer, in his little parlour, curled his lip when I explained the situation and said, 'I'm not in the business of providing a holding pen for wet art.' His expression shifted, though, when he turned his attention to the Van Eyck, and I knew he would find no fault with it. It was perfect. I had laboured over it as I had no other copy, had wrestled it from the inside out, and now, finished, it glistened in its precision.

'It will go to America,' he said. 'There is money there. And plenty of people who do not know where the original is.'

I imagined my copy journeying across the Atlantic to a place I had never been and, inspired for a moment by the painting, its freedoms, its scope, asked for double the proposed fee. The dealer paused and looked at me, as though it was me he was buying. 'You want eighty pounds for this?' he said, and sighed. I felt shame rising, a familiar sense of having given myself away. But then, before I could backtrack and apologise, he agreed, and what I felt then was alarm to discover that it could be done that way, that you could simply ask for what you wanted and receive it.

'Really?' I said.

'Don't you want it? I'll revert to forty if it makes you more comfortable, Miss Inderwick.'

'I am comfortable with eighty.'

'And what will you bring me next?'

'I don't know,' I said. 'I don't know. There are some complications in my life.'

'Perhaps a living artist. There are chaps fetching good money in Paris at present, if you care to travel.'

'I don't know,' I said. I tried to imagine what it might be like if all I needed to consider, in that moment, was whether or not I cared to travel. Again I said, 'There are some complications.'

'Caravaggio, then,' said the dealer, waving his hand, as though this were the solution to all complications. 'I can always sell a Caravaggio.'

'I thought I might do a Venus.'

'Whose Venus? Titian? Let it be Titian.'

'No,' I said. I thought of Titian, of 'Venus and the Lute Player'; there were several of them, weren't there, a series, and in each there was a reclining woman, lovely and louche, her beautiful belly draped almost like fabric, and in each there was a man beside her, clothed and leaning in too close, and the thought of it made me irritated at once. I could almost feel the breath of the too-close man right there in the dealer's parlour. It made me want to wriggle and kick out. 'No,' I said. 'Not Titian.'

The dealer looked ready to say something else, but in the end swallowed whatever it was, and fiddled with his cuffs. 'What will it be, Miss Inderwick?'

A Venus. I could see the painting in my mind's eye, but it

was taking me a moment to remember the name. A woman, nude, reclining and seen from behind. I had seen it reproduced in a book, and had lingered over it; there had been some small detail that had fascinated me. Cupid. Drapery perhaps, or a texture? A mirror. Ribbon looped over the frame. Then I had it. Could see the whole thing, and the artist's name printed beneath it just as it had appeared on the page.

'Velázquez,' I said, at last, and he gave me half the money up front.

It had been too late to do anything other than return to my aunt's house as planned, but I knew, at least, what my next steps would be. As I packed up my belongings in Clapham, one of the Annies perched on the end of my bed, keeping me company and kicking her heels against the sideboard. I asked her how much the rent was for her room. 'Don't you know your own?' she'd asked, and I had explained, feeling afresh the indignity of my dependence, that my affairs were all handled by my aunt and cousin, that I had once and once only paid for a night in a hotel room, but it had been expensive and a one-off. She told me about her rent and also how much she spent per week on omnibuses, cabs, entertainment, food, and I felt then that I had a handle on things, could simply add up the numbers she gave me, reduced a little because I doubted I would feel compelled to go out for cake as much as she seemed to, and then I would know what expense lay ahead of me. There would be additional outlays, of course: paint, primarily, but eventually I would need new clothes, and would have to travel to view paintings from time to time. I factored these into my calculations, overestimating costs to be safe. I could predict, this way, how many weeks of life were bought by a single copy, and what my rate of production would need to be in order to sustain myself as an independent woman living modestly in London. I had jotted it all down in the back of my sketch book and felt a jolt of delight and power whenever I caught sight of the little tallied figures, incomings, outgoings, rent, meals, paint. The grand house and the parties would have to wait, but my freedom was imminent. So real it was possible to express it numerically.

'It's true,' said Annie, watching me curiously from the bed. 'You worry about money all the time.'

'Can I ask even more of you?' I said then. 'I know we are not really friends.' We never would be, was what I left unsaid, because I was too awkward and too distracted and could not come back to live at Mrs Roberts's, even as an independent woman, because my aunt and cousin would surely think to look for me there. 'I need a place to store some belongings, while I work on a plan to move out of my aunt's home.'

Annie said they would all be happy to keep things for me at the house, and it was a small thing, really, no huge inconvenience. She had been so quick to say yes to me, had given it so little thought and was so kind, I suddenly thought I might cry.

'Thank you,' I said. 'You're too kind to me.'

'It's nothing,' said Annie, and she offered me a little cake.

My escape plan: I would return to Inderwick Hall. I would bide my time. Little by little I would pack up my things and send them to the Annies for safekeeping. I would look out for advertisements in the newspaper from people seeking a young lady lodger; I would send off surreptitious expressions of interest. As soon as the room was found, though I was unsure how long these things took to arrange, I would be ready to leave, would have already sent away my things, could simply disappear overnight. And until then, I would behave in a way that suggested nothing at all was the matter, in a way that would reassure everyone that I would stay the course, that I would marry Charles and never run away. I would bide my time.

And so on that first day back, I walked into the house in the manner, I thought, of a person who was returning from a short break, ready to resume her ordinary life. I pulled the large front door shut behind me and felt it slam too loudly, shaking the floor and the books on the shelf. Glass stoppers trembled in empty decanters on the sideboard. I walked across the hallway, round past the staircase, past the oak room and the library the way a person might who was anxious to settle herself back into the place she considered her home. Gun room. Passageway. I opened the door to my old bedroom the way a person might who felt nostalgia, or at least a kind of relief, at the words 'my old bedroom.'

I looked at the room and smelled its air and listened to its creaks. The furniture was just as I had left it and everything else, too: a single glove clutching the arm of a chair, a glass of water by the bedside, cloudy with dust, the door to the painting room reassuringly shut. Everything reminded me of Charles and of Ruby more than it did of myself. It was as though I'd been only a ghost there, and when I saw the bed it was Ruby on the sheets, not myself, that I recalled, and when I looked up at my copy of 'The Drag' on the wall, I felt in place of my horror at Grandmother Hodierna's horror, in place of my dismay at the sight of the twisted pheasant at her knees, its neck at an awful angle, Charles's faint amusement as he said, 'That awful painting.' There was something comforting in being a ghost. As though I had never been there, not really, or only as a kind of shadow, and soon I would leave and never come back.

It was quiet and it stayed quiet. In the days that followed my return my aunt would, on occasion, summon me to her to ask about arrangements for the wedding. Charles had asked that it be soon, a matter of one or two weeks (unsurprising, of course, that he was in a rush now), but she was unconvinced that things could be readied in such a short time. It was no small occasion, the marriage of her son to her niece. And while, yes, there were some nowadays who frowned upon marriages between first cousins, it was a centuries-old tradition in our family and in all the old families, and we must rise to the occasion to see off any foul gossip. I think she even used the word scandal.

And she alluded, drily, to what she called the 'small commotion' over Charles's identity, noting that the wedding would be a good way to draw a line under it, but expressing some doubt about whether it should precede or follow his court date. If the wedding came first it would naturally signal the family's confidence, but if there should happen to be any unpleasant commentary in the press following Charles's appearance in court, a wedding shortly thereafter would be a wonderful way to signal that the question should be dropped. I nodded. I expressed no preference on timing. I contributed what I felt was necessary to conversations about trousseaus (modest, since, being family already, the exchange was only symbolic) and honeymoons (Italy, Mr George having sent a postcard from Rome that had captured my aunt's imagination) as though it were real, really happening, and sometimes I caught myself feeling a skin-gripping dread about the whole thing, as though it actually were. I had to shake my head, press cold fingers against my eyelids to snap myself out of it: I was biding my time. I was not getting married. I was biding my time.

I barely interacted with Charles. He seemed to be keeping his distance from me. He was away a lot, in any case, speaking with his personal solicitors in Plymouth, making sure everything was in order for the judge. 'Is he concerned?' I had allowed myself to ask my aunt, when she mentioned this.

She looked up at me vaguely. 'Concerned about?'

'The court appearance.'

'His only concerns are administrative,' she said. 'He wants certain papers in order. But the testimony of his family, his mother and his cousin—his fiancée!—is really the only thing that should concern anyone.'

My aunt was living in an impossible world in which the events of New Year's Eve had both happened and not happened. They had to have occurred, in order to silence those who had persisted in doubting him, and they could not have occurred, because the accusations he had made were preposterous and ruinous. A scandal. I could not tell even then what she really thought, or how she really felt, whether she was as unwavering in her belief in Charles as she claimed, and if so, why that might be. She coughed and complained of fatigue and found fault with small things I did in her presence, the heaviness of my footsteps, the loudness of my breathing, and I said nothing. When Charles returned he and my aunt were cool with each other, but when she asked if all was well and he said that it was, she reached out and patted him on the forearm and said, 'Well that is good. That's good, Charles.'

It was the beginning of February. The court date was set for the day after Valentine's Day. I began to pack faster, paying servants in secret for the use of their trunks. I sent off keepsakes from my parents and childhood, things I could not part from but never used; then light, cool clothes I would not need until the summer; some painting supplies I rarely needed but which might come in useful, depending on the work; finally, almost all of my clothes, all footwear except for my new boots, all of my paint and oil and brushes and canvas. I was left with a tiny closet of three outfits which I rotated as slowly as I could without drawing attention, and nothing to do except watch obsessively for the arrival of post.

A letter came from the landlady of a house in Chiswick regretfully informing me the room I had asked after had already been taken. A man in Bloomsbury requested a photographic likeness of me before he made a decision. Another emphasised that he refused on principle young ladies without references from male persons in their immediate family. And then, beside another inauspicious note from a landlord, I saw an envelope addressed to my aunt in the simpering scrawl of Mr Barnard, and the feeling of dread I had dismissed as misplaced returned with full force.

My aunt read it with no expression, then set it on the table, open and just readable from where I sat. Mr Barnard and Mr George sought confirmation that the court date remained set from the fifteenth of the month, and also wished to inform the family that they hoped they would be received at the house following their return from Italy on the fourteenth.

'What do they mean by it?' I asked.

'They mean only to be home in time to show the family proper support,' said my aunt, and she began to slice her apple into thin slivers, and then thinner, so papery I could see the pink of her fingertips through them. 'I expect after all the unpleasantness they wish to make amends. The court date is merely a formality, Grace. There is no need to look so appalled. The Inderwicks have always adored formality. When Mr George returns from Italy, he will tell you so himself.'

Part Five

Civitavecchia, 1889

PATER

The voyage from Valparaiso took seven weeks. They stopped at Montevideo and at Rio de Janeiro, where the crew changed and cargo was dragged off, dragged on, new rations were got on board and Green scurried ashore in search of good tobacco and fresh bread and oil. Green had a kind of mania for bread; he was surprised not to have noticed it before and found that it was infectious. They passed long hours in their berth together, tearing crusts to dip in vinegar. The steward brought them little pots of sugared plums in brandy, which they ate after supper, spooning the fruit into each other's mouths. At Lisbon, where they spent a week before resuming their journey, he noticed how heavy his luggage felt, though really there was very little of it. He had to pause halfway up steep streets to pant and catch his breath. He had become languid at sea. He had become the opposite of his former seaman self. At their hotel, they asked after a seamstress, and in the end a boy appeared with a needle and thread to let out their coats and trousers. They stayed in Portugal long enough only to make onward plans, which he passed on in a letter to his father. And then, before they could get too comfortable on land, they were back at sea. A new ship. The final leg of the voyage.

And there, astonishingly, was Italy: bright, bright blue and cream and terracotta and a porter who carried their bags—extraordinary strength, back bulging like a pack horse—down to the dinghy and from thence the quay. There was the familiar strangeness of coming ashore, the wrong-footedness and eerie sense of too-much-space, too-much-stuff, not-enough-water, not-enough-walls. If he felt some excitement—which he did: it was a thrill, a glimpse of what had seemed until then still a fantasy—he also felt dread. This was Europe, after all, and he caught himself scanning crowds for his father's face, felt the threat of encountering that glowering brow at any turn. Green tried to calm him, tried to tell him that the world was large and they were just two men in it, that however mighty his father might seem, he too was just a man, just one, angry man who didn't know any better than to rage on the clifftop.

But Green did not particularly want to talk about his father. What Green wanted was to arrange immediate passage to Rome, to find out about art schools and apprenticeships and painting masters, to begin this work they had both decided on, to become artists. If there was a lapse in conversation, even a moment's lull, Green would come out with something like, 'I've read great things of Trastevere. I've heard that many artists gather there. I've heard it is entirely the place to be seen.' He liked to hear Green talk this way, the patter of 'I've heards' that could not possibly be true, since all they had heard for weeks on end was each other's voices and the waves, but found himself still too nervous to participate in making proper arrangements the way he could tell Green wished he would.

'There might be letters waiting for us,' he said. 'We shouldn't make plans until we collect our letters.'

Green looked uneasy, then, and did not say what he so clearly wanted to say: what sort of letter could cause them to change their plans? There was no reason, was there, that they might have to change their plans?

There were no letters waiting for Green. He wasn't sure if anyone except himself knew where Green was. Green had achieved complete invisibility in that way, a vanished man. But there were, as he expected, letters for him. Three. One addressed in his father's hand, one in his mother's, one he didn't recognise and opened first, which turned out to be from a second cousin, mild and conversational, 'I hear you are planning to make a go of it in paint! You must look up my friend Robinson on the Via Bocca di Leone,' nothing of note but it helped to calm his nerves, to remind him of the patter of family life that was not all awful, that there was a recognisable form to it. Green was watching him read; they were in a small café that sold very strong coffee and a kind of sweet bread that Green had already developed an obsession with. 'All well?' Green asked, after he folded his cousin's letter and set it down, where it soaked up a little spilled coffee. He nodded.

His mother wrote in long, run-on sentences with the occasional full stop thrown in, mostly gossip about people he had never heard of, and making no reference whatsoever to anything difficult or unsavoury.

Green peered over his shoulder. 'Whose writing is that?'

'My mother's.'

'What does she say?'

'She says that the Crawford family have sold a large part of their estate to cover the grandfather's gambling debts.'

'And who are the Crawfords?'

'I have no idea.' He shrugged. Took a sip of coffee.

'Read the other one, then,' Green said, and they both looked at his father's letter.

His father's letter. Just paper stained with ink. Nothing in it could harm him.

'You do it,' he said, and pushed the envelope towards Green.

Green's face, as he read, a constellation of twitches: a flicker of the eyebrow, a tiny tensing of the muscle in the cheek. Was his colour heightening a little, or was it just the changing of the light, as the sky outside darkened towards sunset?

'What does he say?' he asked. 'What does he say?' He sipped his coffee, pinched off some bread.

Green's brow tightened and his eyes darted down to the bottom of the page, then he flipped it over and scanned the other side.

'Well?'

Green put the paper down, reached for the loaf. 'He says he is here. He has come to meet the ship.'

They talked quickly as they walked from the café to the hotel where their bags had been left, a little flurry of 'What if's and 'Couldn't we just's bouncing back and forth between them. Green was staunchly of the opinion that he need not go to meet his father at all; that they should go direct to the bank and withdraw all available funds, then proceed direct to Rome. And if not that, then he should simply placate his father in any way possible, say whatever his father wanted to hear, and no matter what dishonest promises he made they could depart at once. But Green's suggestions felt impossible to him, and for the first time he felt himself angry at Green, who had no understanding of his father, his family. He found himself biting his tongue, working hard not to say something abhorrent—'You wouldn't understand because your family is poor'; 'You wouldn't understand because your family is dead'—and therefore saying nothing at all.

His father had specified a date—today's—and a time— seven o'clock that evening—and also a place, a hotel by the waterfront they'd noticed when they'd landed because of its bright yellow awnings, its pretty terrace with starchy table- cloths laid for lunch. Green had said something appreciative about its appearance, he couldn't remember what exactly. It made him shudder now to imagine his father somewhere inside it, coolly noting the arrival, as scheduled, of *The Margaret*. He had the sensation of being a doll, or a character in a play, dutifully moving according to somebody else's design. If only *The Margaret* had been delayed, he thought, or had taken some unforeseen detour. If only he had been vaguer in the letter he'd sent about their travel plans. If only they had not boarded it all, as Green had wanted. Then his father could have waited all he liked and would not have felt so powerful.

Green lay stretched out on the bed of their room. 'I don't see, my love, how anything good can come of you going to see him.'

Green was correct. And yet, surely, one did things sometimes not because good would come of it, but because it was the right thing to do, because one did, after all, owe everything to one's father and they were, after all, eating food and lying on a bed in accommodation paid for by one's father? He felt helpless to express it. 'He's my father,' was all he could say.

'Do you want me to come with you?' said Green.

He almost laughed, but saw how earnest Green was and said instead, 'That's wonderful of you, but no.'

At seven, he went alone to the hotel with the yellow awnings.

And there was his father, his father, like a figure from a child's storybook. It had been so long since he had seen him and there he was, standing on the hotel terrace facing out to sea. *The Margaret* was still in the harbour, men crawling up and down her sides to do repairs. For a second, in the doorway leading out from the hotel, he paused, wanted to extend the moment in which his father had not seen him. He almost retreated but a waiter was behind him carrying a glass of wine on a tray, and he stepped forwards clumsily, and apologised, and the waiter in his hurry to pass almost tripped, almost spilled the wine, and there was a contrite scuffle between the two of them, which was enough to attract the attention of everyone on the terrace, including his father, who turned, rotating on his heel, and looked directly at him.

He raised his arm instinctively to wave and then knew the gesture to be pathetic. He felt himself walking towards his father. He held out a hand. His father shook it.

'How do you do, Pater?' he asked, and it was as though he was thirteen years old again, as though at any moment his voice might squeak boyishly.

They sat at a table and his father ordered a red wine that would have perhaps tasted good in an English winter but which, there in Italy, seemed fusty and unsubtle. Ferris, his father's man, was waiting nearby with his hands folded around a glass of water, pretending not to listen. His father drank fast, refilling his own glass from the bottle twice before Ferris or the waiter could approach. It occurred to him only then that his father had been drinking even before they met, and that there was something unfocused and wild in his father's eyes.

'I'm glad to see you, sir,' he said.

'Liar,' said his father. 'You're quaking. Look at you. Worried your little jaunt has perhaps come to an end.'

'Well I am,' he insisted, 'I am glad to see you.'

His father drank and drank. And the gist of it was predict-able, was what he and Green had anticipated and discussed: the painting was a ludicrous idea and one that would under no circumstances be supported, he would be cut off again in an instant if he were to pursue it, and he should return home at once with his father.

'Your mother at least,' said his father, 'will be pleased to see you.'

'And I her,' he said.

'Oh, well, you two always did love one another, did you not.'

'Naturally, sir, a man loves his own mother.'

'Nothing natural about the way you love. You've not changed in that regard. You're as fat as an air balloon but you're no more of a man. I can see it in the way you walk. Limp. Handshake like a dead fish. A sissy.'

Sissy. He thought it preferable at least to 'sod'. There was something almost sweet about it. A schoolboy's insult. He tried to force a smile. He tried to swallow more of the grating, rough wine. He tried to keep his mind on what Green had said he should do, which was to lie, lie, lie and then to run away.

'I agree with you, Father,' he said. 'The painting was a poor idea.'

'No defence of yourself, then? Not going to tell me you've become a real man in all this time at sea?' His father was raising his voice.

He looked around. People had looked up, surprised by the volume, but were not yet staring.

'Pater,' he said. 'Perhaps a walk along the shore. Will you walk with me along the shore?'

'Embarrassed, are you?' said his father, but followed meekly enough, losing his footing for a second on the steps from the terrace to the scrubby shoreline, Ferris darting forward to steady him. And when the three of them were further from the hotel, walking along jagged rocks and away from the town, his father began talking again, a drunken, rambling invective that began with more insults but soon veered off, became unfocused.

He listened to his father rant, first about his brother Teddy, who was foppish and unintelligent, and then came a familiar refrain about his mother's infidelities and whether Teddy was even a true Inderwick, which he had heard many times before and never knew whether or not to believe, and then about his father's mad brother locked up in an asylum and the burden of raising the weird niece, and then back, once again, to his own failings. He was braced for the word, and then it came.

'Sod,' said his father. He said it as though he had kept it in his mouth too long, and needed spitting out. 'They used to hang men like you. One of my earliest memories in fact. My father taking me to view the sods, dangling on their gibbets. As limp in death as they were in life.'

And that was when Green appeared, almost from nowhere; he must have been there at the hotel, must have followed them down to the rocks at a distance, sweet, silly Green, who couldn't keep away. His father looked up as Green approached, bemused at first and then afraid; Ferris leant forward as though he might swing a punch then faltered and stepped back. Green: close, enormous, glowering.

'Don't talk to him that way,' said Green.

He had never thought of Green as any kind of force, had only known him to be gentle, loving, delicately dipping a piece of bread into vinegar, smoking his pipe and wondering out loud about something harmless like paint, or money. But he saw now that Green was who he had said he was: a boy from Borough, who grew up rough, abandoned, with very little to lose.

Green stepped closer still. 'Don't talk to him like that.'

His father looked between the two of them and gave a

curt nod, jutting his chin towards Green. 'Is this your wife? Or are you his?'

Green, so close to his father they were surely breathing each other's breath, glanced towards him, was pretending to be casual. 'You never told me your father was a drunk, darling.'

It was more violent than a blow. It was a masterstroke, really, the coolness of it, the insult, the 'darling' at the end the pièce de résistance. His father reeled, almost lost his footing on the rocks, then staggered away from Green, towards him.

He saw clearly that his father was about to hit him and didn't feel afraid, not really, since the blow seemed inevitable, almost embarrassingly obvious, had been destined for him since his father had first set eyes on him at the hotel, before, even, and because his father had hit him plenty of times before. Nothing about the situation seemed extraordinary, except, of course, that this time Green was there, Green was with him, and this would be the last time his father would hit him, and this would be the end of it—there was relief in that, too—because after his father struck him, Green would pick him up, dust him down, and together they would go to Rome.

Part Six

Spring, 1900

TROUSSEAU

There were, in fact, two trousseaus, both diminutive. There was the one my aunt was preparing for me, symbolic only, since my marriage would involve no new household, no sudden need for linens and gowns, everything being in place in the house already, including the bride and groom. And there was the one I was guarding for myself, the true trousseau, which I would use not for my married life but for my real life, the one I would live after running away. This comprised very little, since I had sent most ahead to the Annies, keeping only those items that were either too precious or too essential to part from: some letters my parents had written in more lucid moments from their asylums, a drawing I had done, as a child, of Horatio the rat, my few remaining items of clothing, the note Ruby had scrawled to me during her stay at the house, the filthy, delightful little sketch she had drawn, and, of course, my money, which I kept in a purse, wrapped in several layers of undergarments, inside a leather bag, inside my painting room.

It was unseasonably warm that February, so warm that it began to feel spring-like though in other years we'd been under snow at that time: the first lambs had come at the end of January and the fields around the house were dotted with them, silly and jumpy, long-tailed, flitting about like blossom. I found a crocus by the back gate that led out to the cows and felt stricken by it for a moment; I had spent so much of my life in that house, after all, and had come, if not to love it, then at least to find some reassurance in its familiar bricks, familiar rhythms; the little purple flower appearing out of the mud seemed almost indescribably precious. I took it all in and thought of my leaving. I went to the cows and sat on the wall and looked at each one of them, their enormous haunches and dung-caked backsides and their sweet downy ears and almost burst into tears, as though I knew those cows far better than I really did.

As days passed, Charles became increasingly adamant that our wedding should precede the court date. I took to visiting my secret trousseau, looking through it, stroking the case almost as though I was petting an animal. I was reassured and inspired by the knowledge that, if necessary, I could leave in a heartbeat and never come back. I thought of my late uncle, who had always kept a hunting bag ready at all times, in case the opportunity arose at short notice. Here was my hunting bag, I thought as I patted the case, unbuckled and re-buckled the straps. Here was my gun, my leash, my crop.

I went to the stables to find Bobby, who was still avoiding me; he saw me coming and half turned as though his instinct was to run, then stopped.

'Hello,' he said. 'I got your letter.'

'Bobby, I need to ask you for something.' Panic flashed across his face. 'No, no, it's not the money.'

I worried he'd start crying again, but he took a tight breath and nodded.

'I don't know that I mentioned in my letter,' I said, 'but I'm engaged to marry Charles.'

He nodded again, still struggling to meet my eye. 'I heard about it.'

I wondered how to phrase the request. 'I need your help.'

'You'll be running away, then?' he said, and at last looked at me.

'Is it so obvious? I don't want—it can't be obvious.'

'I expect it's not,' he said, 'to those that don't think about you much.'

'You'll take me to the train station?' I said. 'When the time comes? I don't know when. Very soon. It will be sudden.'

'Of course.' There was excitement in his voice when he said, again, 'Of course.'

'I'll pay you for it, Bobby.'

'You don't need to do that.'

'I do.'

'I'm glad,' he said. 'I'm glad for you.'

'Thank you.'

'Where will you go?'

I'd had the idea of going first not to London but to Yorkshire. I was thinking of the Velázquez I'd promised the dealer, which was listed in my uncle's encyclopaedia of provenances as being in Rokeby Hall, the home of the Morrit family, near Barnard Castle. And since things would surely be cheap in Yorkshire, cheaper at least than in London, and since my family would never think of looking for me there no matter where I stayed or what I did, I thought of going there first, getting the Venus copy underway while continuing my search for a permanent place to live. It all felt a little unlikely, as though the plan was a game, but since I could not think of a better one, it became fixed in my mind. I had no idea what Yorkshire was like, but I was going to go there, alone, a runaway, and do my work. I wrote to the Annies in Clapham, apologetically requesting the return of my painting supplies; I was on high alert for the delivery, anxious that the arrival of a large trunk would attract attention and give the game away.

In the end, it wasn't the trunk—nobody even noticed it arrive, and I gave it to Bobby to keep for me—it was 'The Drag' that ruined everything. Unease over 'The Drag', about its destruction and rebirth, had remained unvoiced for years, since long before Charles's return. It was a subject nobody could broach, everyone scared of madness coming for them, everyone doubting themselves, their memories, the sights they had seen with their own eyes, worrying that if they mentioned what they recalled it might be revealed that none of it had happened. Nobody ever wanted to be told they were the mad one. But my imminent wedding had reminded my aunt of the painting, of its continued presence in my bedroom and therefore of its connection to me. She had felt moved to see it again, and so—horrifying—I came back from speaking with Bobby to find her—horrifying, horrifying—standing in my room, gazing distractedly up at the canvas.

'Aunt!'

If I'd taken the time to think, I would have simply backed out of the room in silence and waited for her to leave.

'Grace,' she said, not averting her eyes from 'The Drag'. 'Here is that dreadful painting.'

'Yes,' I said. 'There it is.' I looked up at Grandmother Hodierna's awful face, and then to the face of my aunt, and only then saw how ill my aunt had grown, how similar they looked.

'As though it had never been taken away.'

'Yes,' I said. 'Just as though.'

'As though it had never been burned to ash.'

'Yes,' I said. 'As though it never had been.'

'And you are,' my aunt turned now, taking in the corners of the room, the emptiness of it, and finally resting her eyes on me, 'responsible for that, somehow, I suppose?' She coughed, bending forwards, and then righted herself and fixed me with her eyes. It was as though she was looking at me, really looking at me, for the first time.

'Responsible?'

'The business with the painting.'

'I don't know what you mean.'

Something was happening to my aunt. I couldn't remember the last time she had come to my room, and now she was there and something was happening, a horrifying clarity was emerging in her expression, almost a smile, almost triumph, and when she coughed again, she did so standing upright.

'This room is very empty, Grace.'

'I don't have many belongings.'

'And it is rather dirty, Grace.'

'I'll ask the maid to clean.'

'And see, here, all along the floor, what is that, Grace?'

'I don't see anything, Aunt.'

'Paint, Grace. There is paint everywhere, splashes and stray drops and look, here, a dreadful smear upon the woodwork.'

I thought then of the small mole at the inside corner of my left eye, the one I hadn't known was there until my uncle pointed it out to me. How astonished I had been to be confronted by the details of myself like that, something so intrinsic and enduring that had been invisible to me. How many times had I looked into a mirror and seen myself without really seeing myself at all?

Now I looked around the room I had carefully cleared, in which I had kept so many secrets and which I had trusted to guard them, and saw that it was absolutely covered with paint. My aunt was right. Flecks of green, cadmium, umber and black from 'The Drag' were all along the floorboards reaching away from the threshold to the painting room. There was a large area daubed with white and cream and rose madder, still unfaded, from where I had done the Courbet, and that, too, seemed formed like an arrow towards the place where the work had been done. The more I looked the more I saw the ghosts of all the copies I'd ever made, footprints and smears and flecks that had been tracked through or dripped: blues and reds from the robes of Madonnas, the distinctive glowing yellows of 'The Music Lesson'.

'Open the door to that room, Grace.'

'Aunt, I prefer to keep some privacy.' My voice sounded weak, even to myself, girlish and faint. I knew there was no point fighting it; what was happening would keep on happening, but couldn't help myself. 'I prefer not to.'

'Shall I open it myself?' she said.

And now Charles was there, standing in the doorway and then approaching, saying, 'Mater, she prefers not to.'

'I shall open it then,' she said, and she did, flinging open the door so violently that it slammed and bounced back towards her hand. Inside, the painting room was a riot of colour: wide daubs, wall to ceiling, that I had never noticed or thought to clean. And there was nothing else there, no furniture or decoration, to distract from the paint: there was only the leather bag containing my trousseau, and all that space everywhere else. My aunt stepped in just far enough to reach it and I ran at her; I thought I might hit her, but Charles blocked me.

'Grace,' he said. 'Just let her.'

'No,' I said. 'It's mine. It's private. Aunt, stop. Aunt, I forbid you to open it.'

My aunt laughed. Stepped back from the doorway, bag in hand. Stopped laughing. Seemed to hear afresh what I had said and started again. Then she opened my trousseau.

There was nothing inside that was not mortifying when I saw it through my aunt's eyes. Clothes, including underwear; my parents' letters, precious and weird; my own childhood drawings: these things mattered to me, though perhaps nobody else. But, worse: Ruby's letter, Ruby's drawing. Worst of all: the money. It was impossible that my aunt should see it. It had to be impossible. It had to be a dream, my night-time mind rehearsing a worst-case scenario; it could not be happening that my most precious and private self was about to be uncovered, and with it all my hopes for a new life evaporating, not then, not by my aunt, my aunt, my aunt who was right there, not by her hand, which was reaching into my bag, leafing idly through my parents' letters and my sketches as though they were insignificant, as though they were simply paper packaging for whatever else she hoped to find, and then resting, horribly, over Ruby's letter.

I felt myself go white. Charles shot me a look of urgent enquiry.

She was pulling the page towards her. She was reading. She was frowning. She was reading. She was turning the page. Any second now she'd see the drawing. She was about to see the drawing.

Then she saw the drawing.

My aunt at first looked bemused, squinted, turned the paper ninety degrees and back again—and then it seemed to become clear for her. She dropped the page. Lifted her hand to her mouth. Swallowed. Coughed, and then coughed harder. She began to twitch her head in little sideways shakes, the way horses do when flies get near them, and how badly I wished I could be with Bobby again in the stables rather than where I was, in my room, watching my aunt discover me. I sat down on the bed and waited for her to say something.

She said nothing. She reached, instead, back into the bag, and took out the bundle of my under garments, which she untangled to reveal my purse. The room was silent, the only noise the musical rattle of the buckle, my aunt's fingers rubbing against the leather. She stared at the money inside the same way she had stared at Ruby's drawing, and then, instead of dropping it, she was folding the notes. She was tucking them into the belt of her dress. She was taking my money.

She was taking my money.

Money belonged to nobody. That was what I believed. Those notes from the dealer were simply visiting the inside of my purse, as transient as air briefly drawn into the lungs. But I could not help thinking of how often money seemed to leave me: coins left in the hand of the girl outside the White Lion, the notes missing from my room in the inn. The twenty pounds stuffed through the letterbox of Mrs Clawson, counted firmly into Bobby's hands. Before that: my parents' house, nothing grand but made of brick and thatch and belonging, as much as anything belonged to anyone, to me, which had burned down without a trace while Inderwick Hall still stood. I could not help thinking, too, of how often money seemed to find its way towards my aunt's family, a tidal sweep of wealth washing over their history. And now it was happening again. Here was my aunt grabbing my money, grabbing it, as this family had always done, taking and taking and taking from everyone and now specifically from me.

Charles looked from his mother to me, and then to the painting room, and seemed to understand everything. Every tiny muscle in his face seemed to be tensing and releasing, possibilities darting through his mind, and then he broke the silence. 'Mater.'

She looked at me, not at him. 'Grace. Where did you get this? Who have you stolen this from?'

Charles, insistent, 'Mater. Please.'

'Whose money is it? Have you been blackmailing that girl?' She nodded towards Ruby's letter on the floor.

'Mater,' said Charles. 'Please.' He put a hand on his arm. 'I gave it to her. It was me who gave her the money.'

She shrugged him away from her. 'Don't lie, Charles, for God's sake, you must stop—'

His eyes widened. Hers did too. For the first time since he'd come into the room they really looked at each other. A separate, wordless conversation was happening between them and I didn't understand what exactly it was, but in that moment could barely think about it. The only thing that seemed clear to me was my money, its crisp edges extruding from behind my aunt's belt buckle, my money, mine, pressed against her stomach.

'Don't,' she said.

The talking began then. There were questions, endless questions, and to watch Charles lie was to watch a virtuoso at work. It was almost wondrous to see. He was a master of his art. It was money he had given to me, he said. I had stolen it from no-one. He had wanted me to have it in case some emergency purchase was needed for the wedding, it was nothing strange, nothing suspicious, and yes he conceded it was a very large sum but he had wanted to make sure there could be no anxieties on a financial front, he wanted me to feel completely at ease, and he had advised me, too, to undertake a spring clean of my belongings, so that when we returned from our honeymoon he could have ready and waiting for me a new wardrobe of items befitting a married woman of my status. On and on he went, the very picture of an attentive fiancé, a man who had, hand on heart, wanted to make everything simple. My aunt was annoyed and then sceptical, and in the face of her scepticism and annoyance he continued to lie and lie and lie.

I held my breath and let him save me. That there would be a cost attached to this favour seemed inevitable, but I was happy to take the deal and pay later. At least, I thought, the paint on the floor had been forgotten, 'The Drag' had been forgotten. Occasionally my eyes drifted to Ruby's letter on the floor, the drawing face up, unashamed of itself, and I thought how, had my aunt not found the money, the uncovering of that alone would have been the greatest disaster of my life.

My aunt let Charles speak. She frowned. She seemed if not to believe him then at last to be so exhausted by the barrage of falsehoods that she gave in to them, saying grudging, grumpy things about how unnecessary it was to give me money, how I had no right at all to get rid of good clothes without asking her, not now, not while I was still a guest in her house and dependent on the family's charity, how she really should be lying down now, since she was not well, not well at all, and these kinds of anxieties might be the thing to kill her once and for all. Charles agreed he had been foolish in handing over such an extravagant sum without consulting her first and expressed a desire to send for my aunt's doctor, but reiterated that I had acted according to his instruction. I was mute. I simply waited for them to finish their performance and hand me back what was mine.

But then the conversation seemed to be ending and the money was still in her possession. She was saying, 'Well, I need to go and speak to Cook before I can rest,' and Charles was nodding and saying that he himself should be getting back to his papers, and they both turned to leave my room as though something had been finalised.

'Wait,' I said. And though I had been the focus of their entire argument, my belongings, my behaviour, my freedoms, they both looked a little surprised to be reminded of my existence. 'Wait.'

'What is it?' My aunt looked irritated and was coughing again. There was nothing she needed to say to the cook; I could tell she was anxious to be elsewhere for the sake of being elsewhere. 'What do you want?'

'My money,' I said.

She looked astonished. She opened her mouth and let it stay open, her tongue rising to words she didn't speak.

'Grace,' Charles said. His eyes said: stop. His eyes said: don't push it.

'Give me my money,' I said.

And my aunt said, 'No.'

Behind her was the open door and beyond that was the house. I thought my way along the passage, the gun room, kitchens, dining room, all the way round the library, the oak room, past the green room to the entrance hall, past the foot of the stairs where Charles had held forth on New Year's Eve and out of the front door. It would take, perhaps, thirty seconds if I ran flat out. I crouched to pick up Ruby's letter, replaced it in my bag, did up the buckle, looped my arm under the strap. And then, before I could think of a reason not to, I charged full tilt at my aunt. As I lunged forwards I began to roar, and it was throat-grating, a real lion's roar, a weird wild woman's roar; it filled all the space inside my head so I could think of nothing except roaring, the roar of a mad person, and she shrieked and flattened herself against the wall, which made it easier than I'd anticipated to loosen the money from her belt and take it, and even as I did so I saw clearly for the first time how ill she was, how frail and limp, and then I ran and I ran and I ran through the house, past Charles, past everything, and out, and all the way round to the stable block, where Bobby when he saw me jumped into action, retrieving my trunk and preparing the carriage, as though it was he who was being pursued.

And so we drove away from Inderwick Hall. Nobody tried to stop us. We passed yew tree after yew tree and I turned in my seat to look back at the blank windows of the house, glass planes reflecting only the white and grey clouds, revealing nothing. Was Charles's face there, looking out from behind one of them? I couldn't see; it was hopeless to try. As we reached the gatehouse, I breathed in the air of the estate for the last time, the warm spring earth and damp and cow dung and wood smoke, wood smoke, the lovely promise of it which reminded me of the bonfire that burned 'The Drag', and in that moment struck me as an assurance that all great houses would, one day, burn down.

On the road to the station I wrote out, hurriedly, a character reference for Bobby to show to new employers in case his role in my escape cost him his position at the stables, and I folded into the letter enough money to pay for half a year's living and I knew it was not enough and told him so, and he said it was, it would be, it would all work out just fine. He was thinking of leaving in any case, he said, because he had realised he was in love with a girl in the village, perhaps he had mentioned her to me once or twice, her name was Rosamond; she had family in Canada and had said they should get married and move there, she and Bobby and Bobby's mother and sisters, and he thought it was a good idea. He seemed in high spirits, asking, optimistically, whether he should drive me as far as London and seeming a little disappointed when I told him to go only as far as the train station.

'Where will you go?' he asked, since I had not answered his question the last time.

'Yorkshire,' I said.

'What's in Yorkshire?' he asked.

Copy of Diego Velázquez's, 'Venus at her Mirror', Oil on Canvas, 1647–1651

Later in my life, long after I left my aunt's house for good and long after Charles died, I flew in an aeroplane. It was a flight from California to London, a journey that would otherwise have taken weeks of travel by land and sea. In the air, it lasted merely hours. I had the sensation of being raised up from myself, of being lifted out of my own life, and in floating above it all I felt I could see everything terribly clearly. There were the little trees and roads below us, the fields like the pages of books, toy houses. And there were the clouds above us, and then all around us, and then, astonishingly, below us, white and ornate, baroque, and it all seemed so precise, so exact and obvious, quaint really. The edges were so neat. It was as though I could see everything I had ever done and would go on to do from up there, and I felt a kind of detached sympathy with myself, a feeling of not being myself but instead a person with a moderate investment in my wellbeing. It was peaceful up to a point, and then sad, and I was glad to reach the ground again, to be in the thick of it all, unable to see anything clearly anymore, or to know anything other than the present moment, the smell of a London street, cigarette smoke and exhaust fumes from the buses.

And though it was nothing like anything I'd ever experienced before, that soaring flight into thin air on the plane, the thing it resembled most precisely was the moment after I roared at my aunt, and the moments that followed that moment. The train journey north, which I took in stages, stopping as necessary at inns that made me somewhat nervous, and seemed to exist only in the dark—dark station roads to reach them, dark corridors, candles that spluttered and then, before daybreak, the next train coming darkly. The arrival at Barnard Castle, having had no time to look at maps or plan how I would get to Rokeby Hall, or what I would say when I got there to persuade them to let me see the painting, or where I would stay in the meantime. Finding a ladies' boarding house signposted from the train station, giving my name, in a panic, as Mrs. Charles, and then, panicking more, making up a story about being a widow and visiting friends at Rokeby Hall. The landlady gave me an uncomfortable look and said, 'Why not stay at Rokeby Hall then?' but didn't wait for an answer, merely showed me to a room. Sitting in that room in an unfamiliar town, so far from my life I might as well have been thousands of feet in the air, thinking, and thinking, and thinking of what I had done.

The painting made me feel better, when I was with it. Faced with the Rokeby Venus, I almost forgot everything else, and in almost forgetting could feel more like myself again, my old self, for whom everything had been a secret and there had been, therefore, no way to fail. The people at Rokeby Hall let me view their painting with almost no questions asked (a student of art, I said, remembering the letter I had written about the Courbet, a special interest in the female form) and only brought me cups of tea at intermittent intervals and kept offering me meals, biscuits, sausages wrapped up in ham, dried figs. And the truth was that I was hungry, that meals at the boarding house in Barnard Castle were agonising affairs, full of people asking questions about who I was and what I was doing there, and I missed the Annies and the Bonnies horribly then, though I'd never really known them, either, but I felt there had been a warmth there that I now yearned for. I had found myself avoiding the dining room, making up engagements in order to skip dinner and then hiding in my room. Eating sausages in front of the Velázquez was almost euphoric.

The painting itself: startling in colour, nothing like the etching I'd seen in the book. It reminded me of the Courbet, the nudes amongst draped bedsheets, except this time the woman was alone and portrayed from behind, the upwards jut of her hip almost the exact centre of the canvas above the sweet, dark parenthesis of an upper buttock. There was a Cupid attending her, winged and silly with a toddler's round belly and thighs, and he held up a mirror to show to Venus, and to me, as I ate and looked up at her, the reflection of her face. And it was the face that I had remembered, or rather, had failed to remember; it was the face I had been thinking of when I named this painting to the dealer.

It was softly done, so softly you could barely make

anything out of it other than its face-ness, just the hint of pink on the woman's cheek, though it was in fact an apricot tone, almost orange, and shadows for eyes, a general plumpness. But there was something correct about it nonetheless. It seemed entirely as it should be, the unknowable face, that sensation that I had always had of seeing in my own reflection not myself, nor even a stranger, but something incomprehensible, and of seeing in other people everything, just as it was, nose, eyes, mouth, only for it to slip through my grasp like water, or money.

But then: what I realised as I looked and looked and looked was that the face in the mirror was not the face of Venus at all. The frame was angled too much towards the viewer so that it could not be showing her face, and neither did it reflect her stomach and breasts as a real mirror, positioned that way, might. The face in the mirror was another face altogether, and the Venus saw it, this hazy stranger, and so was not alone. The face in the mirror was a mystery.

I mapped the whole thing at Rokeby Hall, and continued to think about it in my room at Barnard Castle, where the rain got in through the walls in a way that reminded me of Inderwick Hall, the wallpaper curling over itself from the corners, wind twisting through a gap in the window frame, shrill as a flute, familiar and unnerving and reassuring all at once. I thought: there were two very dark sections in the painting, one behind the right-hand side of the mirror and the other below Venus's leg, the thigh's shadow being darkest of all, and echoed by blacks in the folds of the grey-blue sheet, Payne's Grey. I spent a long time on those creases, which were the bulk of the whole painting, and if I could get those right I was almost done, the fabric under her waist where the sheet was most rumpled, as though her maid should have spent longer pressing it, a pale dove grey where the light hits the top of the crease and the brushwork surprisingly fine.

I didn't a paint single stroke, just recited the painting to myself over and over. I told myself this was for practical reasons. I had canvas with me at the boarding house and all the necessary tools to stretch and prime it, but I had the feeling that I was in a hurry to go south again, that I couldn't wait all that time in Barnard Castle while I painted the thing, and then let it dry enough to transport it, stretched to an enormous frame or rolled up and inevitably damaged, and in any case the trains on the way up had been bad enough with only a small bag and a trunk; I could not face it with the painting, too. I was filling my brain with it, even as my thoughts hurtled back to Oxfordshire, to London, ahead of me.

The real reason was that I knew that the minute I allowed the painting to escape me, I would have to face my situation, which was a thing I did not know how to do. There was a lovely insulation in thinking about the Venus, its soft greys and creases, gentle and absorbing, and there was something so comforting about not having started yet. The potential untapped. The money unspent. Procrastination a kind of hoarding. Once I began the work, or, worse, finished it, what would I do? What was I going to do? I had nowhere to go, and no friends, and I found myself missing not only the Annies and Bonnies at Clapham but also the view from my room of the Common and trees, the cluttered normality of it, and most of all Ruby—Ruby!—sauntering in, unbuttoning her blouse as though it was nothing to be ashamed of, the sanest thing in the world. Where was Ruby? What was she doing at that very moment, and was she still angry with me, and would she ever forgive me?

I looked in the little mirror above the washbowl in my room and saw my own blurred face and thought: is that really me? I felt so strange to myself, out of context, and the only things that brought me any comfort were the painting and the snacks at Rokeby Hall.

I sat in a blue upholstered chair before it, alone in a room with high windows. The people there always lit the fire for me; after my first day, the room was always warmed before I arrived, which was a kindness I did not know how to acknowledge, or whom I should I thank for it. I felt I should offer money for the room, the warmth, the sausages, for the way they left me alone simply to look and didn't ask too many questions, but I also knew this was the wrong thing, that nobody in Rokeby Hall thought about money as much as I did, or at least not the people whom it would be rational to pay. So instead I slipped sixpences to the maid who brought the food, to the boy who scurried ahead of me opening doors, to the woman who came in, every day, to ask if I would like to be driven back to my lodgings.

I was aware, without explicitly acknowledging it to myself, that the days were sliding one by one towards Charles's court date, six days to go, five, four, and then suddenly only one, and I was finding it harder and harder not to think about Charles. It was Valentine's Day. Somebody slid a card under my door and I opened it ready to burst into tears, anticipating that my aunt had somehow tracked me down and would, even now, try to take my money from me. But it was only a card, a lobster in pink lying across the lap of a forlorn cupid; if you lifted the body of the lobster it read, 'I have a lady in my head,' and I didn't know what to make of it at all, sat on the edge of my bed and stared at it entirely bemused. I thought for an optimistic half-second that perhaps Ruby had sent it, though I knew Ruby could not have sent it; would not have even if she could. It seemed too ornate and too particular to be something Charles had done, and yet I could think of nobody else who would do such a thing. When I closed my eyes the long body of the lobster began to shift into the body of the Venus, orange-pink to white-pink, and the little Cupids flapped and pranced and held up mirrors, *I have a lady in my head, I have a lady in my head*.

I went out, not really sure what to do, and wandered a little around the town, which looked dark in the drizzle, the ruins of the castle black above the houses. The river was high, loud under the bridge, and I had been alone for so long. Alone in all sorts of ways, with all sorts of people, but mostly alone locked up in my own head. A carriage passed by, sending up a plume of water from a puddle, drenching my shoes.

If I left at once and was lucky with the trains, I could be there in time to see Charles in court, and I don't believe I ever decided to do it, there was no moment of clarity about it, I simply packed my case and decided to leave the boarding house ('You're off so soon, Mrs Charles?' and then, once I'd settled the bill, 'And did you care for my Valentine card? I give a Valentine to all my ladies. Which one did you get? The lobster?'), and then I decided to go to the train station, and then I decided to take a series of trains south. What I thought about as I went was Charles, of how much I loathed him and also of how, since his re-emergence in my life everything had entirely transformed, of how I was there alone on a train, hurtling past strange fields of sheep with a bag of my worldly possessions stored above me and a Velázquez in my head, a whole painting, a whole sweep of pink fabric, pale body, grey sheet, of how all of this was what I had dreamt of the years before his return and was now real: nobody knew where I was and I had money to my name, at least for now, and even though I felt lost and bemused and still trembled when I thought of the encounter with my aunt, the cupboard flung open, the roar, it was a dream, a dream and real. I stayed the night in an inn at Corby, as dark and alarming as the others I'd found, but this time there was a lightness to it that must have—could only have—come from me.

A Brief Discourse on Faces

That it is not Venus's face in the mirror is, once you see it, the whole point of the painting. At first you might think the point is the fabric or the buttocks, you might think it is the fleshiness of the pink sheet hanging up behind her; your mind might turn, once again, to rose madder and to crevices. But all of this, the body, the bed, is only a kind of frame. The point is the face, Venus's face that could not be hers, and so vague! It is so unforgivably vague, and the vagueness feels deliberate, incredibly precise, as though to say: do we ever know who anyone really is?

A face is simply a collection of shapes, no more or less complex than any other thing: a tree, the front of a building. I had no trouble recalling those other things. And a face in a painting was no problem at all: I could reproduce it as easily as I could write my own name. When I try to explain my difficulty with faces, I find myself saying something like: *It is like being distracted at the most important point. It is like reading the climactic scene in a book and realising only afterwards that you took none of it in. It is like a word on the tip of your tongue, and you never remember it.*

I was surprised, every single time I noticed it, by the mole in the corner of my left eye.

The face in the mirror in the Rokeby Venus seems all wrong for the woman whose body we are shown from behind. Even if the angle were right, it could not be her face. There is a leanness to the body, a kind of restraint, and what is shown of the face is different altogether. It is a generous face, generous in the cheeks, generous in its very existence.

I could not recall my parents' faces.

I could not recall my aunt's face, though I would know it when I saw it. The same was true for Charles—I could picture only the scale of it, the broad forehead—though I felt myself propelled towards it.

I could not recall my parents' faces, but I thought perhaps I remembered other things more vividly in their place, the sensation of sitting up beside my mother in bed and the mattress tilting down towards her hips, the mushroomy smell of her breath, my father's laugh, honking and jubilant. I could not even remember the face of Horatio the rat, but I remembered how his claws felt as he twisted around my forearm, toothy and light, and the surprising cool of the skin of his tail.

There are people who keep faces locked in their memory like addresses in an address book, or like—better, more apt—specimens in a collector's catalogue, dried flowers or insects or butterflies, ordered and preserved for posterity and pinned in place. There are people who see the world in faces, for whom faces are the wallpaper of every experience and who, having seen a person once and only briefly would recognise them decades later, and not only that, would recognise that person's brother, their sister or their son. Nobody is ever lost to them, which seems to me an almost audacious wealth. I have met only a handful of people like this, those whose great talent lies exactly where my weakness does. It took me many years to understand that Charles was one of them.

I became aware that, when I sat down, at last, to paint my copy of the Rokeby Venus, it would be the closest thing to a self-portrait I had ever attempted.

FORMALITIES

At King's Cross Station in London on the day of Charles's court appearance I handed in my trunk for storage and decided to walk a little, just to meander through the streets, enjoying their breadth and their upheavals and smells and the two children scattering seed for pigeons and the boy pasting up big sheets of advertisements on the sides of parked cabs. A gentleman walked ahead of me with two little dogs; a woman caught my eye and smiled and passed on into a crowd. I gave money to a man collecting donations for the education of girls. The day was cold and clear. The shadows of trees and buildings were very sharp on the pavement.

This was my life. I repeated it to myself. This was my life. I could simply stay here, in London, amongst all these other people, and I would find a place to live, surely I would, I could go to a hotel in the meantime, I could paint, and I felt a soaring giddiness at having done it. I had done it. I had escaped. It had somehow not felt real in Barnard Castle. It had not felt celebratory, everything as strange and unsettling as the lobster on the Valentine's card, but now here I was in London, here I was by myself and I could do whatever I wanted, forever. Couldn't I?

Then I thought perhaps that what I wanted was to turn to-wards Trafalgar Square and go again to the National Gallery, but then perhaps, how about, what if the thing I wanted was to go this other way, and this way, and to ask one or two people for directions until I came upon—what a surprise!—the courthouse where Charles would be. What if I wanted to go inside? What if I wanted to see Charles? I had not planned to go there. I had not intended to see him. But I had arranged everything exactly so that I could.

Inside the courthouse the air was freezing and smelt of paper, and my steps echoed too loudly on the smooth stone floor, and I felt at once that I didn't want to be there after all. I'd been feeling giddy and frankly a little silly wander-ing through the sunshine; things had seemed easier than they were. But by then I was set on my course and I tried to stay calm, to walk on towards the room where I could already—I felt my step quicken—hear his voice. The door of the courtroom creaked and then slammed as I came through it, but nobody looked around at me, because Charles was there, broad and tall at the stand, wearing his brown mono-grammed jacket, and he was speaking, and speaking hotly, his face red and his knuckles white where he gripped the rail.

'And to be asked to defend myself *against* myself, your honour, is an unspeakable thing, a maddening thing. I cannot deny my own self, and anyone who seeks to deny me does grave injury to my family's name and reputation, and to my own name, though it is over and over denied me, and yet such grave injury has been done and done again, since my return to England. To be required, both in private and now in a court of law with newsmen and strangers watching, to affirm that I am who I am and then to be told that despite my affirmations I am a liar, it is a kind of madness. I am made to feel like a criminal merely for asserting that I am who I have always been. Or rather for the crime of, what, having been to sea for many years? Having gained some girth around my face and middle in that time? I am sorry not to be the slender young man I once was, but I do not find that to be anyone's business but my own. None of this—none of this, your honour—is anyone's business but mine.'

A formality, my aunt had said. Merely that. And the Inderwicks have always loved formality. The family and its hangers-on had gathered for the enjoyment of this particular one. There was Mr George, sitting, formally, beside my aunt, who seemed thinner than ever and tilted to one side like a blown-over tree, and there was Mr Barnard, scribbling notes in a little book, and there were the uncles, the distant cousins, there was Ferris, straight as a board, the back of his neck a deep puce; there were all of them, and people I did not recognise, and for a second I wondered if Ruby might be there, wondered if this occasion would have collected everyone together like a funeral. I scanned the backs of all the heads and saw none that belonged to her.

It was clear from Charles's demeanour that something had gone gravely wrong, as I had, on some level, known it would. He had been so wonderful at lying for me, that was the thing. He had lied so beautifully to my aunt about where I'd got the money from. And Charles, the original Charles, had been above all a terrible liar, hopeless, could never bring himself to do it, even when his honesty caused him enormous trouble. 'Mr George has been to Italy,' the new Charles said to me in the pub those weeks ago, and Mr George was back now, and it was obvious that there had been something discoverable in Italy, something Charles knew would ruin him, and it seemed likely that it had been discovered.

I felt newly expert in being discovered. I had experienced for myself the naked horror of it, and I also knew that on the other side of it was a kind of relief. I fidgeted in my seat and coughed a little and found myself hoping I would attract Charles's attention, would be able to tell him that it was quite all right to give up, even at the last, and I found when I looked at him that I didn't hate him as much as I had thought I did, and in fact wished him well, and in fact wished him more than well, wished him success and joy and perhaps even, why not, money, because he and I seemed so alike, liars, both of us, and anxious, both of us, and strivers, both of us. We were oddities and ill-matched to everything except, perhaps, each other.

Mr George was speaking again now. Irrefutable evidence, he said. A marked gravestone in a remote spot, though known to locals of Civitavecchia. Witnesses who had seen the young man arrive and give his name as Charles Inderwick, and then later had discovered the body of the same young man in the water, this being 1889, and presumably occurring shortly before the late Charles Inderwick senior arrived to seek his son there. The real Charles: dead. This Charles: an imposter, a charlatan, impersonating a dead son to the man's own mother, unspeakable evil.

Charles, on his feet again, demanding to know how, in this outlandish version of events, he could possibly know the things he knew, how he could be standing here before them in Charles Inderwick's monogrammed jacket, waving Charles Inderwick's monogrammed pen, speaking in Charles Inderwick's own voice? He demanded evidence, demanded anything whatsoever to support this story of a gravestone, and even were there to be such a stone, was it not possible for anyone to put anybody's name upon it, had these so-called witnesses had any authority whatsoever to pronounce the identity of the drowned man, had any efforts been made then to inform the family of this loss? No, there had been none, the reason being that this was a fiction, malicious and relentless, designed to discredit the rightful heir and so on and so on, everybody speaking too fast and the judge looking rather dazed, having presumably entered the courtroom expecting a straightforward formality and encountering instead the dreadful formal chaos of the Inderwick family, and of Charles, who was speaking still, and still speaking, and I wanted to tell him that it was all right, that he could stop, that it would be fine, it would really be fine, to give up.

At last it seemed the judge reached the same conclusion and bellowed a demand for silence. It took him three tries to succeed, and then everybody stopped, Charles's mouth still open and my aunt tilting even more acutely, and the only sound was of over-wrought breathing. The judge shuffled some papers, cleared his throat. The certainty with which he had ordered quiet was fading, and he seemed at a loss as to what he should say next. Charles, seeing an opening, said,

'If I might add—' but was silenced by the judge's glare, then Mr George tried, 'If it please your honour to—' and received the same.

I stood up.

I said, 'Charles.'

Everybody turned, even my aunt, almost sideways in her chair. Mr Barnard's expression: horror, and, despite himself perhaps, hope. Mr George: irritation. The uncles: indignation. The judge: further confusion. And Charles. Charles, a blurred face in the mirror, raised his hand and waved.

'Charles,' I said, 'might I speak to you?'

Nobody tried to stop him as he made his way from the front of the courtroom towards me, and nobody spoke at all, and it seemed to take a very long time, his footsteps very loud, my aunt wheezing horribly, for him to reach me.

'Might I speak to you?' I said, when he was close, and I beckoned him still closer, so that I could bend my head towards him. He crouched a little so I could speak into his ear.

'What is it, Grace?'

'I think you are like me,' I said. 'I think you are like me.'

Everything I wanted to say was muddied and evasive, vague, except for that. But I wanted him to know that I saw him as clearly as it was possible for me to see anyone, even as I wondered who on earth he really was, that I saw him the way he had seen me. All the rest of what I wanted to say, about how in giving up the act there was freedom to be had, and how there was a way that we could, both of us, come out of this as winners—which he had been trying to tell me all along in his own way, but which I hadn't understood until that moment—and better still we would never have to think of the family ever again, and could go anywhere and do anything, and be anyone, all of that I found I couldn't put words to. I hoped he knew it anyway, because he was Charles, and Charles always seemed to see these things in me, could see them even when I couldn't.

He stepped back so he could meet my eye and seemed to want to check something there. He gave a small twitch of a nod, glanced over his shoulder at the rest of the family. I moved my face back into his line of sight, tried to see if he was understanding what I meant him to. He nodded again.

I held out a hand, and he took it, and we walked together out of the courtroom almost like a real man and wife.

Part Seven

Saint Helena, 1899

CHARLES THE FIRST

It was they, after all, who had come to him. That was how he thought about it. It was as though they had extended a hand and tapped him on the shoulder right there, in his own kitchen, when he'd seen the obituary in the newspaper. Mr Charles Inderwick of Inderwick Hall. Survived by a wife, one son. Remembered for his enthusiasm for countryside pursuits, his dedication to his family. They might as well have slapped him, the lot of them, might as well have sauntered into his house and assaulted him. After all these years. After all these years, and it was they who inserted themselves back into his life in this way. It took restraint not to spit on the page.

Charles had once told him, on the voyage from Valparaiso, that of all the members of his family, he felt most sorry for his mother. He'd said a lot of things about his family over the course of those long, shapeless weeks at sea, about his father's outbursts and cruelties, about his strange little cousin who was so good at copying, but the comment about the mother stood out. Charles's mother, who had always loathed his father. Who had been absent, even when Charles and his brother were home from school, even at Christmas. Who had only ever really loved her daughter. Charles's mother, who had slept with the family lawyer, so uninhibited that her own son knew about it, an affair that had lasted years and years and to which Teddy likely owed his existence. But he felt sorry for his mother, Charles said, because she was a dreadful combination of loyal and awful. To be perfectly loyal would make things simple for her, and to be perfectly awful would be likewise straightforward, but being a mix of the two made her life unbearable. It would probably, eventually, drive her mad.

A dreadful combination of loyal and awful. He felt it so keenly he almost thought Charles was accusing him. It was exactly how he felt himself to be. But no, Charles was being Charles, meaning only what he believed himself to mean, was talking of his mother and nothing else. Charles never insinuated; Charles never even lied. He only ever said what he thought.

It would have been so much easier if Charles hadn't loved his family. That was what caused everything to fall apart, that damned loyalty, even to his awful father, which meant that when they'd reached Civitavecchia and read that letter, summoning Charles to a meeting, Charles had dutifully attended, despite everything. He'd done his best to stop it from happening, but Charles was unstoppable about his family, had insisted on going and insisted on going alone.

He'd followed Charles to the hotel regardless, slipping past the concierge and the waiter and seating himself in a corner, below one of the yellow awnings. It was easy for him to make himself invisible; it always had been. There was something about the way he moved, covert but not ashamed. People's eyes seemed to glance off him. The table he chose hadn't yet been cleared; there was a plate of half-eaten cheese that he picked at and two glasses, one empty, one with enough wine for him to swill and sip from. Charles and his father were far enough away that neither looked his way; he could hear nothing of their conversation beyond occasional coughs. They were drinking—or at least, the father was, knocking back glass after glass. Charles was struggling to swallow. Charles was holding himself in a way that made him seem smaller and younger, and his father, who was old and frail and likely couldn't even piss in a pot without a servant to guide his aim, seemed buoyed up by his son's submission. Whatever was being said, it was being said mostly by the father, Charles shifting distractedly and nibbling the skin around his fingernails.

The father was getting heated. Starting to spit a little as he spoke. And then at last he raised his voice enough that it was audible, and he caught snatches of sentences, 'sissy' and 'real man,' something longer that ended 'all this time at sea.' Charles looked embarrassed, was glancing over his shoulder, and then shortly afterwards they both stood up. If they walked back through the hotel Charles would surely see him, and he began to panic, to shift in his chair so at least his back could be turned, but they didn't come towards him after all. They approached the steps that led down to the water, and it was only then that he realised a servant was with them, some man of the father's, who after a moment's hesitation went down the stairs after them. He counted out five slow breaths and then followed. They were a little way down the shoreline by the time he finished the descent, walking in a triangle, the father and son at the front, servant behind, and he began to trail them, sticking close to the rock face, flattening himself into crags whenever he worried they were about to turn.

He was downwind and could suddenly hear everything being said, the father slurring insults and Charles saying nothing, or saying only mollifying little apologies, but it was unbearable listening to it go on and on like that, his sweet boy being ridiculed and degraded, and in accepting it all so meekly Charles allowed the degradation not only of himself but of the two of them together, and so when the father said 'sod,' starting talking about hangings, 'sods dangling on their gibbets' and so on, he could take it no longer and stepped out of the shadows towards them.

The father looked only confused, Charles horrified, the servant uncertain. 'Don't talk to him that way,' he said. The father's face showed a little fear, and seeing it energised him, made him remember himself, an option he'd forgotten: things could be got by cunning, of course, but they could also be got by violence. The father seemed to recognise this. 'Don't talk to him like that,' he said. He was standing very close to the father now, could smell the rank alcohol on the man's breath. He could extend a single finger, jab it forward, and the old man would fall.

The father found his words. He looked at Charles. 'Is this your wife? Or are you his?'

Unbearable, intolerable, to allow Charles to hear this, to let Charles think for a second that it was relevant to him, to them, to their life. It was just noise, noise, the wind coming in off the water. It was nothing to them.

Cunning? Or violence? He chose words, at least for a little while longer. 'You never told me your father was a drunk, darling.'

The father looked aghast, took a step back and almost tumbled. It hadn't even required a prod. The servant seemed unsure where to direct his attention, whether to say something indignant or simply take his master's arm. But the old man righted himself unaided and changed course, moved towards Charles and it was just bad luck, just chance, that the father was closer to Charles than he was in that moment, that he couldn't get there in time to stand between them, that it was so windy and getting dark and hard to hear all of a sudden, hard to see clearly, but the father had abandoned words, was raising a fist, was about to—must have—he couldn't see—Charles was suddenly not there, the father was standing alone, impossible—and then of course there was Charles, there he was, knocked over only, about to get up, about to get up, surely about to get up, and yet: not getting up.

'Charles?' he said, aware of the name in his mouth, how rarely he'd used it. 'Darling? Are you all right?'

The father seemed confused, was looking around rather wildly. The servant was with him, guiding him away towards a cranny where there was respite from the wind. So he was alone when he got to Charles, alone when he crouched down and touched Charles's face. There was the faintest bruise, nothing really, where the old man's fist had hit him. It was barely visible in the fading light.

'Darling?' he said again, softly. He put his fingers through Charles's hair, moving it out of his eyes, and that was when he felt the blood seeping from the back of Charles's head, and he rolled Charles onto one side to check, saw the dent in his skull, the sharp rock jutting up from the ground beneath him. He let Charles's body slide back again. He took a step away, wiping his hands on his trousers.

'You've killed him,' he called to the father, who had been watching him and saying nothing. 'He's dead and you've killed him.' He felt there was something wrong with his voice, with the way he was speaking. It was as though he was saying, 'You've forgotten your hat.' He tried again, 'His head,' he said, and in trying to get it right, to get the words to mean what he wanted them to mean and sound the way he wanted them to, he felt himself come apart, 'his lovely head,' he said, 'his lovely head is,' he said, 'his beautiful lovely head is—' but it wasn't possible.

After that it was the servant who did everything. Who stripped the body and rolled it into the water, waded in after it to nudge it out to sea. Took away the bloodied clothes, returned with money and told him to fuck off. Told him that if he ever spoke of what had happened, the father and servant would both testify that it was he who had done it. Told him never to show his face in England. Led the father back along the shore to the hotel steps, guided him up them as though it was the father who was the victim, the father who needed care, the father who should be brought back to life.

And then, all those years later, it was *they* who had come

to *him*, sending their self-satisfied death notices right into his kitchen, mourning the wrong Charles.

He had stared at the words on the paper, half convinced it was some kind of hallucination. Charles Inderwick. His lover's name, there in print, right there, except they didn't mean his lover. Charles Inderwick, the father. And it was 1899, it said so right at the top of the page, and he was himself, he was in his own home, the landscape outside the window was the same yellow-green rocky scrubland leading down towards Jamestown; everything was real and as it should be except that his dead lover's name was in the newspaper, because his dead lover's family had as good as strolled into his house.

CHARLES THE SECOND

He considered himself a pragmatist. He'd learned at a young age that there were men who would pay well for boys like him, boys who could make themselves invisible upon demand, who could be summoned to perform and then vanish and seem to have never existed. His early business ventures had been crude ones: money changing hands in alleyways and abandoned buildings and, sometimes, the backrooms of taverns, and the men treating him so sweetly beforehand—they seemed awed by him, even—and then roughly during, and then afterwards they seemed to loathe him, such was their shame and disgust at what they seemed to feel he had forced them to do against their will. They paid him all the same and if they tried not to, he used his fists until they behaved fairly. It was all he asked in those early days: fair behaviour. Later he became more sophisticated.

He studied the gentlemen he worked for and began, without any design, any scheme, to copy them. He simply liked the way they looked, their neatness, their cleanness, the way they raised their knuckles to their lips to clear their throats, rocked forwards on the balls of their feet; these small, gentlemanly mannerisms charmed him. He took notice of the cut of their undershirts, the way they tied their cravats. If any of them had some little item he particularly admired he took it, fingers snaking through fabric to loosen a handsome belt, for example, while they were distracted by his mouth, his other hand. He found nice cufflinks that way, a purple scarf, pocket handkerchiefs and rings. He guarded those treasures while he assembled the rest, saving his earnings to buy, at last, a perfect shirt and a double-breasted frock coat in wool with a bright red lining. These things were his, were really his, paid for with his own money. He added a folding opera hat stolen from a sweet elderly gentleman who had wanted nothing but to hold his hand, and there it was: he was fully dressed. It did not feel like he was wearing a costume, which is what he'd feared. He felt he was finally appearing as himself. A gentleman. Whichever way he turned his head, frowned, smiled, strutted in front of shop windows, he found himself indiscernible from the real thing.

He moved in different circles then, which was when his work became more complex and more lucrative. In no time at all he found that, as a gentleman, he could do less and gain more simply by being the friend of other gentlemen. He could dine at their clubs. He could smoke their tobacco. He could even, after a little while, borrow their money, so long as he made frequent enough references to his father, his inheritance, said a few casual things about horses and hunts. They'd loan him extraordinary sums, these men, and then all he had to do was vanish afterwards to some other corner of London, some other set, and start the whole thing going again. It was the easiest thing in the world. He found himself almost bored of it after a while, until he met Arthur and—it was too late by the time he realised—they fell in love.

Arthur wasn't even wealthy, he was just very sweet. They met at the White Lion, which was just a regular man's pub, nothing fancy, but still when he met Arthur he started to talk about his family, his big house, all of that, just out of habit. Arthur had been horribly impressed and had asked naïve questions about how many horses he had, how many servants, how many rooms in his great house. He'd spent a lot of his own money on Arthur in the end, and then when that had run out, he'd found himself telling one of his usual tales: his father had cut him off in a temper for something forgivable, a little rakish (he varied the particulars each time, a gambling debt, a tactless word spoken in anger), and though the old man would change his mind in a week or so—always did, this had happened before—he found himself a little short in the meantime, and would it be possible—he'd pay it all back by Monday, Tuesday at the latest—to trouble Arthur for enough to tide him over, just enough to cover his suppers and cabs and theatre tickets until then? Arthur had looked first aghast and then anxious, knitting his brow and biting his lip until at last saying, 'I'll find it for you somehow.'

How was he supposed to know that Arthur would take the money from his sister? Or that the sister was a widow with children to feed? How was he supposed to know all the damn trouble Arthur would cause in getting it that way? He hadn't asked Arthur to do any of that. Arthur could have simply said no.

He had felt so ashamed, so sick with himself, once all that

came to light. The sister had appeared at his door, must have followed him home from one of his meetings with Arthur, and when he couldn't bring himself to answer it she had explained, quiet enough to be respectful of the neighbours but very firmly through the keyhole, that her children were hungry and could she please have the money returned to her. And since he had nothing to pay her with in any case, the money having been spent in an instant on fripperies, and since there was nothing he could say to make it any better, and since he knew, had always known, that Arthur was a kind man who was not rich and who deserved only easy good things in his life, it felt easier to disappear than to try to make it right. He was good at disappearing.

He went first to Liverpool and took work on a ship to Australia. He drafted a letter to Arthur from Sydney explaining that he had gone to sea and would send some of his wages to settle the debt, but found that he couldn't send it. Whichever way he worded things it sounded inexcusable; the project of excusing it was beyond him. He moved on to the next port, and the next, taking money for his labour on the ships, seeing the world from every corner and coming to understand the ways, previously unseen by him, that everything had always been about trade. He recalled arguing as a boy with other boys on the street in Borough over a sugar lump; now he saw the whole entangled history of the thing, how that sugar lump had come in a great barrel on a ship full of barrels from the West Indies, had been bought from plantation owners who, now they were obliged to pay their workers, did so barely, using foreign labour at cheap rates.

He thought of the many, many hands who had touched that sugar; how, as a boy, he had seen none of it, had thought only of how hard he should punch in order to keep it for himself. It was exhausting to see the whole, exhausting to be part of it, loading and unloading cargo, working to transport the products of others' labour, and he found himself yearning for his old life, when he had been a gentleman.

And that was when he found himself in Valparaiso, where he had come upon a familiar type, an English gentleman who looked lonely and forlorn and easy to befriend, and he had found himself going through the old familiar motions, the 'how-do-you-do's, the 'how-about-we's and 'would-you-care-to's, and the beautiful thing about Charles was that he always said yes, right from the start, yes to everything, yes to taking a walk, yes to falling in love.

He convinced himself it was possible to swindle and love a person at the same time; the one did not negate the other. He could want Charles's money for money's sake, and want Charles's love for love's sake, and yes it was true he had spotted Charles at the port and thought, *That's a man who's been around money; I wonder what money can be got from that man*, and yes it was true he had continued to wonder it, all the while that he and Charles had spent together, but it was also true that to look at Charles was to feel a lurching sensation, like being about to sneeze, and to have him look at you back was explosive. How wonderful it had been then, to know that money and love could slot together so easily, could rub alongside one another like that in the form of this beautiful man, who was his mark and his sweetheart in one.

It had been the truest joy he'd ever known. He had felt almost entirely like himself walking arm in arm with Charles around Valparaiso, water sparkling, wine flowing. When Charles said his father had cut him off, it hadn't seemed disastrous; it was a familiar story to him after all, one he himself had told countless times. The thought—fleeting, amusing—crossed his mind that perhaps Charles was attempting to swindle him. Then Charles said it again, that he really was cut off, and their money dried up and with it the wine and the food, and he wondered whether love was enough to keep going, and felt, almost, that it was. Beautiful, Charles was beautiful, and he'd almost made up his mind about it when he realised it needn't be a choice. There was a way to get the money back, surely. Fathers like Charles's never meant to keep their sons cut off. It was only ever a way of controlling them. All that needed to happen was a letter or two, a few well-chosen words, and things would go back to being golden again.

There was a moment, some weeks into their life together, when he realised Charles didn't know his name. And when he told him his name was Charles, Charles hadn't believed him, had laughed, and then looked baffled, and said, 'You're not joking?' and he said no, not joking, Charles was a good and common name, and his surname was Gray, a little like Green, not so far off. 'Charles,' Charles had said, reaching out and touching his face as though it were his reflection in a mirror. 'Charles.'

But they'd never really used each other's names in any case. Charles could not break the habit of calling him 'Green,' after his hat, stolen from a gentleman in Cadiz, and for him Charles was always darling, sweetheart, my love, or else silly nonsense sorts of things, jam tart, bunny rabbit, my little loaf. So the queerness of both of them being Charles hadn't really struck him until later. Then, in years after Charles's death, he'd thought so much about it, had taken to writing their initials side by side, Charles and Charles, CC, he could draw it a certain way so it looked like one man embracing the other.

Charles the Third

He decided to become Charles. It was not so much a decision he made as a decision that happened to him. It seemed it had already taken place, the whole thing had already been determined and he was simply playing the part he had been given. The letter he wrote to the solicitor in Jamestown had already been written, as though someone had whispered the words to him long ago. He was Charles Robert Inderwick, long estranged from his family, and had noticed his father's obituary in the *St Helena Guardian*. He was anxious to reacquaint himself with his mother Irène, his brother Teddy, his cousin Grace. He had such happy memories of Inderwick Hall, he wrote. His lovely old horse Roger. He sealed the letter.

He thought: that should do it. Should be more than enough.

He thought: what could they do? He defied them to deny him. They would accept him because he would force them to, because they would have no other choice. He had spent a decade loathing them, thinking of them daily, fantasising about ways to punish them for what they had done to Charles, done to him, done to their beautiful lives. And here was this possibility: he could simply walk back into their world and insist he was a person he was not. He could be unwavering in the face of any and all doubt. He could make a dead man walk.

He had spent the first weeks after Charles's death drunk, and had then found his way to opium, which he loved because Charles had loved it (Charles had never once mentioned it, but he had the look of the opium eater all over him, the way his hands shook, his mouth twitched, the way his eyes would glaze sometimes and it was clear that he was dreaming of it; it had been the one unspeakable thing between them), and he had given in to it entirely. Sober, he would see again and again the bloody rock beneath Charles's head. Intoxicated, he saw only Valparaiso, the golden weeks, the yellow house, funiculars sliding up and down the hillside. And then—how tedious, how familiar, how exhausting—he had run out of money. He had been hungry and thirsty and wide, wide awake, unsure as he wandered the streets of Civitavecchia where he had been sleeping, where his belongings were. He might have died, wouldn't have minded dying, if the servant hadn't found him: the man of Charles's father, Ferris, the one who had been there, who had taken care of everything. The servant fed him, took him to a hotel, asked where he had been and what he had been doing, and when he said he didn't know, had lost everything, had spent all the money they'd given him, the man had disappeared for a while, then come back with clean clothes, more money.

'You'll leave Italy,' the man said. 'There's a passage booked in your name, departing in at the end of the week.'

'Where to?'

'Alexandria.'

'Ha!'

But he hadn't minded where, really. Packed up his belongings, and Charles's too. Boarded the ship. Began what became months, and then years, of travel again. He took jobs below deck without even particularly minding. On occasion, for a holiday, he stayed some time in a port town—in India, Singapore, Madagascar—and told a tale or two for a nice lump sum from a gentleman, and then when that was exhausted, he began again, set off for somewhere new. He had even studied painting for a while with the idea that it might somehow honour Charles's memory, but he was better at talking than drawing and his creative efforts depressed him, so he had given it up and set off again. There had been no reason to stop at Saint Helena other than that it suited him, the scrubby landscape and the cheap living, the washed-up weirdness of the place, half English and half unfamiliar, far from anywhere at all. At first it was an odd sensation to him, this misery, comfortable because he had no hope of alleviating it, but soon it became gentle and reassuring, like wrapping himself in Charles's old brown coat, running his fingers across the embroidered initials. There was nothing at stake. There was nothing to be lost. He could simply endure.

The closest he came to happiness in all those years was to think of Charles's family and the ways in which he'd like to ruin their lives.

He thought, too, of the money, of Charles's money, and of what Charles's father had said about wives, about which of them was the wife, and of how, really, he *had* been Charles's wife, or Charles his, or should have been. He thought about how, if that could have somehow been the case, then the money would have been his already. They had stolen his money from him when they took Charles.

So when he sent the letter to the solicitor, and when the solicitor forwarded his response the family, and when the family in turn sent funds and an invitation, he was certain of his purpose. He was not stealing their money. He was reclaiming his own. He repeated that as he packed up and readied himself for his journey, to Senegal, to Morocco: *It is my money. It is already my money.* When he stayed the night in Casablanca he took the priciest room he could find, and when, in the morning, they presented a bill in the name of Charles Robert Inderwick, he offered to buy the whole hotel. Why not? It was his money. He could do what he liked.

It was like being drunk. He bought wine. Then he was properly drunk.

He took Charles's jacket, Charles's hat, Charles's scarf, holding them up to his face, pushing his nose into them though they smelled only of mildew and his own tobacco and the musty Saint Helena house. When he put them on, knotting the scarf just the way he remembered Charles doing it, angling the hat deep over his brow, shrugging into the coat the way he might shrug his whole body towards Charles, he felt a change come over him. It was almost like sobriety: clarity, a sense that he was moving differently, and when he approached the mirror he was half afraid that it would show Charles's face, though all he had wanted for ten years was to see Charles's face, had dreamed about it so vividly he'd wanted to do nothing but sleep.

He need not have worried: there he was, framed in the glass, inescapably himself. And yet. He turned his head one way, another. His features, his nose, chin, ears. His pores. The mole on his chin. And yet. He opened his mouth, cleared his throat. 'My name is Charles Robert Inderwick,' he said, and it was Charles's voice. And when he spoke, it seemed to him it was Charles's mouth, too, the way it had moved around words, and Charles's tremulous eyebrows, and Charles's darting eyes.

Charles, who he had carried with him for all these years. Charles, who loved him, whom he loved. He thought of the body on the rocky shore, the wind lifting stray locks of hair up from his forehead and blood soaking through the rest. He imagined that Charles, that sweet dead Charles, stirring, coughing, opening his eyes. What if that Charles had picked himself up off the beach and wandered back into town? What if that Charles had been the one who had lived and he who had died, and it was Charles in the house in Saint Helena, idly turning newspaper pages, suddenly confronted by his own name?

He said it again, 'I am Charles Robert Inderwick,' and this time scared himself, the voice was just alike, had been waiting in his throat all this time.

He mopped his brow with Charles's handkerchief, embroidered C.R.I. He tucked Charles's pen and leather-bound diary into his pocket.

He slipped a foot into one of Charles's boots, a size too large and worn down at the outside edge. Stepped back from the mirror, towards it again.

There he was: Charles, coming back to life. A new Charles. A vengeful Charles. He was going home.

'I am Charles Robert Inderwick, and I've come for my money.'

Epilogue

Some Truths About Copies

A copy is a way of carrying on in the face of adversity. A copy is a promise to the future.

A copy is heroic.

Charles and I got married, in a small and covert ceremony in front of a vicar and two strangers dragged in off the street, during which I found out, for the first time, Charles's real name. I was reluctant to call myself Grace Gray, which seemed a sort of a joke name with no punchline, and in any case Charles preferred to take my name for his, so we became the Inderwicks, as in some ways we always had been.

'I want nothing from you,' he said, before we wed.

'Except for all my money,' I said, and he said yes, that was true, except for that.

This all happened after Charles had explained who he was, of course: who he was, who he was to my cousin, who he was to me. That is to say: a copy, all along.

A copy stands up to be counted.

My aunt died two months after the wedding and I never discovered what she really thought of Charles, if she had always
believed in him as she said she did, or had only wanted to,
and whether she had wanted to because she thought it was
possible he really was her son, or because she had known
all along that he was not. I thought perhaps that all of these
things were true for her at the same time: he was her son and
he was not her son; she knew what had really happened and
did not know.

The Inderwick money came to me and thence to my husband.
By that time I had painted my Velázquez, the blank backside
of Venus and the even blanker face in the mirror, and I had
talked to Charles as I did it, explaining that to my mind it was
a self-portrait. He had said, 'Do you really not know yourself,
Grace? Are you really so mysterious to yourself?'

When I looked at my husband, I sometimes felt that I could
remember another face, could picture the face of my cousin
Charles as he had been before he left. It happened only fleet-
ingly, but when it did I felt the shock of the original, and
enduring gratitude to the copy for bringing him back, albeit
diluted. The vision faded but I loved it while it lasted.

Once Charles and I had found somewhere to live—in London,
a large enough place that we could keep entirely separate and
still meet at breakfast—I wrote to Ruby and invited her to

come. I sketched out a life of extraordinary freedoms, a front door opening right onto the street, and bicycles, and nobody watching. I said that yes I was married and yes I did know how that seemed but that Charles and I were friends only, and alike, so alike. I was free to do as I pleased, as was he.

She took several weeks to reply. It was a polite, earnest kind of letter: she had met somebody else, she said, who was rather straightforward, which she liked, though she would always think fondly of me. But at the end, she drew a perfect picture of a cunt and I cackled when I saw it, a horrible, delighted sound I didn't know I could make, and Charles came in from the other room to find me laughing and laughing and when I showed him the picture he backed off, looking alarmed.

'From Ruby,' I said.

He said, 'No business of mine,' as he retreated, though he returned a while later to say, 'I'm glad she has written to you,' and again a little after that to say, 'I'm sorry she will not come,' though I had told him nothing of what she had written.

Later, after Charles had died, I thought of going back to Oxfordshire, of trying to make something of Inderwick Hall. What I imagined for it was very arty and surprising, somewhere I would throw the sorts of parties I'd once fantasised about. I felt sentimental about the cows. But the reality was that it would bankrupt me: needing new roofing, new windows, new floors, needing to be almost entirely re-built in its own image. And I could not justify it, could not imagine living under the weight of all that long-grabbed wealth. I felt almost nothing when I sold it and I gave the money from the sale away. A new family lived there for a while, changing its name from Inderwick Hall to Oxford Manor, though it was miles from Oxford, and then wisely decided that to try to live in that house was madness. It was some kind of training camp for soldiers during the war, I believe. Later, a hotel. I requested the brochure. Very beautiful, very expensive, a passing mention to the house having a great history.

In 1916, Charles was forty-seven years old, too old to be a conscript. He went back and forth about joining the war but in the end decided he should go, would do half a year in the navy and then come home. Within weeks he was dead at Jutland. I found out months later, when a letter addressed to Mrs Charles Inderwick arrived and I knew at once what it must be. I think I mourned him almost like a real wife would mourn, ragefully, the way Charles had mourned my cousin.

I had a wife of my own by then, or at least, that is what I called her and she called me the same. We had been living in the house alongside Charles, meeting at mealtimes and some-times smoking together after dinner. He had been wary of her at first and she him, but they found they shared an interest in bread with salted butter and became friends.

For a while at the beginning, my wife had asked me to paint her, to paint Charles, to paint myself, and I had said I was a copyist, and she had said yes, of course, now copy Charles's face onto the board. Later, she laughed at herself for having thought I could do it.

The only portrait I have of Charles is the ink sketch drawn by Ruby's father without seeing him, and which was really just a copy of a photograph.

In all the years before he died, I was so glad the Inderwick money was Charles's, that it had only passed through me to him. I was only ever a conduit. I could never think straight about money: who should have it, who should be denied it. Charles felt more simply and took pleasure in buying things. I kept out of it. I sold my copies. I gave too much away.

A copy is a kind of currency, after all.

Is it so different, my wife used to ask, to copy from a body instead of a canvas?

When I think of portraying my wife, I see a copy of Corot's 'Interrupted Reading'.

When I try to remember Charles's face, his wide forehead and the way he would catch my eye unsmilingly when somebody said something he found funny, though he was on the brink of laughter, what I see is a copy of Andrea del Sarto's 'Portrait of a Man Wearing a Large Hat.' When I think of Ruby and the way her hair caught under the scarf she tied around her neck, what I see is a copy of Botticelli's 'Portrait of a Young Woman'. And when I look at myself, my own specific lips and chin, my own specific brows and eyes, my mole nestled by the left tear duct, and I try hard, so very hard, to really see myself, it is a copy of the face in the mirror of the Rokeby Venus, only that, only a suggestion, an idea of a person, a copy of a painting of a reflection in a hazy looking glass.

A copy is a way of holding what cannot be held.

A copy, as if to say: I have made something of myself.

A copy: a propagation of love.

By which I mean, a copy is an extension of love, from the original out into the world, and so it is a kind of hedonism, a fantasy, as if to say: there is plenty, look, there is enough for everyone. Please take what you need. There is more than enough, for you, for you, for you, and even for myself.

ACKNOWLEDGEMENTS

[to come, six pages available]